Te

It is amazing how God can take a person like Richard, who was not thought capable of much, and enable him to accomplish so much over the last 40 years. By the world's standard, Richard would be the most unlikely to succeed... a high school dropout, drug addict, totally consumed and lost. God took Richard's weaknesses and turned them into strengths through Christ, calling him to evangelize throughout the world. My brother's story shows what God can do with a vessel that is totally surrendered to Him. I've seen Richard hurt, upset, frustrated, disappointed, and tired, but I have never seen him waiver in his faith. That in turn has built my faith. God doesn't call the qualified; He qualifies those He calls, and Richard is a prime example of that transformative power.

My hope is that this book will encourage those who feel too far-gone, to help you know that God will meet you where you are. He sees *your* potential and longs to reveal Himself to you.

–Phyllis Garrett
Sister to Richard
Brunswick, Georgia

Ricky and I have known each other since 1976. We were members of the boilermaker union together and worked at the old shipyard in Brunswick, Georgia, as machine operators. We both lived lifestyles that brought much bondage and enslaved us to the darkness of this world. His book, *Such a Worm As I,* accurately describes the life we both lived.

One Saturday afternoon in July 1979, I went to visit Ricky. I had a lot of drugs with me and planned to party with him. Ricky was standing on the front porch as I was getting out of the car. The first words out of his mouth were, "Hey Darrell, Cheryl and I accepted the Lord into our lives last week." Not knowing what he was talking about I said that that was good.

He asked me if I wanted to come in, and I accepted. Although it seemed that only a few minutes had passed, I was still sitting at their kitchen table five hours later listening to them share with excitement about God's love.

You see, I knew Ricky well, perhaps better than anyone, so I knew this had to be real. God had truly delivered him from all his bondages. When I left their home, I felt strong conviction deep within my soul. As I was driving home, I looked out of the window and all I could see was Jesus hanging on a cross. I started throwing my drugs out, and I experienced something that night I had never experienced before. The hand of God had touched me.

In a couple of weeks, I attended church with Ricky and Cheryl. When the altar call was given, I responded, and Ricky was right beside me, crying and praying.

They introduced me to Kathryn, and we have now been married 40 years. Ricky and I have remained friends for nearly 45 years.

–Darrell Lee
The Baker's first convert
Brunswick, Georgia

One of the many wonderful attributes of our Lord and Savior Jesus Christ is His ability to toss our past sins, "into the Sea of Forgetfulness," where he remembers them no more. Our human frailty at grasping this reality many times leaves us burdened with guilt which He has promised to lift when we confess our sins and commit to a life dedicated to Him. Richard Baker is a testament to grabbing hold of this promise and not letting go. His book title is taken from a line of the old hymn, "At the Cross where I first saw the light and the burden of my heart rolled away!" How appropriate and uplifting! *Such A Worm As I* will lift your spirits as you read the testimony of a man who completely surrendered his all to the King of Kings and Lord of Lords, turning his life completely in the direction of Christ-centered living and service.

–Timothy M. Hill
Administrative Bishop, Church of God
Chattanooga, Tennessee

I have known Richard Baker for more than two decades. His life personifies a transformed and dramatically changed life that experienced a foundation of living in the real world of a poor and drug-infested environment. But God's grace intervened in Richard's life and provided unbelievable favor and empowerment. In short, Richard Baker is an overachiever. Richard is in touch with the everyday trials of the ordinary man or woman but also testifies to the overcoming and transformational power of Christ. Richard has literally traveled the world representing orphans and widows, preaching the gospel of Jesus Christ, and modeling the servant leader lifestyle—he cares! Richard's story will both inspire and challenge any reader, at any age.

—Fred Garmon, PhD
LeaderLabs, Inc.
Cleveland, Tennessee

One Sunday afternoon, I received a phone call from a man I did not know, had never heard of , and had no idea where he came from, let along how he knew about us. It was Pastor Richard who, along with his daughter-in law, Mia, was on his way home from an extended trip traveling to seven countries in Africa and Asia. After making a special stop in Thailand, where a missionary shared our ministry with him, he wanted to visit Baan Zion. Although I had no idea what to expect when I saw the car pull up at the children's home, the moment Pastor Richard stepped out of the car and we shook hands and looked each other in the eyes, the Holy Spirit that was clearly upon him took over. It was an amazing encounter. We shared, I showed him around, introduced him to our girls, and we had an emotional Holy Spirit time of prayer. Mia, a professional photographer, was interacting with the girls taking photos. Seldom in my life, or in our 25 years of ministry, have I had the privilege to meet such a loving and compassionate man.

That day everything changed for us. The Lord by His hand and by His Holy Spirit sent a truly amazing man of God to Baan Zion. Pastor Richard's visited resulted in us not only receiving an immediate offering of $2,000, which we desperately needed, but also in us being accepted into the SOW family. After all these years, we are still blessed with this indispensable monthly support. Over the years, we have developed a special relationship with Richard and SOW and were blessed by his visits to Baan Zion. He is an amazing man working for an amazing organization serving children. Without Richard listening to the leading and direction of the Holy Spirit and visiting us, and without SOW welcoming us into their family of supported projects, I would not know where we would be today.

—Rev. Dr. Jan Smit
Founder of Baan Zion
Chiangrai, Thailand

The end of the twentieth century and the beginning of the twenty first century proved to be very difficult times for the Ukraine. The Collapse of the Soviet Union, which caused the economy to nearly collapse, was devastating for most Ukrainians. This led to an increase in alcoholism and drug addiction which caused many children to be abandoned or orphaned because of the death of the parent/parents from alcoholism or drug overdose. Many children, at times over 100,000, had nowhere to live and gravitated to the streets. In the winter months some had to live in the sewage systems just to stay alive. These precious children, through no fault of their own, had become hostages to their situation. How could we as part of the body of Christ view the helplessness of these children and do nothing?

In 1999 we started feeding street children and helping them in other ways to have a better life. We rented a dilapidated unfinished building. It was difficult times as the path we took was one of trial and error, but also one of successes. We had no regular funding coming in but God put some kind souls in our path to support us, which allowed us the opportunity to survive, but it wasn't enough; the need was too great. In the spring of 2009, I was handed a note with a couple of the numbers and the words, "You must call this number and speak to this man, as this is concerning the Pearl orphanage." In the past we had many people who admired what we were doing to alleviate the suffering of the homeless children and made promises, but most we never heard from again. But this time I felt in my spirit something was different.

We called and made an appointment with Richard Baker, which was held at the Church of God World Missions headquarters located in Cleveland, Tennessee. He gave us a short tour and then invited us into his office, where he shared a little about himself and his ministry. He spoke about his recent trip to the Ukraine and his visit to Pearl orphanage. I was not present during his first visit. We had shared with him that the building we were renting belonged to the government and at any time they could ask for it back. Richard shared with us about the Lazarus Foundation, which he served as the executive director and about its president, Dr. John Gregory. He explained that the Lord had burdened his heart to help Pearl Children's Home acquire a facility of its own and assured us that he would be asking Dr. Gregory to consider us. This was an amazing new page in the history of our ministry to orphans in Ukraine.

There are not enough words to describe what has been accomplished through the Lazarus Foundation donation in purchasing the land and building and having the building completely renovated. Because of this support, our children have been able to enjoy a permanent home. And if that wasn't enough, Serving Orphans Worldwide has come along beside us faithfully supporting us monthly all these many years. We thank God for putting Richard in our lives to help these disadvantaged children, and we believe that God has a very special reward in store for him for this tremendous contribution into His Kingdom.

–Sergey Drok
Co-founder of Pearl Children's Home
Ashville, North Carolina

Richard Baker is a diamond–not a diamond in the rough but a diamond OUT of the rough. His salvation and transformation of life is a miracle. But he didn't stop there; he went on to bring salvation and transformation to thousands of others: Lead pastor of four churches; 15 years a missionary leader; partnership with his beautiful wife, Cheryl, to care for thousands of orphans. Pastor? Yes. Missionary? Yes. Visionary? Yes. Man of God? Yes. Diamond? Indeed!

–Raymond F. Culpepper, D.D.
Executive Director of Care
Iris B. Vest Spirit Care Center
Sevierville, Tennessee

Richard Baker loves people and loves our Lord Jesus Christ. This book reflects these two factors. I am honored to know this man who has left an indelible mark on thousands of orphans living in abject poverty. His life is one of selfless dedication and love to see the lives of children totally restored. *Such a Worm as I* will help anyone to rediscover "the God beyond man's rules" by offering a deeper understanding that will fill them with confidence to step beyond the box of past failures and hurts and live out the life for which Jesus Christ so dearly paid. This is a book you need! It is unequivocally one of the best books written by a man who has lived a life marked by ignoring rules of favor and promotion. Every chapter is biblically accurate, historically accountable, and culturally insightful. It's impossible to read this book and see God the same way.

–Fatima Maruta
Founder, Rose of Sharon Welfare Organisation
Harare, Zimbabwe

Richard W. Baker, Sr., has been a wonderful friend, not only to some of us, but also to many orphan children around the world. It is not easy to have such concerns for those unfortunate children. The story in this book portrays Isaac Watts' amazing grace so vividly. I encourage everyone to read this autobiography of Richard Baker to enhance each of our lives far greater and to realize how destitute we are in the sight of God. It is only by the grace of God that we believe through Jesus Christ who died on the cross and made us righteous in God's sight.

–Dr. Billy Kim
Chairman, Far East Broadcasting Company
Seoul, South Korea

I met Missionary Richard Baker and his family in the year 2003. I observed in Brother Baker a man consecrated to God and to the ministry the Holy Spirit placed on his shoulders. He possessed obvious compassion for the lost and an irrevocable love for children.

He and his wife, Cheryl, served as directors of Casa Shalom for several years. During his administration, Casa Shalom experienced holistic development never seen in the history of this ministry to orphaned and abandoned children in Guatemala. He took care of 107 children in all their needs--balanced nutrition, clothing, shoes, education, but above all, unconditional love from he and his entire family to children who never had a mother or father to love them. One can say with no reservation, the Bakers were loving parents to the unprotected children of Guatemala.

I also observed him as director of special projects for Central America when I was serving as regional superintendent. He promoted new projects and administered them with a high level of responsibility and transparency. The truth is, Missionary Baker was a significant blessing and help to me as superintendent of Central America.

I express my gladness and give thanks to God for the book Missionary Baker has published. It is worth the effort to read his book and learn much regarding the life and ministry of this pastor, administrator, and servant of Jesus, Richard Baker. You will be enriched, motivated, and inspired by the reading of his book.

–Dr. Roberto Aldana Sosa
Pastor of 2,000-member Church of God
Coatepeque, Guatemala

SUCH A WORM AS I

SUCH A WORM AS I

RICHARD W. BAKER, SR.
WITH BOBBY DUNCAN

For more information and additional
copies of this book, contact Richard at:
suchawormasibook@gmail.com

Books can also be purchased at:
Amazon.com

Serving Orphans Worldwide
Phone: 866.580.5700 ext. 0
PO Box 1403
Bristol, TN 37621
soworldwide.org

Proceeds from book sales will go to Serving Orphans Worldwide, which presently serves more than 8,000 orphans (84 orphanages) in 33 countries.

As long as funding permits, this book will be sent without cost to jails, prisons, and rehab centers. Contact Richard for more information.

ISBN: 978-1-64288-126-4

Although the following story is true, some names
have been changed to protect the privacy of certain people.

Revised 2025

Printed by Derek Press
Cleveland, Tennessee 37311

Richard & Cheryl Baker

Richard & Cheryl Baker family - 2020

Table of Contents

Foreword

Richard Baker's life story is a wonderful example of how God can take an individual heading toward destruction and totally change that person and then utilize that new life for the benefit of tens of thousands of people around the world. I have personally known Brother Baker for over 15 years and during that time, whether he was serving as a director of an orphanage, or as a director of a benevolent program, or as a pastor, he has always been willing to accomplish whatever job the Lord called him to do to the best of his ability and with excellence.

Specifically, Richard Baker worked with me for over nine years as executive director of my family's personal foundation called the Lazarus Foundation. During this time he traveled the world checking on different orphanages, feeding programs, and other projects which the Lazarus Foundation had the privilege to fund. He also worked with me to found Serving Orphans Worldwide (SOW) in May 2010 and served as its chief operating officer until September 2015. His willingness to travel anywhere in the world in order to help people, along with his great compassion for those who were suffering, but yet his tenacity to discover the truth about the situation of any project, proved invaluable for the Foundation.

Also, like most successful men of God, Richard's wife, Cheryl, has been a full-time partner in his ministry, and Richard would not have been able to accomplish half of the work that he did around the world if it had not been for Cheryl. Furthermore, the Lord proved faithful to both of them when he provided a miraculous healing in their lives by totally curing Cheryl from stage IV cancer at age 32.

In my life as a Christian, Brother Baker is one of the few believers I have known that has a great compassion for the suffering of humanity, along with a huge zeal for the salvation of their souls. I believe this will become obvious to you as you read this wonderful story of how the grace of God changed a man and how that life impacted the world for good.

–Dr. John M. Gregory
Chairman & CEO, Gregory Pharmaceutical Holdings, Inc.
Bristol, Tennessee

Acknowledgments

Writing my autobiography, *Such a Worm as I*, has brought a renewed sense of God's love and mercy, and a deeper understanding of just how amazing His grace really is. I cannot find any adjective that describes my love and appreciation to the Lord for sparing my life and giving me the opportunity to be used by Him in some incredible ways. This could not, would not, have been possible if it had not been for my parents who prayed for me and loved me unconditionally, and for my wife, Cheryl, who, apart from my salvation, has been the best gift God has ever given me. For years my sister, Phyllis Garrett, has encouraged me to write my life story. Also, my good friend and first convert, Darrell Lee, has constantly encouraged me in this endeavor. It would not be an overstatement to say that 100 people have mentioned it or encouraged me to write it. One was Dr. Bill George who has gone on to be with Lord and who, in his own right, was a prolific writer. He was also a mentor and close friend who mentioned it often and even offered to help with the project. When he passed away, I thought I should have taken his advice and the advantage of his skills. Now, I won't have the privilege of his vast writing abilities and insights.

In 2014 Bob Duncan, a pastor, former state youth and Christian education director, and writer interviewed me for a book he was writing on the history of People for Care and Learning (PCL), on whose board of directors I was presently serving. In the spring of 2015, our paths would cross again when I was invited to speak at the Hosea Conference in Siem Reap, Cambodia, and Bob was in attendance. After my session, he immediately came up to me and asked, "Richard, have you ever considered writing your life story?" I shared with him that he was the 101 person who had asked me that question. He offered to help in any way he could. A few years passed and, in the fall of 2019, I felt the release of the Holy Spirit that the time had now come to begin the project. Cheryl and I drove up and spent two days with Bob in Columbus, Ohio. After giving me some guidelines and suggesting that we put the book in the third person, I started writing. Bob has proven to be such a blessing and an encouragement to me by taking my manuscripts, transcribing them into the third person, correcting grammar, when necessary (often), and working on sentence structure and helping develop the flow. I simply could not have finished this project without his patience, guidance, unwavering encouragement, and support. I am eternally grateful for God putting him in my path and life.

I offer special thanks to Dr. John Gregory, for his friendship, and for affording me the privilege to travel around the world to meet with key religious and governmental leaders, and to serve many orphans in many countries. Special appreciation also goes to Ken Anderson, one of my dearest friends and colleagues in the ministry of world missions, for his complete devotion to his calling, and for his full support and assistance in the work that I have been privileged to do. And many thanks to my daughter-in-law Mia Baker—teacher, graphic designer, and web developer—for the cover design of this book.

Time, pen, and paper prohibit me from mentioning all the many family members, friends, and associates who have contributed to my life and to the writing of this book. My prayer is that God will richly bless them all in incredible ways.

—*Richard Baker*
Bristol, Tennessee

Reflections

Magnanimous, faithful, bold. For this brief reflection, I forced myself to think of three single-word qualities that best describe my perception of one of God's best, Missionary Evangelist Richard Baker. Beginning in 1998, I have known him not only as a missionary but also as a friend.

He is *magnanimous* because we have witnessed a bankrupting of himself, more than once, to rescue the world's most vulnerable from extreme poverty and imminent death. Richard's heart is larger than Texas and Alaska combined. In taking personal responsibility for lost and hurting people around the globe, his example of reckless abandonment as a disciple of Jesus is equal to first-century believers who sold everything in order to lift the poor.

He is *faithful* because his level of commitment toward God and His assignments are nothing less than extraordinary. In both large and seemingly small tasks, Pastor Richard's work ethic challenges and convicts. Whether nailing shingles, pouring himself out in preaching, or charging toward unknown dangers in a mission to expose and correct, he passionately stays the course as a faithful steward of his Lord until the job is finished.

He is *bold* because there is an uncommon deposit of God's grace and spiritual gifts operating in Pastor Richard's life and ministry. The amazing stories shared in this book are a testament. Along with being physical, masculine, and strong, he possesses a spiritual sensitivity and discernment that set him apart in ministry. An interesting quality that casual observers may not see, in regard to his boldness in tackling complex problems, is his constant seeking counsel both with God and trusted friends in every decision. In getting acquainted with Pastor Richard through this book, your life will be greatly enriched as mine has been.

—*Ken Anderson*
Vice President, SOW
Minneapolis, Minnesota

Preface

Each January, Cheryl and I spend time in prayer and fasting, seeking God for the year ahead. This past January (2022), we both felt the Lord lifting His mantle from us as pastors of Grace Point Church. In mid-February, I shared this with Cheryl. She responded, "I was wondering when you were going to share it with me, as I have been feeling a release since early January, also." I am so thankful for Cheryl who has always been so sensitive to the Holy Spirit, especially when the Lord is about to move us in a different direction of ministry.

We spent five and a half years as members, before serving six and a half years as pastors of this great and wonderful church. We witnessed over 200 conversions, over 200 new members added, and nearly 200 water baptisms. Several people were set free from demonic bondage; marriages were healed and restored, with more than 15 people receiving the call into the ministry. We witnessed over one million dollars spent on much-needed remodeling and property acquisition, and well over one half million dollars given to world and home missions projects, and with the church remaining debt free during our entire pastorate.

Grace Point is a giving church with giving coming from the poorest to the richest. It was our honor and privilege to be a part of the Grace Point family for 12 years. However, we believe the Lord spoke to us to return home to Coastal South Georgia. I felt impressed deep within my spirit that the Lord wanted to use us for a deliverance ministry. We are already beginning to see the doors open in this area.

Our niece, Chasity, along with her sister, April, lived with us when they were children and young teenagers. Chasity was a drug addict, and a little over a year ago entered Shane's Crib, a rehab in Jessup, Georgia, for women. She just graduated from their one-year intensive program and is totally set free and filled with God's Holy Spirit. I will have the joy of baptizing Chasity in three days (Sept 18, 2022).

The director of a small ministry that recuses children and young adults from sex trafficking here in the coastal area of Georgia approached me asking that I consider helping them with their rescue operations. He shared with me that last year different ministries in the area had rescued 400, mostly young females.

Last, God is bringing me back to my first calling, and that is being a revivalist. The best way I can describe the word *revivalist* is to say that it is a mixture of two of the ministry gifts, that of evangelist and prophet. The first printing of *Such a Worm as I* has sold out as of the writing of this article—2,050 copies in total with more than 1000 copies going to prisons, jails, rehab centers, and a few schools. The book has generated over $41,000 in sales, all of which went directly to Serving Orphans Worldwide. Cheryl and I could not be more elated. But the greatest blessing has been those that have come to the saving knowledge of Jesus through reading the book. I have received countless letters from jails, prisons, and rehab centers. This has encouraged and touched me to the core of my being. And once again, God has used SUCH A WORM AS I.

The Father wants to use you too. No doubt, someone is reading this that God desires to accomplish more through than He has through me. SURRENDER! If you do, it will certainly happen. I ask that you help us pray over this second printing, so that the Holy Spirit will send the spirit of peace and deliverance to so many who are bound by Satan's devices.

The last two and a half years have been turbulent times, to say the least. The pandemic, social unrest in our country and throughout the world, the downward spiral of the economy—caused by hyperinflation that has negatively affected 80 percent of the population—have all contributed to great unrest. In addition, many natural disasters are affecting the entire world.

People may wonder just what is happening, what has caused this spike in violence, this deep hatred, and prejudice, and what is bringing about this intensifying of natural disasters. The answer is this: The Lord is soon to return (we do not know the day or hour, but He says we would know the seasons), and the professing church is not ready! In the Old Testament, when Israel backslid, God would allow pagan nations to conquer them in hopes that they would repent and call on His name. Sometimes they did; sometimes they didn't. America and the world at large have forsaken the living God. We call evil good and good evil.

One of many examples in our nation is the 63.5 million (63,500,000) abortions since 1973. To bring humanity to repentance, God removes, in some measure, His hand of protection. This allows the spirit of the antichrist, which Paul and John said was already in the world in their day, to work greater havoc. We know that God loves us all regardless of our nationality, the color of our skin, or our social and economic standing. He also loves us the same irrespective of where we are in our personal relationship with Him (John 3:16).

But a Holy God, who gave His only Son Jesus to die on a cruel cross for the sins of the world, requires that we accept the sacrifice of His son and repent, make Him Lord of our lives, and serve Him. Failure to do so results in judgement. I believe we are already experiencing certain judgements of our loving God who is endeavoring to get our attention before it's too late.

Jesus declared in Revelation 3:20 (NLT), "Look! I stand at the door and knock. If you hear my voice and open the door, I will come in, and we will share a meal together as friends." Jesus is *knocking, calling, urging,* and *pleading* for all of us to come to Him and eat of the Bread of Life that gives eternal life.

Introduction

In 1707, Isaac Watts—English minister, hymn writer, and theologian—published his second collection of hymns, which included *Alas and Did My Savior Bleed.* This well-known hymn contains the words, "Would He devote that sacred head for such a worm as I."

Using the word "worm" to describe sinful man in today's culture has become so objectionable and politically incorrect that some modern versions of Watts' song have replaced the phrase "for such a worm as I" with "for sinners such as I." Supposedly, the word "sinners" is more palatable than "worm." Anyway, how can a culture that promotes self-worth and self-esteem justify calling someone a miserable maggot? This seems to be going too far. There surely must be some way to mitigate the implications of man as a worm. As distasteful as it is to think of ourselves as sinners, it is even more revolting to think of ourselves as worms. Yet, Job would say, "If even the moon does not shine, and the stars are not pure in His sight, how much less man, who is a maggot, and a son of man, who is a worm?" (Job 25:6, NKJV) Two Hebrew words are used here, the first one referring to a worm bred in putrefaction, which means corrupt and despicable, and the second, which speaks of weakness and groveling.

Interestingly, singing certain gospel songs the way they were written cuts across the grain for some worshipers making them feel uneasy. For example, the "worm" in Watts' song and the "wretch" in John Newton's *Amazing Grace* tend to create some level of discomfort among today's believers. Someone said that we have taken the "worms" and "wretches" out of our theology. Words like "evil" and "immoral" are swept aside for words like "dysfunctional" and "maladjusted." Others may have been worms and wretches, but surely not us! Others may have been repulsive degenerates, but certainly not our circle of acquaintances! We would like to think that we were simply ignorant of the truth until Christ found us.

The truth is that we all were miserable and wretched worms. We all have sinned and have fallen far short of God's glory. Every believer has in the past been a cursed and marred vessel. There is just no way we can dress up sin, however hard we try. Sin is ugly, detestable, and loathsome. Sin is a stench in the nostrils of God. Was Watts, then, justified in using the phrase "such a worm as I" in his hymn? Absolutely! Just as correct as Job was in using the word "worm" in Job 25:6.

Despicable worms? Really? Indeed, we were–that is, until Christ searched us out, found us, and elevated us into his eternal kingdom. The supreme glory of Divine grace sees man as elevated from a contemptible worm to a position higher than the stars or the angels: "To him who overcomes I will grant to sit with Me on My throne" (Rev. 3:21, NKJV).

Richard Baker knows that identifying himself as a worm is an apt description of his life before Christ. He cringes at the thought of what he once was, but weeps at the thought of what he has become through the grace of God. Baker's story is not only one of plunging the depths of sin, it is also a story of reaching the heights of Christian service through the redeeming power of God's grace.

His and Cheryl's prayer is that their story will make a life-changing impact on people still steeped in sin, and that many, who feel worthless and without hope, will come to the knowledge that God loves them and stands ready to forgive their sins, cleanse their hearts, and empower them for service.

–Bobby Duncan
Brunswick, Ohio

1

Family Roots

On a hot and muggy Tuesday afternoon, August 27, 1957, in the coastal port city of Brunswick, Georgia, Dorothy Mae and Gilman Wesley Baker welcomed their second child, a son, whom they named Richard. Their first child, daughter Phyllis, was two-and-a-half years old at the time.

Dorothy (better known as Dot) was born in Coffee County, Georgia, in 1929, to Jim and Minnie Mae (Tyson) Kirkland. Jim, a carpenter by trade, and a farmer, built the house in which she was born. Although a builder, he was also a bootlegger. When Dot was only six months old, Jim was arrested, jailed, and while behind bars became so ill that the sheriff released him to return home to his family. Tragically, he died at home a few days later while holding little Dot in his arms. The last words Minnie Mae remembers her husband saying were, "She's so beautiful!"

Because of losing her husband at such an early age, 21-year-old Minnie Mae had to move back in with her parents, Jacob and Minnie Lee Tyson, who lived on a farm in the neighboring county of Erwin. Dot's grandparents raised her until she was nine years old, but the passing of her grandmother compelled her to live with her mother, who now had married a man with several children.

Although by the time Dot had entered high school, she had developed a desire to become a nurse, such a venture seemed out of the question, mainly because funds were not available. Her family, like so many others, subsisted on a meagre fare and was unable to provide that kind of education for their daughter. To help Dot fulfill her dreams of nursing, members from both sides of the family sacrificially pulled together enough resources for her to attend nursing school. Smart and hardworking, Dot graduated from high school one year ahead of her class and, at 21 years of age, finished a four-year nursing degree at Grady Hospital in Atlanta, Georgia, in only three years.

Gilman Baker, who also grew up on a farm in Coffee County, Georgia, quit school halfway through the ninth grade to help his family on the farm. In rural America even into the 1940s, such early exits from school were not unusual. Making ends meet often meant arduous work from everyone, including the children. Consequently, survival frequently trumped formal education.

Upon graduating from nursing school, Dot went to work for the hospital in Douglas, Georgia, and soon began attending the Westward Street Church of God, the church where Gilman attended. Immediately attracted to each other, Dot and Gilman quickly fell in love and, in time, married. Shortly afterward, they moved to Brunswick where Gilman secured a job as a butcher at a small independent grocery store. Because both worked, they hired a daytime nanny, Lucille Singleton, to take care of Phyllis, and later, Richard.

Lucille was a dear African American woman who, unable to have children of her own, treated Phyllis and Richard as if they were her flesh and blood children. Richard's mother related to him that when his father came to the hospital to pick her and their newborn son up, Lucille insisted on going. As soon as the nurse brought them out, Lucille took Richard from Dot and held him all the way home.

As Phyllis and Richard were growing up, they awoke each morning to the aroma of a hearty breakfast, as Lucille prepared grits and eggs with bacon, sausage, or ham, along with toast or biscuits. And they would never forget the delicious preserves. Lunch contained meat, a starch, two or three vegetables, and was served with cornbread or biscuits. There was little junk food in the Baker home during those growing-up years. In fact, the only cereal Richard remembers seeing was cornflakes, and they were generally eaten as a snack with bananas and/or strawberries.

When Richard reached 11 years old, he received a much-coveted BB gun for Christmas, one akin to the Red Ryder on *The Christmas Story.* Anxious to put it to good use, he said to Lucille one day, "I'm going hunting for our lunch. What would you like for me to bring back?"

Amused by Richard's confidence to provide a meal with his BB gun, Lucille replied, "It will be good if you can get us a couple of squirrels."

Since his BB gun was not powerful enough to bring down a squirrel, he chose to shoot a few robins. After delivering them to Lucille, who dressed and fried them, they sat down to a meal of songbirds. With his chest swelling with pride at his hunting skills, Richard, along with Phyllis and Lucille, enjoyed this pleasant change from the normal fare.

Lucille was a godly woman who prayed over the children daily. Richard recalls hearing her crying out to God in a small room just off the living room—a room that later became his bedroom.

While still a young boy, he contracted the mumps, and the only thing that seemed to relieve his suffering was Lucille holding him and rocking him for hours, praying over him and singing to him in her sweet voice. Thoughts of her today still bring tears to Richard's eyes, as he reflects on her warmth and kindness. She was most certainly a God-sent second mom to him and his sister and was a good teacher to Phyllis, who took it on herself to rock Richard during his bout with the mumps.

Richard's father and mother were good Bible-believing parents and worked hard to see to the needs of their children. Understandably, that alone took much of their time. Consequently, having someone in their lives like Lucille meant much to Phyllis and Richard, as well as Gilman and Dot. The memory of her presence and influence indelibly etched itself into the minds of the entire Baker family.

2

Elementary School Days

In the Deep South in the 50s, 60s, and into the 70s, racial tensions ran high. However, Gilman and Dot, being devout Christians with high moral standards, taught their children by example that truly all men are created equal. Use of the "N" word was unheard of in the Baker home.

Since the school was only a five-minute walk from Richard's house, any number of students would pass it on any given day. On one occasion, several junior high boys walking by on their way home from school saw Lucille sweeping the front porch. No doubt influenced by their own bigoted parents, they hurled a volley of racial epithets in her direction.

That was too much for Richard to take. The next day he lay in wait for just the right opportunity to exact his preferred method of revenge. Several large evergreens stood in his front yard adjacent to his house. It provided just the right cover for an avenging boy clasping as many rocks as his hands could hold. As the mischievous students walked by, Richard launched his arsenal of projectiles, hitting a couple of the boys in the head and back. Turning to identify their attacker, they spotted him and chased him, as he ran for his life through several neighbors' yards. Thankfully, just as they were about to catch him, one of his neighbors saw the action and came to Richard's rescue.

From an early age, Richard displayed a significant work ethic and, through his actions, expressed a desire to succeed in life. As a first grader, he would set up a stand in his front yard to sell homemade candy and lemonade to earn a little cash. At age 11 he went with his father to a Western Auto store and was quickly drawn to the push-mowers. He begged his dad to buy him one so he could earn money by cutting yards in the neighborhood.

Although Gilman continued refusing his son, saying, "No, Ricky," Richard persisted. Interestingly, they left Western Auto with a beautiful emerald green lawnmower. Gilman's industrious son immediately acquired several clients and began making money. Richard's mom took him to First Federal where he opened his first banking account with an initial $25.00 deposit.

Not only did Richard start his own grass-cutting business, but he also developed a plan to pay his dad back for his investment in the lawn mower. Since Gilman had been paying a young boy $3.00 a week to cut the yard, Richard offered to cut it without charge to pay him back for the purchase of the mower. The plan worked beautifully, and both were satisfied with the arrangement.

Gilman with Richard & Phyllis.

Since the family lived only 20 minutes from the beach, many Saturdays, and sometimes Sundays after church, found the Bakers on Jekyll or St. Simons Island picnicking and enjoining the warmth of the sunshine and the beauty of the beaches. It was in preparation for one of those outings that Dot swung by a KFC that had just opened in Brunswick and purchased a bucket of chicken. The family headed to Jekyll Island and soon all were sitting on the ground in anticipation of a delicious picnic. As seven-year-old Richard bit into that new recipe greasy chicken, he thought it was the tastiest food he had ever eaten. He believed on this day that the food and the atmosphere just could not get any better than this.

Richard entered the first grade in September 1963 at the age of six. Kindergarten was not required in Georgia and, for one reason or another, Dot chose not to send him and his sister. This placed them at a disadvantage over the kids that had attended the pre-school program.

As soon as he entered the first grade, Richard realized that there was something different about him. He may have been the only child in the class that could not say the ABCs from A to Z without getting them mixed up. In the second and third grades, he struggled with spelling and reading. He also had a stuttering problem, although it wasn't severe. However, it was serious enough for other kids to make fun of him at times. For years, he could not properly pronounce his sister's name, Phyllis. So, he called her Sus. She didn't mind that so much around the house, but she didn't like him to call her that in public.

When Richard reached the third grade, a bully began to pick on a boy who was autistic, had bucked teeth, and whose clothes were usually shabby. Watching the bully make fun of this poor mentally challenged boy so infuriated him that he leaped on the bully's back, taking him down. After an unceremonious landing on the hard ground, Richard began punching the bully as hard as he could, while making sure that his blows didn't miss their target. A teacher, upon seeing the ruckus, quickly came, pulled the boys apart, and took the two offenders to the school office. The principal told Richard that he would have to paddle him for his transgression and called his mother at work to get her permission. The paddle looked like a Ping-Pong paddle with four holes drilled through it for greater effectiveness.

Something snapped in Richard that day, and a spirit of anger possessed him—a spirit that never left him until, some years later, he became a Christian. Receiving punishment for helping a poor underprivileged kid who could not defend himself simply did not set well with him.

Determined to prepare himself for any future battles he may have, he soon asked his mom for a set of weights and joined the Boys Club down the road from his house, which had an incredible weight room. By the time he finished the third grade, he could bench-press more than his body weight. He also had gotten into a couple of more fights over the bullying of some kids.

During his fourth-grade year, conflicts began to intensify for him. The fights became more the rule than the exception. For the first time, he was expelled from school for a day. He became aggressive with kids in his neighborhood and choked one boy until he almost lost consciousness. The boy's mother called Dot, who immediately ran to their house to check on him and to render any medical attention needed. When she returned home, she was beside herself exclaiming, "Ricky, what has happened to you? The impressions of your fingers are still on his neck! You could have killed him!" Yet, Dot's son felt very little remorse.

Richard's school integrated when he entered the fifth grade. On the first day of school, he witnessed several African American students—four boys and two girls—enter his class accompanied by the principal and two other people. As he looked into their faces, he saw utter fear. Years later, Richard remarked, "Even today, I can't imagine what thoughts and anxieties must have been going through their minds."

At lunch that day, a few white boys approached him and informed him that at recess they were going to jump the "black boys," as they put it, and "teach them a lesson." They wanted him to join them. Although he told them that he would be there, his motives were completely different from what they were thinking.

When recess time came, eight or more white boys approached the Black people, and the predicted fight ensued. As Richard fought on the side of the Blacks, two teachers tried to stop the brawl, but to no avail. Only the arrival of additional teachers brought the students under control. From that day forward, Richard had very few friends left at school and, once again, he received a suspension, this time for three days.

The sixth grade was just as turbulent as the fifth. Once, one of his teachers sent him to the office, but instead of going to the office, he decided to walk home. That brought another suspension and brought his parents to their wits' end. At the time, he felt convinced that every fight he had was justified, because he saw himself as defending the cause of those continually exposed to bullying. Years later, he remarked, "I know my thinking was completely wrong; I actually had become a bully myself."

While still in the sixth grade and 12 years of age, Richard tasted his first beer. While staying with one of his uncles for the weekend, his uncle asked him to fetch a beer from the refrigerator for him, while he worked on his car. Richard simply couldn't resist the temptation of popping the top of the Budweiser can and taking a swallow before handing it to his uncle. Regrettably, he actually liked it, and from that day forward, sought out every opportunity to drink a beer. Taking one sip from his uncle's can of brew started him on a journey that would nearly cost him his life.

The seventh grade brought Richard to a new school. He was now in junior high and thought conditions would get better. Unfortunately, his hopes were soon shattered. In fact, his troubles intensified. Just before the opening bell rang one morning, he got into a fight with a boy that bullied him. During the fight, he broke his right hand. His mother had to pick him up from school and take him to the emergency room at the hospital. Two days later, he returned to school, but he had gotten off on the wrong foot. It quickly became apparent that this school year would not be a good experience for him. He struggled on all fronts–socially, academically, and emotionally. When the school year finally ended, no one was more greatly relieved than he was.

That summer his dad let him work with him a little in the butcher market. It was the old-style market with sawdust on the floor and the meat in a case. Steaks were cut to order, and the meat was weighed and wrapped in butcher paper for the customers.

Richard learned several things that summer. First, he learned his dad was the hardest working man he had ever been around. Second, he discovered that his dad's customers, 90 percent of whom were African Americans, loved and respected him. Third, he found his dad to be a compassionate person and a giver. For example, Gilman had a beautiful leather jacket that his son coveted. Richard had asked him on a couple of occasions if he could have it, but his dad declined to part with it. One morning, a woman came up to the meat case and placed an order. During the conversation, she asked Gilman to agree with her in prayer for her son, who had been accepted in a college in New York. She explained that he did not have a jacket suitable enough for the wintry weather he would find in the north, and she did not have the funds to purchase one for him.

Gilman wrapped her meat, handed it to her, and asked her to wait for a minute. He went back into the storage room, returned with his leather jacket, and handed it over the counter to her, explaining, "Tell your son this is a gift from me."

At that moment Richard became furious with his dad. Although he had often mentioned that he would like to have it, he now stood by as his dad gave his jacket to someone who, in his mind, was almost a stranger. The woman burst into tears thanking Gilman and giving God praise.

When she walked out of the market, Richard angrily asked, "Dad, why did you give the jacket away when you knew I wanted it?"

Gilman looked at his son and replied, "Ricky, son, you didn't need it, but her son did."

About one hour passed and a handsome 18-year-old African American man walked into the store sporting Gilman's jacket. He walked up to the counter and with a broken voice and teary eyes thanked Richard's dad for the gift. Unexpectedly, tears filled Richard's eyes as well. He had to admit that there was something moving about the experience.

A bowling alley sat at the end of the Bakers' street, and Richard's mom encouraged him to join the league for teens. Reluctantly, he did as she asked. He was assigned to a team called the Screwballs, a name that most certainly fit. Interestingly, he was the only boy on the team, which caused him to think that his mom had had a clever idea after all. The workers, and even the owners, reached out to him, at times allowing him to bowl free so he could get in more practice.

One of the staff members was a man in his 70s who was a top bowler in the nation during the 50s and 60s. After watching Richard practice one day, he walked over to him and remarked, "Son, you have what it takes to be a pro bowler. If you like, I will train you for free."

He taught Richard not to look at the pins but focus on the dots and arrows. His score instantly began to climb and after only bowling for a couple of months, he was consistently bowling 170 and over. In his first tournament, he bowled 206, with his highest lifetime score being 242. Despite his success, he soon lost interest in the game and quit.

Lamar, a good friend from church, lived in a rural area, and Richard enjoyed spending weekends with him. They spent the summer between the seventh and eighth grades hanging out together and exploring the canal that ran behind Lamar's house. On one occasion, they walked under a railway trestle and found one of Lamar's older cousins smoking marijuana. When he asked Lamar and Richard if they wanted to try it, peer pressure kicked in and both did. A new chapter in Richard's life opened, as he lived for the next high.

That same summer while staying with Lamar at his house, he saw the most beautiful girl he had ever seen. Her name was Cheryl, and she was Lamar's cousin. Her mom, stepdad, and Kenny, her younger brother, were moving from Virginia Beach to Jacksonville, Florida. They had stopped by to visit Lamar's family while in transit. Although for the moment the shortness of time did not give them much of an opportunity to get to know each other, Richard felt deep inside that the future held something special for the two of them. Cheryl felt the same way and periodically asked her cousin about him in the weeks that followed.

Like the previous school year, the eighth grade proved to be a total disaster. He still had problems with his pronunciation, and the school put him in a special speech class. He refused to have anything to do with it and completely rebelled. After getting into a couple of fights, he once again received a suspension. A school year that did not begin well, did not end well either. Yet, more trouble lay on the horizon.

3

School Woes

During the summer following the eighth grade, Richard visited his Granny Paulk, his maternal grandmother. He talked her into letting him spend the night with a cousin, who was a couple of years older than he was. Of course, his grandmother had no idea what they had planned. He had just gotten his driver's license, and after driving outside of town a few miles, they purchased some Boons Farm wine. Richard said that "it went down sweet and came up sour."

This was the first time he experienced being drunk. He and his cousin tried slipping into the house but got caught. A family member took him to his granny's house, and he knew what that meant. She was an old-time Pentecostal who believed in godly living and in the power of prayer. She took one look at Richard and began praying and rebuking Satan and his demonic forces. It was amazing how quickly he sobered up.

That same summer he and his family visited his Aunt Shirley, his mother's sister. She lived in a small community in west central Georgia, close to the Alabama line. His cousin, Randall, who was three years older than he was, wanted him to go to the movies with him. After getting his parents' permission, the two boys drove 25 miles to Eufaula, Alabama. Just as other such outings with cousins gave opportunities to drink, so did this one. Both boys came home drunk. Randall's bedroom had a door which opened to the outside that provided the means for them to slip into the house without his parents being wiser. But Richard had to frequently go the bathroom. That caught his Uncle Marvin's attention, and he came into his son's room and asked, "Randall, did you take Dot's boy off and get him drunk?" Knowing that he didn't want to have this conversation, Richard pretended to be asleep. He breathed a sigh of relief when his uncle finally went back to bed.

Academically, Richard's grades were not good enough for him to advance to the ninth grade, but the school administration decided to promote him anyway. At the beginning of the ninth grade, the school started sending him to a psychologist, with his parents' consent. Some of his classmates found out about it and began taunting him, which caused him to lash out, just as he had done many times before. He got into more fights which brought about more suspensions.

Richard did not consider his science teacher to be a likeable person. Once, the teacher asked him to step into the hall and called him a SOB to his face. His only transgression was simply making a failing grade on a science test. He had never been disrespectful to him but quickly explained to him that his mother was no dog. Richard instantly walked away from the teacher, went to the office, reported his offense to the principal, and asked if he would call his mother.

When Richard's mother arrived, the principal summoned the teacher to the office for a meeting. The teacher denied any wrongdoing and called Richard a liar. He became so irate that he jumped up and lunged at his student. The principal had to physically restrain him. At this point, Dot asked that the principal assign her son to another class. Once she had his assurance that he would, she took her son home.

During Richard's ninth grade year, a major riot broke out one morning between the Black students and the White students. The people embroiled in the fracas were not just students; adults were also involved. Neither the school officials nor the police were prepared for trouble of this magnitude. As hundreds of people faced off, Richard began searching for a place of safety not wanting anything to do with the unrest that was unfolding.

A student named Ted, with whom Richard had attended school since the seventh grade, along with four other boys, jumped him. Three of them held him while Ted began pounding him. Fortunately, Richard was able to break free and outrun his attackers. That day, the deep spirit of bitterness and revenge that had gripped him earlier strengthened its hold on him and remained until Christ, years later, set him free.

A couple of years following that incident, Richard was hanging out at the bowling alley, which had now expanded to include a pool hall and an arcade. As he shot pool, Ted approached him as if nothing had ever happened and tried to sell him some cocaine. Richard quickly went home, got his rifle, and returned with every intention of killing him.

A canal with vegetation growing along its bank flowed on the right side of the facility providing good cover for a surprise attack. Richard positioned himself in the thick vegetation and waited for his nemesis to come out. In about 30 minutes, Ted exited the pool hall and casually walked toward his car. Carefully, Richard took aim for a head shot when suddenly a car pulled into the parking lot. With headlights brightly shining in his direction, someone saw him with the rifle and shouted, "Look out! Somebody has a gun!"

Richard scurried away and no one ever knew who the would-be assassin was. Their paths never crossed again, and that, no doubt, was fortunate for both men. In time, Richard's animosity toward Ted, and anyone else with whom he had had serious conflicts, vanished because of his decision to follow Christ. But that would take some years to materialize.

One morning, just after the first class, a couple of Richard's friends asked him to skip school and join them for an outing to the beach. One boy was 16 years old and had his driver's license. Richard quickly agreed, but as the truant boys walked to the parking lot, he became extremely nauseas and had to bow out. His friends departed for Jekyll Island and soon were traveling on the causeway at speeds estimated to be over 100 miles an hour when a car decided to do a U-turn. With no time to react, the boys broadsided the car instantly killing all its occupants and them as well. One of Richard's friends was decapitated.

This tragedy was the first of many dangerous moments that prompted his mother to ask him what had happened at a certain time, because the Lord had stopped her from doing what she was doing to intercede for him. Richard will always be convinced that his mother's prayers caused his upset stomach that day, and if she had not been sensitive to the Holy Spirit on that occasion, he would not be alive now but would be in hell totally separated from all hope of ever being saved.

When Richard was 14 and still in the ninth grade, his next-door neighbor, Leslie, spent a particular night with him, after they concocted an idea to take Dot's car and run away. So, when his parents went to bed, Richard slipped into the kitchen and quietly took her car keys. The two boys pushed the car down the road a way to keep Dot and Gilman from hearing them or seeing the lights and as they took off.

Richard and Leslie drove all night covering about 300 miles, which brought them to east central Alabama. When morning came, they realized the serious mistake they had made and headed for Richard's Aunt Shirley's house. Of course, Dot was surprised to find her car missing when she got up to go to work. Shirley called Richard's mother, who, along with his sister, her husband, and Leslie's mother came to get them. Predictably, the ride back to Georgia did not prove to be as exciting and fun filled as their foolhardy ride to Alabama was.

Considering that Richard had squandered his time and had made countless unwise decisions, it is not surprising that he failed the ninth grade. Certain that the school would hold him back, he prepared for the worst knowing that he had only himself to blame. Unexpectedly, the school administration promoted him to the tenth grade, no doubt to get rid of him as soon as possible. However, a warning was attached to the promotion. To have enough credit hours to graduate, he would need to go to summer school.

Unfortunately, Richard had no interest in summer school. Once again, he made an unwise choice and refused to show up. On the first day of the beginning of the new school year, he proudly reported to his tenth-grade homeroom class, and no one said a word. He chose as one of his electives FFA (Future Farmers of America) thinking this would be an easy class for him.

Soon, Richard's FFA class went to a large tract of land, across from the school, assigned to plant pine tree saplings. The teacher broke the class into groups of four. As luck would have it, a boy who did not like Richard was part of his group. Once they were alone, his adversary jumped him from behind knocking him to the ground. Richard bounded back to his feet and the fight was on. Although he knocked his attacker to the ground, two more boys jumped in against him. As Richard once again fell to the ground, he espied a four-foot piece of wood about three inches in diameter, which he thought would work quite nicely as an equalizer. About the time he put it to use, Mr. Grindstead heard the commotion and came running. Fortunately for Richard, the teacher witnessed part of what happened and knew he was only defending himself.

He marched the four boys to the principal's office, where the nurse was summoned to look at the two boys he had hit with the piece of wood. Because they were injured, the principal had to call their parents, and the news of the event quickly circulated throughout the school. The principal felt it was not safe for Richard to remain at school and asked Mr. Grindstead to take him in his personal vehicle to one of his parents. It being his dad's day off, when they pulled up in Richard's driveway, they found his dad working in the front yard. Richard felt greatly relieved when Mr. Grindstead shared with his dad the altercation and explained that his son had no choice but to defend himself.

The following day, the school called Richard's mother and communicated to her that they felt that it would not be wise for him to return to school, recommending that he stay home for the remainder of the week.

As he returned to school the following Monday and walked to his first class, a brawl erupted that involved more than 50 students. Before he knew what was happening, he found himself in the middle of the fracas. Knowing that he attended school on borrowed time, he bolted out of the door to get away as fast as he could. One of his friends shouted, "Ricky, let's get out of here!"

They quickly jumped into his friend's mustang and sped away. Thinking they had amazingly escaped trouble, they turned into Shoney's. Within a few minutes, other students began showing up. His friend saw someone with whom he had had an altercation earlier, grabbed a machete from the trunk of his car, and approached the boy, threatening to cut his head off. This happened around 8:30 in the morning, in the broad view of all the customers and workers. Richard jumped out of the car, ran up to him, and pleaded with him to stop. Fortunately, his friend relinquished and backed off. They left Shoney's and his friend dropped him off at his house. The next day, the school permanently expelled Richard from the Glynn County school system at the age of 15.

4

A Dark Place

The rejection Richard felt from the school's decision to permanently expel him affected him to the core of his being. To say he was a troubled person is a glaring misjudgment of where he really was, and that was not a good place for anyone to be. It was an extremely dark place that was about to get darker. He would later find out just how true the warning of John 10:10 was: "The thief cometh not, but for to steal, and to kill, and to destroy."

Years later, Richard came to believe that he was suffering from demonic oppression, which he is convinced began to disturb him when he was around 10 years old. The spiritual stronghold that Satan set up in him was only going to get stronger. For the next few years, Satan's control over his life would become increasingly apparent, especially to those closest to him.

After his expulsion from school, Richard had a lot of time on his hands, and boredom was not good for any 15-year-old boy. Consequently, his father spoke to the owner of the store where he worked and asked him if his son could start working there. Mr. Mock hired Richard at $70 a week for a 45-hour week. That's a whopping $1.55 an hour—not too bad, considering the minimum wage in Georgia in 1973 was $1.60 an hour. He enjoyed working with his dad, who was a workaholic. Since Gilman was not into sports, this was the most one-on-one time his son had with him. Under his dad's tutelage, Richard learned to make certain cuts of meat and became adept enough to cut up a fryer and wrap it in about one minute.

Richard had somewhat settled down, was banking some money to buy a car, and would be turning 16 in August. In June, Dot and Gilman took a long weekend to visit both their mothers. Gilman's boss had provided him with a company vehicle, but Gilman made the mistake of leaving the keys in plain sight over the kitchen sink. That temptation proved too much for Richard.

He invited two girls to go to the beach with him on Sunday. The car was a Volkswagen beetle, and he thought that he surely could not get into trouble with a Volkswagen. But trouble seemed to have a way of catching up with Richard Baker.

The three friends went to the beach, where they spent several hours enjoying the sun and the water. On the return jaunt home, Richard began playing a game with the girl sitting in the front passenger seat. He would let go of the steering wheel, and she would have to reach over, grab it, and keep it in the road. It's no wonder insurance rates are so high for teenagers!

Richard kept up the dangerous game until they came to a sharp curve. This time when he let go of the wheel, the girl panicked and didn't grab it. The car went into the other lane and, as fate would have it, a deputy sheriff was driving toward them. The law officer had to run off the road to prevent being hit by this Volkswagen that was alternately piloted by two reckless teenagers. The deputy ran into oft sand, and Richard seized the moment and sped away, turning down different roads to confuse anyone who might be following them.

As the car approached one turn, Richard was driving too fast to avoid a parked three-quarter ton pick-up truck sporting a huge bumper. The Volkswagen was no match for a truck that, at least on this occasion, seemed more like an army tank. While the truck suffered little or no damage, the Beetle's front end almost sat in the laps of the front-seat passengers. Although the girl suffered a slight injury to her leg, she and her friend scurried away at Richard's request. He figured he would be in less trouble and would have less explaining to do if the police found him alone.

In less than five minutes, the police located the wrecked Volkswagen. They pulled Richard out, handcuffed him, and put him in the back of a cruiser. Upon arriving at the city jail, he was fingerprinted, photographed, and booked. After spending the night in a cell, his parents bailed him out, and he received a date to appear in court.

A few weeks passed and the time came for his court hearing. Wanting to make the best impression possible, he cleaned himself up a bit. He got a haircut, put on white dress pants, added a nice dress shirt, and even put a vest on for good measure. As he and his mother walked up the steps to the courthouse, they met a friend of his coming out with his father.

Looking at Richard all dressed up, he laughed and said, "Ricky, sorry to tell you, but the judge is blind!"

Upon entering the small courtroom, Richard felt an overwhelming sense of uncertainty. He had several serious charges against him that included driving without a license (he only had a learner's permit), speeding, reckless driving, causing an accident, and driving someone's car without permission.

Although the judge was surprisingly cordial, he let Richard know how dangerous his actions were and noted that people could have been seriously hurt or killed. He continued, "I could sentence you to three months in a juvenile detention center, but I have decided to cut you some slack, with the hope that you won't be back in front of me again." He suspended his learning permit for three months, fined him $200, and gave him six months' probation.

Richard's dad had to pay to have his boss's car fixed, so there would be no insurance claim. The man whose truck he ran into came to talk with Gilman saying the collision damaged the transmission. He made it clear that the only way to avoid going to court was to pay the several hundred dollars needed to repair his vehicle. Gilman had asked his son to be in the living room when the man came, so he could apologize to him. However, when Richard heard the man threatening his father, he verbally lashed out at him and had to be sent out of the room. But the wheels were turning in his head, and he devised a plan to get this man back for strong-arming his father into paying him for a truck repair he didn't think he needed.

With revenge in mind, Richard asked a friend to go to church with him on a Sunday night. Once the service got underway, they slipped out, stopped at a nearby store, and purchased a bag of sugar. The man only lived about a mile from the church. Richard planned for his friend to drop him off and drive around the block, while he poured sugar into the man's gas tank. He would then pick him up on his way back around, and they would return to church. As they approached the man's house, they saw it totally engulfed in flames. They got back to the church as fast as they could and never knew what caused the fire. Richard felt the man had suffered enough and never followed through on his twisted plan to get even.

Two months later, he turned 16 and got his driver's license. Although he tried to do better, he still was drinking and smoking marijuana every chance he had. He applied for a job at Big Star as a stock clerk and was hired. Now needing a ride to and from work, he talked his mother into signing for him to get a brand new 1973 Yamaha 500 street bike. For the next few months, all seemed to go smoothly. He was working 40 hours a week and was enjoying his bike.

Richard soon met a man, Charlie Davis, who had served his country fighting in Vietnam. Even though Davis was six years older than he was, they became close friends and drinking buddies. In fact, Charlie was a brother to the beautiful girl, Cheryl, who he had met some time ago. Through Charlie, Richard and Cheryl would one day get to know each other much better.

At the time, Richard was dating a girl who had been on his bowling team several years earlier. Her parents did not want her to ride on his bike, except only in their neighborhood. Consequently, when they went on a date, he had to find a car. Once, his sister, Phyllis, let him use her brand-new Volvo. Because of the trust she put in him, he didn't drink or speed while using it.

Because Richard's parents were under the impression he was turning his life around, they began letting him use one of their cars. Their 1964 Chrysler 300 was in mint condition. It had a 413 cubic inch engine and came from the factory with two four-barrels, which boosted the horsepower to 400. The state of Florida used this car for its state troopers.

With the '64 Chrysler at his disposal, Richard drove to pick up Lamar for a time of drinking and smoking pot in Darien, a coastal town about 20 miles up from Brunswick. As they departed the city and headed back to Brunswick, Richard sped along the highway well beyond the legal limit. Glancing in his rearview mirror, he observed a Georgia State Trooper pulling in behind them. Not wanting the trooper to catch him and Lamar in their condition, and not wanting to get a ticket for speeding, he pressed the pedal to the floor and pulled away from the officer on a straight run. The trooper had wisely radioed ahead, and the county sheriff's department was waiting for them. But the sheriff provided no more competition for this high-powered Chrysler than the state trooper did.

Richard decided to get off Highway 17 and turn onto the county roads in the hope of finding a place to hide. He had already turned a couple of times and was making one more turn when he ran headlong into a car sitting at a red light. Knowing that the police had not caught up with them yet, and realizing that his car was still functioning, Richard thrust the gearshift into reverse and, once clear, took off again. The last time he looked, his speed was around 100 miles per hour. Suddenly, Lamar screamed, "Lookout!"

His frantic exclamation came too late. They rear-ended a Pontiac driven by a teenage girl. Literally, they pushed the trunk into the back seat. Miraculously, no one was killed. Although she was injured, her injuries were not life threatening. Once again, law officers arrested Richard and locked him up, this time in the county detention center.

Within a few days and with more charges than he wanted to contemplate, Richard stood before a juvenile judge to await his sentence. The state trooper told the judge that he estimated that the teenager hit speeds on a state road at between 135-140 miles per hour. Both cars he hit were totaled, with the occupants suffering injuries. Because he was under the influence of alcohol and drugs at the time, if he had been 17 years of age, the prosecutor would have charged him with three felonies.

The judge placed Richard on probation, suspended his driver's license for two years, and fined him over $1,000, a huge amount in 1974. Neither of the victims appeared in court or tried to sue him, which, of course, helped his case immensely. Gilman's insurance company covered all the damages and medical expenses, but then abruptly canceled all his policies, including his homeowner's policy. He had difficulty finding an insurance company that would write him a policy, if Richard continued living in the home with his parents.

Amazingly, Big Star did not terminate his employment. Lee Bruce, the store manager and a dedicated Christian, saw something in Richard that Richard did not see in himself. But evil was waging a war in his heart and, for now, evil was winning.

5

Intensifying Darkness

Richard Baker's life was spinning out of control. He foolishly thought he could handle whatever problems came his way, but it seemed that every day he slipped farther from his Christian upbringing. He began snorting cocaine and took his first hit of LSD. On a Sunday afternoon while under the drug's influence, he and several friends drove around the countryside and happened upon a commercial poultry farm. Upon entering one of the poultry houses, the rabblerousing teenagers began throwing eggs at each other. Not satisfied with only having an egg fight, they began grabbing chickens and wringing their necks. Either the caretaker or owner came running toward them with a shotgun, yelling out threats. The boys barely escaped without being shot.

In August, Richard turned 17 and already had had too many close calls and run-ins with the law. His friend, Charlie, received a call from Cheryl saying that she needed him to come to Jacksonville, Florida, and get her and their younger brother Kenny. She shared with Charlie that their mother had left them and had gone to California. When Charlie told him the situation, Richard's mind drifted back to the only time he remembered seeing Cheryl some years before. Admittedly, he was excited about seeing her again.

Although his driving privileges had not been restored, Richard was still riding his motorcycle. Seeing Charlie returning from picking up his siblings, he fell behind them on his bike. When Charlie stopped at a convenience store, he pulled in behind him and waited for him to exit the store and continue his drive. When he did, Richard followed them to Charlie's trailer.

As Cheryl climbed out of the car, she refused to make eye contact with Richard. She retrieved a medium-sized cardboard box from the trunk, which contained all her earthly possessions. At the time, Richard could not understand the emotional trauma she was going through. He just knew that he was drawn to her and even thought in that moment that he would one day marry her.

Cheryl and her siblings were products of a broken and dysfunctional family. Her father was an alcoholic and drug abuser. For the most part, he was a kind person but was bound by these strongholds. He and Cheryl's mother divorced when Cheryl was around eight years old. Her mother was raised in a dysfunctional family herself and continued looking for happiness and contentment in all the wrong places.

Cheryl and Kenny had only been with Charlie for a week or two when their father, who was living in Texas, sent for them. Although Richard was sad to see them go, he knew that because Charlie had no official documents on them, he could not register them in school. After a brief time, their father sent them back to Brunswick to live with their Aunt Dorothy Mosely. Interestingly, they began attending the same church Richard's parents attended.

Almost immediately, Richard asked Cheryl for a date. Her aunt gave her permission to go out with him and, once again, happiness filled his heart. Cheryl enrolled in Brunswick High School, the same one from which Ricard was expelled. When her first school day ended, he was waiting with his motorcycle to give her a ride home and continued the practice every day.

On one occasion as he picked her up at school, she casually mentioned to him that a boy in her class was bothering her. The following day, Richard boldly walked into the classroom and confronted the boy, but embarrassing Cheryl in the process. Evidently, he got his attention, because he left her alone.

After dating for only a couple of months, Richard asked Cheryl to marry him when he turned 18. She looked at him in total disbelief and exclaimed, "Marry you!"

One of Richard's friends had gotten married about the time he and Cheryl began dating. He and his wife enjoyed hanging out with them, and drinking and doing drugs became a regular routine. Once when they were all drinking and smoking pot, Richard said to his friend that he had some THC to lace the pot with. THC is the principle psychoactive ingredient of cannabis. In its extracted and more concentrated form, it can cause hallucinations and create a sense of an out-of-the-body experience.

As they rode together to their friends' house, Richard and his friend gave the girls joints laced with the THC without telling them. By the time they arrived at the house, Cheryl was already tripping. She had never done much more than drink a little and smoke a little weed.

After a few hours, Cheryl came to her senses and was furious with Richard. She almost quit dating him because of it. From that day forward, she never wanted to touch anything stronger than a mixed drink.

Cheryl's mother, ever on the move, had now relocated to Brunswick and had purchased a new mobile home. Cheryl and Kenny now lived with her. At first Margaret didn't like Richard, and he would later admit that the feeling was mutual. But after Cheryl and Richard were married, their relationship became pleasant. In fact, Richard began to think that she actually started liking him. Time would prove that she did.

Richard & Cheryl with Cheryl's mother, Margaret (1976).

Frustrated that he still had not gotten his driver's license back, he paid a counterfeiter to make him a false one. While driving inside the city limits of Brunswick, a policeman stopped him and charged him with a DUI. The fake license worked. The city judge, before whom Richard appeared, dropped his DUI down to reckless driving and released him after one day in jail, and after paying a $300 fine.

Another one of Cheryl's brothers, Joey, moved from California to Brunswick. His presence did nothing to change Richard's lifestyle, as they began running together, drinking heavily, and doing drugs. Amid his run-ins with the law, he was able to hire a lawyer, who succeeded in having his driver's license reinstated. He soon purchased a 1971 Oldsmobile Cutlass 442.

The law shortly caught Joey and arrested him for possession of drugs with intent to distribute. Having obtained bail, he fled to California. After a few months had passed, he called his mother's house. He was a few miles outside of Brunswick and wanted Richard to come to get him. He had an idea that he would be there visiting his sister, Cheryl. Although she did not want him to go, he ignored her pleas and went anyway.

Apparently, someone had tipped the law that Joey was back in Brunswick, because as they reached the outskirts of town, a state trooper pulled in behind them and turned his lights on to pull them over. Not being a stranger to police chases, Richard jammed the pedal to the floor and broke through a wooden barricade. He outran the trooper, who later said that he clocked Richard doing 135 miles per hour. He called ahead and county and city law enforcement agents gave chase.

Richard pulled into an alley hoping to hide in someone's garage, but there were too many officers looking for them. The city police soon surrounded them but waited for the state trooper who had called in the boys' escape attempt. He cautiously approached the driver's door with gun drawn, shouting commands to Richard. But heavily influenced by drugs and alcohol, he couldn't understand the trooper's commands. The trooper took his failure to properly respond as resisting arrest.

Enraged by Richard's reckless attempt to escape him and by his apparent lack of respect, he grabbed him by the hair of his head and stuck his pistol barrel into Richard's mouth. As the trooper began dragging him out of the car, Joey, who was also under the influence of drugs and alcohol, bolted from the passenger side of the car and headed for the trooper. A 300-pound city police office stepped in his path, grabbed him by the seat of his britches and the back of his neck, picked him up, and forcefully drove his face into the hood of Richard's car.

The two troublemakers were taken to the city police station where they were booked, fingerprinted, and photographed. Foolishly, Joey began mouthing off at the cops. They quickly handcuffed both the boys once again. Apparently, Joey's disrespectful action pushed one police officer over the edge. He took his pistol in his hand like a hammer and hit Joey in his face with the butt of it. The impact knocked Joey's eye out of its socket. When they took Joey away, Richard assumed they did so to get him the medical attention he needed. He found out days later that they locked him up and refused to take him to the emergency room for a couple of days.

Years later Richard wrote, "I appreciate law enforcement. The tremendous stress that officers are under sometimes causes some to negatively react to a situation. What the office did to my brother-in-law was certainly unwarranted, but his action was the exception, not the norm. My son, Ryan, is a police officer in Chattanooga, Tennessee. I am proud of him and every other officer who serves to protect the citizens of this great country we live in."

This time when Richard and Joey were locked up, the judge denied bail, and understandably so. An attorney appointed by the court informed Richard that he had one of two choices. Either he could request a trial by jury–in which case he would have to stay in the county detention center for about four months–or he could take his chances before a judge, knowing his verdict would be final. The advantage of the latter was that he could appear within three or four days. He chose the latter.

This was quite a fix for Richard to be in on May 4, especially considering that he had asked Cheryl to marry him. They had scheduled the wedding ceremony for the end of the month, and this was certainly not the way to begin life together.

Court day came and Richard, handcuffed, climbed into the paddy wagon for the short drive to the courthouse. His escorts marched him inside and placed him in a holding cell located in the lobby of the second floor. His mother was too distraught to attend the trial. When his father walked into the lobby and saw him in the cell, he broke down and began weeping uncontrollably. Although Richard motioned for him to come to him, his father ignored his appeal and walked into the courtroom.

Richard's guard brought him into the courtroom, sat him in the proper chair, and handcuffed his right wrist to the arm of the chair. His court-appointed attorney did not have much he could use to help in his client's defense, other than leading him to throw himself on the mercy of the court. He had seven major counts against him: harboring a known fugitive, a felony DUI, driving 135 miles per hour in a 45-mile zone, failing to heed police sirens, failing to heed police lights, reckless driving, and resisting arrest. Additionally, he had run several red lights, many stop signs, and had driven through the courthouse grounds tearing up the beautifully landscaped lawn and gardens.

As each charge was read, Richard pled guilty. The judge proceeded to tell him what an incorrigible person he was and noted that he felt he was a menace to society. He began the sentencing process, starting with the lesser offenses and working his way up. The first ones brought fines. Next, his driver's license was revoked for another two years, followed by a six-month prison sentence. Suddenly, Richard felt like all hope was gone.

When the judge pronounced the prison sentence, Richard's father again broke down and wept profusely. Normally, he was a quiet man, and for the most part reserved. The judge looked at him and asked, "Sir, you didn't raise him this way, did you?"

Gilman could only shake his head. The judge sat back in his chair and put his hands over his face. After a brief contemplative pause, he leaned forward in his chair, looked directly into Richard's face, and announced, "What I am about to do, I have never done before. I am not doing it for you but for this gentleman that you call your father."

In addition, the judge generously reduced his fines from $10,000 to $2,000 and reinstated his driver's license, with the understanding that he would attend driving school and take some classes for drug and alcohol abuse. After commuting his prison sentence to five years' probation, the judge declared, "You will be back in front of me and when you are, it will be a very bad day for you. Now get out of my courtroom!"

Richard promptly obeyed and exited the courtroom as quickly as he could. As he walked out with his father, he could not find any words to say. He had already cost them thousands of dollars, and they were not wealthy by any stretch of the imagination. His mom and dad were just hard-working people, doing their best to make good lives for their children.

Now beginning to sense the anguish and embarrassment that his actions brought upon his parents, Richard finally got the courage to tell his father how terrible he felt about all that he had done. He assured him that he fully intended to straighten out his life and that, by June or July, he would be moving into his own place.

Gilman took his son to the impoundment lot and loaned him the $250 he needed to retrieve his car. His dad may not have played sports with him or taken him fishing very often, but that day he showed his son unconditional love. Gilman's tears of genuine brokenness in front of the judge had much to do with the reduction of Richard's sentence. And Gilman's work with his hands provided the means for his son to get his car out of police impound.

6

Marriage and Mayhem

Somewhere around May 10, Richard got out of jail and on May 30, he and Cheryl married. Because he was only 17 (minimum marriage age in Georgia was 18 for men and 17 for women), they had to travel to Ridgeland, South Carolina, to legally wed. His mom, dad, sister and her husband, along with their infant son, Tony, attended the ceremony. Pastor W.G. Abney officiated. After obtaining their license at the courthouse, they found a First Christian Church that was being painted. The painters stepped outside for 10 minutes while pastor Abney married the young couple. Upon returning to Brunswick, the small entourage joined for a reception at the Bakers' home church. Richard's mother, along with Lucille, who was like a second mother to Richard, hosted the reception.

Richard and Cheryl's wedding (1975) 1971 Cutlass 442–Just Married.

Gilman and Dot loved Cheryl and treated her like a daughter. Gilman had even taken Cheryl to an upscale boutique and had purchased her wedding shoes. They saw the same thing in her that Richard saw—a kind, loving, and truly compassionate person.

Richard and Cheryl went to Silver Springs, Florida, for their honeymoon. Upon their return, they rented a one-bedroom apartment. Since Gilman and Dot were in the process of updating some of their furniture, they almost completely furnished the apartment with their old furniture. Richard stayed true to his word and was out of his parents' home by the time he told him he would be. Having now married, he could get car insurance at an affordable rate.

Gilman & Dot with newlyweds.

Richard & Cheryl with Lucille.

When Richard was only 12 years of age, his mother had taken him to a company picnic. Wanting to spend more time at home, Dot had transitioned from hospital nursing to industrial nursing for a large company. Richard was captivated by the size of the plant and fascinated by all the complex machinery he saw. The plant had been a shipyard during World War II but now had become a factory for building components for power plants, paper mills, offshore oil rigs, and engines for ships, including aircraft carriers. At the company picnic, Richard boldly walked up to the assistant plant manager and asked, "Sir, when I turn 18 will you hire me?"

Probably not thinking much about it at the time, the supervisor responded, "If I am still here when you turn 18, you have a job!"

As soon as Richard turned 18, he made a trip to the offices of Babcock & Wilcox and asked to speak to Mr. Steve Szwast. A secretary called the supervisor on the phone and then handed the phone to Richard. Eagerly, Richard sang out, "This is Ricky Baker. I am 18 years old, and I am here for the job you promised me." Since a few years had passed, he had to refresh Szwast's mind. The process took a little while, but he was hired six months later, in February 1976.

Wedding (1975).

For the time being, he worked at a grocery store and did some roofing with a cousin's husband. Since the cost of living on his own was quite high, he jumped at an opportunity to work at a package liquor store doing security. He started in September just after he turned 18 and worked from 6:00 pm to 11:00 pm. On arriving for his first day of work, he asked the store clerk why the black wreath was hanging on the door, to which the man responded, "The store was robbed last week, and the security man was shot and killed. The wreath is in remembrance of him." That was most certainly not the welcome he expected to receive on his first day of work.

Not only did they hire Richard, but also hired a good friend of his, a man named Jimmy. He was six years older than Richard and was a power weightlifter, who held the Georgia weightlifting record in his weight division for a couple of years. He could bench press over 500 pounds. They worked the same shift. Imagine two druggies and heavy drinkers overseeing a package liquor store!

During the three months they worked there, there were at least three attempts to rob the store. Jimmy always worked at the cash register, while Richard was mobile. Richard would sometimes be in the stockroom and at other times, he might be walking around outside. They had a code word they used if they sensed something wasn't right. On one of those occasions, Richard heard Jimmy speak that word in a loud distinct tone. Upon hearing the code word, Richard eased out of the stockroom with his pistol drawn. His eyes at once fell on a man and a woman standing at the counter, with the man brandishing a large pistol.

Richard slipped up to within 10 feet of them and shouted, "Drop it or die!"

After the man obediently let the pistol fall to the floor, Richard and Jimmy thought about calling the police. After all, that was the protocol. But Richard had a better idea. He said to Jimmy, "Let's rob them!" They did just that, thinking that the two would-be robbers were not about to call the police on them. They were right.

On several occasions, Richard would see his mother parked in the extreme left corner of the parking lot. Repeatedly, he would walk out to where she was parked and say, "Mom, this is not a safe place for you to be. I can't watch over the store and you at the same time. Just go home."

Her response was always the same. "I'm just worried about you, son," she would say. Richard knew that she was sitting in the parking lot praying over him. He knew deep inside that God had given him an amazing mother.

During this time, his and Cheryl's marriage began to suffer. The issues that surfaced increased the tension between them to the point they decided to separate. Although they both were young and immature, the problem rested mostly with Richard and his selfishness. In a short time, they reconciled, and Cheryl moved back in.

In February 1976, Babcock & Wilcox finally hired him and started him as a Level One Laborer making $5.05 per hour—equivalent today (2020) to around $23.00. Within two months, he bid on a Group C Machine Operator position, which he really didn't expect to get. He rose all the way to level five, and his pay jumped to over $7.00 an hour.

Unfortunately, although working in this job brought many benefits, it would also expose him to a deeper darkness that led to some of the blackest days of his life.

Richard was 18 years old, married, and working his dream job. The personnel manager never wanted to hire him, mainly because he didn't have a high school diploma. But the assistant manager had overruled him, called Richard in, and hired him on the spot.

He and Cheryl were living with his sister, Phyllis, during the first few months of 1976, trying to save enough money for a down payment on a home. His new job required him to work the second shift—3:00 pm to 11:00 pm. After arriving home from work one night, Phyllis came into their bedroom and said that someone was at their window. He grabbed his pistol, walked outside, and started around the corner of the house. Just as he turned the corner, a man jumped up and Richard let loose with five rounds. The police arrived and found blood in the backyard but never found the intruder. When he walked back inside, Cheryl and Phyllis, thinking that maybe he had been shot, were hysterical.

Cheryl began working at the counter at a dry cleaner during the day, while Richard worked in the evenings. Consequently, they didn't see much of each other except on weekends. He bought a 1973 442 Oldsmobile, which Cheryl drove to work, and for him, a new 1976 F-150. They also purchased their first home and closed on it just a few days after his 19th birthday.

They made it into a lovely home furnished with an American Indian style living room suit from Rhodes Furniture Store, at a cost $2,000. In addition, they spent $3,000 on an 820-watt disco stereo system with four-foot-tall Stonehenge speakers. That $5,000 in 1976 would calculate to $22,663 today (2020). They were surely doing well financially.

Richard began hanging out daily at a bar called the Quarterback Club, a place where a lot of men in the Boilermaker Union hung out. His passion was shooting pool, and he tried to play some every day. One day as he and Joey were drinking and shooting pool there, one of the lady bartenders was also shooting pool with a male customer. Unfortunately, her beating him so enraged him that he took a pool ball and began hitting her in the face. Richard and another man intervened, roughed the attacker up a bit, and proceeded to escort him and his wife out the door.

Second wedding anniversary.

A few moments later, they also decided to leave and walked outside. The man they had roughed up was waiting with a shotgun pointed directly at them, about 50 or 60 feet away. His wife was trying to talk him in to putting the gun down and leaving. Since the man seemed to be fixated on Joey, Richard at once dropped to the ground and began to crawl to his truck, where he retrieved his rifle and took aim at the man's head. His wife glanced in Richard's direction, saw him with the rifle, and shouted at her husband, "He has a gun!" They fled to their van, as Richard fired a shot that appeared to hit the top of the vehicle. Fortunate for all involved, the man and woman fled the scene.

Richard had made friends with a man named Darrell. He was hired just before Richard, and both were Group C Machine Operators. They began spending a lot of time together drinking, doing drugs, and selling them as well.

Another man that came into Richard's life was Mick. By far, Mick, who was a welder at Babcock & Wilcox, was the darkest person with whom he would ever associate. He needed help moving and Richard offered to help. That act sealed their friendship. Mick was 29 and Richard was still 18. He looked up to the older man, who was involved with drug dealers in the Savannah, Georgia, area only about an hour north of Brunswick.

Richard and Mick began spending a lot of time together, drinking, doping, shooting pool, and dealing drugs. Mick introduced him to taking drugs intravenously–that is, shooting up, mostly cocaine and liquid speed.

Soon, Richard made an acquaintance shooting in a pool tournament. The man was the manager of a local drug store that was part of a nationwide chain. They were having beers together and Richard jokingly said, "You should let us rob your store. You could give us a map of where the narcotics, Quaaludes, and black beauties are located."

The manager responded, "What kind of cut would I get?"

Richard answered, "I will get back with you."

He spoke with Mick, and the three of them met to discuss plans. They decided to pull the robbery one night when the store manager was scheduled to close. Mick told him they would have to ruff him up a little to make it look like he was not a suspect.

They picked a date a few weeks away and, frankly, Richard was nervous. Amazingly, before the planned date arrived, the manager became a Christian and shared with his superiors what he had been planning. They fired him but did not file charges against him. Fortunately for Richard and Mick, he did not mention them. Richard felt relieved and, although Mick never mentioned it, he feared the manager would get more than a little roughing up.

An acquaintance of Richard's asked him about arranging to buy ten pounds of marijuana. He sent him to Mick and, through contacts in Savannah, they gave him the ten pounds, with three weeks to pay back the $3,000. No long after, Mick reported, "Mark hasn't paid for the weed, and his three weeks are up. The only reason we fronted him the weed was because he was your contact. You need to handle it."

Richard asked Mick to give him a couple of days more and he would speak with him. The next day, he had a cup of coffee with Mark and asked him what was going on. Mark explained, "Ricky, I was robbed. I don't have the marijuana or the money."

"Mark, you have three choices," Richard countered. "Get the money somehow by Sunday night (which was in two days), commit suicide, or it will be done for you." His body was found early Monday morning on Jekyll Island with a slug in his head. His death was ruled a suicide. Proverbs 18:21 says that death and life are in the power of the tongue.

Richard realized that his tongue had power to bring fear and death to a person. He also realized that he was involved with some men who were far more ruthless than he could have imagined. He now knew that he was in way over his head, as Mark was not the first one to die, neither would he be the last. Satan's purpose for Richard's life was going exactly as the enemy planned.

Richard became friends with Bill, an African American, who was 15 years his senior. They hit it off and spent several days a week with each other smoking weed and drinking. He would come by Richard's house frequently to watch ballgames with him. Bill also owned a nightclub outside of town. Occasionally on Sunday afternoons, Richard would pay him a visit. Most of the time, he was the only white person on the premises. Considering that this was in the 1970s when there were still a lot of prejudices between Black people and White people, this was quite unusual.

One afternoon, a Black man walked into the club and began harassing Richard. Bill took a rod and beat him as he ran out of the club. Just his association with Bill allowed him to move freely inside the Black community. On more than one occasion, when Richard was in a part of town that was predominately Black, someone would start to bother him. Soon, someone would speak up and say, "Hey, that's a friend of Bill's!" They always backed away immediately. This friendship continues until this day, more than 40 years later. His path would later change just as Richard's would.

From 1977 until the day Jesus Christ came into Richard's heart, he doesn't remember having a completely sober day. Amazingly, he was a good employee, as far as work went. He stayed busy and did what he was told to do. He eventually would learn to operate 15 different machines and advanced to Level 11 Group 1 Large Machine Operator. But he seemed incapable of making it a day without drugs and alcohol.

He finally offered a bid and was moved to the third shift—11:00 pm to 7:00 am. There was only a skeleton crew of machine operators working, with only one supervisor. Being on this shift made it much easier to drink and smoke pot. Each shift he would consume two half pints of 60-Proof gin and would smoke one to two joints of weed. He kept the alcohol proof low so he wouldn't get too drunk to do his work.

With shooting pool being one of his favorite past times, Richard entered a tournament. He was pleased when he learned that his mother-in-law had come to watch him compete. The rules stated that a person losing two games would be eliminated. He was doing well and had not lost a game. While playing a guy named Mac, who had already lost one game, Richard was poised to make an eight-ball shot that both knew he would not miss. In desperation, Mac offered him $20 to miss the shot. Richard responded, "Man, you're crazy!"

After he made the shot and won the game, Mac yelled out, "You are a (expletive)!"

Richard shot back, "Do you want to step in the bathroom or outside?"

Mac chose the bathroom, and the fight was on. He suffered a couple of broken bones, and one of his friends, a rather large guy, came in and reached to grab Richard from behind when suddenly his mother-in law, Margaret, bolted in. She grabbed Mac's friend by the back of his shirt collar, dragged him out, and tossed him under a pool table. Since Richard was still engaged in hand-to-hand combat, he did not witness Margaret throwing this big brute under the table. Several bystanders told him the same story, including his brother-in-law, Joey. It's not surprising that his respect for his mother-in-law rose to a whole new level.

A couple of weeks passed, and Richard and Darrell pulled in to the Quarterback Club. Darrell was at the wheel, and Mac came out with his hand and arm bandaged from the earlier fight with Richard. He came to the driver's side, looked past Darrell at Richard, and announced, "I'm going to get my pistol and kill you, if it's the last thing I do! I am going to kill you!"

Richard grabbed Darrell's 357 from the glove box and pointed it at Mac's forehead. Darrell grabbed the pistol from him, and Mac, caught off guard, fled. Richard felt at that moment that the feud between the two of them would end with one of them dying.

In the latter part of 1977, Richard was once again stopped for a DUI, which would be his fifth one. And once again, his license was suspended, his car impounded, and he was fined $350. He bailed out the next day, got his car from the impoundment lot and had to get someone to drive it to his house, since he now had no license.

Shortly after losing his license, as he and Cheryl were taking a drive with Richard at the wheel, a county policeman fell in behind them and turned his lights on. Apparently, Richard was speeding, and with no license, he shoved the pedal to the floorboard and managed to outrun the officer. They hid in a section of woods for about an hour.

Cheryl was petrified and exclaimed, "If we get caught, I will go to jail, too!" Although she wanted to get out of the car and walk home, Richard, believing the coast to be clear, cranked up the car and headed back before she could exit the vehicle. As soon as they turned onto a main road, they found the officer waiting for them. The chase was on again and for the second time that night, Richard outran the police.

When they finally arrived home, Cheryl was a nervous wreck. The next morning, she got up and dressed for work realizing that the car she had to drive was one with which the police were now quite familiar. She had another meltdown fearing that a policeman may pull her over and charge her with the events of the night before.

The tension in their marriage once more reached a breaking point, and Cheryl left him again. There were even times when he told her to leave. In the first four years of their marriage, they separated at least seven times, usually for two to three weeks.

During one of those alone nights when he was drinking, snorting cocaine, smoking pot, and listening to some rock music, he had a surreal and virtually unbelievable experience. All the lights in the house were off except the blue lights and the strobe light in the living room where he sat. There was a 100-pound German police dog in his fenced-in yard, and only he and Cheryl could enter the yard without him attacking. They had a closed-in front porch with a solid wood door at the entrance, with another solid wood door coming into the house. Both were shut and locked.

Richard heard the door open and for a split-second thought Cheryl might be coming home. A figure emerged taller than the eight-foot ceiling in the house and appeared darker than the darkness around him. Because of his height, he moved closer to Richard in a crouched position and spoke in a voice unlike anything he had ever heard before. The voice projected authority and strength. Richard recalls verbatim the words the figure spoke: "What will it take for you to sell your soul to me completely? Will it take you being a millionaire? Will it take being as popular as the group you are listening to? I made them into what they are. Bow before me, and I will empower you, giving you great desires."

Here he was, a young man raised by godly Christian parents in a Bible-believing, Spirit-filled church, and Satan had come so boldly into his home asking for his soul. He bowed that night at his coffee table and submitted himself, in some measure, to this evil spirit. The next morning after he had sobered up a bit, he thought about the previous night's encounter and passed it off as the result of drinking and taking drugs.

Only days later, he was transporting five pounds of drugs and still without his driver's license. His hair was longer than Cheryl's, he had no shirt on, and he was driving his 442 with dual cherry bombs–a dark blue metallic automobile with a one-foot white strip down the middle of the hood and trunk. He came upon state troopers doing a random license and insurance check. The drugs in his possession he had placed on the passenger-side floorboard.

As Richard approached the checkpoint, he saw that there were several cars in front of him waiting. His first thought was to do a U-turn and try to get away. Instead, he did the unthinkable. He prayed to Satan, saying, "If you have any power, get me through this checkpoint. If you do, I will give you a little more of my life." Through this twisted exercise, the demonic strongholds became stronger in him. Nonetheless, every car in front of him was stopped, and he could see the drivers handing their licenses to the trooper who was doing the checking. When he pulled up, the officer just waved him through.

At that point, Richard could sense that something had changed deep in his spirit. He had just escaped trouble, perhaps even miraculously. Through his forthright submission to the Prince of Darkness, he opened the door to spiritual depravity in a manner unprecedented in his life. Demonic forces now entered with more control than before.

Richard had been taught Proverbs 4:23, which says, "Keep thy heart with all diligence; for out of it are the issues of life." However, for the time being, he paid little heed to it. He snorted cocaine, took hits of LSD, smoked pot and hash, ate black beauties, and drank substantial amounts of alcohol. None of that seemed to be enough anymore, so he started using the needle to shoot up cocaine and Blue Hawaiian (street name for liquid speed). In all honesty, he really did not know what he was injecting into his bloodstream.

He and Cheryl were constantly fighting, and she continued to leave him for two or three weeks at a time. Eventually, he started missing her so much that he tried to talk her into coming home. But Cheryl just did not want any part of the life Richard was living.

The Georgia coast has a lot of marsh grasses and countless inlets and tributaries, which make ideal areas for smuggling marijuana into the country. Most of the marijuana in the 1970s came in from Colombia. Shrimp boats would travel offshore to meet speedboats that would be waiting to offload their cargo. The shrimp boats would then come to within a few miles off the Georgia coast where smaller boats would retrieve the cargo to bring to various landing points. Someone like Richard could make $5,000 to $10,000 in a single night.

Most of the cocaine was processed and distributed from a few places on Martin Luther King Boulevard in Miami, Florida. From Miami it would be transported up the eastern seaboard by various means. One common method for carriers was to secure a rental car and fill the spare tire and/or other compartments with kilos of the drugs. Richard had seen 30 kilos (66 pounds) transported to Brunswick in this manner. In 1979, 30 kilos of uncut cocaine had a wholesale value of $660,000, with the street value several times that.

On a Saturday morning in early May, Richard began snorting cocaine and drinking alcohol that continued throughout the day. Mick came over later that night, and both went to a party in the home of one of Cheryl's cousins. Upon arrival, they socialized for a while drinking beer and just hanging out. Sometime in the early morning hours of Sunday, they began shooting up cocaine. Seeking a higher high, Richard asked Mick to give him a shotgun—a syringe with cocaine injected into a person's arm, quickly pulled out, and forcefully rammed back in. It gives a super rush, but because he had been snorting so much during the last 18 hours, he collapsed against the refrigerator and slid down onto the floor. The syringe was still in his now bleeding arm. The last words he remembered saying, or thinking, were, "Oh God, let my mother pray for me!" He recalls:

> I immediately felt my spirit leave my body. I could see my body lying on the floor with the syringe still in my arm. Something was taking me backwards. I couldn't see where I was going, but I could feel two

> massive hands on each of my upper arms pulling me backwards, and it was the darkest black I have ever seen. We traveled for what seemed to be a couple of minutes, and then I began to hear such awful screams and loud groaning. It is hard to describe the darkness that surrounded me; it looked and felt much different than the darkness on earth. As dark as it was, you could see the silhouette of the landscape.
>
> As I looked down, I saw hell, and I knew it. I kept praying, "Oh God, let my mother pray for me!" The landscape was barren and hilly. The ground was very parched, and I saw what looked like round cylinders filling the landscape. Then I witnessed the greatest horror of it all—souls of men falling into these cylinder-looking holes. As the souls were falling, they appeared to be cone-shaped, larger at the top, and tapering down at the bottom. I didn't see flames, but I began to feel intense heat.
>
> Suddenly, the creatures that were pulling me backwards stopped. I looked down and saw directly below me an empty cylinder-shaped hole. I knew that I was about to be released, and that would be my eternal destination.
>
> Then just as suddenly as I had traveled to hell, the creatures brought me back. I could see my body again and witnessed my spirit reentering it. As I lay there for a moment, I heard a voice speak to my heart, "This is your last chance; your mother is interceding for you."
>
> I got up, took the syringe out of my arm, went home, and crashed, sleeping for many hours. When I awakened, I convinced myself that I had only hallucinated from all the drugs I had taken.

Sometimes, Richard's mom worked at the hospital on weekends. At the end of a 12-hour shift to end this particular weekend, Dot went home around 7:15 and lay down to sleep. After drifting into a deep slumber, she was awakened by a fear of something terrible happening. She clearly heard a voice speaking to her heart saying, "Mother, pray; your son is heading to hell!"

Dot quickly arose from bed, knelt, and began to intercede for her son. She cried out to God, praying for more than two hours, before she felt a release in her spirit. Several days passed before she was able to share this experience with Richard. When she did, he was shaken to the core of his soul, but not enough to surrender his life to Christ.

Near the end of May in 1979, he was working with a drug cartel out of Indianapolis, Indiana. They wanted 1,000 pounds of high quality Columbian marijuana delivered monthly to them. He met them at a Holiday Inn in Brunswick. He had one guy with him and two more for backup in a vehicle close to the hotel. He took a pound of the product for them to sample and began negotiating the price. Richard was just the middleman and would be paid $10 per pound, if the deal went down.

A friend of his, James, heard about these guys and undercut Richard's price. James showed them one quality but delivered a poorer grade. Richard and Mick went to see him. Richard usually carried two firearms on him, but he was comfortable with James. They had worked at the same place, and James and Cheryl's friend, Kim, had even double-dated once with him and Cheryl.

As he and Mick entered James' dwelling, they found at least 10 thugs there, some of whom he knew. They threatened to kill the two men and dispose of their bodies. As Richard and Mick quickly departed and walked away from the house, they felt that the men were going to open up on them at any time. Fortunately, that did not happen, and both men felt they had narrowly escaped with their lives.

In July, someone doused James' home with an accelerant, and he and several others were burned alive. Richard had gone to warn him that day that the Indiana guys didn't play around, but he wouldn't listen. As Richard related this story, he again reflected on John 10:10: "The thief cometh not, but for to steal, and to kill, and to destroy: I am come that they might have life, and that they might have it more abundantly."

In June of 1979, Richard and Mick went to collect a past due drug bill from a man who worked at a lumberyard. After spotting him loading lumber for a delivery, they pulled alongside the delivery truck. Mick, who was 6-feet 3-inches tall, weighed 230 pounds, and was a fighting machine, got out of the car and asked for the money the man owed them. The customer begged, "I don't have it. Please give me a couple of weeks."

Mick answered with a solid blow to the side of the man's head nearly knocking him out. He instructed the man to bring the money to a certain location by 6:00 pm, or else–whatever "else" may have meant. As they pulled away, the man cursed them prompting Mick to get back out of the car and approach him again. When the man picked up a two-by-four and started toward Mick, Richard immediately pulled his pistol and cocked it.

Seeing Richard's pistol drawn, he dropped the board and fell to his knees begging for his life.

Richard cried out, "No! I'm going to shoot you! Where do you want it—in the belly or chest?"

Mick, who was now standing close to Richard, reached over and grabbed the pistol just as he was squeezing the trigger. Mick's thumb got caught in the breach preventing it from discharging. Jumping into the car, he shouted, "Man, 10 people are looking on! Let's get out of here!"

They sped away angry that they had not collected the money, but glad they had not done something stupid. Later that day, the man brought the money he owed them before the 6:00 pm deadline.

Not all stories have good endings. Thankfully, some do. Years later, in 1991, after Richard had gotten his life together and was pastoring in Manchester, Georgia, the Holy Spirit brought this incident to his remembrance. He felt deeply impressed to find this man and make things right. A couple in his church, Ricky and Faye Smith, wanted to go on a short vacation with him and Cheryl to St. Augustine, Florida. As they passed through Brunswick on the way back to visit family, Richard took the opportunity to look up this man.

After driving to the lumberyard, he and Ricky walked into the office and up to the counter. Richard shared the story of the incident back in 1979. All three of the employees in the office were there on that day and had stood on the porch watching the entire scenario unfold. Today, they were utterly speechless, and one woman started crying. They shared with Richard that the man in question had had his hip crushed by a forklift and was unable to work.

After he had gotten the man's address from the office personnel, he and Ricky went to his house and knocked on the door. His wife opened the door thinking they were bill collectors. Once he assured her they were not, he told her that he was a pastor and God had sent him to speak with her husband. She informed him that he would be home in a couple of hours, and they were certainly welcome to come back.

When Richard and Ricky returned, the man answered the door and looked at Richard with great despair. A bit reluctantly, he invited them inside. As they entered his home, Richard began to weep at once. Through his tears, he announced, "I am the man who almost killed you at the lumberyard 12 years ago."

Richard fell on his knees, placed his hands on the man's feet, and begged forgiveness. He shared with him about his amazing transformation, about how Christ was now the Lord of his life and about how he had now come to make things right. He reached into his pocket and returned the money that he had taken from him years before.

The man, deeply moved by Richard's act of humility and kindness, related his own amazing story. A few weeks earlier, he and his wife had decided to start going to church, as their lives seemed in shambles. They started attending a Church of God in Christ, which, remarkably, used to be Richard's home church, and the one in which he and Cheryl had been set forth for the ministry. That congregation relocated and sold the facility to this body of believers.

The man continued, "We immediately accepted the Lord on our first visit. We were struggling financially, and this past Sunday, we went and spoke to the pastor. He took a dollar bill from his wallet, anointed it with oil, and prayed over it. He told me to place it in my Bible and claim my need every day. Brother, the money you have given us today is exactly what we were praying for!"

Richard and his new fellow-believer hugged each other, shouted, and danced around the man's living in joyous celebration. He never could have scripted such an ending to this story—only God could have. He later found out that after hearing the story, his own precious mother, Dot, took an offering to them a couple of times.

But now in June of 1979, Richard and Cheryl had little to do with each other. They had separated at least seven times over the last four years of marriage. Although they shared the same house, he was hardly ever at home. He had become loosely affiliated with a couple of drug cartels and lived for the excitement of doing the next drug deal and, of course, staying high.

7

The Darkness Broken

Cheryl had attended church a couple of times at her in-laws' church, a church where her grandmother and other family members also attended. She set up a meeting with the pastor, Joe Muncy, and shared with him that she was tired of the life she and Richard were living. Although she felt that her husband was ready for a change, she still was thinking about leaving him for good. Pastor Muncy asked her if she would give God a couple of more months to work out their problems, as he assured her that he would be praying. She agreed.

In late June of 1979, Richard announced, "Cheryl, let's go to Disney World. We will stay in the Contemporary Hotel and will have a great time." The hotel was the best one there at the time. She told him later, after both had accepted the Lord, that she hated him by then and did not want to go anywhere with him, but something would not let her say no.

Since Richard had not seen his Granny Paulk, his maternal grandmother, in a couple of years, he suggested a visit to her first. She lived in Fitzgerald, Georgia, which was about two-and-a-half hours from Brunswick. Cheryl thought it would be good. They packed up, called his granny to let her know they were coming, and headed out on Friday, June 29.

When they arrived around 4:00 pm, his granny was getting ready to fry chicken for their supper. After a delicious meal and an enjoyable visit, Richard's granny dropped a bombshell. She turned to her grandson and announced, "Ricky, we are in revival tonight, and I would love for you both to come. But if you decide not to, I should be home around 10:30."

He offered some feeble excuse, and he and Cheryl went to the bedroom. As soon as the door closed behind them, Cheryl, a bit put off, censured Richard, exclaiming, "That's rude to come, eat, and spend the night with your granny and not go to church with her! I am going and I hope you will too!"

Realizing that Cheryl had rightly backed him into a corner, he loaded Cheryl and his granny into his car, with his granny in the front seat, beehive hairdo and all. He cranked up the 442 and his granny asked, "What's wrong with your car?"

"Oh nothing, Granny. That's just the cherry bombs making that noise," he answered.

She exclaimed, "Bombs!" He couldn't help but chuckle.

Richard and his boys with Granny Paulk.

One thing his granny failed to tell them was that the revival was being held in a large tent set up in what looked like a cow pasture. Nine churches from three different denominations had come together to hold a regional revival. Herb Winegar from Kingsport, Tennessee, was the evangelist.

An area near the tent had been designated as handicapped parking, and for his granny's sake, that was where he had to park. He was definitely not a happy camper. As he exited the car and helped his granny out, he felt that all eyes were upon them. In his words, "It must have been a spectacle to witness—a Pentecostal woman in her 70s with a beehive hair-do getting out of a sports car, being escorted by a long-haired hippie looking dude, with a beautiful blonde following along!"

Just before entering, Richard seemed unable to force himself to step under the tent. Cheryl followed his granny all the way to the front, but he stepped back outside and spent the entire three-hour service sitting on the hood of his car. He heard the singing, the worshipping, and the preaching, but it only agitated him. He impatiently waited for Cheryl to come out so they could continue their planned trip to Disney World.

After what seemed like an eternity, he saw her coming. She informed him that his granny was staying and that his Uncle Jerry and Aunt Jeanette had invited them to spend the night with them. As they started down the highway, Cheryl rolled her window down and began tossing her Salem 100s out.

Richard asked in a strong voice, "What are you doing?"

Cheryl replied, "I don't need them anymore!"

"What did that preacher tell you? Did he tell you to quit smoking?" Richard asked.

She answered, "No, I just don't need or want them anymore."

A bit perturbed, he responded, "You will have me going to the convenience store by midnight buying you more cigarettes!"

Cheryl confidently declared, "No, I won't!"

After arriving at his Uncle Jerry's house, he and Cheryl went at once into their bedroom. Desperately wanting to resume their trip, Richard pleaded, "Cheryl, let's leave early in the morning so we can be at Disney World by lunch, get checked into the hotel, and start partying for a few days."

He did not get the response he wanted. Instead, she answered, "I would like to stay and go to church tomorrow night."

That did not set well with Richard, and he reacted, "No, we are leaving in the morning!" He began to taunt her by pretending that he was smoking and saying, "Don't you want one!?"

As they were lying in bed that night, she rolled over, looked him right in his eyes, and whispered, "Ricky, I love you."

He had not heard those words in a couple of years. In later years he reflected, "Her eyes had a sparkle to them almost like little flames of fire burning. And those three words pierced my heart with such conviction."

The next morning as his uncle was getting ready for work, he suggested that his son, Randall, take his cousin bass fishing on their boat. It sounded like fun to Richard, so they went. After returning to the house in the early afternoon, he said to Cheryl, "Hurry and get ready. We still have time to get to Orlando today."

Cheryl replied, "I want to go to church tonight."

Reluctantly, Richard agreed. That night when they arrived at the tent for service, he decided to sit in the back. Still not happy, he was at least closer to the action than sitting on the hood of his car. When he sat down on the back row, Cheryl kept walking all the way to the front row. He was embarrassed and somewhat agitated by her apparent determination to move into the inner circle of the worship service.

Richard's mother had gotten word about what happened to Cheryl the night before, although Cheryl still had not shared with him that she accepted the Lord. Dot and Phyllis drove from Brunswick to be in service, walked under the tent, and seated themselves on the back row with him—certainly, a surprise.

As the service got underway, spirited worship quickly followed. Richard was amazed at how large the tent was once he got inside. He thought that perhaps it would hold 2,000 or more, and it was almost full. The tent belonged to evangelist T.L. Lowery, with whom Winegar often traveled ministering in music.

When Winegar began preaching, Richard became uneasy and restless. The evangelist walked from one side of the platform to the other, came off the platform, and moved a few rows down the aisle to where Richard was sitting. He felt as if Winegar was preaching directly to him. Before he realized what he was doing, he had stood to his feet. He wanted the evangelist to shut up, and he wanted to run as far as he could from that tent meeting.

Winegar stopped preaching, looked at Richard, and asked, "Son, do you want to know the Lord?"

Richard responded, "I am not a Christian, and I don't want to be one, but here's $100 for your ministry!" Winegar sent an usher to receive his offering.

When he sat back down, the evangelist shared some closing thoughts and gave an altar call. This was the moment Richard saw his opportunity to inconspicuously escape this most uncomfortable atmosphere. After slipping out to his car, he once again waited impatiently on his wife. By the time she arrived, he was in a terrible state. The demons inside him were disturbed and provoked. Richard vehemently declared plainly, "Tomorrow morning, we are going to leave for Orlando!"

Not to be outdone, Cheryl quickly exclaimed, "Ricky, I know the revival ended tonight, but I want to go to church with Granny Paulk in the morning!"

Knowing he was in no position to push her, he agreed to stay but made it clear that he had no intention of going to church the next day. That Sunday morning, July 1, 1979, Cheryl got up and started dressing for church. Greatly irritated, Richard declared, "I am not going to church, and I am asking you not to go!"

Without any hesitation, she responded, "Ricky, I am going to church with your granny. I promised her I would go, and I am!"

Cheryl left for church, along with everyone in the house, except Richard. Fretfully, he paced the floor for over an hour and became so enraged that he drove to the front of the church and parked at the entrance of the sanctuary. In his fevered mind, he planned to go inside, forcefully remove Cheryl, and leave for Disney World.

When he walked inside the church, he surprisingly found it completely full. He stood there for a few seconds trying to locate his wife but was unable to spot her. He did see his mother and sister, but they were too close to the front for him. A man sitting on the back row moved over and motioned for him to sit next to him. Not sure what his next move would be, he accepted the offer.

The choir was singing its last song. As the song ended, the tent revival evangelist, Herb Winegar, took the pulpit. Richard, as uncomfortable as ever, thought, "Great! Him again!" He thought the local pastor would be preaching. After all, Cheryl said the revival was over.

He had no idea what Winegar preached, but he noticed that most of the people seemed extremely happy. When Winegar asked everyone to stand for the altar call, Richard felt something warm inside. Several people responded to the invitation to come to Christ. As he stood there with his hands on back of the pew in front of him, he began to think about the transformation he had seen in Cheryl and knew deep inside that he had no peace. Instead, he was miserable.

When he started to move his body, his hands seemed glued to the pew. Then he saw something that shook him to the core of his being. He saw the imprint of two hands on top of his hands pressing down agonizingly hard. He heard a voice, whether audible or not, he was not sure—a voice saying, "You can never be saved; you sold your soul to me that night in your home when you knelt down and prayed to me!"

Richard had never experienced such a feeling of hopelessness. He stood in a Pentecostal church where people were in the altar accepting the Lord, and where others were rejoicing. And here he was bound and seemingly unable to do anything about it. He again tried to move his hands, but they appeared welded to the pew.

At that moment, an elderly man that had been sitting on the front row began to make his way toward the back of the church. Richard initially thought he was leaving. He was holding on to each pew as he slowly made his way to the back. When he came within a few pews of him, Richard could see tears streaming down his cheeks and made eye contact with him. Immediately, the demons released the hold they had on his hands and demanded, "Quickly, run out of here!"

This elderly man reached Richard, laid his hands on the top of his hands, and simply declared, "In the name of Jesus, be thou set free!" The instrument used that night was Raymond Chambers, a retired Assemblies of God bi-vocational pastor. He later told Richard that just a few days before, the Lord laid on His heart to fast four days telling him that He would show him the reason why at the Ocilla Church of God on Sunday. At that time, he had no plans to be there. He lived close to Atlanta, but God had directed him to that church for a divine purpose. It is amazing how God orchestrates events to bring about His purposes.

Immediately, Richard experienced a sensation of something leaving his innermost being. This happened three times in rapid succession, with each succession sounding like, "Swoosh!" The joy and peace that filled his heart at that moment was indescribable. People reported that he literally leaped to the altar. Although he was sure that God had wondrously saved him before he ever reached the altar, the local pastor, Earl Merritt, still took time to pray with him.

As Richard continued on his knees in the altar, someone came up behind him and spoke, "Young man, you need to allow the Lord to sanctify you, so you will be able to stand against the attack that is coming." Although he did not fully understand sanctification, especially considering the debate among theologians as to whether it is a first or second definite work of grace, one thing he knew for sure was that when he raised his hands to heaven and asked the Lord to sanctify him and take the love of the world out of him, something dynamic happen. Years later he testified:

> I felt as if someone had poured hot honey all over me and all the desires for drugs, alcohol, and illicit sex–in short, all my narcissism–was instantly washed away. That's not to say I have not been tempted; we all are, but the deep desires I once had to sin were taken away on that Sunday morning, and now after 40 years, they are still gone. (For Richard's testimony of how to receive Jesus Christ as Savior, turn to page 417 at the end of the book.)

Someone else came to him and declared, "God will use you in mighty ways. You will need extraordinary strength and power to accomplish His calling on your life. Ask the Lord to baptize you with His Holy Spirit, and He will."

In response, Richard raised his hands again and said something to the effect, "Lord, this man said I needed the Holy Spirit baptism. If it's for me, I want it!" There was no one directly praying for him at the time; he simply felt awed by all the love and grace he had experienced over the last few minutes. He related:

> With my hands raised, as soon as the words fell from my lips, I felt fire erupt in my soul, and my lips began to stammer. At first, I tried to stop speaking, but every time I would try to praise Him in English, the heavenly prayer language would flow through me.
>
> I know this is another hot doctrinal issue for many but let me emphatically say that everyone who is born again has the Holy Spirit living within them. Paul tells us in Romans 8:15-16 that the "Spirit Himself bears witness with our spirit that we are children of God."
>
> But to be baptized in His Spirit is to allow the Holy Spirit to empower you in ways you never thought possible. Some Pentecostals and Charismatics will have to answer to God one day as to how they have misrepresented the purpose of this amazing gift Christ has given to the church.

At the conclusion of the service, I was asked to give a short testimony of what God had done for me. I just thanked the Lord for saving me and asked the pastor if I could be baptized. He answered, "Last night I felt impressed to fill the baptistery, but didn't. But if you will come back tonight, I will baptize you." Believe me, when I say nothing could have kept Cheryl and me from returning that night, I mean nothing.

We had another wonderful service and, yes, Pastor Merritt baptized me, as he promised. Brother Winegar took the pulpit and informed the church that one of his drivers had to leave suddenly due to a death in his family. He wanted to know if anyone could pull one of his 40-foot trailers to Atlanta the next morning. Anxious to start working for the Lord, I eagerly raised my hand—to which he responded, "Would there be someone else?" Wow, the air was knocked out of me! But no one else responded, and he gave in exclaiming, "Son, I guess you will have to do!"

We departed at 6:00 am with a convoy of five vehicles, with me in the middle. I was pulling the platform/stage that also carried the organ, piano, and sound equipment. We were going to stop at a certain truck stop along Interstate 75 to fuel up and eat breakfast.

When we stopped to have breakfast, we sat down near 10 or 12 members of the Outlaws, a notorious motorcycle gang. After our food arrived, Brother Winegar, in a loud voice, said, "Son, will you please give thanks over our meal? —and please pray loud enough for us all to hear!"

It suddenly hit me that I had never prayed out aloud. Intimidated a little by the Outlaws sitting so close by, I started praying. I don't remember what I prayed, but when I ended, I glanced over at the table where the Outlaws were sitting. One of them gave me a thumbs-up. I almost viewed this as my first sermon and him as my first convert!

We made it to Atlanta, and I shuttled back to Ocilla. Later that week Cheryl and I returned to our home in Brunswick, Georgia. We never made it to Disney World.

Richard was coming to the end of his two-week vacation. Sunday night at 11:00 pm he would start back to work, and a rash of emotions began to overwhelm him. He thought of his many friends with whom he ran and with whom he worked at Babcock & Wilcox. He wondered what he would say to them and how they would react. Also, he pondered what they would say and questioned if his life was in danger, or even worse, if Cheryl's life was in danger.

He wouldn't have to wait long to find out. On Saturday evening, Richard heard a car pull up and stepped onto the front porch to see Darrell exiting the car. Richard knew he had to tell him what had transpired over the last week with him and Cheryl. He remembered that Darrell had told him before they had left on vacation that he was getting some prime hash and wanted to come over and smoke it in Richard's hookah pipe. The one he had featured four hoses, which allowed four people to smoke simultaneously.

Before Darrell could open the gate, Richard shouted, "Darrell! Cheryl and I accepted Jesus as our Savior last week!"

Richard clearly remembers thinking that he shouldn't hesitate to tell his friend what had happened to him and Cheryl. He invited him in, excused himself for a minute, and went looking for Cheryl, seeing he needed help. He found her in the bedroom and told her that Darrell had stopped by. Looking for all the support he could get, he asked her to come and help him share with his friend the change in their lives they had experienced.

They all sat down at the dining room table, and Richard began telling him what had happened over the past week. According to Darrell, five hours later they were still talking. Although Darrell kept saying, "Man, that's great," he was astounded and was struggling to comprehend their experience. After he left, Richard felt strengthened by sharing his testimony.

On Sunday morning, he and Cheryl went to Sunday school and church. It all felt so strange. They began attending a young adult class, which had 40 to 50 attendees. Frankie May served as the teacher, and at least once a month, the class got together for outings. This was exactly what they both needed and drew so much strength and encouragement from the fellowship.

When Richard arrived at work on Sunday night he didn't see Darrell. At the time, they were Group Two machine operators and worked the same shift and sometimes worked together. The supervisor told Richard that Darrell had been in a car accident and was in the hospital.

Darrell lived approximately one hour away in Waycross, Georgia. When he left Richard's house on Saturday night and was driving home, he came up behind a utility truck hauling telephone poles and crashed into them. The poles came through the windshield destroying his car and almost killing him.

Richard made his first hospital visit on Monday. As he entered the room, he really didn't know what to do or say, considering compassion wasn't something he was used to showing. Darrell looked a mess and was clearly in pain. In the bed next to him was a young man who was having minor surgery, whose father was a pastor. Every time the pastor visited his son, he would minister to Darrell. The seeds were being planted.

After Darrell was released from the hospital, Richard invited him to church. He accepted the offer and came on a Sunday night. When the altar call was given, Darrell headed for the altar with Richard right behind him. He became Richard's first convert. What an amazing feeling he had knowing that God could use a worm like him to help someone find eternal life.

The blessings didn't stop there for Darrell. Richard introduced him to a young woman in the church named Katherine. They began dating and later married. Today they have three children and six grandchildren. Darrell still serves the Lord and is a member of Richard's home church, Golden Isles Church of God, in Brunswick, Georgia.

Shortly after Darrell's conversion, he came to visit Richard the same day that Richard decided to burn all his rock albums and drug paraphernalia. He dug a hole in the backyard, got a good fire going, and began tossing in his Foghat, Kiss, Lynyrd Skynyrd, Electra Glide Orchestra, Pink Floyd, David Bowe, Led Zeppelin, Deep Purple, Grateful Dead, and others. Darrell exclaimed, "Hey man, if you don't want them, let me have them. I can sell them!"

Richard shouted, "No!"

The two people he was most concerned about were Bill and Mick. Bill was the Black man 15 years his senior, with whom he had become close. Bill was connected to people who moved a lot of drugs, and Richard was privy to some of these contacts and transactions. He wasn't sure how Bill would react to the news of him becoming a Christian. He also worked at Babcock & Wilcox and, at the time, worked the second shift as Richard did.

Richard came in a little early on Monday night so he could tell him the news. As he walked up to him, he remarked "Bill, I need to share something with you." He proceeded to tell him about his and Cheryl's accepting the Lord and made it clear that no one needed to worry about him ratting them out.

"I will not be going to the authorities concerning anything I know," Richard continued.

Bill just looked at him and his exact words were, "Hey man, that's cool. There's no problem here."

Richard moved to second shift, and Bill offered to come by and pick him up, since he drove by his house. Appreciative of the offer, he said, "Bill, I don't smoke pot or drink anymore; furthermore, I don't want to be around it either." They had worked the same shift before, and Bill would pick him up to smoke pot and drink before going to work.

Bill responded, "We don't have to smoke pot or drink, but I still want to pick you up."

Mick, on the other hand, was not as understanding. Although they were close–at one time Richard had even saved Mick's life–he had no knowledge of God and was a ruthless man. Richard kept trying to get up with him, then one day he and his wife came by the house and, as destiny would have it, Richard was not home. Cheryl invited them inside and shared with them about accepting the Lord.

Following that encounter, he did get word to Richard that if he ever divulged any information about their drug dealings in the Savannah area, it wouldn't end well for him. He moved to Louisiana to work on oilrigs, and Richard never saw him again, although he did call him once about seven years later.

His life had now been changed, and Richard wanted all his friends to make the same decision he had made for his eternal future. Clearly, not everyone understood or even cared. Some did. For sure, he genuinely believed that God had set a course for his and Cheryl's lives, and he was determined for them to pursue that course with all their hearts.

8

A New Journey Begins

As word spread about Richard's conversion, he received applause by some, ridicule by others, and threats by still others. In mid-July, he received a tip that some power player had possibly ordered a hit on him—a hit that would come in the form of a drive-by shooting at his home. Out of concern for Cheryl's safety, he sent her to stay with his parents for a couple of nights. Thankfully, the drive-by shooting never materialized.

Only a few weeks after his conversion, he was invited for an interview on Christian television. PTL had many satellite stations, one of which was located in Brunswick, Georgia. After the interview, calls started coming in inquiring if he was available to speak at youth gatherings and other events. The local station manager told him that 60,000 people watched at least part of the interview.

Richard spoke to his first youth group at a local church in Brunswick soon after the interview. A man that also worked at Babcock & Wilcox and was involved in drug trafficking had a girlfriend whose younger brother heard him speak. He told his sister that a former drug dealer talked to them about his drug dealings and conversion. "I think he's a friend of your boyfriend," he said. When the man heard about Richard speaking at the church his girlfriend's mother attended, he approached him at work, stomped on his foot, and spit in his face. He then told him what would happen to him if he ever revealed information or mentioned names during his speaking engagements.

One of the hardest things Richard had ever done was to walk away from that kind of humiliation. In his earlier life the fight would be on. A few days later, the man apologized to him saying "Religion is not for me, but I definitely have seen a change in you, and I respect you for it."

Someone later shared with Richard that the man's initial action was a test to see if he would retaliate, since he was known to fight first and ask questions later. He and his cohorts felt that if he didn't retaliate, he would probably be quiet about any drug operations or drug dealers he was privy too.

On the Sunday that he had accepted the Lord, the Holy Spirit prophetically spoke through the evangelist, Herb Winegar, three times. First, "If you come to me, I will set you free and put my Spirit in you." Second, "If you come to me, I will bless everything you touch for My name's sake." And third, "My Spirit is calling you for the last time." The church was full and although Winegar didn't mention his name, he knew the Holy Spirit was speaking directly to him.

In late August or early September, Richard and Cheryl found out that she was pregnant with their first child. The doctor said the child would be born March 20, but his mother, a registered nurse, counted from July 1, 1979, and said the baby would be born on April 4. Ricky came into the world early Sunday morning on April 4, 1980, just as Dot had predicted.

Pastor Muncy had scheduled a revival with Evangelist Dan Brockman in mid-September. Richard began asking Bill to come to the revival one night. Bill responded, "Man, do you know what would happen if I walked into that white church and heard someone say something derogatory to me?"

Richard answered, "Bill, if anyone says anything derogatory to you, Cheryl and I will walk out together with you." Considering this was 1979 in the Deep South, that scenario was possible.

Concerned, Richard went to Muncy, shared his burden for Bill, and related how he had responded when he, Richard, had invited him to church. Muncy said, "Get him on the phone and let me speak to him."

Richard called Bill and told him that his pastor wanted to talk to him. When Muncy got on the phone, he explained to Bill how heavy Richard's burden for him was and how much he wanted Him to come to the revival. In turn, Bill shared his concerns with the pastor that he had shared with Richard.

Muncy declared, "Bill, if anyone asks you to leave or says something derogatory towards you, I will personally walk out with you!"

With that, Bill agreed to come on Sunday night. Richard and Darrell met him in the parking lot and escorted him into the sanctuary. They all sat close to the front with Cheryl, Phyllis, and her husband, along with several others. After the evangelist preached and gave the altar call, Bill walked all over Richard's feet to get to the altar. Richard fell in behind him and knelt beside him. Tears were flowing freely from both men, as the evangelist knelt and prayed with Bill to accept the Lord.

The following week, a couple of very unhappy friends and associates of Bill approached Richard. They strongly suggested, "If you want to have religion, that's okay, but just keep it to yourself." Continuing, they declared, "There are a lot of people not happy with what has happened to Bill, so you need to be careful!"

Richard visited 75-year-old Bill in September 2019. Forty years had passed since his conversion, and he served God as a deacon in his local church until his death on October 20, 2021, at age 77. Richard had asked him about a certain person wondering if he had stayed in contact with him. Bill had answered, "Yes, I have. He is serving God and is also a deacon." That person was one of the men that had threatened Richard.

Revival fires had begun to burn in Richard's home church mainly through the young adults. They had begun having weekly prayer meetings at different homes, usually on Friday nights. James Carroll, a cousin to Cheryl, offered to host one of the prayer gatherings in his home. About 20 to 25 people attended. He had moved most of the furniture out of his living room to accommodate the crowd.

As the attenders formed a circle, joined hands, and began praying, Richard opened his eyes and saw a woman standing only inches in front of him. She was a mother to one of Phyllis' friends who had invited her mother to join her for the prayer meeting. Immediately, Richard discerned through the Holy Spirit that she was demon-possessed. Although he did not, in himself, know what to do or say, the words came out of his mouth, "How many are you?"

A man's voice spoke through this tiny stature of a woman and declared, "We are three, and we are not coming out!" With that, over half of the people attending the prayer meeting literally fled.

Richard anointed her with oil, and the remaining people began to pray. After a few moments she fell to the floor. As everyone began to rejoice thinking she was set free, something strange happened to Richard. He felt a powerful force pulling him to his knees, and he began to pray. As he did, he saw the image of an opossum. Being from Georgia, he knew what the Holy Spirit was conveying to him. Often when an opossum senses danger, it will roll over and play dead—hence, "playing 'possum." The demons had not departed but were trying to hide behind a façade only appearing to be cast out.

Richard rose to his feet, walked over to the woman lying on the floor, and reached out his hand to place on her head. She quickly grabbed his wrist with both of her hands and forcefully tossed him to the other side of the room. Understandably, he was briefly overwhelmed with fear and unbelief. But the Lord spoke to his heart and said, "Don't fear. I have given you authority over all unclean spirits. Go in the power of My name!"

He got up from the floor, walked back over to her, and stretched his hand toward her forehead once again. And once again, she grabbed his wrist with both her hands, but this time she could not move him. The band of believers prayed in the name of Jesus that the demonic strongholds in her life would be broken. This time, she rose to her feet cloaked with a look of peace and tranquility.

On Sunday morning, Richard was assigned to the greeter's team at church and saw a new guest sitting in the front row. He went to greet her and to hand her the visitor's packet. As he walked away, she asked, "You don't remember me, do you?"

He answered, "No, I don't think so."

The guest replied, "I'm the woman you prayed for Friday night, and I want to thank you for helping me get set free." Her countenance had changed so much that Richard simply didn't recognize her. This would be the first of many such encounters he would have with people bound by demonic powers.

A few weeks after Richard and Cheryl's conversions, one of the female bartenders who worked at the Quarterback Club missed seeing him come to the club, since he was there almost daily. She asked some customers who knew him, "Hey, where has Ricky been? I haven't seen him in a while."

After they told her that he had gotten religion, this woman knocked on the Baker's door one Sunday afternoon. Cheryl was in the bedroom, so Richard went to the door. To his surprise, there stood the bartender. She looked inquisitively at Richard and said, "Tell me if it's true. Did you get religion?"

Richard replied, "No."

Disappointedly, she responded, "I was hoping it was true."

"I said I didn't get religion!" he continued. "I got a whole lot of Jesus!"

She broke down, started weeping freely, and pleaded, "Ricky, you know what kind of life I live. Will Jesus save me?"

He quickly answered, "If He would save me, He will save you also!" He invited her inside and took her into the bedroom where Cheryl was, whom she also knew. As she knelt beside their bed, they led her in the sinner's prayer. She left their house with a beautiful glow and started attending church. This was the second person they led to the Lord in less than a month.

Cheryl's cousin, Mary Alice O'Neal, was over the children's ministries of the church and asked Richard if he could help a few weeks in the puppet ministry. In all honesty, that was the last thing he wanted to do. But he had already started praying for the Lord to use him in any way He chose to. The first Sunday was awkward and embarrassing. He had two worms as puppets, one on each hand, but he somehow made it through that portion of the children's church.

Mary Alice had scheduled the children's workers to do a children's revival in a church located in Jessup, Georgia, about 40 miles from Brunswick. Richard thought to himself, "Great! I have to be two worms for four mornings straight!"

The team arrived on Monday morning to set up the stage. He pulled the worms from their storage box in preparation for rehearsal. After rehearsal, the pastor, Elmer Golden, Jr., came out to meet them and thank them for their work. Seven years later, Richard would become his associate pastor.

Around 100 children poured into the sanctuary for Vacation Bible School that first morning. The program began and Richard tried to synchronize the mouths of the two worms with the words of the songs. That only increased his frustration level, considering that he really did not want to be there anyway.

At the end of the puppet ministry part of the program, Mary Alice, standing in front of the puppet stage, began giving an altar invitation. She asked each of the puppets what Jesus meant to them. The puppeteers were to answer in their own voices. When she got to the worms, Richard shared what Jesus meant to him and how he had recently accepted the Lord.

Mary Alice then asked the children who wanted to ask Jesus into their hearts to come to the altar. Richard pulled the curtain back just enough to witness several children coming forward. He fixed his eyes on an eight or nine-year-old boy who had tears streaming down his cheeks, as he made his way to the altar. One of the workers prayed with him to accept the Lord into his heart. Then Mary Alice let each child testify. When it came this little boy's turn, he said, "It was what the worms said that made me want to ask Jesus into my heart."

Richard walked up to him, got down on his knees, and gave him a big hug. He also told the Lord that if He wanted him to be a worm for Him, it would be his pleasure and honor. He later wrote:

> In Matthew 18:1-4, Jesus said that we must become as little children to inherit the kingdom of God. Verse four emphasizes that we must also humble ourselves as a little child. I experienced this humbling in the VBS service that morning and have never been the same since.

Throughout the fall of 1979, Richard and Cheryl thoroughly enjoyed going to church. They also enjoyed the outings with other young adults and found those times tremendously encouraging to them. Cheryl's Aunt Sally Mae began a Friday night prayer meeting in her home, which they began attending. For two to two-and-a-half hours every week, they would conduct Bible study, pray, and have fellowship. She had a large den and sometimes there would be 40 or more in attendance. People were saved and filled with the Holy Spirit. Miraculous healings occurred, and some experienced divine deliverances from demonic possession and oppression.

The second Monday in January Richard was on Christian television again giving his testimony. A Methodist pastor was watching. That Friday while shopping at a Western Auto store, the pastor saw him, approached him, and said, "Richard, I heard you Monday night, and the Holy Spirit spoke to my heart that you were to preach in our morning service this Sunday. And, oh, by the way, I don't want you to give your testimony. I want to share with us from the Word."

Richard quickly responded, "I am not called to preach. I'm not sure about preaching for you on Sunday."

The pastor replied, "You will need to take that up with the Holy Spirit. He has already spoken to me, but if you can't, let me know by 8:00 Saturday morning."

From that moment, Richard was in sheer shock and filled with considerable apprehension. He began praying and trying to figure out what a sermon would look like. Friday night came and he still had no peace. James was the first book he had read after becoming a Christian, so he started reading it again. When he got to James 1:22, 23, he felt what he called a "ping." "But be ye doers of the word, and not hearers only, deceiving your own selves. For if any be a hearer of the word, and not a doer, he is like unto a man beholding his natural face in a glass..."

He began doing his best to put together a message from these verses. By 11:00 that night, he had outlined his first sermon. He called Pastor Farris at 8:00 Saturday morning and shared with him that although he didn't feel called into pulpit ministry, he did feel peace about coming and speaking for him. The pastor was elated.

Richard paced his bedroom floor almost the whole day Saturday praying and going over the few notes he had. He struggled with overwhelming anxiety. Awaking at 6:00 on Sunday morning, he couldn't believe that he had gotten talked into doing this. Cheryl had nursery that morning at their home church and couldn't go with him. He was going to a church that he knew little about, as far as their order of service and how they worshiped. Consequently, he was not sure just what was expected of him. This only added to his anxiety.

He arrived 30 minutes before the service, and he and Pastor Farris had the opportunity to meet for a few minutes. Farris was a tall, stately man dressed in a clerical robe, with a distinctive moustache complete with handlebars. Richard had never seen a pastor wearing a robe, and the thought of having to wear one himself struck fear into his heart. Thankfully, that didn't happen, and he breathed a sigh of relief.

Farris went over the order of service with him, and promptly at 11:00 am, the service began. This was the first time Richard had ever attended a liturgical service and found that it had a solemn beauty to it.

At 11:45 am, the pastor presented Richard to the congregation, as Richard wondered if the Methodist only had 15 minutes of preaching. Simultaneously feeling fear and joy at being able to minister to this congregation, he shared that he was honored to have been given this opportunity to share God's Word. The next words out of his mouth were typical Richard. He declared, "Two things will happen this morning. You will either get up at 12:00 and leave, or you will stay and hear the Word of the Lord, for I will not be through by 12:00."

He read his text from the Book of James and shared what the Lord had given him. The pastor sat behind him, so Richard couldn't see his expressions. About two-thirds of the way through his message, he heard a commotion and turned around to witness the pastor on his feet, hands raised, tears streaming, and crying out, "This is what I have been praying for!"

Not surprisingly, that reaction elevated Richard to another level of expression. Now more impassioned, he preached another 10 minutes and felt impressed to give an altar call. But having an altar call was not something he and the pastor had gone over. Consequently, he turned to the pastor and asked, "May I give an altar call?"

Pastor Farris shouted, "Yes, yes, please do!"

Richard gave an invitation for salvation, and two men in their 50s came forward. The pastor met them and led them to Christ, while he continued the invitation. On the front row sat a woman in her 60s weeping uncontrollably, with her 12-year-old grandson sitting beside her. She motioned for Richard and explained, "My grandson has terminal juvenile diabetes. Can God heal him?"

"Absolutely!" Richard answered. He proceeded to anoint him with oil and pray over him in the name of Jesus. Farris called him two weeks later and told him that they took the boy for testing, and he was diabetes free. God had completely healed him.

On a humorous note, during the altar service, Richard became extremely thirsty and grabbed a large glass of liquid sitting on the side of the pulpit. The glass had an ornate metal lid, and he thought how helpful that was to keep flies out, considering this was South Georgia. He lifted the lid and took a shallow. According to him, what filled his mouth was the most rancid taste to pass his lips. And considering everything that he had swigged in the past, the taste must indeed have been foul! He soon discovered that Methodist sprinkle when they baptize, and he had drunk their baptism water. For sure, he got some shocked looks. An usher quickly retreated to get him some pure water, for which he was thankful.

According to Richard, "It has always been amazing to me how God can use the least of the least to accomplish His plan here on earth. And when He chose me, He chose one of the least. After Cheryl and I had been saved only six months, we had already had the joy of leading 12 people to the Lord, not counting those who called in to the TV station and prayed with one of the counselors while I was sharing and giving my testimony. Now, the Lord healed this precious boy because of my obedience. But as crazy as it may sound, I still didn't feel a call into the pulpit ministry. I just assumed that was a onetime occurrence."

The third Friday night in January, while attending the prayer meeting, Richard turned around and kneeled in front of the chair on which he was sitting, when prayer time came. He had only been praying for a few minutes when he felt a sensation come over him, and he received his first vision. He dimly saw Jesus from the neck down standing afar off. As He started toward Richard, he beheld a beauty unlike anything he had seen before. The Savior's presence overwhelmed him, as His hands reached out to him. He heard in a powerful but warm voice the words, "My son, I called you. Will you carry My Word?"

Richard at once cried out, "Yes, my Lord!" In his vision, the Lord began moving away, as His presence became smaller and smaller, until He was no longer visible.

As doubt filled Richard's heart, the Lord's presence reappeared. And once again He spoke, "My son, doubt Me not. I have called you. Will you carry My Word?"

Again, he responded, "Yes, my Lord!"

The Lord asked, "Will you be willing to leave your home?"

Once again, Richard exclaimed, "Yes, my Lord!"

As the Lord's presence once again began to fade away out of sight, Richard felt doubt filling his heart once more. The Lord reappeared, came close, and repeated, "My son, I have called you. Will you carry My Word?"

Still struggling to grasp the full importance of the question, he again cried out, "Yes, my Lord!"

"Will you be willing to leave your home?" the Lord again asked.

When Richard answered in the affirmative, the Lord asked one more question of him, "Will you be willing to labor for $90 per week?"

Without hesitation, he answered, "Yes, my Lord!"

After the Lord again departed, the doubt did not return to Richard. He, now knowing that God had called him into the ministry, realized that his life was about to radically change.

9

Ministry Opportunities

When Richard and Cheryl left the prayer meeting, he was filled with such excitement that he had to tell his pastor. He drove to the parsonage, rang the doorbell, and waited for an answer. Almost before Muncy could open the door, Richard blurted out, "Pastor, God called me to preach tonight!"

Muncy laid his hand on Richard's shoulder and calmly remarked, "Let's give it some time, and we will see." They talked for a few minutes and the previously excited couple left somewhat disheartened. Richard had expected the pastor to show a greater measure of excitement and rejoice with him over his calling. But that had not happened, at least not in the way he thought it would.

A couple of months later, Muncy asked Richard to meet with him. As they sat together, he explained, "Richard, I knew you had a calling on your life, but I wanted you to make sure of your calling. Consequently, I didn't show you much support or enthusiasm when you first shared it with me." Indeed, Muncy's wisdom had pressed Richard to spend time in prayer and fasting to confirm the calling he felt on his life.

When he returned to work on Monday, the first person he told about his experience was Pastor Mathis, a Wesleyan Methodist minister 30 to 35 years his senior. They worked in the same area. Since the time of Richard's conversion, Mathis proved to be an excellent source of encouragement to him. Richard respected him and loved him as a true brother in Christ. After he began preaching, and when some services were recorded, Mathis always wanted cassette copies (early 1980s) of his messages.

Although Richard always obliged him when he could, he was always anxious, as he anticipated coming back to work the next day to hear what he would say. Mathis would kindly offer a critique of his messages, and once, laid his hand on his shoulder, and said, "Ricky, you need to preach a little slower. Let the people have time to soak it in." On another occasion he asked Richard, "Did you give an altar call?"

Richard answered, "No."

Once again, Mathis gently placed his hand on his shoulder and declared, "I believe souls would have been won to Christ if you had. Never preach God's word without giving people an opportunity to come to Christ." From that time, he sought to practice that word of wisdom from his precious brother. Every time someone received the Lord in one of his services–a service Mathis would listen to on tape–he would approach Richard the next day weeping with joy.

He preached his first message at his and Cheryl's home church, Norwich Street Church of God. It was during a Wednesday night service and his level of nervousness was exceptionally high. When the service ended, he received overwhelming support from his fellow members. He went home that night filled with passion and desire to serve the Lord to the best of his ability.

Invitations began to come more often. Grover Meeks, a Southern Baptist pastor, who also worked at the plant but in a different department, invited Richard to preach for him on a Sunday morning. The anointing was powerful upon him that day, and he let God use him as He saw fit. Several people responded to the altar invitation. Richard still remembers seeing Pastor Meeks, who was a big man around six-foot four-inches tall or more, with his hands lifted shouting praises to God.

On Thursday, April 3, Richard worked the 3:00 pm to 11:00 pm shift, and on the drive home, was deep in thought concerning Cheryl's Cesarean section scheduled for the following morning. On Friday evening a week before, she and Richard, along with others, met at her Aunt Sally's house for a cottage prayer meeting. During the gathering, the believers prayed for God to touch Cheryl knowing that her baby was breeched. As they prayed, she said she felt something happen with the baby, perhaps an unusual movement.

They were to be at the hospital at 6:00 am. Around 2:00 am, Cheryl awakened Richard and announced that she was having contractions. Her mother, Margaret, who was spending the night with them, began timing her contractions. When they occurred five minutes apart, Richard called his mother, a registered nurse, and asked what they should do. "Get her to the hospital immediately," she replied.

Around 4:00 am they reached the hospital and, within an hour, Ricky, Jr., was born. Because both parents had attended special classes at the hospital, Richard was allowed in the delivery room. In 1980, this routine of allowing the father to be in the delivery room was relatively new. They were two proud and happy parents, as the Lord gave them the first of their five children. The doctor had said the baby would be born in mid-March, but Richard's mother had rightly predicted that the child would be born on April 4. And her delivery was natural, only an hour before she was to have the Cesarean section.

Cheryl was scheduled to be discharged on Sunday, and Richard realized that he was about to miss his first church service since becoming a Christian. Since the discharge was not until after lunch, he attended his first Easter service as a believer. He was blessed that day being able to celebrate Christ's resurrection, take Communion, and bring his first child home.

A couple of months after Ricky's birth, Meeks asked Richard to preach again, this time at a youth rally that the Southern Baptist churches in his area were hosting. When he arrived, he found over 500 teenagers gathered in a large family life center. He took his text from James 4:13-14: "Go to now, ye that say, Today or tomorrow we will go into such a city, and continue there a year, and buy and sell, and get gain: Whereas ye know not what shall be on the morrow. For what is your life? It is even a vapour, that appeareth for a little time, and then vanisheth away." He challenged them saying that just because they were young, they had no promise of tomorrow. The Spirit of the Lord moved mightily throughout the service.

Another minister who also worked at the plant, Edenfield, served as pastor in a Church of God about 30 miles from Brunswick and invited Richard to preach a Sunday through Wednesday revival. This would be the first of over 200 revivals that the Lord would bless him to preach. Edenfield was perhaps the humblest man he had ever met. He would often stop by the machine Richard ran and would lay his hand on him and say, "Brother Richard, I love you with the love of the Lord. You are such an inspiration to me!" The Lord put so many encouragers in his and Cheryl's lives during those early years of their ministry. The revival went well with several people accepting the Lord or rededicating their lives to the Lord.

In the summer of 1980, Meeks invited him to speak for the third time. He had planned a time for ministers to come and pray together from 7:00

pm until 12:00 midnight. There were somewhere between 75 to 100 ministers who assembled, mostly pastors. The evening began with a minister preaching approximately 30 minutes. After a time of prayer, another minister preached from 20 to 30 minutes, and the group prayed again. Richard was the third minister to speak, and the time was about 10:30 pm. He preached about 30 minutes, and the presence of the Lord came upon the gathering of mostly Baptist pastors in a powerful way. They were weeping on their knees in prayer and worship.

When the fourth pastor arose to speak, he began crying and announced, "I haven't anything to say other than I need what the previous brother has."

Meeks got up and took the microphone exclaiming, "He has the fullness of the Holy Ghost!"

When the minister declared that he wanted the same fullness, Meeks called for everyone who wanted a deeper presence of the Lord in his life to come to the altar. The first one was the brother who said he didn't have anything to say. When Richard prayed for him, the Holy Spirit came upon him and he began shouting, "It's real; it's real!" Richard found out later that Meeks had received the Holy Spirit with the evidence of speaking in tongues.

In the fall of 1980, the Sunday school superintendent asked Richard to start teaching the older teens, ages 15 to 17. He immediately agreed and took the teacher's manual offered him. He was thrilled and could hardly wait for his first Sunday to roll around. Arriving for class early, he anxiously waited for the students to arrive. That first Sunday, eight or nine students attended. Within nine months, he was having more than 30. No one was more shocked than he was. Parents came to him and told him that their children now wanted to come to church, because he could relate to them.

Richard preached in several other churches during the remainder of 1980. He and Cheryl were genuinely happy having accepted the Lord and having experienced a cleansing from their sins through His precious blood. They were part of a great church and part of a thriving young couples' ministry that they just loved. The Lord had called him into the ministry and had opened so many doors the first year that he was overwhelmed with amazement. And then their first child, Ricky, was born, which brought them additional joy.

As the Bakers moved into 1981, Richard continued preaching, as opportunities presented themselves. Mostly, he preached on Sunday nights and in midweek services, which allowed him to continue teaching his Sunday school class.

Muncy asked to meet with him to discuss his plans for the future. He began by telling Richard that he had no doubt that God had placed His hands upon him and Cheryl and that probably one day they would become involved in full-time ministry. After suggesting that they begin thinking about their long-range plans, he asked, "Have you considered attending Lee College (now Lee University) or some other accredited Bible college?"

Richard responded, "Brother Muncy, I was expelled from school in the 10th grade and don't even have a high school diploma!"

Muncy had two masters' degrees and in all their conversations, the subject never came up that he had not graduated high school. Clearly, he was taken aback by Richard's revelation. After pausing a moment, he said, "Richard, you need to go take the GED test as soon as possible. When you get your GED, come back, and let's talk more about your next steps."

He enrolled in night school just to see where he was. He knew English was going to be the most challenging for him. After five or six classes, the facilitator came to him and informed him that he thought he was ready to take the test. Since the test was being given the following Wednesday morning, Richard signed up for it. Upon arrival, he learned that the exercise was five tests, which would take between six and seven hours to complete. Although he wanted to run for the hills, he took the tests, finished, and anxiously awaited the results.

Upon receiving his results in about a week, he discovered that he had passed every class, including English, which he would have failed had he missed just one more question. He only missed four questions on math, and his overall score was high enough to get him accepted into most colleges and universities. Doing better than he expected was a major source of encouragement to him.

Richard reported to his pastor, shared the good news with him that he had passed, and together they rejoiced. Muncy spoke, "Richard, I know you and Cheryl have a baby now, and it might take you a year or more to make arrangements, but you need to make plans to attend Lee College."

"Pastor, I don't see myself as a pastor or a full-time minister. I don't think I need to do that," Richard explained.

"But you don't know that, and I see you doing greater things in ministry than you presently are," Muncy replied.

After talking it over with Cheryl, he discussed it with his parents at lunch one day, and they offered to pay his entire first year's tuition and book fees. He called the admissions office at Lee College, shared his situation, and asked for their recommendation. The representative informed him that he would have to take some non-credited classes in the first semester and possibly even into the second. Knowing that in his first two years he would mainly be taking core academic classes, the risk just seemed too great for him to quit his job, sell their home, and move his wife and baby six hours away, especially considering that he believed at that time in his life he didn't have the academic abilities to succeed.

Nonetheless, he ordered all the books he needed, read them, and studied them. Forty years later, he still has some of them. His pastor was a little upset with him and expressed his belief that it would affect how far he would go in the ministry.

Muncy asked Richard to preach on a Sunday night in early 1981. Before service began, a peculiar acting woman entered the sanctuary, walked toward the front, and sat down. Several people shared with Richard and the pastor that she refused to shake anyone's hand or look them in the face. Richard approached her and greeted her as he held out his hand. She responded by reaching out and taking his hand in a firm handshake. He at once felt coldness in her clasp and realized that he was holding a hand full of metal, seeing that she had several rings on each finger. She also had a dozen or more necklaces around her neck. Although he didn't want to stare, he observed that some of them were occult related–human skulls, upside down crosses, and such like. She sported tattoos with similar demonic images, including the number 666. As she looked intently into his face, she quickly let go of his hand.

Start time for church arrived and Muncy and Richard walked onto the platform. As they took their seats, the choir began singing. A powerful service followed, and the altars filled with worshipers and seekers. Soon after the meeting, Richard and Cheryl left for home. As they entered the parking lot, Muncy's wife, Elaine, approached him saying, "Brother Baker, please go back into the sanctuary. That strange woman is talking to the pastor, and there is no one else in the sanctuary."

Richard quickly returned to find the guest sitting in the back row with Muncy seated on the row in front of her. When the pastor saw Richard walk in, he invited him to join them. He said, "This is Sue, or that is her name for now. It was Rusty a couple of minutes ago."

Sitting down next to the pastor, Richard turned and faced her. As he did, she looked directly into his eyes and declared "Do you know why I am here? Our master sent me to bring you back. We will defeat Jesus at the last battle, so if you want to be on the winning side, you need to come back into the darkness." She continued, "I am our master's most trusted servant in this region. He has given me powers that you or any other Christians do not possess."

After asking Richard to step outside, she announced, "The first bird that flies by, I will cause to fall to the ground dead to show you the power our master has entrusted to me." She bowed her head and began to pray in satanic tongues in a man's voice. Once again, she looked up at Richard and spoke in her natural voice saying, "The master has invested too much in you; you must come back. The kingdom of darkness needs you."

Richard looked directly into her soul and boldly declared, "I through Jesus have greater power than you and your master!" He then quoted 1 John 4:4, "Ye are of God, little children, and have overcome them: because greater is he that is in you, than he that is in the world."

Immediately, all the necklaces fell from her neck and landed on the floor in 100 or more pieces. It was as if the hand of God had plucked them from around her neck and destroyed them, which is precisely what He did. Under the heavy anointing of the Holy Spirit, Richard asked, "Whose God has the most power now?" Without hesitation, this demon possessed woman bolted from the sanctuary. The week before, the Lord had led Richard into a three-day water-only fast. He often thought how that encounter would have ended had he not obeyed the leading of the Holy Spirit to sacrifice food for that time.

Infuriated at the rebuke she had received from the man of God, Sue went looking for trouble. Finding an Assemblies of God church that was having a fellowship after their evening service, she went inside, grabbed a large butcher's knife from the kitchen, slipped up behind the pastor, and placed the knife around his neck threatening to kill him.

R.L. Hall, next-door neighbor to Richard's parents and a member of that church, was working second shift at a paper mill only about a 10-minute drive from the church. Like Richard, he also had felt impressed to fast three days the week before. On this night as he worked, the Holy Spirit impressed him to leave at once and go to his church, stopping for nothing. Without taking time to get permission to leave, he bolted for his car, hurriedly jumped inside, and drove as fast as he could to the church.

Sensing the urgency of the moment, Hall wheeled into the church parking lot, brought his car to a screeching halt, and rushed into the fellowship hall in time to witness his pastor being held with a knife to his throat. With glazed eyes and a vindictive voice, Sue turned to him and cried out, "Just in time to witness your pastor's demise!"

Hall proclaimed, "In the name of Jesus, I command your hand to become paralyzed!" As he spoke the words, his pronouncement became reality. The knife at once fell to the floor, along with Sue, who now began begging for help. Believes quickly gathered around her, invoked the name of Jesus, and cast out the demons that possessed her. In that moment, the church witnessed the mighty power of God, as His outstretched hand and munificent love transformed Sue's life.

Richard had the privilege of speaking with Sue after her deliverance. In fact, she came and heard him preach a few months after being set free from the evil influences in her life. She secured a job with Jobs Core and began working with delinquent teens. When the Bakers moved to Manchester to pastor their first church, Richard lost contact with her. He later declared, "This much I know, darkness lost two soldiers, and for that amazing work of God's grace, I will forever praise the mighty name of my Lord and Savior Jesus Christ."

In June, a ministers' conference was held in Orlando, Florida, and Muncy invited Richard to accompany him to the meeting. He had never been in a setting of this size, a meeting where more than one thousand ministers attended. He was overjoyed to be there and attended all the main sessions and took in as many breakout sessions as he could. He bought conference manuals, books, and a new study Bible. During the two-hour break in the afternoon, he retreated to his room, read, and prayed until the next session started. In that conference, he determined to educate himself at a pace he could manage and attend as many additional conferences as he could.

After he and his pastor returned to Brunswick, Muncy announced, "Richard, it's time for the church to set you forth for the ministry as an Exhorter. On the designated Sunday morning in July, when the Bakers arrived at church, Richard was a bit nervous knowing that the church body had to vote to confirm them. Muncy asked for a motion and a second to set them forth, and 100 percent of the church voted in favor. He and Cheryl walked down to the altar and knelt to be prayed over.

In the service that morning was a former pastor of the church, Reverend W.G. Abney, who also was the pastor who had married him and Cheryl. That was such a special honor for them even though they were not attending church at the time they got married. Although he didn't know Abney that well, having him as part of the setting-forth ceremony was deeply meaningful and encouraging to both him and Cheryl.

In a couple of weeks, the study material for the Exhorter's test arrived, along with the Minute Book for the Church of God, Cleveland, Tennessee. The test was scheduled for February 1982, and Richard studied those two resources voraciously. In fact, he studied so much that the pages were falling out of the two resources he had.

A co-worker and close friend to Richard, Raymond Drury, had arranged to take his test at the same time and offered to drive him the two-and-a-half hours to Tifton, Georgia. They arrived at the Church of God State Offices and checked in as applicants for the ministry. Members of the licensing committee gave instructions and passed out the tests. According to procedure, following the written test applicants went before a panel of experienced pastors for an oral examination—an interview to determine if the applicant was truly called of God and to determine if they were prepared to pursue pulpit ministry.

Raymond and Richard were the first two to finish. Richard's test was quickly graded, but he did not yet know how he scored. When he sat down in front of the panel, one of pastors informed him that they would give him three questions: one concerning salvation, another on sanctification, and the third on the baptism in the Holy Ghost. He made it through the first two without a problem, and then the third question came.

"Brother, in your opinion, how old does one need to be in order to receive the baptism in the Holy Ghost?"

Richard thought a minute and answered, "John the Baptist received Him three months before he was born, in his mother's womb." Perhaps because he was just nervous, or because he was just being Richard, he added, "Is that early enough for you?"

One of the examiners quickly admonished him saying, "This is a serious matter and not to be taken lightly!" Richard got the message. Both men made 100 percent on their test and returned home rejoicing.

In November 1981, he got off work at 7:00 am and headed for the gym to workout. As he turned into the parking lot, a truck t-boned him on the passenger side and pushed him into a telephone pole. The impact was so forceful that he hit his head on the side glass bursting it out. Following a brief unconsciousness, he came to and felt like his head was in a barrel.

After being taken to the hospital and treated for a slight concussion, he was placed on observation for eight hours. His mother came to the hospital, picked him up, and took him home. That was on a Wednesday night and since he had not yet missed a service, he asked his mother to take him to church. They stopped and picked up Cheryl and Ricky and got there just in time for service. As now had become his pattern, he sat up front.

As the pastor prepared to receive the offering, he noticed a shortage of ushers and called upon Richard to help, not knowing he had been in an accident. Following the offering, he returned to his seat and put his arm around Cheryl, or so he thought. Feeling something lightly touching his back, he turned around to see Cheryl holding Ricky, who was mouthing "Dada" and reaching out to him. Confused, he turned back to see who it was that he had his arm around. Surprised, he saw that it was one of the senior ladies with a beehive hairdo looking up at him with a bewildered look on her face. Some people in the congregation saw what had happened and could not contain themselves. As they laughed, with some bending down between the seats, Richard, embarrassed, got up and went to sit with his family. As he sat down, Cheryl asked, "Are you sure you needed to be released from the hospital?"

As fortune would have it, in December 1981, Babcock & Wilcox announced they would be closing the plant by June 1982. It came as a shock to the nearly 1,000 employees. Richard decided that when his turn came to be laid off, he would make an effort at preaching revivals, and the weeks he had no place to preach, he would roof houses and do other construction work. One of his cousins, Frankie Tyson, who pastored a church in Barnesville, Georgia, located about 50 miles south of Atlanta, had invited him back in November 1981 to preach for him on February 21, in his morning and evening services.

Following the announcement of the plant closing, Richard, who had been a Group 1 Large Machine Operator, was reduced to a lower level and, in January, cut back to a machine operator helper. Finally, he was given a two-week notice that February 19 would be his last day.

When that last day came, he became more emotional than he thought he would be. At the end of his shift at 3:00 pm on Friday, he headed to the parking lot and stopped to look back with tears in his eyes at a place where he had enjoyed working.

As he later wondered why he was so emotional, he felt that he discovered the answer. The subject in school which he excelled in was math. To be a machine operator, a person had to know fractions, radiuses, degrees, decimals, and tolerances. Richard was in his comfort zone but now he was about to embark into an area of service that required skills he did not possess. That fact created in him a great deal of apprehension.

10

First Pastorate

Amazingly, the timing of his cousin's asking him to preach for him on February 21, long before employees knew Babcock & Wilcox was closing, worked out perfectly. Richard walked out of the plant on Friday, February 19, and on Sunday, February 21, he walked into a pulpit for the first time as a full-time minister.

Although he received an invitation to preach only on Sunday, his appointment turned into a revival that saw many people coming to Christ and finding deliverance. On Monday night, Bobby Tatum, who was a pastor and the district overseer for that area, came to the service. Another powerful meeting ensued and after the service, Richard returned to his cousin's home, where he was staying.

As he retired for the night, Tyson knocked on his bedroom door, announced that Tatum was on the phone and wanted to speak with him. When Richard answered the phone, Tatum offered a positive comment on the service and then asked if he would be interested in pastoring a church on his district. Richard was speechless. Tatum informed him that the pastor was planning to retire in early summer of the following year. He noted that the church had dropped considerably in attendance and any salary would be small or non-existent. He made it clear that the new pastor would have to get a job.

At that moment, Richard felt the Holy Spirit come over him and felt some peace about pastoring the church. But he was filled with so much uncertainty that he quickly answered, "I haven't been called to pastor, but to evangelize."

Tatum replied, "Well, you will have to take that up with Lord."

The following morning, Richard's cousin offered to take him to Manchester to see the town and to ride by the church. As they entered the city limits, he observed a little red brick church on the right. Tyson pulled up to the building and stopped. Richard had prayed the night before, "Lord, when I put my hand on the door handle, if this is Your will, let me bear witness."

Frankly, he didn't want to sense anything, because he didn't really want to be a pastor. But as soon as he touched the door handle, he felt a warming and tingling sensation go through his right hand like what he sensed when Tatum had called him after the revival service. When the meeting was over, Richard returned home to share with Cheryl what had happened. She quickly exclaimed, "We can't pastor a church!"

After praying for a few days, Richard reached out to Tatum to share his and Cheryl's limitations, noting how young they were physically and spiritually. Still, he wanted them to take the church following the present pastor's retirement.

An unexpected double blessing came to the Bakers when Cheryl discovered she was pregnant with their second child. Of course, the first blessing was the pregnancy itself. The second blessing came when Richard, after having his health insurance expire because of being laid off from the plant in February, discovered the company agreed to cover the complete pregnancy. His mother, Dot, who worked as a nurse at the plant, had mentioned the situation to one of the plant managers. Within a few weeks, she received word that the company would assume all medical expenses related to Cheryl's pregnancy.

The following November when their son, Ryan, was born, the Bakers did not have to pay one cent to the doctor or the hospital. Clearly, God had a plan for them and was systematically working to bring His plan into focus. They had already experienced several miracles since their conversion, but these were only the beginning. God would increasingly use them in signs and wonders in the years ahead.

A large construction company located in Brunswick, Drigger's Construction, seemed the best place to apply for part-time work to support his work in the ministry. He talked with Terry Drigger and shared his situation with him. Drigger replied, "Anytime you are in between revivals, and I have work, you will have work. And presently, I have plenty."

The company developed higher end sub-divisions and had a couple underway–one on the mainland and one on St. Simons Island. A couple of houses were ready for roofs, and after agreeing to a fair lump sum, Richard began roofing the first house by himself. It took him three days to install the flashing and shingles and prepare for the second one.

The thought came to his mind as he was roofing, "Paul made tents in order to carry the gospel, and now I am roofing houses in order to carry the gospel."

Richard received a call the second week of March from a pastor in Pensacola, Florida, who pastored a servicemen's center. These centers/churches were strategically located near military bases. This one had a bunkroom to accommodate soldiers on their days off, a game room, and the sanctuary—all housed in one complex.

The pastor shared with Richard that he had had several speakers, but none was able to relate to his mostly military congregation. He wanted to know if Richard could conduct a revival for them starting Easter Sunday, April 4, through Wednesday night. Without hesitation or without checking with Cheryl, he agreed. When he did share it with Cheryl, she quickly reminded him that April 4 was Ricky's second birthday. But since he was not getting a lot of invitations, although he intended to enter full-time ministry, he knew that he didn't need to turn down any opportunities.

Excited about this prospect, he embarked on the 10-hour drive from Brunswick to Pensacola early Saturday morning bearing some sadness in his heart for not being there for Ricky's birthday. He arrived around 4:30 pm exhausted, only to have the pastor inform him that they were going to a Church of God in Christ revival service at 7:00 that evening.

Upon arriving for the service, he walked into a rather large church with over 1,000 attenders. He was introduced to the pastor as Evangelist Richard Baker, to which the pastor responded, "Evangelist, I am going to give you 15 minutes to preach tonight." Exhausted and without notes, his mind went blank. All he knew to do was pray and depend on the Lord to give him something to share.

He was seated on the platform with 20 others, including the pastor. After a few songs, the pastor introduced him and called him to the pulpit. To this day Richard is not sure just what he said, but he noted, "The organ stayed lit up, and in a Black church, that's a good thing!"

Following the service, an elderly lady approached him and reached her hand out to shake his, held onto it for a moment, and expressed, "I got the most out of what you shared tonight." Those words provided significant encouragement to him. At the same time, he felt an object of some kind as she held his hand. When she pulled her hand away, she left some tightly folded money in Richard's hand.

Richard instantly declined, exclaiming, "No, ma'am, I can't take this from you!"

The saintly woman replied, "The Lord told me to give it to you, and I ain't taking it back!" He learned a valuable lesson that night.

When Richard arrived back at the servicemen's center, a couple of servicemembers, who would be staying in the bunkroom with him, warmly welcomed him. The next morning was Easter, and when Richard went down to the sanctuary, the pastor was preparing for communion. The pastor said, "Brother Baker, if you are okay with it, I will introduce you, let you say a few words, and I will preach this morning. You can start the revival tonight."

Richard was a little disappointed having expected speaking in the morning service. However, he knew that he couldn't say to the pastor that he couldn't preach in his own morning service.

The revival went extremely well, extending for 10 days. Several people were saved, and some rededicated their lives to Christ. Most nights, at least one service member would be in the bunkroom, sometimes several. They kept Richard up asking questions till two or three o'clock in the morning. But he enjoyed the time he spent with them. This was his longest revival yet.

As he returned home, his mind was racing as he thought about all that had happened in the short two months since losing his job due to the plant closing. He thought, "What's next, Lord?" He had scheduled a few Sundays for the rest of April and May but nothing after that. He kept roofing to put food on the table and pay the bills.

At the South Georgia State Camp Meeting in June, he had several pastors offer to introduce him to a few friends, some of whom assured him they would book him for revival meetings. He excitedly reserved a hotel room for the week. On the first day of camp meeting, he noticed that the same pastors who had offered to help him began avoiding him. They didn't even schedule him as they had promised. Friday came and he had no revivals scheduled. This was his first lesson in church politics but it would not be his last.

He called the state office to schedule a meeting with B.J. Moffett, state overseer for South Georgia. Fortunately, he was able to see him at 10:00 on Monday morning. When the secretary took him into Moffett's office, he nervously entered. Once he sat down, Moffett asked, "What can I do for you?"

Richard responded with his own question, "Do you have a struggling church you need someone to pastor?"

Moffett answered, "If I did, you would have to work and support yourself."

"That's no problem. I can do roofing and other carpentry work," Richard replied.

Interested, and for the sake of verification, the overseer asked, "You can roof?"

Once again, Richard answered, this time more emphatically, "Yes sir, I am licensed and bonded."

Hearing that response, Moffett took him to the swimming pool that was in an enclosed building. He asked, "Can you install four skylights in the roof of this building?" Richard answered in the affirmative.

When asked if he could do some light remolding on a couple of the smaller dorms and have them ready by the beginning of youth camp the following Monday, he announced that he could. Moffett let him know that he would pay him for his work.

Richard went home, donned his work clothes, gathered his tools, and started working on the projects Tuesday morning. He finished the work on Saturday afternoon in plenty time for the beginning of youth camp.

He never heard another word from the overseer about an opportunity to pastor a church. This was the first time, as well as the last, that he ever asked to pastor a church. When he returned home, Tatum called and asked him if would still be interested in pastoring the church in Manchester, Georgia. Richard answered, "If you feel I am the man, and the church could wait until late August, I will give it strong consideration."

Tatum explained, "Please understand that there is no parsonage, and the church can't presently pay any salary."

Richard shared the news with Cheryl, who was now four months pregnant. Although she was quite anxious, she agreed to move. He found a couple of men who needed work and started roofing from daylight to dusk, through all of July and into the first part of August. God blessed so bountifully that a few of the homeowners who knew what he was doing even paid him over what he charged. He wrote later:

> I have discovered in this Christian journey that God honors and rewards raw faith that believes what others won't and a willingness to follow hard after His will, no matter the difficulty one faces to get there. And I thank the Lord so much for the raw faith He has given us, and the tenacity to see it come to fruition in so many ways.

In early August, Richard and Cheryl drove to Manchester to find a house to rent. Manchester is a small town of about 4,000 residents. They stopped at a realtor's office but found no rentals available, nor did they find anything available after searching into the afternoon.

As they drove, Cheryl felt impressed to tell Richard to turn down a particular road. There they discovered a small four-room house, checked it out, and found that it was available. Not knowing what the future held, they leased it for three months, paying in advance. After returning to Brunswick, Cheryl busied herself packing, while Richard worked as much as he could.

In a couple of weeks, Richard rented a moving truck and enlisted Darrell, his first convert, to help him load. Cheryl's cousin, Benny, along with Darrell, would be riding with him in the truck. Their wives would follow accompanied by Cheryl and Ricky.

The entourage stopped by to see Richard's parents and say goodbye. It was an emotional tear-shedding moment. After hugs and good-bye kisses, the group began the six-hour journey to the Bakers' new home, stopping about 10 miles from Manchester to spend the night at a hotel.

After helping unload the truck the next morning, Richard's and Cheryl's friends exchanged good-byes and departed on their return trip to Brunswick. As he held Ricky, with Cheryl standing beside him, they watched somberly as their close friends drove away. At that moment, reality struck him. He had not met one member or the pastor he was following. Nor had he even stepped one foot inside the church. He had now moved his family to a town he had only briefly visited once. Although they didn't know a single person, and although Richard was dealing with some uncertainties, he had an abiding peace that they were in the center of God's will.

He scheduled a meeting with the pastor on Monday morning at the bank to change names on the church bank account. At 10:00 am the pastor approached him and asked, "Are you the new pastor for the Church of God?" When Richard answered in the affirmative, both went inside the bank to make the necessary changes.

As they were changing the signatures on the account, the vice president confronted the pastor and asked, "How do you want to handle this delinquent loan?" He then opened the file in his hand.

Clearly, everyone was embarrassed. The pastor pulled out his checkbook, wrote a check for part of the balance, and asked the banker to give him a little time for the rest, seeing that a new pastor had just arrived. After walking out of the bank, the pastor shook Richard's hands, handed him the church keys, and departed.

Richard went back inside and asked to see the vice president. To assure the banker of his trustworthiness, he declared, "I plan to seek a loan to expand the church within a year, and I want you to know what kind of person you are dealing with. What is the payoff on the loan?" When the bank officer gave him the figure, which was a little less than $1,000, Richard wrote a check to pay off the full amount. Impressed by this new pastor's forthrightness and honesty, he shook his hand and said, "When you need a loan, come see me."

Even though the Bakers had not yet met a member of their congregation and had not been inside the church, he had paid off the church's loan and built creditability with the banker. They were now ready for their first note-burning service.

The departing pastor had also informed Richard that the church didn't have a piano player. To help her grandson in his first pastorate, his Grandmother Paulk agreed to come up for a few weeks and play. On Tuesday he drove down to Fitzgerald, Georgia, to get her.

His first service was on Wednesday night, and he was quite nervous. There were only nine people in the service that evening, and that included Richard and his small family. Regardless, he preached like the house was full.

He managed to contact a few members between Thursday and Sunday. That first Sunday, 16 people showed up for Sunday school with the same number for morning worship. When Cheryl took Ricky to a classroom to teach him, he looked up at his mother and asked, "Where are all the children?"

That was a tough day for both parents. Richard admitted his disappointment, after hearing and expecting that the church was averaging between 25 and 30 in attendance. He soon learned that the church had not seen 25 people attending in several years and was on the brink of closing.

The overseer appointed Cheryl as clerk until such time that Richard could appoint one.

After he and Cheryl counted and totaled the Sunday school offering and the morning worship tithes and offerings, the amount came to exactly $90. When Richard remembered the night the Lord called him into ministry and asked, "Would you labor for $90 a week?" he literally shook. That experience reinvigorated his faith, as he received affirmation that they were in God's will, regardless of how bleak things looked at the time.

He didn't take the $90. In fact, it would be six weeks before the church could give anything. His first check was $75. But this interesting and challenging beginning brought confirmation that God had indeed called them to Manchester.

The church was in disarray. The fascia boards were dangling, the grass was knee-high, and there were electrical and plumbing issues, as well. He spent a couple of weeks and used his and Cheryl's personal finances to do the repair work needed.

Richard's grandmother, after being with them for three weeks, expressed that she needed to return home but believed that God would provide someone to play piano for them on a permanent basis. He drove her home the following week and returned concerned about not having a musician for service on Sunday.

The following Sunday morning, he noticed a car in the parking lot that he didn't recognize. A young man in his early 20s got out and came in before Sunday school began. After introducing himself, he explained to Richard, "The Lord spoke to me in prayer this week that I was to come help you if you need my help." He continued, "I play the piano and am a member at the Assembly of God. I met with my pastor and told him that I felt the Lord leading me here, and he gave me his blessings. So, here I am, if you need me."

Woody Dunn began playing that morning, soon joined the church, and became involved in other areas of ministry. Richard explains, "True faith plus tenacity equals one piano player!"

With financial needs beginning to press upon them, Richard began earnestly searching for work. He would drive around, find some construction project underway, and inquire about a job. Disturbingly, no one would hire him. With their funds now under $1,000, he began to worry. Just as he and Cheryl neared the end of their resources, someone told him that the Nazarene church was building an addition. He drove to the church and talked with the contractor but received a rather rude response. The contractor exclaimed, "I don't need any help!" As an afterthought, he asked, "You're not from around here, are you?"

Richard answered, "No, I'm from Brunswick. I came here to pastor the Church of God on Hwy 85." He added a "thanks" and headed for his car. Before he reached it, the contractor called him back and said, "My dad is a pastor. Can you roof?"

"Yes sir, I can," Richard answered.

"Be back in the morning and I'll have the material delivered," the builder responded.

The structure was large, and Richard needed one more person to help him. Woody Dunn, his new piano player, told him that his cousin worked for roofers at times and that he probably would be glad to get the work. Woody put him in touch with his 19-year-old cousin, Randy. Richard picked him up the next morning, and they worked together Thursday and Friday. He had been witnessing to Randy off and on throughout those two days wanting so much for him come to Christ. When Richard dropped him off on Friday afternoon, he invited him to come to church on Sunday.

Randy replied, "I had already decided to come. I have never met a pastor like you. You are easy to talk to."

That same night Randy and some friends were drinking and driving. They crashed their car in front of the home of one of Richard's church members that happened to be a nurse. She heard the crash and, living on a gravel road, instinctively grabbed a spoon knowing she may need it. She ran to the accident site, saw Randy lying alongside the road, and heard him making gurgling sounds. Although she tried desperately to get the gravel out of his mouth with the spoon, he passed away at the scene.

His largely unchurched family asked Richard to conduct the funeral service. During his message, he shared something Randy had said to him as they worked together on the roof. "Pastor Baker, does God love me like He loves you, and will God save me like He saved you?"

Continuing the story, Richard had answered, "Absolutely!" Sadly, he replied that he wasn't ready to pray. His death had an effect on Richard for months, leaving him wondering if there was more he could have done.

Needing a more economical vehicle, Richard went to the local GM dealership looking for a suitable automobile. As a salesman approached him, he explained, "I need the lowest priced new car that is four-door, automatic, and has air-conditioning."

Taking him to a Pontiac T-1000, he exclaimed, "Here she is!"

Richard had sold his Buick Electra 225, which was enough for a decent down payment. After agreeing on the price, the salesman started filling out the credit application and asked where he worked. Richard told him that he pastored the Church of God. He immediately looked up, tore the application apart, and announced, "You get the car for $100 over dealer cost. Mr. Meadows (the owner) believes if he takes care of the man of God, God will bless him." The favor of God just kept coming to the Bakers.

Someone connected to the church needed a roof put on and contacted him. He surveyed the project, gave them a price, and they accepted. Cheryl was now past seven months into her pregnancy and was going to have to go back to Brunswick to have the baby. She planned to stay with Richard's parents. As Richard talked on the phone with Darrell, Darrell declared, "I will come up and help you roof the house, and Cheryl and Ricky can ride back with me." His first convert was already paying off in service rendered.

It was hard for Richard to watch as Cheryl and Ricky left for Brunswick. He had been working hard just to make ends meet and pastoring a struggling church at the same time. But each Sunday the attendance increased slightly over the previous week, and the small church was now averaging around 30 in morning worship.

Richard had booked Raymond Drury for a revival meeting set for the first part of October, since he did not want to get too close to Cheryl's delivery date. Drury arrived on a Saturday evening and his companionship was much welcomed. The meeting was to last from Sunday through Wednesday but continued for a week and a half. God opened the floodgates and sent a mighty revival. Twenty-nine people accepted Christ as their Savior, and Richard and Raymond baptized 24 in a local lake. On the Sunday following the revival, there were over 50 in attendance. In only two months, the church had grown from 13 to 50, and no one was more amazed than Richard was.

On what now seems a lighter note, Granny Horton, who was close to 90 years old and lived with her daughter, Velma Cooper, in a three-room mill village house, invited Richard and Raymond for dinner one evening. Their only income was their Social Security checks. The two men arrived at 5:00 pm and Velma apologized, saying, "Our checks haven't come in yet, so we were limited on what we could serve."

When the men sat down at the table, the hosts placed their plates in front of them with the food already on them. It truly was simple fare—

pigtails, collard greens, and cornbread. Raymond looked at Richard, who immediately knew that his evangelist was struggling. With a measure of hesitancy and an ample portion of determination, they ate the meal, politely excused themselves, and departed. As they got into the car, Raymond looked over at Richard and declared emphatically, "You couldn't pay me $10,000 to eat what I just ate, but there was no way I would have offended those two widows who gave us their best!" Richard confessed that he actually enjoyed it.

Approximately a year later, Granny Horton, and her daughter, Velma Cooper, moved a couple of streets behind the Bakers. They dearly loved this saint of God who stood about four feet 10 inches tall. She was reportedly a full-blooded Cherokee Indian. After every service, she would grasp Richard's right hand between her two small hands, pat it, and say, "My little preacher man."

One morning he received a call from Velma informing him that earlier that morning she could not get her mother to fully wake up. Velma had three sisters who all lived close by, and she had called them, as well as a son who pastored a church in the Atlanta area. Velma continued, "It's not looking good pastor."

Richard hung up the phone, ran out the door, crossed the neighbors' yards, and jumped a fence or two. When he arrived at the house, he entered to witness four daughters all weeping and sitting on the bed around their mother. Velma looked up at him and whispered, "Pastor, she's gone."

His heart sank knowing that he had lost a dear friend and his greatest encourager in the church. He walked to the bed, started weeping, and began praying for peace over the daughters. Of the four, only Velma was faithfully serving the Lord. On occasion the other daughters would attend church—on days like Mother's Day and Easter.

Suddenly a presence filled the room as Richard prayed. It was a peace like he had never witnessed before. Then an unimaginable thing happened. Granny Horton sat up in bed, began looking around at her four daughters, and started speaking. She declared, "Girls, I have done my best to raise you right and teach you about God and His love. Mommy has done all she can do for you, but now the time of my departure is here." She pointed to the ceiling and exclaimed, "Can't you see them? They are waiting for me, and I must return now. I hope you girls will start living for God, so we can see each other again one day."

With that, she looked around at each one of them and looked up at her pastor. For just a couple of seconds, he saw a small smile on her face. She then lay back down, and the angels ushered her back into the presence of the Lord. Richard simply could not find the words to describe what he had just experienced. The glory of the Lord that had filled that small house was like nothing he had ever experienced.

A few days later, he had the wonderful privilege of preaching her homegoing, which, in part, he had witnessed. He had to move the service to a larger church, which quickly filled. As he shared the story he had witnessed with her daughters of her transitioning from this life into life eternal, the funeral service turned into a revival service with people coming forward, weeping, and crying out to God. Her three wayward daughters all began attending church more often, with two of them joining the church. Granny Horton could not read or write much, but she knew how to touch the throne of God when she prayed. The following Sunday just did not seem right without her being there. He had lost his greatest supporter and prayer warrior and knew that he would not feel her hands holding and patting his hands each Sunday, nor would he hear the words again, "My little preacher man."

Since Cheryl's due date was approaching, Richard went to Brunswick the week after the revival hoping the baby would be born while he was there. After returning to Manchester to preach the last Sunday in October, he went back to Brunswick knowing that Cheryl could deliver anytime.

Friday rolled around and still no baby, so he told Cheryl he was returning to Manchester to preach Sunday morning and would return to Brunswick that same day. She responded, "Richard, don't leave. I feel the baby will be born this weekend."

Thinking that one day wouldn't make a difference, he didn't listen and returned to Manchester. A son, Ryan, was born early Sunday morning with his sister, Phyllis, beside Cheryl's bed instead of her husband. He felt a rush of emotions. He was proud to have a second son born to them, but then he started thinking about not being there and felt a rush of guilt. He didn't preach that morning; the congregation just sang a few songs. As soon as the service was over, he took off to Brunswick, where he found that Cheryl had had a difficult delivery, with the doctor having to use forceps. It took Cheryl some time to forgive him. And on more than one occasion, he has asked Ryan to forgive him. He says this is one regret he will take to his grave.

11

God's Power and Protection

Richard had leased a larger house in Manchester, and while he was in Brunswick, the church completely moved them in. About a week after Ryan was born, the family loaded up and returned to a different house from the one Cheryl had left. When they arrived at their new residence in the early afternoon on a Monday, Cheryl was exhausted. To add to her discomfort, the heat was not on, and the house was cold.

A retired pastor, Reverend Hardy, along with his wife, lived across the street. The wife came over to meet the Bakers and quickly appraised the situation. Seeing that the house was cold, and that Cheryl was not feeling well, she declared, "Pastor, bring your family to my house so they can be warm. I will look after them."

Scooping Ryan up in her arms, this sweet pastor's wife headed across the street, as Richard helped Cheryl and Ricky. She put Cheryl in a warm bed and then fed Ricky, while making over him like a grandmother. Richard returned home to get the heat going and to straighten up a bit.

With a cold November and not much construction going on, the Bakers were nearly broke—something he had never experienced before. He had always made good money, and he and Cheryl had never really struggled financially during the seven years they had been married. His biggest check yet from the church, $125, came the week before. The following Sunday, the family was able to attend church together and experienced a beautiful service. That week he received $75. When Friday came, he had $21 to his name.

After driving to the service station, he pumped $10 worth of gas into his car. Since there was not much food in the house, he visited the grocery store and purchased beans, rice, grits, and eggs, along with some milk and cereal for Ricky. When the clerk at the register tallied his bill, the total came to $10 and some change. Seeing he had 75 cents left, he returned and, for 67 cents, picked up a ham hock to flavor the beans.

Freezing rain began falling that night causing the roads to ice over. The following afternoon, Cheryl informed him that they were reaching the end of the baby formula. Knowing he had no money for formula, Richard asked her how long their supply would last. When she answered, "Until early Monday morning," he suddenly realized just how desperate their situation was.

The roads remained iced over all day Saturday, and Richard knew that the churchgoers would face a challenge getting to church on Sunday. But he was in a dilemma and chose not to cancel the service. Wisely leaving Cheryl and the boys at home, he went to church, where less than 10 people showed up. And although he desperately needed money for baby formula, he simply could not bring himself to ask anyone for help. Furthermore, the small amount of money the church had was in a checking account and, this being Sunday, he would not be able to cash a check anyway.

When Richard glumly returned home, Cheryl pleaded with him saying, "I can go without, but our baby can't! You need to do something!"

Not used to asking for help, he walked across the street to request a loan of $20 from the retired Hardy. They talked for an hour, but he still could not bring himself to ask for money.

Since he had deflated his tires a bit, which helped him to successfully negotiate the drive to church, he decided to drive a little farther to the grocery store. His intention was to explain his predicament and offer to leave his driver's license for a few cans of formula. He took Ricky with him thinking that perhaps the store clerks, seeing he had a two-year-old child, would have more compassion.

There was only one main grocery store in town, and it had closed early due to the icy roads. His last option was to drive to a convenience store hoping to find the needed formula. Unfortunately, the retailer didn't sell formula.

As Richard drove home, his mind raced to find a solution to his and Cheryl's growing dilemma. To add to his misery, as he climbed a hill, his car lost traction because of the icy roads. Once it came to a premature stop, the car began sliding backwards while spinning out of control. Fortunately, they didn't hit anything, but he did have one scared two-year-old.

After finally arriving back home, he reluctantly told Cheryl the bad news and exclaimed, "If God is not big enough to take care of us, we will leave!" He felt now that adversity was pressing his faith to its limit.

Around 6:00 pm he announced, "I am going into the front bedroom to pray, and if God doesn't meet our need, we will leave at 10:30 and head for Brunswick. So, pack up and be ready."

Settling into the quiet of the bedroom, he began seeking God for an answer. When he felt that he had prayed for an hour, he looked at the clock and saw that he had only been praying for 20 minutes. Ignoring the clock, he returned to his petition and persevered in prayer for nearly four hours.

Cheryl knocked on the bedroom door around 10:00 pm, but he cried out, "Don't interrupt me!"

She responded, "Richard, some lady is at the door asking for you!"

Grudgingly, he stopped praying, walked to the front door, and looked into the face of a woman he had never met before. She was in her 60s and asked, "Are you the pastor of the Church of God?"

Still feeling a bit put off by this interruption to his desperate praying, Richard answered, "I am."

The mysterious visitor then asked, "Will you step out to my car for a minute?" After leading him to the trunk of her car, she stated, "If this is not of God, please forgive me for intruding so late."

With that, she opened the trunk, and the first thing Richard saw was a case of Enfamil fortified with iron, exactly what they fed their baby, Ryan. In addition, her trunk was full of groceries.

Richard and Cheryl soon learned the whole story. This unknown Good Samaritan was at the commissary at Fort Benning, Georgia, some 45 miles away, buying groceries. As she passed by the baby formula, the Lord impressed upon her to buy a case of the product and take to the pastor of the Church of God in Manchester. Thinking it to be such a strange impression, she just passed it off as a crazy thought. As she checked out, the impression returned, this time so overwhelmingly that she knew she had to do it.

After taking her groceries to the car, she returned to buy the baby formula. As she stood before the formula, she prayed, "Lord, I don't know what kind!"

She instantly felt an impression filling her mind, "Enfamil with iron."

Sensing the answer was from God, she quickly grabbed a case and put it in the buggy. Suddenly, another thought came to her: "Maybe the family needs food too." In response, she filled the buggy full of all kinds of groceries.

When she arrived in Manchester with no idea where the Bakers lived, she stopped and asked someone at a service station. Although the attendant didn't know, he did know someone who attended the church and gave her directions to that person's house. Interestingly, the woman in the Bakers' church to whom this visitor was sent lived on the same street as they did. As Richard later said, "Real faith plus tenacity equals Enfamil with iron—baby formula plus two weeks of groceries for the rest of the family."

The precious woman's name was Virgilina Bridge, whose husband was a disabled World War II veteran. They lived a few miles from Manchester in a small community. Although Richard later visited them on several occasions, his first visit had the greatest impact on him. It was then that he more fully realized that the pension of a disabled war veteran had sustained his family for two weeks. And just as touching was the fact that they were not people of real means. It's amazing that God often uses people of limited resources to provide for the greater needs of some of His other children, just as the poor widow of Zarephath fed the hungry prophet Elijah.

When Richard tells this story, people usually ask him why his family didn't help them. The answer is that he truly felt in his heart that if God called them into the ministry, He would provide for them. Consequently, he never let his family know what they were going through during those lean years. On more than one occasion, his mother would ask him if everything was all right, or did they need her to send them anything. He always replied that they were fine, and that God was in control. Later, when his mother did hear this story, according to Richard, "She tore into me big time and literally cried!"

All these years later, he honestly believes that this was God's plan all along. God knew the calling He had placed on them, knew where this journey would take them, and knew that it would take extra-ordinary faith to fulfill His plan in their lives. These first three years of full-time ministry were a proving ground for him and Cheryl. It was a time to see if they were willing to pay the price and walk in the perfect will of the Lord.

Richard managed to keep enough money coming in to make it to Christmas. A few weeks before Christmas, his district overseer, Tatum, called him and announced that he and his wife wanted to help buy some gifts for the boys. It touched his heart, but his parents had already signed up to do it.

Since the Bakers planned to stay two weeks in Brunswick, Richard asked a retired Baptist pastor—whose son was the contractor that hired Richard to roof the addition on the Nazarene Church—to fill in for him. They had a great Christmas with family and just enjoyed being home.

They went to church the Sunday after Christmas, and a brother walked up to him and said, "I felt led of the Lord to give you this." He then handed Richard $350.

That night following service, the church held a reception for a couple going into full-time ministry, and the congregation was encouraged to give them a special going-away offering. Richard had already shared with Cheryl about receiving the $350, which brought no small measure of peace to them. However, as they walked through the reception line, the Holy Spirit spoke to Richard's heart to give everything he had to them. That meant not only the $350 he received that morning but also the rest of what he had with him.

He knew he had to obey God, even as he wondered what Cheryl, who was behind him, thought. When they had a private moment, she asked, "Did you give them everything we had?"

Richard answered, "I sure did!"

Cheryl reacted, "Why?"

Answering now with more detail, Richard declared, "I sensed the Lord telling me to give it to them."

Knowing how God had repeatedly and miraculously supplied their personal needs, she simply replied, "Okay," and didn't mention it again.

Richard had been invited to preach the following Sunday at a church close to I-95. He arrived that morning with great excitement about the opportunity to minister. God powerfully moved, and the altars filled with people crying out to God. After the service, the pastor handed him an envelope containing an honorarium. He also had a few people personally hand him love offerings.

As he stepped outside the church, a man in his 50s asked for a few minutes of his time. He began by saying, "I was raised in a Pentecostal church but strayed away from God many years ago." He continued, "I am a superintendent for Miller High Life, and we are building a new distribution center in South Carolina. I stopped at this exit to fuel up and saw the church. I felt an overwhelming urge to come to service today, but I got in my truck and pulled back onto the interstate. Two exits down, I turned around and came back. I am so glad I did. Your message was for me, and I just wanted you to know that." He then placed $200 in Richard's hand.

When he arrived back at his parents' home, he counted all the money that he had received. All that he had given to the couple going into the ministry, plus a little extra, came back to them within one week. The golden rule of giving is that you can't out give the Lord, if you are giving with pure motives.

The Bakers returned to Manchester feeling revived and refreshed, even though along their trip, their new car started leaking water onto the passenger floorboard. Richard drove to Meadows Motors the next day, where the service department explained that the repair would be a minor one. Considering that the repair would only take about 45 minutes, he chose to wait.

Having the time to spend, he walked into the showroom and was approached by the salesman that sold him the car. The man said to Richard, "Preacher, don't go anywhere."

Within a few minutes, the salesman returned, along with Meadows, the owner of the dealership. After introductions, Meadows said, "Preacher Baker, may I talk to you for a minute in my office?"

Once inside the owner's office and after taking a seat, Richard listened as Meadows explained, "I don't want to offend you, but I know you are pastoring a small church. Could you use a job?"

Richard responded with his own question, "Doing what?"

Meadows answered, "Selling cars."

Tentatively, Richard replied, "Mr. Meadows, I don't think I could tell someone that a certain price is the best price, when I know it probably isn't."

He laughed and said, "We don't operate like that here. We are a wholesale dealership. You will not be paid commission, but you will be placed on a salary. You will have medical insurance on yourself and can purchase it for your family if you choose. We will train you to take the customer all the way from the purchasing process, including the financing. All invoices have one non-negotiable price written on them. We never reduce that price for anyone except pastors, who get the car for $100 over cost."

Richard asked, "What if I have a funeral or someone is having surgery, will I be able to get off?"

Meadows laughed and declared, "I own three of the five funeral homes in the county, so when you have your pastoral duties, just take off. Your pay will never be docked."

He continued, "I am opening a Ford, Lincoln, and Mercury dealership in a few weeks, and I want you to be one of my first employees." Richard agreed to give it a shot and filled out the application before he left. The dealership was set to open in a couple of weeks.

Near the latter part of January 1983, Richard went to the post office to check his mail. The box contained a letter from Jacksonville, Florida. He opened it and found a brief note saying, "Hi! I am the man who stopped in Brunswick and attended the church that you were ministering in a few weeks ago. We spoke for a few minutes afterward. You know I work for a beer company, but I felt led to send you an offering. I hope you will receive it."

Inside the letter was a $500 money order. For the next 12 months, Richard continued to receive a money order for $500, with no more notes attached. After one year, the money orders stopped. He never heard from the man again but prayed for him often. He thought, "Real faith plus tenacity equals $6,200 from Miller High Life and a full-time dream job with wonderful benefits."

The questions that stir Richard's heart even today are, "What if I had not prayed for four hours for baby milk? What if I had not given all the cash we had? Would these blessings still have come?" He believes the answer to the last question would be a resounding, "NO!" In his words, "God rewards faithfulness and the first five letters of the word spells F-A-I-T-H."

12

Confronting Evil

When Richard began working at the Ford dealership, he instructed the clerk of the church to no longer pay his salary, since he was making enough to live on, and since the church needed to build up some reserves. The T-1000 Pontiac was now too small for the four Bakers, and his mom was looking for a small car to drive to work in. So, they sold her their car and bought a new Pontiac station wagon. He purchased a used pick-up truck that someone had traded in. Circumstances were turning around, and the days began to look brighter.

On Mother's Day, a middle-aged man walked into the church looking disheveled and sat down. The service was already underway, and people were singing. That morning Richard preached on the family. About 10 minutes into his message, the man stood up, cursed, and told Richard that he didn't know what the (expletive) he was talking about.

A few months earlier, an ex-marine, Johnny, who had served in Vietnam, visited the church and accepted the Lord. He was in excellent physical condition and, on this day, sat in the front row. He at once jumped up and shouted, "You don't cuss my pastor!" With fire in his eyes, the Vietnam veteran bolted for the heckler. The man ran to the back door, yanked on it, and the door handle came off in his hands. With no place to go, he braced himself for the worst.

Richard cried out three times to Johnny, declaring, "Stop in the name of Jesus!" The man fumbled with the door and finally got it opened. When he paused for a moment and looked back at the pastor, Richard, under the inspiration of the Holy Spirit, declared, "Set your house in order, for your days are numbered!" Three weeks later, someone found him sitting in his car, dead.

Later, Richard found out that he was a notably mean man. His wife had cancer, and he made her work until the week of her death. After they buried her, he went by her place of employment and picked up her last paycheck. Why he chose to stop by the Manchester Church of God, Richard never knew. He would be the first of several people to whom the Lord would speak these words to through him.

The church was in dire need of a new roof. With Richard not taking a paycheck, the church had enough funds to purchase the material. He scheduled two Saturdays to replace the roof–one side each Saturday. Meadows allowed him to take off from the dealership to oversee the project.

A new family had begun attending church. The wife and the two grown children seem okay, but the husband, Jim, troubled Richard deeply within his spirit. The man was 6-feet 2-inches tall and weighed 250 pounds with virtually no fat. He showed up to help with the roofing job the first Saturday. Needing to go to the hardware store to get certain items, Richard left the men tearing off the shingles. When he returned after only about 30 minutes, he found Jim alone on the roof. Richard asked, "Men, what are you doing?"

They replied, "Get him off the roof, and we will go back up. He told us that if the Lord told him to, he would throw all of us off the roof!"

Richard climbed the ladder, walked over to Jim, and asked, "Why did you say that to the guys?"

Jim answered, "I will do whatever the Lord tells me to do!"

In response, Richard asked him to get off the roof and leave. He grumbled at the pastor but left.

One woman in the church worked at a furniture store downtown. That afternoon Jim was walking in front of the store, and a man stopped him and said, "I heard you got religion and are going to church."

Jim replied, "Yes, I am."

The man said, "Remember to pray for me."

With that, Jim grabbed his head and commanded, "Come out of him you (expletive). She called Richard and shared with him what she had witnessed.

The following morning Richard was taking new members into the church. He called for those that had spoken to him about membership to come up to the front of the sanctuary. When Jim joined the group, Richard was at a loss as to what to do, but the Lord impressed him to stand his ground. Walking up to him, he said, "Jim, you can't join until you meet with me first. You will need to take your seat." He gritted his teeth but returned to his seat.

Every Monday morning Richard opened the church from 6:00 to 8:00 for men to come by and pray before they went to work. Jim had never shown up but did that morning, somewhere around 7:15. By 7:30, the only ones left were the pastor, the church clerk, and Jim. The clerk, Randy, a large man in his 20s, came over and knelt beside him and whispered, "Pastor, I have to go to work. This man is up to no good. He has stabbed people and has spent time in prison. He is waiting for me to leave."

Richard appreciatively responded, "Brother Randy, the time of prayer doesn't end until 8:00. God will be my protector."

As soon as Randy drove away, Jim approached the pastor and boldly stated, "We need to talk!"

Jim sat on the second pew, with Richard on the front one. He began to tear into the pastor and even started threating him. Richard dropped his head a little in silent mediation. Jim shouted, "Look at me when I'm talking to you! I am no dog!"

When Richard looked up at him, he saw that his eyes had completely turned red, and he began contorting. At that moment, Richard knew that he was dealing with a heavily bound demon-possessed man that Satan had sent to attack and oppose him. Richard stood to his feet and declared, "There are two doors in the back of this church. Exit one of them and never return, in the name of Jesus!"

Jim arose and made it about halfway to the door but turned and charged Richard, shouting, "I am going to break you in two!"

Richard pointed his finger at Jim and once again declared, "In the name of Jesus!" It was like an invisible force field surrounding him that kept the livid Jim from coming to within five feet of the man of God.

Again, Jim turned and started for the door. But again, he turned and charged Richard. Just as before, the pastor pointed his finger at him and exclaimed, "In the name of Jesus!" And one more time, a powerful force stopped him five feet short of Richard.

This time Richard proclaimed, "Jim, you're fighting against a power much stronger than you are." Upon reaching the door, he threatened to kill the pastor and his family when nobody was looking. For the third time, Richard pointed his finger at Jim and this time spoke, "Set your house in order; you days are numbered!" He died within a month, a healthy man in his 40s.

It is a dangerous thing to defile the house of the Lord and to touch God's anointed. It was Richard's desire for Jim to call out to God for mercy, but he refused and met with God's judgment.

13

A New Challenge

Lee University started offering extension classes in Macon, Georgia, a 70-mile drive from Manchester. Woody Dunn wanted to attend, so he and Richard enrolled. They met on Tuesday and Thursday nights for 12 weeks, taking two classes at a time. Upon completion, both received certificates. Now Baker had six credit hours with Lee. This was a milestone in his life, and he was heartened to reach it. The next year, he signed up for two more classes and received six more credit hours. The extension program soon stopped.

By the summer of 1983, the church in Manchester had grown to an average of 60 attenders. The church received a plaque from the North Georgia State Office for having the greatest percentage of increase (475 percent) for a one-year period.

Muncy came in September and preached a one-week revival. The church thoroughly enjoyed his ministry, but not as much as Richard and Chery did. His fellowship and encouraging words were a sweet-smelling savor to the Bakers. Their spirits soared as he freely poured into them his years of experience and wisdom.

The Bakers lived only five miles from Warm Springs and the Little White House where President Roosevelt spent much of his time battling polio, and where he would eventually die. One of Baker's favorite places to pray and mediate was the highest peak in the Pine Mountain range, where Roosevelt had a stone barbecue pit built overlooking a majestic valley bounded by the beautiful mountains. This was one of the president's choicest places to go and mediate during the turbulent years of World War II. Baker took Muncy there, and he returned every day to pray and mediate.

The church managed to make all necessary repairs and upgrades to the facility and purchased a mobile home for a parsonage. In October, J. Frank Spivey, who was related to Richard, came and spoke at Manchester's homecoming. Spivey, a renowned leader in the Church of God, had retired in 1982 from full-time ministry, which was the same year Baker and Cheryl entered full-time ministry. Baker remarked concerning Spivey, "He probably was the wittiest man I had ever met, and also one of the most intelligent. He poured into our ministry up until his death. He gave me over 500 books from his library and spent time mentoring me. Some of the wisest council I ever received came from his lips. He preached on grace in such depth that it made you just sit in wonderment of the Father's love for us. On one occasion, he shared with me that a minister had to experience grace at a deep level to be able to preach on it at a deep level."

Baker continued working at Meadows Ford, Lincoln, and Mercury Dealership. God had given him favor with Congressman Meadows, who was the wealthiest businessman in the county. He showed considerable kindness and friendship to the entire Baker family.

In January 1984, Baker went to the Church of God campground in Doraville, Georgia, a suburb of northeast Atlanta, to spend a week fasting, praying, and seeking the face of the Lord for His direction. At the end of the week, he met with J. Frank Culpepper, the state overseer for the churches of God in Northern Georgia. He shared with him that unless the Lord directed him differently, he would be returning to the evangelistic field in June. Culpepper not only expressed appreciation to him for giving him plenty time to find a replacement pastor for Manchester, but he also assured him that he would recommend him throughout the state.

When he returned to Manchester after meeting with Culpepper, he shared the news with Cheryl and began reaching out to pastors concerning his decision to return to the evangelist field. A number of pastors began booking him for revivals, giving him a sense of confirmation that he had indeed heard from the Lord.

He had worked hard to build a strong financial reserve at the church, so the next pastor would not have to struggle like he and Cheryl had. God had blessed him with an excellent job, and he didn't need to draw a salary from the church. However, the church did take care of their housing, and that was a win-win for both the church and for them.

Not long after, the Bakers heard that Culpepper had been diagnosed with terminal cancer. His and Cheryl's hearts were saddened, and they spent time interceding in his behalf. On Tuesday, May 1, he received a call from Culpepper. At first, he thought someone was imitating the seriously ill overseer, but then thought that no one would be that cruel. It dawned on him that it must really be his overseer speaking to him. Culpepper's words are etched indelibly in Baker's mind more than 36 years later:

> Brother Richard, this is Brother Culpepper. I hope that you and your family, along with the church, are doing fine. I have been praying for the last two hours concerning a church in the Augusta, Georgia, area. The pastor has resigned and is moving to Africa as a missionary. I know you shared with me back in January that you planned to return to the evangelistic field, but you are the only pastor the Lord has laid on my heart for this church.

As Culpepper's words trailed off, Richard was crying. Cheryl was standing in the kitchen not knowing with whom he was speaking or the cause for his tears.

He continued, "Brother Richard, I can't give you much time to pray about it. I will need an answer by tomorrow morning."

Richard responded, "Brother Culpepper, if you feel so strongly that I am the man for that church, I will submit to you and accept it as God's will."

"Pastor, is that your firm answer?" he asked.

"It is," Richard replied. Only then did he share with Richard which church he was talking about.

Culpepper continued, "When could you move to Augusta?"

Richard answered, "I will resign tomorrow evening and will move on Thursday, May 10."

Pleased at Richard's acceptance, Culpepper exclaimed, "Fine! I will contact the clerk and let them know to expect your arrival next Thursday evening. I will send someone to fill in at Manchester until a pastor can be found."

Richard hung up the phone and explained to Cheryl what had just happened. He announced, "Start packing. We are moving to Augusta next week!" He later expressed, "God bless this precious woman that He gave me for a wife, since I don't believe there are many who would have been so willing to chase the will of God with me as hard as she has."

Now realizing just how hard leaving the church in Manchester would be, the Bakers resigned their pastorate with heavy hearts. Early Thursday morning, May 10, they pulled out of Manchester headed to Augusta, all the way on the other side of the state, near the South Carolina state line.

After traveling for a couple of hours, they stopped and Richard called to check on his overseer, Frank Culpepper, only to hear that he had just passed away about 30 minutes earlier. He cried the rest of the way to Augusta thinking that just 10 days before his death, in excruciating pain, his heart was still on the churches over which God had placed him. Richard was the last pastor this great man of God would appoint to a church, and still to this day, this memory is truly humbling and emotional to him.

The Bakers arrived in Hephzibah, a small community five miles from Augusta, early in the afternoon with two exhausted boys, four-year-old Ricky and two-and-a-half-year-old Ryan. Since the church had no parsonage, the Bakers stayed with a family in the congregation for a few days. They were independently wealthy and lived in a huge house in the country with significant acreage.

Richard convened a meeting with the church and pastor's council the following evening at 7:00 pm to discuss, among other things, living arrangements, and salary. The church, a two-story structure with the sanctuary on the upper level and classrooms, kitchen, and fellowship hall on the lower, was only seven years old. It sat on seven beautiful acres and was debt free. Although the congregation was small, between 60 and 65, it was strong financially. The former pastor, who, along with his wife, was a schoolteacher, never took a full salary. Additionally, they owned their own home.

The seven members of the council, along with Richard, all seemed a bit apprehensive as the meeting got underway. One of the members was a railway engineer who, from the beginning, didn't seem to like his new pastor. His first question appeared to harbor a measure of cynicism as he bluntly asked, "Just how old are you?"

"I will be 28 in August," Richard answered.

"Too young to be pastoring a church," the railway engineer sarcastically replied.

The council finally decided on a salary package, with some members beginning to feel a little better when he told them he was a carpenter and could work some if he needed to. They also discussed the issue of housing. Until now, they simply had not given any thought to the housing needs of their next pastor. After deliberation, the men decided to buy a singlewide mobile home and place it on the property next to the church.

The tension that Richard felt before the meeting was not assuaged after the meeting ended. He didn't feel overly welcomed by the majority of the council, and having to live with complete strangers until the trailer could be set up only added to the stress.

Sunday morning arrived, and Richard prayerfully felt impressed to preach about the sufferings of Christ from Isaiah 53. The attendance had increased to over 80—quite common for a new pastor, with people showing up to check him out. After the singing, Richard stepped up to the pulpit, shared for a few minutes from his heart, and began preaching. About halfway through his message, he saw around 20 people stand up at once and walk out. The response seemed so choreographed that Richard was sure it had been planned. He wondered how any true Christian could get offended at hearing that God loves them so much that He sent His son to suffer and die for them.

Recovering from that insensitive and unbiblical action was not easy for him, but he was determined to complete his message. When the service was over, most of the remaining 60 people gathered around him and Cheryl and warmly welcomed them. Richard found out later that the former pastor was having difficulties before he resigned. Furthermore, the previous pastor displayed more of a teaching style, while Richard ministered more with an energetic evangelistic style. By the end of July, the church had dropped another 10 people and was drawing only around 50 in the Sunday morning service. Richard began struggling with his emotions, feeling so unworthy and sensing that he was out of his comfort zone.

The church clerk, Walt Harris—who had been the postmaster for Los Angeles, California—had retired and moved to the Augusta area. He and his wife, Esther, were wonderful people who loved the Bakers and supported them unconditionally. They were remarkable encouragers. Walt kept saying to Richard, "Pastor, your ministry and the former pastor's ministry are so different that it will just take a little time for everyone to get adjusted."

Harris was right. By September, the church began to experience revival and started growing. Within six months, they had broken three tithe records, and the attendance came back to where it was before the Bakers came. God sent faithful workers, many of whom were seasoned Christians.

T.D. Mooneyham, who pastored one of the larger churches in the Augusta area, retired and started attending the Bakers' church. He met with Richard and shared that it was his desire to return, after one year, to the church he had pastored. Wisely, he wanted to give the new pastor the time and space to settle into his new area of ministry.

Mooneyham was a theologian who often wrote lessons for the denomination's Sunday school commentaries. And although Richard didn't struggle too much with preaching in Sunday worship services, he did struggle with teaching on Wednesday night with this scholar sitting in the congregation. Yet, there was no need for him to be intimidated for God had sent two great encouragers to him and Cheryl through Lucille and T.D. Mooneyham. Both poured into them unconditional love and support.

Harold Jones served as Richard's district overseer and every week or two he and his wife, Barbara, would take him and Cheryl to lunch. By this means, the Joneses shared their experiences with the Bakers and provided for them much needed encouragement. Richard looks back on this experience and believes that one reason God sent them there was for them to receive a higher level of mentoring and support that they probably would not have received anywhere else.

14

Struggling with God's Will

In the fall of 1984, the Bakers learned that Cheryl was pregnant with their third child, Christopher. They had no insurance, and his salary wasn't sufficient to cover the medical fees associated with having a baby. A CPA had bought a warehouse in downtown Augusta and wanted to turn it into a two-story office complex. Richard, along with three other Church of God pastors, joined to form a small construction company and submitted a bid. They got the job and, after several months, completed the project. Now, Richard had the money to pay for Christopher's birth.

The church continued to grow as an increasing number of people accepted Christ as Savior. Conditions had so improved that the Bakers now actually began enjoying living in the Augusta area. In May, Elmer Golden, Jr., who was presently serving as the pastor of the Bakers' home church, asked Richard to consider coming home to Brunswick and serving as his associate pastor. The church had bought 40 acres of land just off I-95 and was in the planning stage of building new facilities. He wanted Richard to help them with the logistics of relocating. Although Baker was honored, he didn't feel that it was in God's timing and declined.

A week later, Golden called back and offered a higher package, but Richard replied, "Pastor, it's not the money; it's the will of God. I am not released to leave Augusta."

Only a couple of weeks before Christopher was born, the pastor called again and this time placed additional pressure on him saying, "Richard, we really need you. The pastor's council voted 100 percent to hire you. Please consider coming home and helping us with this transition."

With Golden's persistence, Richard finally conceded that this could indeed be God's will and agreed to come after the baby was born. Cheryl didn't feel the same way and related the scenario to a message he had recently preached. The message was from Numbers 22:21-39, the story of Balaam. Although the prophet refused to see the will of God, his donkey could see the angel of the Lord with sword drawn. Had it not been for his donkey, the angel of the Lord would have killed Balaam.

When Richard announced to Cheryl that they were moving back to Brunswick, she exclaimed, "I don't feel God is in it, but I will go if you insist. I will be the donkey if you are willing to be Balaam!"

They moved in early July 1985 and, as Cheryl prophesied, she became the donkey and Richard became Balaam. The church could not have treated them any better. Golden more than lived up to everything he said he would do. But when a person is out of the will of God, the only way to find peace is to repent and draw back into His presence. Richard stayed busy preaching every Sunday night, teaching a class on Wednesday night, and working with the planning committee. But his peace and joy were not what they were.

In May 1986, he and Cheryl were celebrating their 11th wedding anniversary, and, in appreciation, the church sent them to Jamaica for a week. A pastor in Montego Bay, Pastor Williams, heard they were coming and invited Richard to preach. They arrived on Saturday, rented a car, checked into their hotel, and relaxed until the next morning, when he was to preach. The church was much larger than either one of them expected, with perhaps 1,000 in attendance. As two vastly different cultures would have it, Cheryl was the only woman not sporting a hat.

The service began with one of the most anointed choirs the Bakers had ever heard. After an hour of singing and worshipping, Williams introduced Baker. With the worshipful atmosphere and the receptivity of the congregation, he preached a 45-minute message. Just as he was about to close, the congregation suddenly stood to its collective feet shouting, "Don't quit! Give us the Word!"

He preached for another 30 minutes and for the second time began his closing. And once again, the people stood and shouted, "Don't quit! Give us the Word!"

After preaching for another 30 minutes, Richard was exhausted, almost beyond having the strength to stand. This time they let him give an altar call. Seventeen people accepted Christ. The pastor's sister, who had fallen away from God and was living in adultery, came back to the Lord. It was incredible for the Bakers to witness this hunger in people for the Word of God.

Following the service, they returned to their hotel a few miles from Montego Bay, had some lunch, and decided to go for a walk. As they exited the hotel compound, which had 10-foot security walls, they crossed a busy highway and entered a small village. When they had gone deeper into the village, four Jamaican men with dreg locks approached them and asked, "Hey man, you and your lady want something for the head?" It was apparent that he was trying to sell them drugs.

Richard nodded his head in the negative, took Cheryl by the hand, and headed back toward the hotel. Not giving up so easily, the men followed them and continued trying to convince them to buy their product. Richard whispered to Cheryl, "I may have to confront them. If I tell you to run, run as fast as you can to the hotel."

The thought occurred to him that if they knew he was a minister, they might be inclined to leave them alone. So, he stopped, turned to face them, and declared, "I don't need drugs to get high anymore. I have Jesus. He is the only high I need."

Pointing his thumb down toward the ground, the man that was doing all the talking exclaimed, "No Jesus; only Beelzebub!"

A righteous anger swept over Richard, and he began quoting 1 John 4:4. "You are of God, little children, and have overcome them, because He who is in you is greater than he who is in the world." He boldly declared, "The power of God in us is greater than the power of darkness in you!" He and Cheryl walked at a fast pace back to their hotel and did not venture out on their own any anymore.

By the end of summer in1986, Richard was growing restless. He slacked up in his prayer life, in reading the Word, and rarely fasted. Speaking with Golden, he suggested that he become part-time with the church, since he wanted to start his roofing company up again. The pastor reluctantly agreed.

Richard's brother-in-law, Wayne Holmes, and a good friend, Raymond Drury, joined with him to form a company they called Christian Brothers' Roofing. Each had his own pickup truck and together they bought a dump truck. Richard also bought a van. They right away had all the work they could do.

Hardly a month into their roofing business, Wayne got a job offer and took it. Within a few months, Raymond decided to do something else. Richard hired four or five men, and all were working from morning till night. He was making the most money he had ever made, at least, legally. But he was also the most miserable he had ever been since becoming a Christian. By January 1987, the Bakers were completely debt free–no car payments, no credit debt, and with four CDs in the bank.

Golden had booked a revival for January and had slated Richard to open the Sunday night service with the reading of a chapter from the Bible and prayer. He asked the pastor if he could sit with Cheryl and not on the platform. Golden agreed. As the evangelist preached, the Holy Spirit gripped Richard's heart saying, "You are not doing My will."

Richard began crying and considered walking to the altar but then felt a tugging at his heart to get on his knees and crawl to the altar. When he reached the front, to his surprise, at least 50 people fell in behind him. He prayed through that night repenting of disobeying his Father. It was at that time that he felt the Lord again leading him into evangelistic work.

When he shared with Golden the calling he felt in his heart, the pastor released him. He at once began booking revival meetings. His first three were in Pennsylvania, with the first one starting in early February. The church was in a small community called High House, just outside of Pittsburgh. One of the strongest moves of God he had ever witnessed occurred during this revival, which lasted two full weeks. Although it snowed six to eight inches daily, the church packed every night, with people standing up against the walls on some nights.

In the congregation there was a man and his sister, both in their 70s. One played the organ and the other the piano. The woman was blind. One night the Lord impressed upon Richard, "Put your thumbs on her eyes and command them in My name to open."

Doubt filled his heart, and he hesitated. The Lord spoke to him again, and this time he obeyed. When he touched her, her eyes opened, and she saw her brother for the first time since they were children. Richard still envisions them embracing each other with tears of joy flowing freely.

On the last night of the revival, a retired minister in his 80s followed Richard to the fellowship hall, where he was producing the cassette tapes people had ordered. The minister declared, "Son, you are not an evangelist." Thinking that the retiree was criticizing his preaching, a feeling of hurt momentarily swept over Richard.

Responding to the older minister's statement, Richard asked, "Brother, can you explain what you mean?"

The man answered, "You are a revivalist. You are called to preach repentance to the church and bring her back into right fellowship with the Lord. The New Testament would call you a prophet, but the word has taking on other meanings in our present day." From that day forward, Richard never doubted his calling. And he felt liberated to understand for the first time what that calling from the Lord truly was.

His second revival was in Meyersdale, Pennsylvania, and lasted two full weeks. Not only were he and Cheryl missing each other, it was also the longest he had been away from the boys. In the true spirit of motherhood, his mom loaded Cheryl and the three boys and drove the 756 miles to Meyersdale, where they stayed two nights.

With his next revival being in Williamsburg, Pennsylvania, he departed on Saturday morning headed there, while his mom, Cheryl, and their three precious sons, Ricky, Ryan, and Chris headed back to Brunswick, Georgia. The revival in Williamsburg also lasted two weeks. Although the pastor, who was in his 40s, had congestive heart failure and was unable to attend all the services, his spiritual heart longed for his church to experience revival. He had two teenage daughters and a son in his early 20s. He passed away only a few months after the revival meeting. Richard, who was always amazed to be around people who had so much going against them but never gave up, wrote,

> This pastor stayed faithful to his calling until his last breath. Oh God, let that be my testimony, because so many have inspired me along the way. This precious pastor and his family were no exception. I still have a scarf his 17-year-old bought during the revival, 33 years later. Because of their massive medical bills, they were struggling financially. Cheryl and I sent a couple of love offerings as God prospered us to do so. Even my precious mom sent a couple of generous love offerings. After the pastor's death, I was contacted to see if I had any interest in pastoring the church. But the Holy Spirit did not release me.

Richard left Williamsburg headed for Atlanta in mid-March for his next scheduled revival meeting, after spending six weeks in Pennsylvania. This was another two-week meeting, and he didn't get back home to Brunswick until Saturday, April 4. The following day, he began a meeting in Darien, Georgia, approximately 20 miles from Brunswick, which lasted for a week-

and-a-half. He had been preaching for 10 straight weeks almost every night and was completely exhausted. He felt somewhat relieved knowing that his next scheduled revival was two weeks away.

In May, he conducted a meeting at his parents' home church, Westward Street Church of God in Douglas, Georgia. He also preached at the Ocilla Church of God where he had received Christ as his Savior. In late May, he received a call from a pastor he had never met, a man who pastored a rural church of about 150 members 50 miles from Brunswick. He wanted to know if Richard was available for a week's meeting in the near future. When Richard communicated with him that he had the week after next open, the pastor agreed that that date would be perfect.

The first Sunday morning saw the church almost filled. Richard went home with the pastor for lunch and to rest up for the evening service. The church was almost full Sunday night, as well. God's presence was so powerful that an overwhelming spirit of excitement filled the atmosphere. He preached that night under a heavy anointing and followed with an altar call. People responded to receive salvation, to find healing, to experience deliverance, and some came forward desiring the fullness of the Holy Spirit.

A man in his 40s sat on the second row with his wife. The Holy Spirit impressed Richard to call him forward for prayer. As he stood facing the evangelist, words flowed from Richard's mouth that even shocked him: "Set your house in order for your days are numbered!" The man fell on his knees, wept, and prayed for 20 minutes or longer. Rising from his knees, he walked over to the pastor and gave him a big hug. He then asked Richard for the microphone.

With tears coursing down his cheeks, he confessed, "I have caused so much trouble in this church, have been responsible for running off the last two pastors, and have tried to run off our present pastor. I have asked the Lord and the pastor to forgive me, and now I am asking the church to forgive me."

The church stood to its feet applauding and praising God. As Richard prepared to return home, the pastor thanked him for being obedient to the Lord and said, "I'll see you tomorrow night, Brother Baker."

Richard was glad to be close enough to home to drive back and forth to the services, sleep a little later in his own bed, and spend some extra time with his family. Around 9:30 the next morning, the phone rang. When he answered it, the pastor informed him that the man he had prophesied over the previous evening was eating breakfast with his wife, as both prepared for work. She left first around 7:00 am. At 8:00 am she received a call from her husband's employer asking where he was. She drove home to find him dead, still sitting at the breakfast table where she had left him. He had no known health issues, and the autopsy report did not fully conclude the cause of death. His wife told her pastor that the evangelist had prophesied his death, so now he could preach his funeral.

Two days later, on Wednesday, Richard had the uncomfortable task of preaching a man's funeral he didn't know. In some mystical way, he felt a little responsible for his death. Looking at his family sitting in the front row while he tried to share a message of hope would go down as one of the most difficult tasks he had ever tackled. After the funeral, his wife thanked him for being obedient to the leading of the Lord, as she felt for sure her husband was now in heaven. The revival ended on Friday, and the pastor shared with Richard several weeks later that peace and love were more abundant in the church since the revival.

15

Unexpected Return

The South Georgia State Camp Meeting convened the following week in Tifton. With three small boys, Cheryl decided to stay home. Richard arrived on Monday afternoon, checked into his hotel, and drove to the campground. As the congregation began singing, Richard heard a voice behind him asking, "Are you ready to go back home?"

Turning around, he saw Bobby Tatum and heard him say that Manchester was back on the bottom with only 10 people attending. Richard made it clear that, as much as they loved the people in Manchester, there was no way he would go through those challenges again and noted that it was not even fair to ask him to.

Tatum responded, "I don't blame you. It probably will have to be closed in a few months."

Richard continued booking revivals through the camp meeting and enjoyed the services and the fellowship. When he returned home to Brunswick around 1:00 Saturday morning, he found Cheryl sitting in the living room waiting on him. He asked, "What are you doing up so late?"

She answered, "One of the boys has been sick and, after getting him to sleep, I just felt led to sit here and pray." She continued, "Richard, sit down. I need to share something with you that I don't think you will like. As I have been sitting here praying, the Lord has burdened me for the church in Manchester. Maybe we should consider going back to pastor there."

Richard had not yet shared with her the words that Tatum had spoken to him at the camp meeting. Now he chimed in, saying, "Cheryl, that chapter in our lives is closed. The church is at the bottom again, and I don't have it in me to go through what we went through the first time. I am staying booked up preaching revivals, and we are having amazing services. I just don't see God sending us back to Manchester. Anyway, I am very tired. Let's go to bed."

As both were sleeping soundly the next morning, the telephone ringing suddenly awakened them. Picking up the phone, he heard his mother's voice on the other end of the line. Apologizing that she had awakened him, she said, "Son, I had a dream last night that God called you back to pastor the church in Manchester. I am a little sad since I have enjoyed having the grandkids living so close, but God's purpose must come before our desires or wants."

A bit perturbed over what now seemed like a bombardment, Richard sharply asked, "Mom, what is going on with you and Cheryl? Have you been talking to each other?"

Dot answered, "No, we haven't."

The possibility that this may be God began to settle in, especially considering that he knew neither Cheryl nor his mother would desire this in the flesh. The following week, the pastor who was presently pastoring Manchester, called him and informed him that in the 18 months he had been there, the church had experienced a decline. He also mentioned that he worked for Great Dane, a company that builds trailers for trucking companies, and that they had donated most of the material to build a three-bedroom two-bath home on the church's property, and the work had just been completed. In reflecting on this time, Richard wrote,

> Sometimes, no matter how hard you try, you just can't outrun, or out reason, God's will. It is what it is; you either fully surrender to it or try to endure the consequences of not being submissive to His Lordship. About one year earlier, I had preached a Sunday morning and evening for Pastor Thompson, and when I returned to Brunswick, I had shared with Cheryl how tough things were going for the pastor.

Finally realizing that God was indeed speaking to him about returning to Manchester, he called Tatum and informed him that they would once again accept the position of pastor there and would plan to move in late August. For the second time in five years, Richard resumed roofing work to save up enough money to live on, so they could fulfill God's will and return to Manchester to pastor.

His home church was starting to build on their newly acquired property. Golden asked him if he wanted to bid on some of the work. They began constructing the Family Center first. He turned in a bid on the roof system, which also included running the conduit for the electrical lines, installing insulation, and installing decking and roofing. His bid was accepted, and he put together a crew of five men to help him. Raymond Drury, his good friend and a minister, agreed to help.

They completed the job on Friday, August 23, 1987. The church gave him a couple of thousand dollars more than he had bid, since they knew he and Cheryl were pulling out the following Monday returning to Manchester to pastor. They arrived late in the afternoon, but this time to a new home. The former pastor had left several weeks earlier, and no one was presently attending the church. Richard decided not to start services at once. In fact, he waited three weeks before conducting his first service. He placed a half-page ad in the local paper announcing the formation of a new church and broadcast that they would be having the new launch and first service on Sunday evening, September 20. Richard explained:

> I truly believe God tests us at times to seeing how obedient we really are to the leading of the Holy Spirit and our true desire in fulfilling His will. I have learned that God equates spiritual depth with obedience. There is no doubt in my mind that Cheryl and I would have never experienced the miracles and witnessed the majestic hand of God leading us to accomplish some pretty amazing things, if we had not been obedient in returning to Manchester.

After spending time in prayer, Richard felt impressed to disband the church and reorganize it with a new name. After receiving permission from the denominational leaders, he proceeded to legally change the name and remove all 66 members from the membership roll. The new name would be Victory Temple. He had a sign company design, build, and install the new sign before they had their first service.

Cheryl asked him why he wanted to have the first service on Sunday evening. All he could say was that it was just what he felt. Thirty people showed up for that first service, which would be the smallest crowd they would have. Within six months the small sanctuary was almost full.

Maxi Bullock, a master carpenter who specialized in refurbishing old Victorian homes, heard about him and asked if he was interested in bidding on some roofing projects. After finishing the first project, the two men had bonded. Maxi was a devout Christian and the two of them constantly fellowshipped and praised the Lord as they worked. When he asked Richard if he would be willing to work for him by the hour doing carpentry work when he didn't have roofing to do, Richard agreed.

He began working for Bullock and his two sons, when he didn't have a roofing job. They built and remolded houses and did some light commercial work. Richard bought a dump truck when the roofing work began picking up. He was quickly becoming one of the main roofing contractors in the county. The Farm Bureau Insurance Company asked him to manage all its roofing claims in a three-county area. To meet the demand, he put together a crew of four to five industrious men who worked 10-hour days, from Monday through Friday. Meadows, the congressman who owned the two large car dealerships, tried to hire Richard back, but he was making as much in a day roofing as he would in a week working for him.

Addition to first church (1990)
Manchester, Georgia.

In the summer of 1988, the pastor of a small independent congregation of about 40 members decided to resign and move to Florida. The pastor met with Richard and suggested a possible merger of the two churches. In response, he visited the small church and preached on a Thursday night. In his message, he shared with the congregation about Victory Temple and his vision for the future. The following Sunday, the independent congregation voted to merge with the Victory Temple Church of God. It was amazing how the two congregations complimented each other. Where Victory Temple was weak, the independent church was strong, and where they were weak, Victory Temple was strong.

Immediately, the need arose for expansion. Richard went to the bank, established a line of credit, and Cheryl and the women of the church began selling chicken dinners and having yard sales. The men began cooking and selling barbeque dinners. They laid the foundation and started building onto to the front of the church, adding a foyer, new restrooms, church office, nursery, and a pastor's study. In short order, the church raised one half of the funds needed and borrowed the remaining half. The project took less than three months to complete.

Velma Cooper (Granny Horton's daughter) was one of the church's most faithful members and had been praying for years for the church to grow. She approached Richard and asked, "Pastor, would it be possible for you to loan me $100?"

Without hesitation, Richard answered, "Yes, I will." He retrieved the cash from his wallet and handed it to her thinking that she was struggling to make ends meet. She was approaching 80 and lived alone, with just her social security check for support. Richard did not intend to let her reimburse him for what she called a "loan."

Velma took the $100 and purchased flour, buttermilk, and ground sausage. She then proceeded to visit various businesses and take orders for sausage biscuits, announcing that 100 percent of the proceeds would be going to the building fund for Victory Temple Church of God. On the first Saturday, she sold over 100 sausage biscuits, and orders only increased from there. In fact, her sausage biscuit business grew so much that she came to Richard one day crying and exclaiming, "I can't make as many biscuits as I have orders for this Saturday!"

As word spread of her dilemma, other women in the church got involved and began showing up at her house at 5:30 on Saturday mornings to help this precious widow make hundreds of biscuits. Velma, by far, raised more money for the building fund than anyone else. She even had Richard out early on Saturday mornings delivering sausage biscuits.

Later, she shared with him about how awful she felt in not being able to give anything toward the building fund, especially considering that she had been praying for many years for God to send revival and bless the church. She related that as she prayed, the Lord spoke to her saying, "I have given you something. Give me your hands and I will bless them." She continued, "As I meditated on what I was sensing from the Lord, the thought entered my mind to make and sell sausage biscuits."

Through Velma Cooper's efforts, thousands of dollars came in for the new expansion project. On an amusing note, Richard was at her house one Saturday morning, picked up one of the freshly made biscuits, and began eating it. She looked at him and firmly declared, "Pastor, you will need to give me one dollar before you leave." Of course, he did.

16

Overcoming Setbacks

By the time the improvements had been made, the church found itself in dire need of a new sanctuary. Consequently, in 1989 the congregation voted to build a sanctuary and attach it to the side of their present sanctuary, which in turn, the church could use for classrooms and a fellowship hall. The Sunday attendance was approaching 100, with the city manager and vice-president of the bank attending.

Richard was still not taking a salary or benefits from the church, other than living in the parsonage the church provided. Even though the tithe coming into the church was sufficient to pay him a salary, doing so would have seriously affected the ability of the church to expand.

During the winter of 1989, the men planned an all-night barbecue to raise funds to assist in their expansion. Richard was probably in the best physical shape of his life at the time. So, when some of the men started challenging others in arm wrestling, he quickly enlisted. This was one of his strengths and, quite honestly, he felt a little pride since he didn't think any of them could put him down. He arm-wrestled several men and easily triumphed.

Terry Elliot, who was slightly larger than Richard and worked for Lance Snack Company, was next. Locking hands in a firm grip, Richard quickly realized that Terry was much stronger than he looked. Neither one was able to move the other. About 30 to 45 seconds into the match, one of the men, horsing around, came up behind Terry and grabbed him from behind, which awkwardly pushed their arms. Because Richard was not seated directly in front of Terry but to his side, when their arms were pushed, the immense pressure Richard was exerting caused one of the bones in his arm to snap. Cheryl, who was standing about 40 feet away, said it sounded like a limb had broken out of a tree.

It happened so quickly that Richard didn't know at first what had happened. His arm was completely numb, and he was unable to move it. Instinctively, he reached with his other hand and grabbed his wrist. As he did, he heard Billy, who was a physical therapist at the Roosevelt Institute, shout, "Don't!" but it was too late. When Richard pulled his arm to his chest, the humorous bone protruded from his right arm. Had two men not been standing behind him, he would have fallen to the ground in excruciating pain.

A couple of the men helped him into a vehicle and rushed him 40 miles to Columbus, Georgia, to a group of doctors who practiced sports medicine. They arrived at the emergency room where X-rays were taken, and a specialist was called in. The specialist examined him and the X-rays and declared, "Pastor, you have swung your last hammer." As they chatted, the doctor continued, "Not only do you have a compound fracture, but when you lifted your arm, the jagged bone sliced through the muscles, tendons, and ligaments and has done some serious damage."

The severity of his injury required his admission to the hospital. Because of the swelling, it would be eight days before doctors could perform surgery. On day 11, a Tuesday, he was released to go home provided he could get a hospital bed equipped with traction pulleys. When the bed was delivered and set up, Richard thought, "What have I done now? I cannot work to provide a living for my family. The doctor said I could lose up to 80 percent use of my right arm."

The orthopedic surgeon explained to Richard that he had a one-in-10,000 break, the kind he had only seen a couple of times in his practice. He explained that because he and Terry were not facing each other diagonally, his awkward position caused his muscles to pull his bone apart.

If there was any hint of humor in the whole experience, it was Richard's four-year-old son, Christopher, who constantly walked by his bed and taunted him, showing him his arm and saying, "Daddy, you want to arm wrestle?" He knew his father couldn't do anything to him, and he was having a field day with him.

Phillips, the retired Baptist pastor who had filled in for him when he pastored the church the first time, was now a regular attendee. Baker asked him to take care of the church until he got back on his feet.

Seeing Cheryl and the boys walk out of the house headed for church that first Sunday morning was almost more than he could take. He cried and prayed for the next two hours. When time came for the Sunday evening service, he said to Cheryl, "I am going tonight!" Cheryl tried to talk him out of it but finally relented. She took one of his shirts, cut the sleeve so it would fit over his sling, and off to church he went.

As he sat on the front row during praise and worship, he felt something happening to his arm. Although he didn't feel any greater pain, his nerves started twitching. He stood to his feet and continued singing and worshipping. He even began lifting his arm up a little in the sling. Until this service, he had no ability to move his arm at all. Now he was lifting it up several inches with no pain. As faith rose up in his heart, he stepped onto the platform and declared, "The Lord has just healed me!"

With that declaration, he threw the pillow that was under his arm across the sanctuary, with his left hand lifted the sling over his neck and removed it from around his arm. As he flung the sling to the floor, the music and singing stopped. Richard shouted again, "The Lord has healed me!" He threw both of his hands over his head in praise to the Lord.

Revival broke out that night. The next morning, he went to the church and started cutting molding with a handsaw and nailing it up in the new addition. He called the doctor's office and asked to see the surgeon. They scheduled an appointment for Thursday morning. When he arrived, he was sporting a mauve sports jacket and could hardly wait for the doctor to witness the mighty miracle that God had performed.

After calling him back, they first X-rayed his arm three times. When the doctor came into the room, he looked at Richard twice and asked, "When did I do your surgery?"

Richard answered, "About two weeks ago." He continued, "The Lord instantly healed me!"

The doctor showed him the X-ray which showed the steel plates and pins. But there was no sign of a facture. Now, more than 30 years later, he still has never had one problem with his arm other than not being able to throw a ball very far due to the restrictions of the plates. Although the doctor could have removed the plates, the insurance would not pay for the procedure.

The doctor was a practicing Catholic and shared with Richard that this was the first time he had ever witnessed something for which there was no explanation. He continued, "I would have been happy if you had only regained 30 to 40 percent of your arm function."

Approximately six months later, Richard began having some pain and numbness in his lower right arm and wrist. He went back to the surgeon thinking that perhaps he had begun using his arm too soon. As he expressed his concerns to the surgeon, the doctor interrupted him and reminded him, saying, "It's not that. Remember, the Lord healed your arm." This was a moment when a practicing Catholic taught a Pentecostal pastor a lesson on faith.

After the examination, the doctor diagnosed him with a severe case of carpal tunnel syndrome and said that he needed to have surgery to correct the problem. The doctor told him that he would have to stop swinging a hammer. Richard chose not to have the surgery, but he did sell his roofing business to a member of his church. Meadows hired him back at the Lincoln, Ford, and Mercury Dealership on the same terms as before, but this time with a better salary package. The way God worked with Richard in this situation prompted him later to write:

> Even after serving the Lord for 40 years, it is still amazing to me the favor He bestows on you when you pursue the heart and will of the Father, and when you chase as hard as you can the vision He places in front of you. To experience the blessings of the Lord that literally run you down when you are walking in obedience to His will is still so wonderful to me (Psa. 68:19, NKJ). Jesus said in Matthew 11:30, "For my yoke is easy, and my burden is light." The only time I have found the easy to be hard and the light to be heavy is when I am not carrying His burden, but another burden that He never asked me to carry.

Completing the addition strengthened the church's faith and gave the body of believers a sense of accomplishment. The attendance continued to increase, and the small sanctuary frequently filled. At times, people would even have to sit in the foyer.

Richard called a church conference in the fall of 1989 to discuss the construction of a new sanctuary. The membership voted unanimously for the project agreeing to borrow only one-half of the cost to build, with the intention of raising the balance. Plans were drawn and building permits secured, listing Richard as the general contractor.

In the fall of 1989, the foundation was laid, and, within a few months, the walls were in place. The reality that God was in the Bakers returning to Manchester became clear to them. Because of budgetary restraints, the church ceased construction for a few months.

When Christopher was small, Richard could hardly get out of his sight when he was home. On one occasion while cutting the church grass with his lawn tractor, he held four-year-old Christopher between his legs. A steep embankment ran across the back of the building. As he drove toward the bank, he engaged the clutch, but the tractor kept moving forward. Momentarily distracted by trying to get the tractor to stop, Richard climbed part of the way up the embankment before he realized it. The steep incline caused him to fall off backwards, with his small son in his arms. Richard landed on his back and Christopher landed on his father's stomach.

In horror, Richard looked up to see the lawn tractor, with blades of the older model still turning, flipping over backward onto them. He instinctively thrust his legs upward just in time for his feet to catch the mower's seat. His action caused the mower to roll over and fall toward them in an upright position, with blades still spinning. The drama was not over, because he saw the lawn tractor coming toward them again. Clinging tenaciously to his four-year-old child, Richard barely managed to roll both out of the way as the tractor rumbled past them.

Cheryl happened to be standing nearby and saw the shocking episode as it unfolded. To Richard and Cheryl, this escape was nothing short of another miracle of God.

17

Disturbing Diagnosis

Cheryl had two nieces that had been placed in the Smokey Mountain Children's Home about a year earlier, April, 13, and Chastity, 12. Her brother, Joey—who was serving time in prison on drug charges—and the girls' mother were unable to properly care for them. Richard and Cheryl would get them for two weeks in the summer and two weeks during the Christmas holiday. Taking them back to the children's home was getting increasingly difficult, because the girls were not adjusting well to the environment. The Bakers decided to take them into their home and make them part of their family.

From a family of five that included three boys, the family grew overnight to seven that included two girls, which was an entirely new experience for the Baker household. They had to put all three boys in one room and the girls in another. But they made the necessary adjustments, enrolled them in school, and did their best to make them feel like they belonged. Richard knew that Cheryl saw herself in her two nieces and so much wanted a better life for them than she had growing up.

In the summer of 1990 as the Bakers were planning their yearly vacation, Cheryl asked Richard if Carroll Copeland—a young single woman who had come to their church through the merger and had become a dear friend—could accompany them. Knowing that Carroll enjoyed spending time at their home and loved being around their children, Richard quickly agreed.

The Bakers planned to take an extended vacation and travel to Kings Island in Ohio, continue to Niagara Falls in Canada, and finally visit Plymouth Rock and the surrounding area on the return trip to Manchester.

In June, Richard rented a U-Haul trailer to pull behind their van to accommodate the luggage, coolers, and other incidentals needed for the trip. After loading up the van and trailer, the entourage—three adults and five children—headed north. Although being confined to a vehicle for hours on end, driving over 3,000 miles in less than two weeks, and rarely staying in the same motel more than one night provided a certain measure of stress, the trip was nonetheless enjoyable.

Richard noticed that Cheryl was not her normal self. Most days by lunchtime, she had already grown tired and wanted to return to the hotel to rest. This was to be the first sign that all was not well with her. They returned to Manchester exhausted and glad to be home.

The women of the church had planned a yard sale in July to raise money for the building fund. As was usually the case, Richard joined them the day of the sale to help in any way he could. When a particular man stopped by to look around, Richard engaged him in conversation. The man mentioned that he drove a school bus and noted that the school system was nine drivers short, with school beginning in just a month. Richard casually mentioned that he had a commercial driver's license (CDL) with a bus endorsement but had no desire to drive a school bus.

The following Monday, the director of bus operations for Meriwether County called and asked him if he indeed had a CDL. When Richard confirmed that he had did, the director asked, "Would you please consider driving one of our routes this year? We have had nine people apply who either can't pass their physicals or can't pass the new CDL testing."

After much coaxing and with the director agreeing to give him a short city route, Richard signed up to drive a school bus. After he filled out the necessary papers, the school officially hired him on August 13, 1990, with his insurance taking effect on September 13.

Cheryl's mother, Margaret, had moved to Manchester six months earlier and served as a caregiver for an elderly woman in her 90s. In July, the woman died having had no children, her closest relative being a great-niece who lived in Atlanta. She had lived in a smaller Victorian style house, and Cheryl loved it. Now with five children, the Bakers had been talking about looking for a larger place to live. With the church growing, it needed to use the parsonage for classrooms, and as a place where the youth could hold their services on Wednesday nights.

Cheryl asked Richard about making an offer on the home. Knowing that it needed significant repairs, Richard said that they simply could not afford it. Not ready to give up so quickly, as they were preparing on Saturday morning to take the children on picnic, Cheryl pressed Richard to call the great-niece and just inquire about the house. Finally giving in, he called. The woman's husband answered, and Richard expressed an interest in the house that belonged to his wife's aunt. Still not greatly interested, he casually asked the selling price for the house.

The man answered with a price that Richard felt was almost twice what it was worth. Feeling relieved, he thanked him for speaking with him and hung up the phone. Confident he was off the hook, he shared with Cheryl that the price they were asking, along with all the renovations needed, was extremely high. Persisting, she countered, "Call them back and make an offer."

A bit agitated, he called back and asked if they would consider an offer. The man answered, "Sure."

Richard responded with a lowball figure and then added a caveat. He said, "We will need to finance it with no money down."

The man replied, "Let me speak with my wife, and I will give you a call later this afternoon."

No sooner had Richard and his family arrived home from their picnic that the phone rang. The great-niece's husband announced, "We accept your offer and the terms."

Stunned, Richard almost fell to the floor. Within 10 days the Bakers were the proud owners of a home that he later found out Cheryl had walked around seven times praying for and claiming. The niece and her husband even offered to pay for the utilities for two months, keep insurance on it for the same time, and have the home treated for termites. They later discovered that the couple owned a commercial sewing machine factory in Atlanta and just wanted to bless a young pastor and his family.

The Bakers began moving into their almost 100-year-old house in late August. Some of the men in the church helped Richard move the furniture in. Once he and Cheryl had set up the living room furniture, they sat down to rest for a few minutes and planned their next undertaking. Cheryl began rubbing her neck and discovered a knot she had not noticed before. She asked Richard to look at it and tell her what he thought.

Closely examining the protrusion, he suggested, "You probably need to have it looked at by a doctor."

Cheryl replied, "My annual appointment is next month. I will mention it to the doctor then."

As Richard's concern for Cheryl heightened, he also knew that he needed to install a new and complete roof system for the old house. The roof was large and steep and was a major undertaking. He hired James Gresham, a member of his church who had also worked for him in his roofing business. They tore the roof off in small sections and installed decking as they went along. They did the entire roof that way and installed flashing, shingles, and insulation in the attic.

When time came for Cheryl's appointment, the doctor decided to do a biopsy of the lump in her neck. Within a few days, the report came back positive for Hodgkin Lymphoma cancer. With that revelation, the Bakers' world turned upside down.

Dr. Bassett, an oncologist whose office was in Columbus, Georgia, came highly recommended to the Bakers. After making an appointment with his office, Richard took Cheryl to see him. The doctor described for them the type of cancer Cheryl had been diagnosed with. He further explained that she would have to have staging surgery, which included removing the spleen to slow the spread of the cancer. After setting a date for the operation, the Bakers returned to Manchester and to a home still needing a lot of repairs. It also meant returning to five children from ages five to 14 and to a church to pastor.

When time came for Cheryl's surgery, Richard's mother came to help in any way she could. Cheryl's mother, Margaret, who lived in Manchester, also lent a hand by keeping the children and helping around the house. The Bakers' former pastor and wife, Joe and Elaine Muncy, surprised them with a visit just before the medical staff took Cheryl back for surgery. Their presence alone brought much peace and encouragement.

Cheryl came through the surgery well and spent several days in the hospital. Bassett determined that the cancer was Stage 2-B, which was isolated in three areas: her chest, the right side of her neck, and her right armpit. He was optimistic in his initial appraisal of Cheryl's condition, explaining that this type of cancer usually responded well to radiation treatment.

As Richard contemplated all the recent events, he realized that God had been at work from the beginning. If the unknown man had not stopped and struck up a conversation with Richard, he would never have found that Richard had a CDL and would never have offered him a job driving a school bus. And if that had not happened, Richard and Cheryl would not have had health insurance. Some may have thought it coincidental, but not the Bakers. To them, it was God working in a timely manner.

As if replacing the roof wasn't enough, Richard discovered that all the plumbing in the house also needed replacing. He simply could not put it off. The house was built around 1904 and still had some of the original cast iron piping. Since he didn't have the thousands of dollars a plumber would charge, he started ripping out the plumbing himself and replacing it. He did have one helper. Five-year-old Christopher volunteered for the job. Since he was short enough to stand up straight underneath the house, Richard would place one end of a ten-foot pipe on his shoulder, while he connected the other end. If he took too long, Christopher would say, "Daddy, it's getting a little heavy." After three long hard days, Richard had replaced every piece of plumbing in the house, including sinks and toilets.

With the original kitchen outdated and quite small, the Bakers decided to turn the dining room into a kitchen. Maxie Bullock offered to help Richard some in the afternoons and together they custom-built cabinets out of three-quarter inch oak.

In mid-October, Cheryl began her 20 scheduled radiation treatments and received treatment each day, Monday through Friday, for four weeks. Not long into the regimen, she began experiencing severe nausea, which required her being admitted to the hospital in Columbus for a couple of days. The radiation not only caused acute nausea and fatigue, but she also developed radiation recall, a rash that looks like severe sunburn with blistering and peeling. To make matters worse, she also had infection and sores in her mouth and quickly lost her hair. Understandably, especially for a woman, the hair loss added a significant measure of emotional distress for her to deal with. Unfortunately, she was allergic to every nausea medicine the doctors prescribed for her.

With Cheryl weakening more day-by-day, her doctor decided to suspend her treatments for a while to give her time to regain her strength. In her debilitated condition, she could no longer take care of the children or the home.

The Bakers got through Thanksgiving, and time came to resume the radiation treatments. Stress increased dramatically for both Richard and Cheryl. For her, the strain had to do with her continued battle with cancer, its unpleasant side effects, and the adverse emotions of not being able to function as a wife and mother, and as the wife of a pastor. For him, the pressure increased as he tried to care for five stressed-out children, pastor the church, drive a school bus, work some at the car dealership, and drive

Cheryl 90 miles to Columbus, Monday through Friday, for her radiation treatments.

Cheryl's brother, Joey—recently released from prison—agreed to take April and Chastity, who were dealing with their own issues, compounded by the stress in the Bakers' home. He picked them up in early December and brought them to his home in Brunswick.

After only a few more treatments, Cheryl had to be hospitalized once again with severe nausea and vomiting. She had become so dehydrated and weak that she could no longer lift her head from a lying-down position.

Richard left the hospital one day around 1:30 pm hoping to get back home in time to drive the afternoon bus route. One of the blessings for him in driving students to and from school was the fact that his children rode his bus and were the first ones to get on and the last ones to get off. He kissed Cheryl goodbye and told her he would return around 4:30. As the elevator opened to the lobby, the Holy Spirit quickened his spirit to rush back to Cheryl's room. Feeling such urgency, he returned as quickly as he could to find Cheryl choking in her own vomit and almost non-responsive. He at once hit the call button and almost simultaneously lifted up her head. The nurse rushed in to find him leaning her forward and patting her back trying to get her to cough up the vomit that was choking her. She instantly called a particular code that brought the necessary personnel to Cheryl's bedside, where they inserted a breathing tube to suction out her airways.

The ladies from the church were taking shifts preparing meals and helping clean the house. Richard's mother came as often as she could get off from work. His sister, Phyllis, also came and helped for two weeks.

Mid-December had arrived, and Richard had not been able to work much. The bills had begun to stack up and, with Christmas only a couple of weeks away, he was at a loss as to what to do. He knew Granny Dot would do whatever she could to see that her grandchildren had a good Christmas. More than that, he knew that God was still on His throne, and he just prayed that God would bless his family during Christmas.

The local Babcock furniture store heard about the Bakers' plight and contacted one of their church members seeking to find out what their children wanted for Christmas. On Christmas Eve, they delivered a top-of-the-line swing set and put it together in the backyard. They also brought all kinds of individual gifts for the children. His mother, along with her sister,

Shirley, came for Christmas, with his Aunt Shirley staying a couple of weeks to help.

Cheryl with Carol Copeland on left with Carol's niece on right (Late 1990s in Manchester, Georgia).

On Wednesday, December 19, Carol Copeland came to stay with Cheryl so Richard and the boys could attend church together. The doctor had been trying different nausea medicines but to no avail. He had called in a prescription for Torecan, a muscle relaxer used to control nausea and vomiting. About 30 minutes into the church service, Carol called the church saying that Cheryl was having convulsions. As soon as Richard received the message, he left the pulpit and headed out the door.

A church member, Ricky Smith, intervened as Richard was leaving the church. He said, "Pastor, I will drive in front of your home, and you bring Sister Baker out. I will drive you both to the hospital."

Richard rushed home to find Cheryl convulsing and wrapped her in a blanket. Picking her up in his arms, he hurried out the door to his waiting ride. After laying Cheryl on the back seat and climbing in beside her, Ricky pressed the gas pedal more forcefully than normal. At times reaching speeds of more than 100 miles per hour, Ricky headed to the hospital in

Columbus. Oblivious to his surroundings, Richard held Cheryl's hand and prayed. Suddenly, she went limp, and her eyes rolled back in her head. Try as he might, he could not find a pulse. He did chest compressions and mouth-to-mouth resuscitations but found no sign of life. After spending more than five minutes trying to resuscitate her, he drew a deep breath and wearily declared, "Brother Rick, you can slow down now. She's gone."

Ricky cried out, "No Pastor, don't tell me that!"

As Richard looked at Cheryl and continued to grasp her hand, his whole life passed before his eyes. He thought about their three boys and wondered how he would tell them about their mother and explain what the future would be like without her.

Even as Richard contemplated just how the scenario with his children would unfold, he heard a slight groan coming from Cheryl and heard her ask, "What was that?" Richard always believed that she had witnessed something most unusual. Once there was a sign of life, Ricky again pressed the pedal forward and sped to the emergency room. Bassett was waiting for them and ran out to the car as soon as they arrived. He treated her for 15 or 20 minutes in the backseat of the car saying that she was too unstable to move. Apparently, Cheryl was having a life-threatening reaction to the medication Torecan.

On December 22, Cheryl's birthday, the doctors decided to surgically insert a Groshong catheter to enable the administering of fluids, medications, and nutrition supplements through an IV. It also allowed for the giving and drawing of blood. During the procedure, both lungs were punctured, which the doctors warned was a possibility. With so much against her, she almost gave up and even prayed for the Lord to take her out of all the pain and suffering. As she thought of her children, she immediately changed her prayer to, "Lord, please let me live long enough to see them all grow up."

The hospital released her on Christmas Eve so she could spend Christmas at home with her family. Richard's mother arrived for Christmas and was nothing short of a Godsend.

He had received training in how to administer Cheryl's medications and nutrition, and his mom was a big help during this time, helping him with giving Cheryl her medication every two hours. Her doctor changed her medicine to Ativan, which caused no negative side effects and virtually eliminated her acid reflux. Dot had to return home a few days after Christmas, and Richard could tell that having to leave was tearing at her.

And the physical, emotional, and spiritual stress he was under was beginning to take its toll on him.

Two women from the church would come and sit with Cheryl while he and the boys attended church. Richard found it increasingly difficult to come up with something new to preach each week. He simply could not seem to find the time to prepare. Reminding Richard that the work was His, God blessed the services with His amazing presence.

In early January 1991, he had gotten Cheryl out of bed, carried her to the living room, and laid her on the couch. After getting her situated, he went to his office, the one he had moved from the church to a room adjacent to the living room. As he tried to study for the Sunday's message, a knock came at the door. Rising from his desk, he walked to the front door, opened it, and saw standing there the Church of God's administrative bishop for North Georgia, Delbert Rose. Without a word, he stepped inside the house and gave Baker a bear hug. He visited for about half an hour and ended his visit with prayer for Cheryl and her entire family. As he took his leave, he turned to Baker and said, "Pastor, walk with me to my car, if you would."

Upon reaching the car, Rose handed Richard a check for $2,000. He then implored him saying, "Pastor Baker, please take Sister Cheryl and your children back to Brunswick where you can have the love and support of your family. I will send a retired minister to fill in and see that you get $400 a week for at least the next six months. The church will be waiting on you when you are able to get back."

Baker knew that his overseer's heart was pure and that he was only thinking of them, but he had his own thoughts. He responded, "Dr. Rose, that's exactly what the enemy's desire has been ever since God called me into the ministry. I fight him by letting him know he is not going to win, and his attacks will not keep me from showing up three times a week and preaching God's Word." Interestingly, during the almost seven months of Cheryl's battle with cancer, Richard only missed one service. Today, he often thinks of the song, *This is How I Fight My Battles,* saying, "Battles are never easy but they are 100 percent winnable if you are in the will of the Lord. And we were right in the middle of His will, and we knew it."

Rose dropped his head and replied, "Pastor, you have my utmost love and respect. Just know that the state office stands with you guys."

After two-and-a-half months of intermittent radiation treatment, Bassett ordered another gallium scan, which showed the cancer beginning to respond to the radiation. Although this brought some encouragement, Cheryl was simply too weak to continue the treatments. Consequently, the doctor suspended the treatment for a month, giving her time to regain her strength.

Even with the suspension of the radiation treatments, Cheryl remained extremely weak and continued to receive her medication and nourishment through the Groshong catheter. By the middle of February 1991, she had gone more than 50 days without taking food, liquid, or medicine by mouth.

Near the end of February, medical personnel performed another gallium scan to see if the status of the cancer had changed. Richard and Cheryl drove to Bassett's office to learn the results of the scan. After being ushered into his personal office, the Bakers sat down and anxiously awaited his report. As the doctor lifted his eyes toward them, Richard and Cheryl could see that tears filled them. Not knowing just what to expect, they listened intently as he spoke. "I have no explanation for what I have to share with you," he announced. "The cancer has intensified to Stage 4-B and has spread to three other areas in the body—two places in the abdomen and one place in the left hip. He continued, "I have never witnessed this type of cancer being as aggressive as it has been with Cheryl."

Richard asked, "What does Stage 4-B mean?"

The doctor replied, "It is the last stage of cancer before death comes." But he quickly pointed out, "Not all people die. Some recover after being diagnosed with Stage 4-B cancer."

"How long does Cheryl have," Richard asked pointedly.

"I am not God and don't like to speculate on how much time a person has left," Bassett answered.

Not satisfied with the doctor's evasive answer, Richard pressed the issue saying, "It's important that I have some idea, with my family being five hours away and with my responsibilities of pastoring a church."

Reluctantly, the doctor explained, "If the cancer remains as aggressive as it presently is, she may have six months. A lot depends on how she responds to the treatments."

As much as he wanted to know the truth, Richard was not prepared for Bassett's answer. The doctor then talked with them about their options and recommended switching to chemotherapy. He asked permission to do half a treatment on Cheryl that day to see if she could tolerate it. After agreeing to and receiving the chemo, they departed for their forty-five-minute drive to Manchester.

18

Nothing Too Hard for God

The February day was cold and rainy, a day more suited for curling up beside a cozy fireplace and sipping hot cocoa than for traveling. They didn't have that luxury. After departing for the trip home and after having driven about 10 miles, Cheryl became deathly ill and began throwing up. Richard pulled over to the side of the road and went to the passenger side of the car to help her. As he took her in his arms, she cried out, "How much longer must I suffer like this?"

With a significant measure of vexation, Richard looked up to the heavens, with the cold rain bitterly stinging his face, and shouted, "God, where are You?" His faith in God was real but, at this moment, his human emotions overwhelmed him. This was truly a trial of faith, for both him and his suffering wife.

After resuming their journey, they arrived home half an hour later. When Richard had positioned Cheryl on the couch, he retired to his office to study for his Sunday messages. Shortly after he had settled into studying, Cheryl called out to him. Walking into the living room to see what she needed, he heard her anxiously exclaim, "You're not only my husband; you're my pastor! What do I do?"

That question landed heavily upon Richard and reached deep into his soul. The only answer he had was to return to his office, get on his knees, place his head and body under the opening of the desk, and cry out to God declaring, "Lord, I am not coming out until I receive an answer to that question!" After remaining in that position for at least an hour, he sensed the Lord speaking to him. He returned to the living room and announced to Cheryl, "The Lord said if you have faith that passes all understanding, then don't do anything else or take any more treatments."

She asked Richard to give her some scriptures on divine healing and faith. He returned to his desk and wrote 40 verses on index cards. He also gave her a small book entitled *Healing in the Church,* a book written around 1919. Cheryl lay on the couch reading the 40 verses repeatedly for hours.

The following day, she asked to be left alone as much as possible so she could spend time with the Lord in prayer and in His Word. She also read the book Richard gave to her and shared with him that she had prayed as she had never prayed before. As she read the book on healing in the church, she came across words to the effect, "God has made provisions for our healing by His stripes, and our healing has been provided for in the atonement."

She related to Richard, "At that moment, a light came on in my mind and spirit, and I knew that the Word had become greater than I had ever known before. I knew immediately that I didn't have to take treatments anymore." She later penned the words,

> I am battling within myself to take more treatments or trust God. No one can help me with this decision, not even Richard. I finally had to go to God on my own. Up to this point, I had relied on others for prayer. But now I had to seek God for myself.

Cheryl continued to experience complications from the half dose of chemo. When Richard called to report on her condition, Bassett instructed him to take her to the hospital, where she was at once admitted. After having started her on medications through IVs, he asked to speak to Richard privately. The doctor informed him that he had been researching different types of treatments for Cheryl and recommended placing her in a semi-coma state and giving her massive doses of chemo. Even with that, he confessed that he could only give her about a 10 percent chance of survival. But if he did nothing, she would have no chance at all. When he informed Richard that he wanted to do the procedure on Thursday and suggested that he notify his family at once, Richard responded that the decision to proceed rested with Cheryl.

On Wednesday, March 6, as Richard visited Cheryl in the hospital, Bassett walked into the room and shared with her the information he had given to her husband earlier. After he had prepared her for the slimmest of hopes, she weakly replied, "Bassett, you have been a great doctor and have shown us a lot of care and love, and we appreciate you so much. But I have tried man's way, and it's not working. Now I am going to trust in God. I am asking you to release me to go home today."

When the doctor looked at Richard for his response, Richard expressed, "It's her choice. Please release her." Somewhere around 3:00 pm, she was released, and they departed for home.

Upon arriving back in Manchester, Richard helped Cheryl into the house and made her as comfortable as possible. As usual, a couple of women came over to sit with her so he and the children could attend church. Cheryl spoke up and said, "Richard, I want to go to church tonight."

Richard answered, "Cheryl, it's Wednesday night. Why not wait until Sunday, and we will try to get you there then."

When he got to church that evening, he had no idea as to what to speak on. He simply seemed to have nothing left to give. The congregation sang a couple of choruses, and Richard opened his Bible to Psalm 91 and began reading. As he read, he made a few comments. Suddenly, the back door of the sanctuary opened, and several women entered carrying Cheryl. At first, Richard felt a little upset, because he had told her to stay home. But he knew this was not the place to discuss the matter.

Cheryl sat down as he continued teaching. In about five minutes, she became violently ill and began throwing up. Some of the women took her to the restroom to provide the care she needed. As they cleaned her up, a couple of men cleaned the sanctuary.

After resuming the service and knowing that he needed to check on his wife, Richard asked the congregation to come down and stand in the altar for a closing prayer. As the people came forward, all he could think about was getting Cheryl home. He began making a few comments before he closed and noticed that she had come back into the sanctuary, with the assistance of a couple of the women. Surely something unusual was happening here, and he asked a couple of the men to get her and bring her to the altar. When they brought her forward, Richard, without any forethought, exclaimed, "Tonight is your night of healing!" As soon as those words left his mouth, doubt filled his heart. There was little doubt, however, that the Holy Spirit spoke those words through him, seeing his faith was not strong enough to speak them.

Richard took the anointing oil and walked up to Cheryl. She was praying and worshiping with her eyes closed as he reached out to touch her forehead with the oil. In that moment, without his hand ever reaching her, she began to experience a powerful anointing of the Holy Spirit. She cried and worshiped for a couple of minutes, and everyone present could sense the atmosphere changing. She tried to speak but could only get out a word or two before the Holy Spirit began speaking through her. Her first words were, "I feel." The Holy Spirit then spoke, "A hand... going down into... my stomach... It's moving around... Now it's coming up."

With that, Cheryl began dancing under the power of the Holy Spirit and shouting, "I'm healed! I'm healed!" The entire congregation erupted in spontaneous praise to God. That night, Cheryl could not walk into the church under her own power, nor did she return home under her own power. She rather returned home under the power of the living God!

When the Baker family returned home that evening, Richard prepared a bowl of soup for Cheryl, the first food that she would eat by mouth since before Christmas, at least 70 days.

The next morning, he called Bassett and recounted the previous evening's occurrence explaining that they believed God had healed Cheryl. He commended them for their faith but reminded him that they had not administered any treatments, and the cancer was still there. He insisted that Cheryl come to the hospital for the chemo treatment he had discussed earlier with them.

After hanging up the phone, Richard felt a little discouraged. His hopes had been high, but the phone call had somewhat deflated him. Cheryl then called the doctor's wife, who had been quite supportive of her during her ordeal. She also encouraged Cheryl to start the treatment option the doctor had recommended.

The following Monday, Richard called the doctor and explained again that they honestly believed that God had healed Cheryl and that he would like him to order another gallium scan. Bassett responded, "Pastor, the insurance won't pay for another scan until there are four more treatments."

Richard offered to pay for the scan with the instructions that whatever the results of the test were, they would submit to his recommendation. He agreed. An hour later, his office called and instructed Cheryl to go to the hospital to begin the two-day process, which required injecting gallium intravenously and the following day performing the scan itself. The technician kept asking Cheryl if she had had any treatment since the last scan, which she hadn't.

The Bakers had an appointment with Bassett the following morning at 11:00 to get the results of the test. They were ushered into the doctor's private office, where they anxiously awaited his arrival. What seemed like an eternity but was only a few minutes, the doctor entered and reported that the hospital had not yet sent the test results to him. However, someone had called to let him know that he could expect the report shortly. After spending the next few minutes in small talk, the fax machine began printing. Turning to retrieve the report, the doctor began reading it with his back still toward Richard and Cheryl.

Not knowing just what to expect but still believing that God had worked a miracle, the Bakers waited expectantly for the test results. Finally, Bassett turned around to face them. That's when they saw tears flowing down his cheeks and heard his words, "All the scan shows are scar tissue in the left hip. I have no medical explanation for you not having cancer."

Bassett's nurse was an African American Pentecostal who could not contain her joy at his announcement. She left his office shouting down the hallway of the complex, "See what my God can do! See what my God can do!"

Richard and Cheryl will always be deeply appreciative for Bassett, his wife, and the entire medical staff that showed them so much love, compassion, and understanding. The Bassetts were themselves believers who exemplified what genuine care should look like.

The good doctor hugged them both and rejoiced with them over the amazing news of Cheryl's miraculous healing. Upon entering the lobby, they decided to wait a few minutes, because the rain was coming down quite hard. Cancer patients almost filled the lobby, and Richard could not contain himself. He began sharing with everyone what God had done for Cheryl. He boldly declared, "Ask Dr. Bassett when you go back to see him. God can do the same for you!"

Some of the waiting patients became a bit encouraged and began moving their arms up and down, as smiles crossed their faces.

As they departed for Manchester, Richard and Cheryl rejoiced in having the proof in their hands for any naysayers that may show up. And some were about to.

Their first stop was at the bank where their church had its accounts. A couple of church members worked there, and the president and vice-president had shown special concern for Cheryl and the Baker family. When Richard and Cheryl walked in, they saw one of their church members, Sister White, who was one of the bank tellers. When he related to her the good news, she said, "Mr. Brent (bank president) is in a board meeting but would not mind you interrupting him with this good news." She then slipped in to tell him herself.

Brent immediately came to the lobby with the biggest smile on his face and asked Richard and Cheryl to come and share the good news with the board of directors. As they walked into the boardroom together, Brent introduced them and asked Richard to share their story with them. When he finished, one man asked, "If God healed her, why did He leave a scar in her hip?"

Without hesitation Richard responded, "He left it there for naysayers who would have said that she was misdiagnosed and never had cancer in the first place." He had even had that thought while sitting in Basset's office, so when he was asked the question, he had his answer.

Richard later wrote, "Cheryl and I would not wish this experience on anyone, but God was faithful all the way and in every way. More than 25 churches, along with businesses and individuals, collected and sent us over $12,000. So many church members, family members, and friends helped with our children, with meals, and with keeping the house clean. Many pastors from different denominational settings sent kind words of encouragement and prayers, along with convening special prayer meetings. Cheryl and I truly experienced the body of Christ being the body of Christ."

19

Again an Evangelist

With Cheryl being healed of cancer, life began to get back on track with some semblance of normalcy. Richard was able to continue freelancing at the dealership working when he had the time. Approximately one-half of his sales were to pastors, some who came several states away to experience the no hassle and special pricing Meadows gave to pastors. Since Richard had been trained in doing dealer transfers, if a customer wanted a certain vehicle quickly that the dealership didn't have in stock, he could go into a data bank and see what all Ford, Lincoln, and Mercury dealerships had in their stock nationwide. His training also included doing appraisals and special ordering Ford trucks for customers and for the automobile lot.

Construction of the sanctuary continued, albeit sometimes at a snail's pace during the time of Cheryl's battle with cancer. Finally in early March, during the time Cheryl was receiving confirmation of being cancer free, the building inspector issued the church a permit of occupancy. Richard set the dedication service for Resurrection Sunday, March 31, at 2:00 pm. District Overseer Tatum, who had appointed Richard as pastor, led the service. Close to 200 people came for the dedication.

As Richard stood to open the service with a welcome to everyone, he began weeping as he remembered how just three-and-a-half years earlier he and Cheryl arrived there and found no one attending. On this day of dedication, he stood in a new sanctuary that was nearly full. Looking at his beautiful wife and three precious sons sitting on the front row, he thanked God in his heart for His amazing faithfulness. He also was thankful that he and Cheryl had obeyed the Lord on returning to Manchester. March 1991 would be one of the greatest months of his life, with Cheryl experiencing a healing from her cancer, having three handsome sons, and dedicating a new sanctuary.

Meadows' brother, Billy, was a member of a Baptist church a couple of blocks behind the church Richard pastored. The church needed a new roof and one of the bank presidents had recommended Richard to the pastor. He had Billy reach out to Richard to see if he would be willing to install a new roof for them. Richard told Billy that he wasn't doing construction anymore but if he could find a couple of guys to help him, he would do it. He knew he needed the money to help pay off medical bills and other debts he had incurred from Cheryl's bout with cancer.

In early April, Richard, along with two men in his church, began roofing the rather large facility. By the end of the second day, he started feeling a bit sick. His usual energy seemed to have vanished, and he found himself struggling to breathe at times. With his entire body aching, he felt miserable. On the third day, the weather changed to a light mist and the temperature had dropped from the 60s to the mid-40s. For some reason, he was working alone that day and felt so bad that he thought he must have contracted pneumonia. But he knew he needed to finish the roof.

Richard clearly remembers standing on the ridge of the sanctuary roof looking out over all the work that remained. With an escalating sense of urgency and desperation, he looked up to heaven and prayed, "Father, I am driving a school bus, selling cars, and roofing this church to provide a living for my family, so I can pastor this church and fulfill your will for my life. But I need You to strengthen me today with Your presence, as I feel so alone."

God answered his plea, and the roof was finished on Friday afternoon. When the pastor handed Richard the check, he expressed, "The deacon board wanted to bless you, so we included an extra love offering."

Still struggling physically, Richard preached Sunday morning and felt at times that he would not make it through the service. As he preached during the Sunday night service, with Cheryl and the boys sitting on the second row in front of the pulpit, he collapsed, fell off the platform, hit his head on the communion table, and turned it over on top of him, as he landed in the altar.

Two men immediately rushed to assist him in whatever way they could. He was not breathing, and they could not find a pulse. One of the men, Ricky Smith, began doing chest compressions and mouth-to-mouth resuscitation. The procedure worked and he began breathing. Someone called 911 and an ambulance transported him to the hospital in Columbus, Georgia, where a doctor diagnosed him with chronic fatigue.

Richard remained in the hospital for three days. His precious mother came and helped, since Cheryl was still getting her strength back. The doctor shared with him that part of his problem was brought on by the extreme stress of fearing his wife would die, by the responsibilities of caring for his family, and by the demands of pastoring a church. He ordered Richard to take it easy for a couple of weeks. He took the doctor's advice.

That spring Ricky and Ryan started playing baseball and loved every minute of it. Their coach had his own baseball diamond next to his home. The boys would eventually go on to play football and basketball. Christopher, the youngest, began playing the next year.

During the summer of 1991, James Gresham offered to take Richard and his sons to a swimming hole he had been frequenting for years. Meriwether County is the largest land county in the state of Georgia but is largely a rural county that is sparsely populated. The Flint River runs through it and feeds several streams. It was to one of these streams that James took them. The party had to navigate their way through high brush and grass to access the swimming hole, an approximately 40-foot-wide creek bordered by a small sandy area. On the far side of the creek, the water swept fast around the sand bar, which prompted the men to tell the boys not to get in over waist deep.

Richard was swimming downstream when suddenly he heard a scream. James was yelling because Ryan had gotten too close to the swift water, which caught him and was rapidly taking him downstream. A tree along the bank leaned over the creek and a lower limb hung just over the water. Ryan desperately reached up and grabbed it but the swift water ripped him away after only a couple of seconds. Richard now was swimming as fast as he could, while trying to position himself in front of his son. He could see that farther downstream a large tree had fallen into the creek, and he knew that if Ryan became entangled in the limbs, the situation could become even more desperate.

James was also swimming towards Ryan, and the current was taking the three of them dangerously close to the fallen tree. To make matters worse, as Richard drew near the tree, he saw a large water moccasin lying on a limb just above the water line. He could see that Ryan was heading straight for the venomous cottonmouth. Turning his attention to the snake, he started swimming towards it but knew he would not make it in time. Fortunately, James caught up with Ryan, grabbed him with one hand just as they reached the fallen tree, and seemingly with one single motion, grabbed the snake with his other hand and tossed it into the water.

Richard approached the tree about the same time, but the current swept him into the area where James had tossed the snake. Thankfully, he and the deadly serpent didn't meet. The men wisely decided to cut their outing short and return home. Richard instructed his boys, an 11-year-old, an eight-year-old, and a five-year-old, not to tell their mother what had happened. Understandably, his instructions fell on deaf ears. As soon as they arrived home, Cheryl heard three different versions of the day's events, with the actual truth being somewhere in the middle.

The remainder of 1991 proved to be a good time for the Bakers. They continued enjoying the pastoral ministry and rejoiced at seeing Cheryl fully recover her strength. The church board met with Richard in the fall of 1991 and offered him a full-time salary package. Although it was less than he was making working his secular jobs, he knew that God had sent him there to pastor, and their offer was a livable wage. So, for the next 18 months, he enjoyed pastoring without having to sell cars or put on roofs. However, he did continue to drive the school bus for the insurance.

For six months he had been studying the 10,000-question syllabus in preparation for his ordination test. When the day for the test arrived, Steve Cox, his associate, drove him to the state office in Doraville for the examination. Feeling extremely nervous, Richard walked into the lobby with Steve to find about 40 other ministers also waiting to take the test. When one pastor asked him if he had taken the test before, he answered that he had not. The pastor replied that this would be his third time. Upon hearing that, Richard turned to Steve and announced, "I am not ready for this. Let's leave. I will come back next time."

Steve responded, "Pastor, I have the keys, and we are not leaving until you take the test."

After the applicants had been called to the examination room, test administrator, Jerry Chitwood, explained that there were three separate tests. Not everyone was getting the same exam. When someone asked which one was the hardest, Chitwood answered that it was the one with the first 100 questions on the Book of Genesis. Richard immediately began praying, "Oh God, please help not to get that one. Please Lord, have mercy on me."

The examiner handed out the exams facedown. After receiving instructions to turn the test paper over and begin, Richard complied, and, wouldn't you know it, the first 100 questions were on the Book of Genesis. He finished his test, turned it in, and waited to hear his grade, before meeting with three seasoned ministers for his oral exam. But first, he sat down with one of the instructors who went over his test results with him. The test was in three-parts–Church Polity, Church History, and Biblical Knowledge. He learned that he scored 83 percent on the first part, 89 percent on the second part, and in the low 90s on Biblical Knowledge.

On August 5, 1992, he received his ordination certificate, a date which also happened to be his mother's birthday. He truly believed that God had a hand in this, especially considering that she was perhaps the one human being most responsible for him even being alive and in the ministry. Richard printed a copy of his test result and sent it to her to express his thanks to her for all she had done for him over the years. No mother could have been prouder of a son than she was on that day. He was certain that no son could have been more appreciative of his mom than he was.

In January of 1993, Richard received a call from Meadows asking him to come and meet with him. During their discussion, Meadows shared with him that he was in the process of petitioning the GM Corporation for authorization to open a Buick/Cadillac dealership. Meadows' next words floored Richard. He said, "Richard, I have complete trust and confidence in you, and I want to invite you to be the general manager of this new dealership. Your starting annual salary will be $60,000, along with health insurance, a 401k plan, and demos every three months for you and Cheryl. In addition, you will receive five percent of the profit at the end of each year."

Richard was speechless. Although Meadows treated him extremely well, he certainly didn't see this coming. Grasping for words, he responded, "Mr. Meadows, what an opportunity of a lifetime! But God has called me to be a minister, and I have to be obedient to what He has asked me to do."

Not willing to acquiesce so quickly, Meadows rejoined, "You can still pastor your church and pretty much set your own hours. And you can take Sundays and Wednesdays for your days off."

Richard replied, "I will pray about it and give it serious consideration." In all honesty, he wanted to take the offer. It seemed almost too good to be true. As he drove home, he was pumped at this opportunity that he knew probably would never come again. "After all," he rationalized, "I wouldn't have to take a salary from the church."

He reasoned that he could possibly bring on Steve Cox as a full-time assistant pastor to help with the day-to-day operations of the church. He had it all planned out in his mind, that is, until he arrived home and announced to Cheryl that he had something to tell her privately. She, suspiciously and with a touch of irony, asked, "Well, what is it now?"

Confident that she would feel just as he did about this offer, Richard related to her the gist of his conversation with Meadow. His notion of how she would respond soon proved misguided. Instead, she just looked at him in disbelief and boldly announced, "That's not why God sent us here, and I don't think it's a good idea!" Clearly, nothing more needed saying.

After Richard reported to Meadows and thanked him for considering him for the position, he informed him that he and Cheryl had discussed it and prayed about it but couldn't get peace about the offer.

Richard admitted that he probably would have missed God's will in this instance if Cheryl had shown any interest at all. He knew that God had given him the right wife, one whose heart always remained pure for the Lord.

In late February he received a call from Rose, state administrative bishop for North Georgia, asking him to consider becoming a member of the state evangelistic team. He wanted Richard to mainly focus on smaller churches in the state with the requirement of preaching a minimum of 14 services monthly (168 yearly) among churches with an attendance of less than 125. The state would provide housing on the campground in Doraville, which was adjacent to the state offices. His family would receive health insurance, and he would be paid $1,500 per month for travel expenses. Rose continued, "We don't want you just to preach revivals, but spend time with the pastors giving them encouragement and offering any guidance you may feel they need."

For several months Richard had been feeling a release from pastoring Victory Temple. This was one reason he had considered Meadows' offer. After spending a week fasting, praying, and talking it over with Cheryl, he accepted the state evangelist position and began making plans to resign his church and put their house up for sale.

The Bakers resigned their pastorate effective the last Sunday in March, and Richard began preaching revivals in April. They waited to move to Doraville, a suburb of Atlanta, until late in May, when the boys had finished school. The boys were thrilled with the move knowing that the campground consisted of nearly 70 acres, with half the acreage wooded. To make the move even better, Richard's cousin, Frankie Tyson, along with his wife, Joyce, and their three sons and one daughter, also lived in one of the homes on the campground. Frankie was pastoring a church just a few minutes away.

It was an exciting place for them to live, especially for the boys. They would leave the house in the morning and sometimes Cheryl wouldn't see them until later in the afternoon. There was so much for them to do—exploring the woods, playing basketball, baseball, football, and, at times, swimming. During youth camps, the campground exploded with hundreds of children and young people, and the Baker boys were usually in the mix, especially Ryan.

John Childers served as state youth director and lived on the property. The Childers had a couple of sons that the Baker boys played with. On one occasion while jumping on a trampoline, Ryan fell on Jeremy Childers and broke his arm. Shortly after his arm mended, Ryan ran into him on his bicycle, and once again Jeremy had to go to the emergency room to get stitches. With a bit of tongue-and-cheek, Childers told Baker if anything else happened, he would be getting the medical bill.

The Lord tremendously blessed the Bakers' evangelistic efforts with salvations, healings, and deliverances taking place in almost every revival. Richard quickly booked up all the way through March of 1994. He even preached the week of Memorial Day, on Sunday, July 4, on Labor Day weekend, and on December 26. He preached over 200 times in 1993, which included every Sunday of the year.

Richard always felt that he was in his true element as an evangelist. He never considered himself to be a great orator and, according to him, rarely ever preached a message in which he didn't stumble over a few words. But he took comfort in knowing that God's anointing always rested upon him. He was asked many times why he thought God used him in the ways he did. He always answered the same way: "I pray, I fast, and I stay in the Word." As an evangelist, he prayed and studied at least four hours each day and fasted at least one day a week most weeks. The last two weeks of August and the first two weeks of January were his times of extended fasting. He usually went to his Grandmother Baker's home in Douglas, Georgia. She lived alone, until age 94, on the farm where she and Richard's grandfather farmed and raised seven children.

Richard & family with his Grandmother Ruby Baker.

Richard loved spending time there roaming the 100 acres, praying, mediating, and seeking directions from the Lord. Many days he could be found sitting on the spillway overlooking a five-acre pond his dad helped his father dig back in the 1940s. His grandmother knew the Bible better than most pastors did having read it through more than 50 times and the New Testament more than 100 times. They would sit in the afternoons and discuss the Word of God for a couple of hours. God blessed him with two godly grandmothers, and for that he will always be eternally grateful.

The Churches of God in North Georgia partnered with the Churches of God in Alaska to render moral, spiritual, and financial assistance, since the denomination designated Alaska as a mission state. The evangelism director for North Georgia asked Richard if he would go and preach a few revivals there if the state office covered the expenses. His motto for many years was, "Have Bible; will travel."

The revival meetings were scheduled for the last week in March and the first week in April of 1994. The Bakers had worked it out for his mom's sister, Aunt Shirley, to come stay with the boys so Cheryl could travel with him. When the time came for their departure, Rose sent word for him and Cheryl to stop by the state offices on their way to the airport. When they entered his office, the overseer shared with them that the pastor at the church in Cumming, Georgia, had resigned the week before, and he felt that the Bakers would be a good fit. Richard had preached a revival for them back in the fall of 1993 that lasted two weeks. He thanked Rose for thinking of them but shared that he had no burden to pastor at the time.

Almost immediately Cheryl gave him a soft elbow to his rib cage. She was tired of him being gone all the time and was ready for them to get back into the pastorate. Rose asked for permission to mention his name to the church. Once again Richard stated that he had no burden at the time to pastor. However, he did agree that if the vote was more than 85 percent, he would accept it.

He and Cheryl had a long conversation on the way to Alaska. She explained how she felt removed from the ministry and how difficult it was for her to raise the boys with him being absent so much of the time. The boys, who were now 14, 11, and eight, needed their father to be home more. Richard explained, "With what I shared with Dr. Rose, we don't need to be thinking about pastoring in Cummings."

Cheryl responded, "I know; you messed up by saying that" (speaking of his threshold of a vote of more than 85 percent).

The Bakers arrived in Anchorage, Alaska, on Friday evening. Pastor Shook of the North Anchorage Church of God picked them up at the airport and took them to, in Richard's words, "A fabulous restaurant where we ate the best halibut you have ever put in your mouth."

On Sunday morning the revival began with a beautiful service. The Sunday night service found Richard, as usual, sitting on the front row meditating on the Lord to get his heart and spirit in tune with Him. Around 5:45 pm, Shook came and told him he had a call from Atlanta. Stepping into the pastor's office, he answered the phone and heard Rose exclaim, "Hello, pastor of Sawnee Mountain Church of God in Cumming, Georgia!"

Richard was almost speechless. Composing himself, he asked, "How is that possible?"

Rose answered, "I will explain it to you upon your arrival back in Atlanta." With that, he hung up.

On Thursday afternoon the state administrative bishop for Alaska, Harvey Turner, invited Richard and Cheryl for lunch. Over a delicious meal, he asked if they would seriously consider coming to Alaska and pastoring a church. When Richard asked him where the church was located, Turner answered, "The North Pole."

Once again Richard felt the all-too-familiar elbow in the side from Cheryl, this time a little harder. The earlier elbow nudge while sitting in Rose's office meant, "You better take it!" The elbow he now felt meant, "You better not take it!"

In just four days, two state bishops had offered them a pastorate, and the churches were 4,171 miles apart. One was in the northern suburbs of Atlanta, and the other rested in the northern suburbs of Alaska.

After the revival ended on Friday night, the Bakers flew to the capital city of Juneau. Pastor Richard Green and his wife picked them up at the airport and took them to lunch. Again, he and Cheryl feasted on the delectable halibut. The congregation consisted largely of American Indians. Green explained, "The people will all show up the first service. If they like you, they will attend every service. Otherwise, only a handful will return."

That Saturday afternoon, evangelist Baker went from the excitement of enjoying the natural beauties of Alaska to experiencing a measure of trepidation. All the apprehension soon vanished when the first service ended. It was apparent that the people liked them. The altar filled with worshipers and seekers, and the fellowship following the service was special. Each night the sanctuary was packed, and the revival went extremely well.

Richard later reported, "I have preached in over 200 churches and experienced some great hosts, but the Greens are up there at the top. Cheryl and I could not have been treated any better."

Following the revival, he and Cheryl prepared to fly back to Atlanta. Speaking with Rose before their departure, he learned that the church was expecting them on the upcoming Sunday. Richard felt like he was on a rollercoaster. He was doing what he really loved to do and felt the most qualified in evangelistic work. However, he had to admit that God was calling them back into the pastorate.

20

Sawnee Mountain and Missions

Upon arriving back in Georgia, Richard and Cheryl immediately shared with their boys all that had transpired since they had first mentioned the possible opportunity a couple of weeks earlier. Sawnee Mountain Church of God was only about 30 miles from where they were living, and Cheryl and the boys wanted to check it out. Richard called the church clerk, who offered to meet them at the parsonage. They were surprised to find such a beautiful home of 3,200 square feet located on a one-acre corner lot in a quiet neighborhood, only about three miles from the church. The boys wanted to spend the night, so the family drove home to get air mattresses and returned to campout indoors.

On Saturday Richard came down with congestion and a fever. The next day was to be their first Sunday, and he was feeling poorly. Rose had also informed him that a small group of members had left the church and started their own church—not the kind of news an incoming pastor wanted to hear just a couple of days before his first service.

Their first Sunday was April 10, 1994. Seven or eight months earlier, the church had experienced a mighty move of God in a revival that went almost two weeks, in which Richard preached. He remembered the people being friendly and exuberant in their worship. Although the church had been averaging between 130 and 150, on this first Sunday morning as pastor and family, they walked into a congregation of about 90 people that seemingly had lost their exuberance and joy. To add to the apparent misery of a wounded church, Richard, still not feeling well, sensed that he too had lost his joy.

He shared with Mark, a young intern studying for the ministry, that he was not feeling well at all. Mark offered to open the service and make the announcements. He had already come up with an order of service for the pastor to approve: Announcements, choir to sing two songs, offering, choir sings last song, Melba Huntley to sing a special, and the pastor to preach.

Mark was sitting next to Richard on the platform and during the choir's last song, Richard whispered, "I will introduce the soloist and make a few comments before I preach. Once again, what's her name?"

He replied, "Melba."

Richard mused, "I hope I can remember her name."

Perceptively, the intern responded, "Just think of melba toast."

After the choir finished their last song, Richard walked to the pulpit and shared a few minutes from his heart. He then encouraged the congregation to "worship with Sister Toast as she comes to minister in song."

At that moment, he witnessed the first display of emotions in the service. Although he was embarrassed by his obvious error, he often wonders if the Lord didn't play a part in it, as even to this day, more than 26 years later, people still remember and break a smile.

He preached and spent some time talking with people after church trying to encourage them. He called for a pastor's council meeting for Monday evening and as the seven men arrived, they engaged in small talk for a few minutes just to get to know each other. Richard then asked, "How did you guys decide on me for your pastor?"

One of the men spoke up and said, "Dr. Rose met with us Thursday a week ago and presented 14 names for us to consider. He then said we needed to eliminate 10 of the names from the list, and he would come on Sunday and present resumes on the four remaining candidates. We knew you because you had preached us a revival, so all seven of us voted for you to be one of the four. When Sunday morning came, Dr. Rose stood before us and went over the four resumes with yours being last. One of the last things he said was, 'Brother Baker really didn't feel led to come be your pastor, but if you vote for him, he will be the best pastor he knows how to be.' The chatter we are hearing is that at least Brother Baker is honest."

The Bakers received all but four votes. Richard was amazed that Rose had shared his hesitancy with the congregation and even more amazed they voted them in as their pastor. If he had any doubts about this being the Lord's will for them, the words he just heard quenched it.

With approximately one-third of the church having left over the previous four weeks since the former pastor resigned, the congregation had begun to struggle financially. Richard met with the clerk on Tuesday morning, who was nervous at having to discuss with him the abysmal financial situation the church was in. She offered to resign her position when he could find a replacement. He strongly encouraged her to remain, at least for a while. He spent a good part of the day going over the financials to see how the church could best manage moving forward.

He decided to take a temporary pay cut and let April play out to see where they were. Over the next three weeks, a few people did return, which brought their attendance to a little over 100 on Sunday mornings. The church closed in April several thousand dollars in the red, with bills due they couldn't pay.

Richard did what he knew would work. He fasted and prayed for a few days for guidance and direction. Some had suggested the church consider refinancing and borrowing extra funds to help with operational expenses. However, that was not at all what he wanted them to do, or felt they should do.

Frankie Tyson, along with his wife, Joyce, was pastoring and felt the call to the mission field. They were in the process of raising their funding and were planning to depart in June for Guatemala. The more Richard prayed, the more he felt led to have them come share with his congregation and ask the church to support them. Yet from the human perspective, it made no sense considering the church was struggling just to make ends meet.

He finally called and Frankie informed him that he was booked for all of May and was planning to take the first week in June off in preparation for their departure to Guatemala. Richard pressed him to reconsider and come be with them on Sunday, June 5. He agreed and Richard began announcing the mission service. Although a few people questioned the timing of the meeting, no one seriously resisted the idea of having a mission service.

The Tysons came, ministered, and shared their vision in going to Guatemala. The ushers had passed out pledge cards and Richard pushed the offering that morning. More than $1,500 came in the morning offering and $300 was pledged in monthly support. He was amazed and thrilled at the response. By the end of July, they were out of the red, and by August, the church had grown to an average of 130 in Sunday morning services, with tithes and offerings increasing weekly.

Later that fall, the Holy Spirit began dealing with Baker about asking Tyson about a small project the church could take. He finally yielded and emailed his cousin to explain how God had been dealing with him. Tyson immediately responded to let him know that there was a church in El Limon, a slum area in Guatemala City, with a growing congregation and nowhere to worship. The church of more than a hundred people had a piece of land with a small metal building that could only accommodate about 40.

The Lord placed a heavy burden on Baker for this pastor and his congregation, but he felt the project was much too large for them seeing that just putting up a block building would cost $20,000 in material alone. However, the Holy Spirit continued to deal with him, surely because He had heard the desperate cries of this church and was moving to answer their plea.

No longer able to ignore the impressions upon his heart, Baker agreed that his church would raise the funds to build the church. Relying on a familiar technique, he had someone draw a large thermometer on a poster board placing a $0 at the bottom and $20,000 at the top. As the church raised funds, he would color the empty thermometer with a red marker up to the amount raised at the time.

Some of the men began to talk about wanting to go to El Limon and help build the church. With increasing excitement about the project, Baker planned a trip for September of 1995. Immediately, he had 17 men sign up. In the early part of 1995, the church sent some funds so the Guatemalan church could began laying the foundation. Baker's church had managed to raise about $8,000 but seemed to be running out of steam.

One Sunday morning during February or March, a family of five visited the Sawnee Mountain church. The family returned for the evening service, which is always encouraging to a pastor. Following the service, the husband asked Baker if he could take a few minutes to speak with him. When the pastor agreed, the two men climbed into the visitor's car to talk in private. The man forthrightly asked Baker about his philosophy of ministry and his vision for the future of the church.

After listening to the pastor's heart, the man then asked about the mission project they were planning and raising funds for in Guatemala. Upon hearing his response, the guest reached into his coat pocket, retrieved an envelope with a check in it, and handed it to Baker. He then added, "I am a local physician, and we are presently attending church in another city but want to find a church closer to where we live."

When Baker got out of his car and walked back inside the church, he opened the envelope to find a $10,000 check for the mission project in

Guatemala. His heart started rejoicing and his eyes filled with tears. He knew God had once again worked mightily.

Before leaving the church that evening, he excitedly took the time to fill in the thermometer, bringing it up to $18,000. It didn't take long to raise the balance of $2,000. And then the planning began on the trip to Guatemala to actually build the church facility.

The church sent the funds to the missionary, Tyson, so he could purchase material and have everything ready for Baker and his men when they arrived. Seventeen men departed Atlanta bound for Guatemala in early September 1995. The excitement and enthusiasm among the men was remarkable to behold.

When the entourage arrived in Guatemala, they were met by Tyson, who had arranged for them to stay at the Wycliffe Bible Translators' compound located in Guatemala City, the capital of Guatemala. The next morning, the team traveled for an hour to get to the job site. After arriving and greeting the pastor and some of the church, the Georgians went to work.

The pastor had asked all the men of the church to try to take off from their regular jobs at least one day that week to assist in the building project. One man could not get off from his work, so he sent his 10-year-old son in his place. The boy stuck to Baker like glue and worked as hard as some men, carrying blocks all day long. It quickly became apparent to Richard that these men were highly excited and motivated to see this project completed.

Every day for lunch, the women of the church would prepare a hot cooked meal. At the end of ten days, they had all the walls up and were working on the rafters. The church was 60 feet wide and more than 100 feet long. Because of the frequent earthquakes in Guatemala, the workers had to build steel reinforced concrete pillars every eight to 10 feet along the width and length of the church. Everyone was amazed to see so much accomplished in such a short time.

Baker and his men took Sunday off and joined the congregation for church. Tyson also took them to visit an orphanage called Casa Shalom. Something happened for Baker on that first emotional visit that ensured that it certainly would not be his last.

Saying goodbye was difficult, considering that the men had formed a special bond with their Guatemalan brothers and sisters. The entire team from Georgia was so appreciative that the Lord allowed them to bless their church family in Guatemala. They agreed that they could complete the church over the next year. As God blessed them, they sent more funds to help accomplish the task and see the vision become a reality.

The mission trip infused a passion in the church for missions and prompted the planning of another trip. The church began a new fundraiser for just a project. The church continued to grow and 18 months into the Bakers' pastorate, the congregation had grown from 90 to over 160 for Sunday morning services, with the income doubling in the same amount of time.

Richard with 10-year-old boy sent to work in father's place.

The Sawnee Mountain church operated a food bank that initially provided food three times per week. At the time, it was the largest food bank operated by any church in the state of Georgia. Additionally, the church delivered boxes of food monthly to the 60 retired ministers and spouses who lived on the campground in Doraville, about 30 miles away.

Baker usually made this delivery with Homer Foster and Jack Till, men who served as co-leaders over the home and world missions' ministries of the church. On this day, Baker made the delivery himself, since he loved conversing with these precious ministers who had such wisdom and so many stories to tell. For example, W.G. Abney, who had married Richard and Cheryl and had prayed over them being set forth in the ministry, had retired and was living on the campground. Baker always made this his last stop knowing that Abney would always invite him in to talk. To listen to the passion and wisdom that came from these soldiers of the faith was an indescribable blessing to him.

21

Casa Shalom

Casa Shalom, the orphanage located in the highlands of Guatemala about 30 miles from the capital city, was in need of transportation for their children. Baker's church had a school bus they were not using, so he contacted Tyson to see if the children's home would like to have it. The answer was a resounding, "Yes!"

The church gladly donated the bus, as Baker's visionary spirit kicked in. He felt like the church should load it down with items the orphanage needed. After contacting the home to get a list of such things, they went to work gathering the needed articles. In preparation for the haul, they took all the seats up and stacked them in the back of the bus to make room for the cargo. The American Bible Society donated 2,000 Spanish Bibles and 20,000 tracts (donated to pastors). Doug and Barbara Ramey, who owned a clothing store, donated cases of clothes and shoes. A local furniture store donated a loveseat so two men of the three-member team, who alternated driving, could have a comfortable place to sit on the trip down.

Initially, their plans were to ship the bus loaded with all the donations. They compiled a manifesto and sent it to the shipping company. Immediately, the church received word that it could not ship the bus with cargo inside. Baker quickly had two men in the church agree to make the trip with him—Homer Foster, fire chief for Fulton County, and Jack Till, an executive with IBM who had recently retired. Time would prove that Baker, Foster, and Till made a good team.

By March of 1996, the bus was loaded to the brim with the departure date of Wednesday, April 3, drawing near. The three men experienced a rush of excitement when they pulled out of the church parking lot headed for Guatemala. It took them two days to reach McAllen, Texas, where they would cross the border into Mexico. The following morning, they headed for the border and quickly encountered a Mexican border policeman who took one look at them and exclaimed, "No, you may not enter Mexico with this bus filled with this content!"

They received instructions to go to an office that specialized in helping people get the right papers for such a crossing. However, there was one big problem. It was Good Friday and most businesses on the border were either closed or operating with a smaller staff. Still, they managed to get the bus properly documented, although no one was sure about the cargo, since it was considered unsecured. Almost everyone on the US side told them they didn't think the Mexican government would let them in with all the donated cargo they were carrying.

Baker, Foster, and Till checked into a hotel and spent a large part of the night praying for the Lord's direction, and praying that He would make the bus invisible. Early the next morning, the men drove back to the border not knowing what to expect but trusting God for His intervention. As they neared the first of four checkpoints, they were still praying for the Lord to make them invisible.

As Baker pulled up to the first checkpoint, the Customs officer simply asked to see their passports. When they stopped at the second checkpoint, the officer just wanted to see the vehicle registration and proof of insurance. The third and fourth checkpoints had no attendants, and the team eased through them into Mexico. For sure, God had answered their prayers.

After driving into midafternoon, one of the tires went flat. As providence would have it, there was a repair shop attached to a home only a few hundred feet from where the bus came to a stop. Two mechanics working there stopped what they were doing long enough to fix their flat tire.

As night approached, they began looking for a hotel that could accommodate the bus and offer security for them. After finding a place, they checked in and went to their rooms exhausted, but still giving the Lord praise for helping them cross through into Mexico. Waking early the next morning, they departed before sunrise and drove into the countryside, where they found a beautiful place to stop and have a short resurrection service. As the sun started coming up, the men worshipped the Lord and took communion. It was a deeply meaningful moment.

The trip across Mexico took three days. Arriving at the Guatemalan border, they were stopped 17 times by either the police or the military. They only had to pay one fine, which some may consider a bribe. They kept a large cooler iced down with drinks and candy bars just inside the bus. When they were stopped, they would immediately offer the officers a cold drink and a candy bar. Clearly, this act of kindness went a long way in helping them to find favor with the authorities.

The men spent their last night in Mexico about one hour from Guatemala. Missionary Tyson was waiting at the border for them when they arrived. They had no problem passing through Customs on the Mexican side but were asked to pull into a fenced in area when trying to cross into Guatemala.

Tyson spoke with the head of Customs and explained to him what they were doing, since they wanted to levy custom fees and taxes on the donations. The Customs official asked Tyson if he could have two cases of the Bibles for his church. The men gladly off-loaded the Bibles, and with that, crossed the border into Guatemala. They knew they had indeed entered the country on the Word of God.

Baker, Foster, and Till followed the missionary for about an hour, until they reached a bridge that had just been blown up by a rebel group. Guatemala had been locked in a civil war from 1960 until 1996, although the rebels did not target US citizens. However, if people were at the wrong place at the wrong time, they could certainly find themselves in harm's way. With no other options, they had to backtrack and take another route to the capital.

The team spent the night in the capital city and had enjoyed a classic delectable Guatemalan breakfast the next morning. Tyson had called the director of the orphanage and shared with her the bus's approximate arrival time. After a two-hour delay, they arrived to find the gates to the home opened for them. What the men witnessed brought tears to their eyes—all the children and staff patiently waiting with big smiles, some with homemade "Thank You" cards held high. As the bus pulled into the compound, everyone began to shout a loud welcome

These short-term missionaries from Georgia spent most of the day with the children. Baker remembers feeling so much at home there and reflects on the burden for orphans that settled into his spirit that day and never left. Within a few years, he would understand that God had a plan all along, and this trip was just part of His preparing him and his family for a much larger role, a role in caring for some of the most vulnerable of our society—the orphans.

After two days, the eight-man team arrived from the church, one of whom was Ryan, Baker's 13-year-old son. He had come to help his dad and other team members build their second church, this one in San Pedro, located about one hour from the capital. Baker was thrilled to have one of his sons on a mission trip with him. Eventually, all his sons would get to experience a mission trip.

Ryan with Homer in Guatemala.

Tyson had rented a house near the church from a medical doctor. The 11 men from Sawnee Mountain, along with Tyson and a few Guatemalan brothers, spent a week building a church 30 feet by 60 feet. They were able to lay all the block walls and install the rafters and metal roofing in a single week. When they left for home, the building was completely dried in.

For Baker, there was simply no way to express the feeling of having this congregation in Guatemala showing such appreciation for the work they did. The church had been praying a couple of years for God to provide the means for them to have a building, and now they had a church in Georgia provide just what they needed.

The men and one teenager flew back to Atlanta filled with joy and a sense of accomplishment. Within a couple of weeks after returning home, Baker received a call from the Mexican Consulate Office inquiring about the bus and wanting to know where in Mexico did he leave it. He had a hard time convincing them the bus was not in Mexico but in Guatemala.

22

Miraculous Provisions

Sawnee's next mission's trip was two-fold. First, Demecio Miranda, a pastor who lived in El Cedro in the mountains of western Guatemala that had no nearby medical care, had been praying for one for his village. Second, there was a pressing need for medical equipment and supplies. Tyson shared this need with Baker, who felt a witness in his spirit that it was of the Lord.

As they developed their plans for the trip, they also discussed the subject of the equipment and the much-needed medicines. Consequently, they decided to gather all the equipment, supplies, and medicines the clinic would need and ship them down before the team arrived to build the clinic. Once the church put the word out, contacts began flooding in. Director of Church of God World Missions, Gene Rice, shared with Baker about a particular ministry located in Bristol, Virginia, called King's Benevolent Fund (now Kingsway Charities), which provided medicines for mission trips and Third World Countries.

Brinkley Goodson, the physician that now attended the Sawnee Mountain church, offered to contact the organization. Within weeks, the church had received $90,000 worth of medicines and medical supplies. Another ministry donated hospital beds, prosthetics, wheelchairs, and other medical items. After all the donations, the church had gotten over $300,000 worth of medical supplies and medicines. They soon realized that they would not be able to ship these items through the normal shipping process without having to pay enormous amounts of taxes, along with a significant amount of red tape. Tyson consulted the denomination's leadership and communicated back to Baker that if they could somehow transport it down, crossing the land border would be much easier.

The church purchased a five-ton Mack diesel box truck from Fed-Ex in almost perfect condition. They began working with Mexican authorities well in advance of their departure sending them an itemized list of everything on the truck, along with letters from the church in Guatemala.

In early summer 1996, Baker, along with his two faithful traveling companions, Foster and Till, climbed into the cab of the Mack and headed for Guatemala. Upon reaching the border, the process flowed smoothly. Mexican authorities put a band and lock on the cargo door to the truck instructing them that it was not to be tampered with until the truck entered Guatemala. They drove through Mexico in two days, since the Mack could cruise 20 miles an hour faster than the bus. Although they were stopped 16 times, the police were not allowed to break the seal that was put on at the border. The three men reached the Guatemalan border later Saturday afternoon, with their faithful missionary, Tyson, waiting for them.

Tyson informed Baker that there had been a shakeup at the border crossing a couple of days earlier, and several border personnel were fired for taking bribes. He let them know that they may have some issues getting the truck into Guatemala. Although they submitted their paperwork, which was all in order, authorities denied them entrance because of the shakeup.

Authorities directed Baker to drive to an impoundment area. Since their main luggage was in the back of the truck, Tyson asked permission to break the seal to retrieve the luggage. After getting approval, they headed to the truck to collect their luggage. As soon as they opened the back door and reached for their gear, Baker noticed two large 70-pound boxes of medicine and felt the Lord impress him to take these two boxes with them. When he told Tyson about what he felt, he replied, "It better be God, because if we get caught going through customs with this much medicine, they may arrest us all!"

They loaded the two boxes, which almost filled up the cargo area of his bronco. Then, they loaded their luggage around and on top of the boxes and pulled in line to clear customs for entrance into Guatemala. Officials thoroughly checked the vehicles in front of them, even to the degree that the inspectors opened the engine compartments and checked under the vehicles. In view of what was happening in front of them, they all experienced a significant level of apprehension. Still, Baker was confident that he had heard the voice of the Lord.

When Tyson pulled up to the checkpoint, the inspectors just waved him through. Once they drove onto the main road, they all realized that they had witnessed another miracle. Clearly, everyone felt complete exhilaration.

After spending the night at a hotel, they rose early the next morning to continue their journey to Tyson's home. Following a short drive, they stopped at a store, where Miranda walked up to them looking quite troubled. He told Tyson that his baby was extremely ill and could possibly die without medical attention. Climbing aboard the Bronco, they resumed their trip to his village, El Cedro, a drive of about two hours and a hike over a 13,000 feet mountain range carrying the two 70-pound boxes of medicines and supplies.

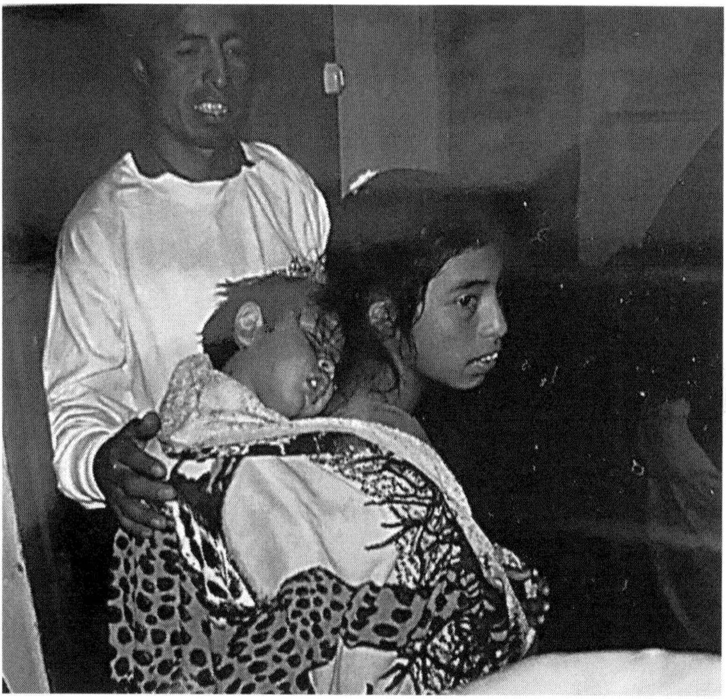

Pastor Miranda with daughter and sick son, Hiram.

Thankfully, Miranda had several of his members waiting to assist them. Baker carried one of the boxes for a while, but it wasn't long before the high altitude and the box's weight drained him of his strength. When he sat the box down on the ground, a 120-pound man picked it up and carried it twice as far as he had, before passing it off to another brother. Baker later said, "This is what they call humble pie—Guatemalan style!"

Box of medicine carried in to the village of El Cedro (Jack Till in front and Frankie Tyson in rear).

Following a one-and-a-half mile hike through spectacular mountains that gave a person the sense of being able to reach up and touch the clouds, the entourage arrived in the village of El Cedro, and to Miranda's home. After quickly meeting his wife and children, their concern shifted to his sick baby boy. Even though they had no idea as to what was wrong with him, they decided to open the two boxes of medicine donated by Kingsway Charities. Each box had a packing list of its contents.

Since it was Sunday morning, Baker called his church in Cumming and asked to speak to Goodson. When he came on the phone, he asked, "Pastor, what's wrong? I was teaching Sunday school."

As Baker explained the situation to him, the doctor began asking questions about the baby. Based on the information Baker supplied, he determined that possibly the baby was seriously dehydrated and had a serious infection. He then asked his pastor to read the packing list to him. Amazingly, the two boxes contained everything they needed to treat the baby. As of this writing (2020), Hiram Miranda is a tall handsome young man in his mid-twenties and ministers in the church his dad once pastored. What an amazing God we serve!

Mike Ramey & Mark Foster (background) with Richard Baker building a medical clinic El Cedro, Guatemala.

Since coming to Christ, Baker has often experienced God using what he calls "pings" to speak His will to him. He expressed, "I just sense deep within my spirit that the Lord is touching me and leading me. During these times, I have acted, and He has never failed to manifest Himself. I have failed Him so many times, but He has never failed me."

Later that day, the team returned to Tyson's home, and together they determined that one of the men needed to stay and work on getting the truck out of customs. Jack Till offered, and Homer and Richard flew back to Atlanta.

23

Medical Clinic and Foster Children

Almost two months had passed and Baker's team of workers was getting closer to departure for El Cedro to build the clinic. At the same time Goodson, Briggs (a dentist), and a local nurse would set up a clinic in the church adjacent to the place where they would build the clinic. The truck still had not been released, but the hand of God moved again. Within a couple of days before the team's departure, authorities released it.

When the construction team of 15 arrived in Guatemala, Tyson was waiting to greet them and transport them the five hours to El Cedro. They arrived at the base of the mountain and unloaded their luggage and tools. Again, members of the church were there to help them carry all their gear across the mountain to the village. Although the team had a few macho men with them, by the time they reached the village, young teenage girls were carrying their backpacks for them.

A temporary clinic was set up in the church. Weeks before the workers arrived, an announcement was made to the villagers about what day they could expect them. Each day a couple of hundred people would line up to see the doctor, dentist, or to be fitted for glasses. The Lions Club had donated hundreds of pairs of glasses for this very purpose.

The foundation to the building had been completed, and under the direction of skilled mason, Terry Addis, a pastor in North Georgia, the men went to work laying the block walls. Within four days, the laborers had finished the wall and had installed the roof.

In the meantime, Goodson saw a number of seriously ill patients. Four men brought a paralyzed woman on a makeshift stretcher to the clinic. She had a large tumor on her back that had grown into her spine and begged the doctor to operate on her. He told her that the facilities were not suited for such a surgery but ultimately decided to perform the surgery, anyway, considering there was no good option. Baker looked on from about 10 feet away in amazement at what he was witnessing. At times during the surgery, the doctor would exclaim, "Preacher, you need to pray!"

Tyson, who served as translator, stood at the head of the patient. She had received an epidural and was awake during the surgery. Goodson confessed that had he known how deep the tumor went, he would not have operated. However, four days later when the team met for a farewell service, they saw this woman walk into the church and sit down for the entire service.

A mother of twins brought her sick undernourished babies to the clinic. Before she arrived, one of them died. The doctor, immediately after hearing the story, took the small two-month-old infant and began working with it. He determined the mother's milk was not sufficient for the babies, and this one was at the point of death. Goodson told brother Tyson to get someone to go and buy formula, which meant a few hours to walk out of the village, a drive to a town large enough that would sell formula and then return. The doctor reached into his pocket and gave enough money for this baby to have formula for six months. Although the team had brought a good supply of medicine, they did not have everything. But when a patient came to the clinic and needed medication that the doctor could not supply, he would always produce his own money and send someone to get it. All that happened made this trip one of the most amazing ones Baker ever remembers.

In the fall of 1996, shortly after returning from Guatemala, the church received word from Family and Children Services that there was a shortage of foster parents in the Atlanta area. The office was asking churches to make their members aware of the pressing need.

Richard and Cheryl discussed the situation and decided to sign up for the 10 weeks of training, which involved going to classes twice a week. After completing the classes, they decided to only take children five years old and up and then waited for the call they knew would come.

As Richard sat in his office at church studying on a Friday, he got a call from Cheryl. She said, "Richard, I received a call asking us to consider taking a newborn." After going home and discussing the request with her, both felt in their hearts that it was the right thing to do. They notified the department and informed them of their decision.

On Monday, they drove over to Gainesville, which was located about 18 miles from Cumming. Walking into a hospital and walking out shortly with a three-day-old infant boy seemed strange but greatly satisfying to both Richard and Cheryl.

The Bakers, especially Cheryl, wanted to become foster parents in the hope of getting a girl. Yet with three boys, God still saw fit to give them another one. A few weeks later, Cheryl received a call from Children's Services asking if they would be willing to adopt the baby, since his birth mother, who had been in the foster care system herself, did not feel she could adequately care for him. Once again, Richard was at church studying when Cheryl called to give him the news. They began the adoption process almost immediately, which took about six months. Their only cost was their attorney's fees. They named him Joshua William Baker.

Shortly before they received the call from the hospital, Richard had purchased a used BMW. He still sometimes jokes with Joshua, telling him, "You're special. We brought Ricky and Ryan home in Pontiacs and Christopher in a Ford Mercury. But you came home in a Seven Series BMW!"

Some 23 years later, as Baker sat in his office at Grace Point putting down his memoirs for this book, he walked to the front of the church to stretch his legs. He saw a homeless man talking with Joshua. After the man walked away, Richard asked, "Joshua, what did he want?"

Joshua answered, "Dad, he is having a rough time, and I told him how you and Mom adopted me and gave me a home. I told him God would help him too." Some may think that to be an amazing coincidence, but Baker knew that it had to do with an amazing God who continued to give them confirmation concerning their decisions about ministry–family, church, community, and missions.

Over time, the Bakers would foster nine children counting Joshua. All were hurting children but, for sure, they were all loved unconditionally in the Baker home. Not one of the children came to them with clothes. Cheryl would not go to the Salvation Army or Goodwill to buy clothes for them but rather insisted that Richard buy all new clothes. Their foster children went on vacations with them and enjoyed all that the rest of the family enjoyed. The Bakers gave the same attention to their birthdays and Christmases that they gave their biological children. Richard confidently declared, "If God ever called a woman to be a mom, it was most definitely Cheryl."

24

Mission Ministry Expands

As the Sawnee Mountain church moved into 1997, the congregation continued to grow, slowly but steadily. The Spirit of the Lord was moving powerfully in every service. The church was located in Forsyth County, which in years past had been a stronghold for the Ku Klux Klan. To Richard's knowledge, in a county with a population of over 100,000 people, there were virtually no African Americans living. He prayed and asked the Lord to let their church be the first to welcome all ethnic groups.

One Sunday morning, an attractively dressed couple, T.J. and Sophia Spencer, walked into the Bakers' church. Both were from Africa–she from Nigeria and he from Liberia. He flipped homes in the Atlanta area and Sophia was a manager of McDonalds. They were members of a large predominately African American church in Atlanta.

When Sophia shared with some of her church friends that they would be moving to Forsyth County, their friends quickly informed her of the history associated with Forsyth County. She later related that when they crossed over from Fulton County into Forsyth County, she felt such an overwhelming spirit of fear.

Baker watched intensely to see how the church would react. To his amazement and in his own words, he said, "They were loved on more than I was on my first Sunday."

They soon joined the church, and Sophia started singing in the choir. Baker booked a black southern gospel group, Charles Johnson and the Revivers. The turnout was so large that seats were not available for everyone. People were placed in the foyer, the side door to the sanctuary was opened, and people stood in the parking lot listening. God had answered Baker's prayers, as well as the prayers of others. And on that day, strongholds were broken. To his knowledge, the church only lost one man who just quietly departed.

There were within the church several husbands and wives who wanted children but were unable to do so biologically. One couple had spent thousands of dollars at a fertility clinic, all to no avail. Pastor Baker called on his people to fast one day the following week for this need. The following Sunday, he called for every woman who wanted to have a child but couldn't to come forward. Five quickly came and stood in the altar. Sophia was among the group. He anointed each with oil and the church prayed for an answer to the desires of their hearts. Within one year, the church's nursery had five new babies. Richard admits that his greatest fear was that one or two would get pregnant and the others wouldn't. He expressed, "It was indeed an amazing thing to experience."

Jokingly, some of the men declared, "Pastor, you're not allowed to even shake my wife's hand!"

The church's Men and Women of Action (MWOA) team was now involved in planning and implementing an average of four major missions' endeavors annually. They raised needed funds, helped build a church on the Navajo reservation in Arizona, and provided funds to build a church in Esquipulas, Guatemala. On the trip to Guatemala, Baker had the privilege of having his dad's younger brother accompany him, his uncle Wayne, along with his sister's son, Tony Holmes.

The drive from the Guatemala City to Esquipulas, which was located on the Honduran border, was a five-to-six-hour trip. They had borrowed the bus that they had donated to Casa Shalom earlier, and when they had gotten approximately half, the engine began sputtering. If the bus hit any kind of incline, it would stall out and stop pulling. As they ascended another hill, the bus completely stalled out. After everyone had exited the bus, their faithful missionary, who had planned and arranged all the logistics for their trips in Guatemala and was accompanying them, called some local pastors to see if they knew of an available mechanic. He found a mechanic in the next town that could look at the bus, but they had to get it there. Unfortunately, they were sitting on an incline in a loaded school bus unable to move.

As the different missions' teams had become accustomed to doing, they prayed to God for His help. As they prayed, the Spirit of Lord moved among the 15 men on the trip and one of them asked, "Why don't we try pushing it to the top of the hill?"

There were a few chuckles, but with no obvious alternative, they decided to try his suggestion. One of the older members got behind the wheel and the rest began pushing. To the surprise of all, the bus started moving. The farther up the incline they went, the easier the bus rolled. After making it to the top of the hill, everyone loaded up and the entourage headed to the town. Baker couldn't help but think, "In Mexico, this bus became invisible. Now in Guatemala, an invisible hand seemed to push it, especially considering it a virtual impossibility for a small group of men to push a loaded bus up any hill." They made it to the repair shop where a mechanic fixed the problem. From there, they drove to Esquipulas without any further delay.

One evening, as the men dined at a restaurant, a homeless man with no hands came to the window and stared at them as they ate. Tony immediately got up from the table, grabbed some tortillas and meat off his plate, and walked outside to the man not thinking about him having no hands to accept the food. As he stood there wondering how to overcome this obvious barrier, the man lifted his arm and Tony thrust the food into his armpit.

Building church in Guatemala with nephew & uncle—Tony & Wayne.

Baker reflected, "Tony was affected by the poverty that surrounded him. I witnessed him walking into a store more than once and purchasing candy or chips, and as he exited the store, small children would come up to him, and he just gave them whatever he had."

Although some days in Esquipulas the temperature would hit 100 degrees, the team worked relentlessly, and at the end of the trip, the walls were up and the roof was on. The men returned to Casa Shalom and spent a few hours with the children before flying back to Georgia and to their normal routine.

The church was experiencing growth on all fronts, numerically, financially, and spiritually. The sanctuary was full most Sundays. Before Baker became pastor, the church only took up an offering for missions once a year. By 1997, they were giving over $100,000 annually to build churches, support missionaries, and continue their support for Casa Shalom.

In 1998 the church raised more than $140,000. Because of its growth, the church had run out of classrooms, which necessitated the building of a two-story addition onto the fellowship hall. Since the congregation consisted of a vast array of skilled craftsmen, the men built the addition with almost no labor cost. By the time the church had dedicated the new addition, the sanctuary filled most Sundays. Since the property was land-locked, the congregation began discussing the viability of relocating.

The North Georgia overseer, Delbert Rose, soon appointed Baker as the director of the North Georgia World Missions' Board. On previous trips to Guatemala, the national overseer, Roque Barrios, would show him a model of a Bible school he had a burden to build. But a project costing hundreds of thousands of dollars seemed unreachable for one church. Now that Baker was the state's missions' director, he had access to nearly 300 churches. Suddenly, the Bible school project in Guatemala seemed within reach.

Baker met with his board, which consisted of six other pastors, and shared Overseer Barrios' request. The men felt it would be good if the board could travel to Guatemala, see the project firsthand, and hear the heart of the national overseer. They made their plans accordingly.

In August of 1998, Baker and the missions' board arrived. Tyson was waiting to pick them up at the airport. For the next few days they were in Guatemala, he served as their host. Tyson informed them that the Guatemalan church had raised some funds, and that he had taken a group of men from the El Cedro church to begin laying the foundation. On their last day in Guatemala, Barrios and his lovely wife hosted the team for dinner at their home. Baker sat next to their youngest daughter, Keren, who was 10.

The mission board completely bought into the project and, with the blessings of Rose, started promoting the Bible school project statewide. Almost immediately, funds began flowing rapidly into the office, which was greatly encouraging considering that educational projects were usually the hardest ones to raise funds for.

A few days after returning home from Guatemala, Baker received a troubling call from Tyson. Tyson informed him that earlier that morning Barrios was taking his 13-year-old and 10-year-old daughters, Cesia and Keren, to school when a vehicle approached, shot out his tires, and kidnapped Keren. Baker's heart sank. He had gotten close to this family and only a few weeks earlier had sat next to Keren at the dinner table.

He immediately called the church to prayer. The Church of God World Missions Department set up prayer vigils. Within a short time, the overseer was contacted with a ransom demand of $330,000. Since he was the national overseer, his name was on the bank accounts for the national church, and the kidnappers had paid someone working at the bank for this information. Negotiations went on for a few days with Barrios telling them he could not come up with that much money, and even if he wanted to, the bank would not let him draw out the church's funds.

In response, the kidnappers demanded a small goodwill payment of $10,000 and assured Barrios that they would give him more time to come up with the rest. But even this was more than he could collect. Mission organizations, including the Church of God, have a policy of not paying ransoms, since it would only jeopardize other missionaries and workers by making them a target. Still, Baker's heart was so closely connected to this family, and the memory of sitting next to Keren just a few weeks earlier still so fresh in his mind, he knew he had to act. He sent the $10,000 to this bereaved father and mother.

The money was paid to the kidnappers, and the ransom was reduced to $250,000. There was still no way for this family to come up with such an amount. The threats were mounting as the days passed by, but so was the mighty hand of God at work. Through Israeli intervention, the phone calls were traced, and the house where Keren was being held was located. Guatemalan law enforcement raided the house, killed one of the kidnappers, and rescued Keren. Her captors had held her for 14 days and had kept her blindfolded the entire time. Guns and even a hand grenade were found behind one of the toilets. It was a jubilant time for the Barrios family.

Because this kidnapping was the work of the Guatemalan Mafia, Barrios was encouraged by Guatemalan authorities to seek asylum in the US, because of the threat of retribution. The US immediately granted asylum, and the Bakers offered to host them. When they arrived in the States, the family moved in with them for a few days. A house soon became available next to the church, and the church leased it for them. Offers of furniture and other items flooded in, more than the family could use.

A friend of Baker's who owned a car lot south of Atlanta had set it up so he could go to the car auction and purchase cars wholesale. He even provided checks on his dealership so Baker could pay for the car/cars until he could arrange financing. Consequently, he took Barrios to the Red Oak auction in Atlanta to help him find a vehicle. Their arrival a couple of hours before the auction opened gave them ample time to pick out two or three cars, just in case the bidding got too high on one or the other.

Baker told him once the bidding started not to raise his hands or make head motions. The car Barrios wanted was third or fourth in line. Baker was standing just in front of the auctioneer, and Barrios stood behind him. A late model BMW was being auctioned, and Baker noticed that the auctioneer kept looking his way and raising the bid each time he did. He turned around to witness Barrios caught in the excitement of being there and was moving around too much. The auctioneer thought he was bidding on the BMW. Baker quickly grabbed him, took him to the side, and breathed a sigh of relief when someone bid higher than his Guatemalan friend had unknowingly bid.

When the car he wanted finally came on the block, Baker offered a bid and won. They did the paperwork, paid for it, and returned to Cumming.

The Barrios were faithful to attend church and worshiped during the singing. When Baker began preaching, Roque Barrios' wife, Magdalena, would get on her knees and stay there the entire time praying for him. He received much encouragement from her unselfish praying.

As the Barrios family settled in and adjusted to life in America, Baker received a call from John Colbaugh, who pastored a church in Lawrenceville about 45 minutes from him. He had a congregation of a 1,000 or more and had started a Hispanic ministry. He explained to Baker that he wanted Barrios to come and minister to his Hispanic group. The rest is history as God's hand moved again to perfect His will in the lives of this precious family. The church hired Barrios, and he became the Hispanic pastor. After a couple of years, the congregation had grown to the point where the Hispanic church family needed its own facility. With the blessing of Colbaugh, the body of believers established its own church. Today, some 22 years later, the Barrios family is still in Lawrenceville, Georgia, pastoring a thriving congregation of more than 500.

The Sawnee Mountain church offered to sell the parsonage and give the Bakers a housing allowance so they could purchase their own home. They agreed and began a search to find just the right home. Richard and Cheryl informed their realtor, Diane Whitmire, who was a member of their church, what their maximum price was. After a couple of days of looking, they had not found a home that met all their needs.

Diane took them to Sawnee View Farms, a new subdivision under construction, which only had nine homes erected at the time. One of the homes was about 90 percent completed, but the price was a good bit over their budget. But Cheryl really loved it. Diana inquired about the house, and the next day the developer informed her that the person who had purchased the lot and was building the home had gone bankrupt. The bank had taken possession of it the day before.

In light of this unexpected development, Diana immediately contacted the Bakers and encouraged them to make an offer quickly. She told them the balance of the loan, and they made that exact offer. The offer was accepted. They purchased the home for $40,000 under what it would have sold for on the open market. They were only a few thousand dollars over their budget. The Baker boys were thrilled considering they now had access to a swimming pool, a clubhouse, and tennis and basketball courts.

In May, Baker received an invitation to the dedication of the El Limon church in Guatemala. Mark Medlin, a friend of his that pastored in the south part of Atlanta, wanted to accompany him. They arrived in Guatemala to find their faithful missionary, Frankie Tyson, waiting on them. He took them to his home, where they spent the night.

The dedication service was set for 11:00 the next morning. As Tyson and his guest drove up to the church, Richard could not refrain from shedding a few tears, as he saw all the people gathering. Frankie had shared with him that the church had increased from three to four times over the past 18 months.

Pastors Mark and Richard sat on the front row, while the El Limon pastor, Armando Yaz, and Missionary Tyson sat on the platform. Pastor

Yaz opened the service with a welcome and a few remarks. The sanctuary was brimming with excitement and overflowing with the joy of the Lord. As the congregation stood to sing, Baker looked around and reflected on the miracle that God had performed and again thought about how God had chosen to use a worm such as he was to answer the prayers of these precious saints.

In this environment rejoicing was easy. He sensed the powerful presence of the Lord beginning to settle on him. For a moment he seemed to lose consciousness. When he came to himself, he was lying in the floor unable to move. As he lay there, the Spirit of the Lord spoke to his spirit in a soft voice saying, "I am calling you to come here."

Shortly, Baker was able to stand to his feet. Immediately, Medlin walked over to him crying and declaring, "Richard, the Lord spoke to my heart. He just called you to Central America!"

As Baker tried to understand all that was taking place, Tyson came to the microphone and, speaking in English, announced, "I am about to interpret something the Lord just spoke to Pastor Armando." The pastor began to speak, and Tyson interpreted.

Although Baker didn't know it, the exact same time that the Lord's anointing fell on him and he found himself lying in the floor, Armando was having the same experience. Armando began to speak, "The power of God overwhelmed me causing me to fall to the floor. As I was lying there, I saw Pastor Baker ministering and working in Guatemala and throughout Central America. The Lord told me he was calling him here and wanted me to confirm it."

Tyson looked at Baker and exclaimed, "Rick, I had nothing to do with this!" In less than five minutes, the Lord had directly spoken His will to him and had confirmed it by two other pastors.

Following the dedication service, Baker and Medlin flew back to Atlanta. On the trip back, Mark kept asking, "What are you going to do? How will Cheryl react?"

For the moment, Richard was simply too overwhelmed to process it all. Furthermore, he and Cheryl had just purchased their dream home, and they were pastoring a growing church. It simply didn't make any sense to him. After arriving home, he kept waiting for just the right time to tell Cheryl, which didn't come until God spoke it to him in a more profound way.

25

Cry From Central America

In the summer of 1998, a 10-man team that included Till, Foster, and Baker, along with Baker's 13-year-old son, Christopher, traveled to the remote town of Kai La Lee, which was located in the northeastern part of Nicaragua close to the Honduran border. They had gone there to build a church. It was in this area that some of the hardest fighting took place between the Contras and the Sandinistas during the Nicaraguan revolution from 1981 until 1990. This region of Nicaragua suffered the highest loss of life during the war, with Kai La Lee experiencing the loss of more than 50 percent of its male population.

Under any circumstances, the seven-hour ride from Managua would be a difficult one, but for the team riding in the back of a pick-up truck, it was especially demanding. About two hours before they arrived in Kai La Lee, they noticed that Sandinistas flags appeared more frequently. Fear struck Baker's heart as he realized his team was entering an area not yet completely liberated from the Sandinistas' influence. Knowing the US backed the Contras, he wondered how well they would be received and questioned just how safe they would be. He now thought that if he had done his homework as he should have and understood where the team would be traveling, he most certainly would not have taken his 13-year-old son, Christopher, along.

After arriving in the village, Baker and his team checked into the only hotel, with rooms that measured six-and-a-half feet wide by nine feet long. Each room featured twin beds. A communal bathroom area containing four showers and several toilets, accommodating both men and women, made it necessary for the men to be sure no women were present before entering. In spite of the good intentions of the team, it quickly became clear that most of the townsfolk did not welcome the men. Even the pastor seemed to have some reservations with a group of men from the US working on his church.

Baker met with his team, shared his concerns, and encouraged them not to be walking around alone. They had prayer and devotions twice daily and asked God to give them such favor with the community that they would see the love of Jesus in them. Day by day they began seeing a little smile and, perhaps, even a wave. By the end of the seventh day, the community's response affirmed their acceptance of them.

The team managed to lay all the block walls and install the rafters for the roof. Christopher worked as hard as any man mixing concrete and cement on the ground with large hoes, while dealing with daytime temperature ranging from 90 to 100 degrees. The spirits of the pastor and his congregation soared as they beheld the church nearing completion.

A pang of sadness filled the hearts of the men on the last day of their expedition. They had met new brothers and sisters in the faith and had made new friends within the village. No doubt many people here had animosity towards the US because of the war. Baker spoke to a young lady in her 20s who had lost her father and two or three brothers. Clearly, the pain of her loss was still fresh in her heart.

The overseer for the Churches of God in Nicaragua later related that the pastor said that the team from Georgia was the first from the US to come since the war had ended. He further stated that he felt God had used the men to bring healing to some of those that had lost family members in the hostilities. Even some of the villagers were saying the North Americans seemed like good men and came to be a blessing to their village.

Baker later remarked, "I truly believe the most important reason the Lord orchestrated this trip was to help start the healing process in the lives of these poor villagers who had suffered so much over the last nearly 20 years. And once again, 'such a worm as I' was humbled."

In October of 1998, a massive hurricane, Hurricane Mitch, struck Central America with fury. Reportedly, it was the strongest hurricane to ever hit the Western Hemisphere, with sustained winds of 180 miles per hour and gusts over 200 miles per hour. The death toll estimate soared above 20,000, with hundreds of thousands of homes destroyed.

As chairman of the North Georgia World Missions Board, Baker received a summons to a meeting in Cleveland, Tennessee, to discuss relief efforts. At the end of the meeting, Rice approached him and asked,

"Richard, with your travel experience and love for Central America, would you consider traveling there to make a firsthand appraisal of just how serious the situation is?"

The timing was not good for Baker, considering plans for his church. The congregation had outgrown its facilities and had purchased a prime tract of land on Highway 20, just a couple of miles out of town. They had hired an architect, had decided on a design for the planned new building, and had put the present church up for sale. Within four days, the facility sold for the asking price, with the stipulation that the congregation vacate it within 30 days.

Having recently relocated, the First United Methodist church had sold their old facility to the City of Cumming for future development. The city allowed the Sawnee Mountain church to use it on Sundays and Wednesdays, but they had to set up and break down every week.

Baker shared with Rice the dilemma and asked him to write a letter to his church explaining the World Missions' need. He assured Rice that if the church agreed, he would go. The church overwhelmingly supported the pastor's decision.

The Lord pinged Baker's heart again, and he called a church conference to recommend that the congregation tithe 10 percent of the proceeds from their building funds to help feed their starving church family in Central America. He reminded them that God had given them their asking price for their property, which no one in the church expected. The church voted in favor of the measure and sent $50,000 to the superintendent's office in Central America, located in San Pedro Sula, Honduras. Ken Anderson served as superintendent.

Baker arrived in Guatemala first and spent two days touring the Atlantic coastal areas, where most of the damaged occurred. The devastation was unbelievable and heart wrenching. He met many pastors who had lost their churches, homes, and, in some cases, family members. Baker could tell many stories from his trip but one clearly etched itself into his mind. He writes,

> I asked a pastor to share his story with me, and he started talking about the heavy rains that began falling, with very strong winds. As the water began to rise, he decided to take his family to the church, which had a higher roof than his house. With the water continuing to rise, he placed his wife and four children on the roof of the church, but the water kept

> rising. There was a large tree next to the church with limbs hanging over the roof. He started placing his children on the limbs and picked up his four-year old daughter. He sat her on top of a highly venomous fer-de-lance pit viper, one of the deadliest snakes in Central America. She was instantly bitten and died shortly thereafter, convulsing in her father's arms.
>
> By this time, I was crying and sobbing uncontrollably, just as he was. We were hugging each other, and I asked him, "Brother, I can't bring your daughter back, but what can I do for you?" His reply was a life lesson which I have never forgotten.
>
> The pastor replied, "First, I need my church rebuilt so I can preach and pastor my people. Second, I need a home for my family to live in as ours was washed away. Third, my three remaining children need school clothes and $100 per child for the yearly school fees."
>
> I saw to it he got everything he asked for. Twenty-two years ago a humble Guatemalan pastor taught me a lesson they don't and can't teach you in seminary, and that is, the calling of God must be the number one thing we pursue and covet above all else, for it is the fountainhead where true joy and happiness is birthed and flows freely. This poor pastor didn't have anything left in this world, no church, no home, no means to care for his family, but the first thing he wanted was his church built back. He did have one thing that Hurricane Mitch couldn't take from him and that was his relationship with the King of kings and the Lord of lords. And through his prayers, God heard and answered all his request using "such a worm as I."

Baker continued to Honduras where Anderson met him at the airport. They spent that afternoon making plans for the next day. Anderson had received the $50,000 and had negotiated to purchase large quantities of food. He had also secured a large truck for deliveries, which was able to haul 6,000 pounds at a time. Because of the logistical demands, Anderson had broken down the affected areas into districts and had appointed pastors to give oversight in their respective areas. For several days, truckload after truckload delivered food to hungry people.

Baker and Anderson had to cross several rivers to reach some of the places that needed supplies. On one of the days that Ken couldn't accompany him, the national overseer of Honduras traveled with him.

They reached a shallow river where the bridge had been washed away. After watching pickup trucks crossing at an angle and seeing the water was only about tire deep, the overseer, who couldn't speak English, got off the truck and talked with a man who pointed them in the right direction. Since Richard's Spanish was not very good, Overseer Lopez walked to the truck window and motioned to him the angle he should use to cross.

Richard took off but about halfway across felt the truck slowing as the water got deeper. By the grace of God, he reached the other side only to realize, when he turned to speak to Lopez, that the seat was empty. He had left him on the other side. As he looked back, he could see his hands lifted with palms up. Within a few minutes, a four-wheel-drive truck came up and took him across. Although they could not easily communicate because of the language barrier, they could laugh in the same language, and they did.

The following day, Baker and Anderson crossed a river by driving over the railroad bridge while straddling the tracks, because the bridge for vehicles had been swept away. Anderson walked a couple of hundred feet in front of the truck to make sure their crossing was safe.

As they backed up to one church and started unloading supplies, Baker saw a little three or four-year-old girl being held by her father. He was standing at the back of the truck, and she was holding a small empty metal cup up toward him. They shared with him that they hadn't had any food in four days. As he looked at this precious child, he thought, "Honey, you will eat today for God has sent His "worm."

After a week in Honduras, Anderson invited Baker to attend church with him on Sunday morning. New Life Church was large with over 1,000 people in attendance. The Spirit of Lord also filled the place, which Baker knew he desperately needed. He spent the rest of the day with Ken and Karen at their home resting. The next day, Anderson took him to the airport for his flight to Nicaragua. About five minutes from the airport, Anderson asked, "Richard, is God dealing with you about coming as a missionary to help me in serving these seven countries in Central America?"

With little hesitation, Baker answered, "No, I don't feel any leading from the Lord to move here, but I will be praying for you and will try to send some teams to help."

They said their goodbyes and Baker flew from San Pedro Sula to Tegucigalpa, the capital of Honduras, to catch his flight to Managua, Nicaragua. As he waited at the gate, he heard an announcement made only in Spanish, upon which most of the people at his gate left. He went to the desk, but no one could speak English. At the time, he spoke virtually no Spanish. He went to another counter, but no one there could speak English either.

Baker began to get a little nervous when a man walked up to him and announced, "Hi, I am John Taylor. Can I help you with anything?"

An anxious Baker shared his dilemma with man, and he asked to see his boarding pass. They went to the counter where he was told that his flight had been delayed for three hours. Taylor invited Baker to have lunch with him and as they were eating, he said, "I saw you yesterday morning at church. I was sitting in the back, and you came walking down the aisle. I thought to myself, 'Who is that man?' The Lord said, 'That is a man who will go anywhere I ask or send him to go.'"

Immediately the question that Anderson had asked him earlier dropped into his spirit. The two men conversed for a couple of hours, after which Taylor boarded his flight for the US and Baker for his flight to Nicaragua.

Bienvenido Lopez, national overseer for Nicaragua, was waiting for him upon his arrival. Going directly to the national offices, they discussed plans for the few days Baker would be in the country. Of all the areas affected by the hurricane, the loss of life was greatest in Nicaragua. As they traveled to the most affected parts of the nation, they witnessed just how much damage torrential rains and winds can cause. A mountain several thousand feet high split into two parts and covered a church with more than 100 people inside. Baker stood near where the church previously had sat but, according to estimates, now rested 70 feet or more below. He saw where raging waters had swept away everything in its path, cutting a swath in the ground 15 to 20 feet deep by 50 feet wide and 20 miles long.

Lopez and Baker distributed food to many pastors and churches. By the end of his visit, he ascertained that in the three main countries that were hit the hardest more than 350 Churches of God had been destroyed, along with thousands of homes. Of course, the greatest tragedy was the enormous loss of life.

Baker flew back to Atlanta emotionally and physically drained. He struggled to find words to adequately describe what he had witnessed over these past two plus weeks. He painstakingly prepared a report to share with the leadership of the World Missions Department.

On November 25, his maternal grandmother, Mae Paulk, passed away at the age of 90. She was a woman full of the Holy Spirit and the glory of the Lord. He had the privilege and honor of preaching her home-going service on Saturday, November 28, in Ocilla, Georgia. Having planned a trip to Cuba with missionary, Tyson, they had to leave immediately after the service and drive to Atlanta to catch their flight. Since there were no direct flights from the US to Cuba, they had to fly to Jamaica and purchase tickets for Cuba.

After going through customs, one of the church leaders met Baker and Tyson and took them into his home. Although they had booked the hotel reservations that were required before a flight could be booked, the church leader offered to host them in his home, which they preferred.

The following morning, officials were knocking on the door of his house inquiring why the two men did not check into the hotel. They now had their first taste of what communism was like. After the conversation, the officials agreed to let the men stay but made it clear that they had to report their movements. They appeared to be under surveillance the entire time. Still, the men had the wonderful privilege of getting to preach in four different churches and meeting some of the most wonderful people in the world.

Knowing the extreme poverty of most Cubans, they offered to go to a grocery store to purchase food. However, almost all food was rationed in Cuba, and every couple of days, a government worker would deliver small amounts of milk and bread that could only be consumed by children under five or seniors over 65. Baker went with the pastor to a vegetable garden that had an eight-foot-high fence around it, with razor wire around the top to protect the green beans that grew there. The worker approached the pastor asking for his document, which let the worker know how many lived in his household. He then picked the beans and handed them to the pastor through the fence. When the pastor asked for a little extra because of his guests, the worker handed him eight or 10 more snap beans.

Baker and the pastor went to one of the few grocery stores in Havana, located next to the Russian embassy. As they entered, he immediately noticed that the shelves were 70 percent empty. The products they did have were ridiculously priced at two to three times the price a person would pay in the US. Nonetheless, they made their purchases and returned to the pastor's house. They had been unable to find meat except for a three-pound roast, which cost over $50.

In Cuba, the law prohibits the killing of a cow, a violation which carries a five-year prison sentence. The killing of a hog carried a lesser sentence of six months. Baker, wanting to bless the pastor and his family, asked him if there was a place he could purchase meat. He mentioned that for $60 they could buy a hog on the black market, and one of his members butcher it for the price of one of the shoulders. Without hesitation, Baker gave the $60, and the next evening for dinner, he, along with the pastor and his family feasted on fresh pork roast.

Although medical care is free in Cuba, there is almost no medicine available for purchase in the pharmacies. For example, one afternoon as Baker and Tyson toured about in a 1955 Plymouth taxi, one of the pastor's members saw them and frantically waved them down. The woman explained that her daughter had a serious eye infection and medicine was unavailable. Furthermore, the doctor had informed her that the infection would eventually cause blindness if left untreated. However, Baker discovered that the black market not only sold hogs but medicine as well. Within an hour the antibiotic was located and for $10 he was able to purchase it. The girl's eyes had begun to improve before he and Tyson left the country.

The hopelessness of the Cuban people, produced by communism, permeated the country. A common worker earned only about $5.00 a month. Baker spoke with a doctor who earned only $25 monthly.

Under certain circumstances, churches could purchase land and even a building from the government, seeing that the government owned everything. One growing congregation that Baker and Tyson ministered to needed a larger facility. Since the government was willing to sell an unused building for $10,000–although some repairs were needed–Baker committed to send the funds once the church leadership in Cuba could substantiate that the government would indeed follow through. Within a week, he received official confirmation for the transaction. He had to send the funds to Mexico and pay the expenses for one of the Mexican church leaders to fly the money to Cuba.

The five days Baker spent in Cuba had a profound effect on him and still moves him today. He continues to sense the intensity of their worship. Church services would last hours as the people cried out to God and worshiped Him with all their hearts. Attending church, which brought uplifting Christian fellowship and the Lord's presence, was one of the few sources of relief the people had from the hardships they endured daily. Witnessing the peace and joy that most had by knowing their hope was in the Lord was nothing short of inspirational.

In February of 1999, Rice invited Richard and Cheryl to attend a mission conference in Toledo, Ohio, and wanted him to speak in one of the services. Two other pastors were also invited to speak, Darrell Rice, a pastor in the Atlanta area, and Alex Tanasuputra, a pastor of a church in Indonesia with more than 100,000 members. They were assigned three subjects: Doing Missions in a Small Church under 500; Doing Missions in a Medium/Large Church above 500; and Doing Missions in a Mega Church.

Troubling to Baker was his feeling of inadequacy to be ministering in such a venue. But God touched him as soon as he stood behind the podium to speak. He sensed the sweet presence of the Lord and quickly felt at ease as he shared what the God had placed on his heart. A few years later, he would come to understand that the many contacts he made at this conference were all part of God's plans for his future.

Since the dedication of the El Limon church in Guatemala, and since Anderson asked him if God was dealing with him about coming to Central America to help with humanitarian projects, Baker struggled within his spirit. There were too many confirmations that God was calling the Bakers to the mission field for him to ignore it. Still, it made no sense to him. He was pastoring a growing church. The congregation had sold the old facility and had purchased a track of land. In addition, they had hired an architect, cleared the property, and were ready to start building as soon as they acquired all necessary permits. They were presently meeting in a temporary facility.

Baker thought, "Surely, God doesn't mean for me to resign immediately and move my family to Central America!"

Finally, he sat down with Cheryl and shared everything with her. He declared, "Cheryl, it doesn't make any sense, but the Lord has given too many confirmations for it not to be His will." She was stunned to think that the dream home and the church she and the boys loved so much could quickly become only a memory. He then added, "I will not do anything until the Lord puts the same calling and drawing in your heart that He's put in mine."

In about two weeks, Cheryl said to Richard, "I guess I at least need to visit first."

He immediately called Anderson and asked what time would be good for them to fly down for a visit. In response to Anderson's suggestion, he and Cheryl flew to San Pedro Sula, Honduras, and spent the next five days with him.

Anderson had a six-passenger Cessna airplane, and on Thursday, the three of them flew to the bay islands, about 40 miles off the coast of Honduras. At the time, the Church of God had about 17 churches located throughout the four islands. Approximately one-half of the churches were English speaking and the other half Spanish. The annual convention for the English-speaking churches had convened, and Anderson, being the superintendent, needed to attend at least a service or two.

As the Bakers, along with Anderson, sat in the front row in one of the services enjoying the music and worship, Richard kept noticing the guest speaker repeatedly casting glances toward him. When time came for him to preach, the minister walked behind the pulpit, made a few comments, and then pointed at Richard and declared, "I don't know you and don't even know if you are a minister, but the Lord told me He sent you here with a message from Him." With that he called him up to preach.

That directive caught Richard completely off guard. Furthermore, he had left his Bible in his hotel room. Today, he admits that, although he doesn't remember what he preached, he does remember being under a very heavy anointing. After the service ended, he and Cheryl received several more confirmations. Still, Cheryl wasn't making any comments as to how she was feeling.

On Saturday morning, they flew back to San Pedro Sula and later that day boarded a plane for Atlanta. As they waited for the takeoff, Richard noticed that Cheryl was looking out the window and crying. He thought she was probably missing two-year-old Joshua since she had never been away from him. Sympathetically, he said, "Cheryl, we will be home in less than four hours. The boys will be waiting on us."

She answered, "I do miss the boys, but that's not why I'm crying. I feel like I am leaving my home."

Her response astonished Richard. Left speechless, all he could think was, "Wow! A hundred times over, wow!" Except for the trip to Jamaica in 1986, this was the first mission trip he could get her to go on with him. Surely, God was at work.

26

Answering the Call

After returning home, the Bakers convened a meeting with their boys and shared the entire experience with them. Christopher, who was 14, melted into his mother's arms crying, as he had aspirations of playing football in the NFL. Sixteen-year-old Ryan seemed to think it would be an adventure, and eighteen-year-old Ricky looked totally bewildered, initially thinking his parents were joking. They assured him they were not and insisted that they keep silent, since it would be several months before they could tell the church.

Baker made an appointment with Overseer Rose and shared the entire story with him. Rose responded, "Pastor, your passion tells me this is indeed the hand of the Lord at work, but maybe you have the timing off. I feel you need to stay and complete the building project, and if you agree, the state office will underwrite your entire mission budget for the first year." Considering that Rose's offer would translate to more than $60,000, Baker agreed to do his best to remain as pastor until the church was completed.

Baker had taken a J-term class (concentrated classes offered in January, June, and July) at the Pentecostal theological seminary in Cleveland, Tennessee, back in January and had signed up for another one for June. He was finding it extremely difficult to concentrate on anything but Central America. The call he felt was strong and undeniable. After completing the class, he made another appointment with Rose to let him know that he and Cheryl had to move forward with what they knew was God's call upon our lives. His plan was to resign the last of August, which would give Rose a couple of months to find a pastor to replace him. To Baker's surprise, Rose was very supportive, no doubt because he also saw the hand of God in the process.

Anderson had already made a request for Baker to be approved as a missionary to Central America, so he set up a meeting with Grant McClung, personnel manager for Church of God World Missions. During the interview, the subject of formal education came up, and Grant shared with Baker that a missionary really needed a master's degree to fulfill the position he would be holding.

After talking for a few minutes, McClung added, "Brother Baker, even if I approved your request, the field director for Latin America, Dr. Costello, would not, since he feels all missionaries should have at least a master's degree."

Richard asked, "Do you know if he (Costello) is in his office today?"

McClung answered, "I am not sure he is even in the country." He then asked his secretary to call and check.

About that time Costello came walking down the hallway and saw Baker sitting in McClung's office. He walked in, laid his hand on Baker's heart, and exclaimed, "Grant, send this man to Central America; he has a heart for the people!" With that, Costello turned and walked out.

Baker piped up, "I think you have your answer!"

McClung, a bit surprised, handed an application to Baker. During the entire interview, he was very respectful and kind. He was simply following the protocol.

A mid-August interview with the World Missions Personnel Committee was scheduled for Baker and his family. The Bakers' oldest son, Ricky, was out of high school and attending Lanier Technical College and working for a maintenance company that maintained federal parks. Richard had helped him get a new Nissan Frontier 4-wheel drive pickup truck and now assumed that he would not want to go to Central America, seeing he was 19 years old, had a great job, a new pickup, and was living with a family he was very close to. His father assumed wrong. Six months later he would join his family on the field.

For the moment, however, it became apparent that at least one committee member was not convinced that deploying the Bakers to Central America was a good idea. They even asked the boys a few questions. The last question asked of Richard was, "Brother Baker, you have two teenage boys. If you stay a few years, they may take a liking to one of the beautiful girls in Latin America. How would you feel about your sons marrying a girl from Central America?"

Without a second thought, Richard responded, "We will have some beautiful grandchildren!" Nonetheless, he felt that the question was out of bounds and sensed that most members on the committee felt the same way. He later had to apologize to him privately.

Following the interview, Costello invited the Bakers to lunch. As they were being seated, Ryan sat next to Costello. Ryan's parents understood that they could never know for sure just what he might say or do. Costello asked, "Ryan, are we going to be friends?"

Ryan quickly shot back, "That all depends on how you treat us!"

Costello replied, "I like this boy; I like him a lot."

The Bakers were scheduled to have a psychology evaluation done while they were in Cleveland, Tennessee. The counselor's first act was to hand them a 500-question questionnaire. Questions included, "Have you ever stolen anything? Have you ever intentionally harmed another person? Have you intentionally broken any laws other than minor traffic citations?" Considering Baker's background, the outcome wasn't looking good for him. When he finished the test, he asked John Vining, the counselor, "Shouldn't the question read, 'since becoming a Christian have you ever...?'" However, the questions stood as presented.

When the results were compiled, Vining went over the findings with Richard and Cheryl over the phone. He started with Cheryl and had nothing but kind remarks to make about her and felt she would have no problems adjusting to life on the mission field. On the other hand, when it came Richard's turn, Vining explained that the test revealed that he had violent tendencies and would not handle well a situation where he was provoked. He shared a few more negative characteristics about what the test revealed about Richard's character.

Feeling unfairly quizzed, Richard responded, "Dr. Vining, the evaluation is not fair for a person like me who lived in open sin and committed crimes before coming to Christ."

Although Vining agreed, he still encouraged him to watch his temper and possibly attend anger management classes before being deployed. Richard noticed that Cheryl loved every minute of it, grinning from ear-to-ear.

The Bakers now faced the hardest part, that of going back and resigning from the church they had grown to love and appreciate. The last Sunday in August 1999, Baker resigned effective the last Sunday in September. As expected, the announcement was a major shock to the congregation. In the five-and-a-half years he had pastored them, he had made 20 trips to Central America. Now they would be moving there to live.

As the Bakers last Sunday approached, they all felt heavy-hearted. Even though they knew they were in the Lord's will, they still felt torn in leaving. Baker did feel good about leaving the church debt free and with $450,000 in the bank, especially considering that the bank returned his first paycheck for lack of funds. He also rejoiced that they had obtained a deed to a beautiful tract of land under development, on which to build the church.

The church voted in Charles Green to succeed Baker as pastor. He contacted Richard to see if he and Cheryl would be willing to lease their home to him. They agreed and in a couple years, he purchased it from them. By the end of his first year, the new church facility was completed, and Green invited the Bakers to be a part of the dedication service, which meant so much to them.

The Baker family moved into a cabin located in the North Georgia Mountains close to Blairsville. They began to raise funds for their missions' budget. Richard had every Sunday booked until the end of December. The World Missions Department required them have six months of funds on hand in their account in addition to raising the funds to move to San Pedro Sula, Honduras. The total money they needed to raise was $60,000 in cash and another $40,000 in pledges.

After setting a goal of January 1, 2000, as their moving date, Baker began working to make it happen. Within eight weeks they had raised more than they initially needed. He also roofed several homes and even a church to sustain them so they wouldn't have to take anything from their missions' budget to live on. Ryan was helping roof the church, which was located in a remote area in the mountains of North Georgia.

On a day when Ryan was unable to go with his dad, Richard went by himself. As he was nailing shingles on with his pneumatic air gun using one-and-a-half inch nails, he saw the evening light beginning to fade and got into too much of a hurry. Wanting to finish one section before darkness completely fell, he began nailing too fast and shot the nail through his left big toe into the roof. At first there was no pain, but he knew the shock would quickly wear off and the pain would come. Without hesitation, he took his hammer and pulled the nail out of the roof and out of his toe. Falling on his back, he cried out in excruciating pain. Once he regained some semblance of composure, he drove the one-hour trip back to the cabin where he and his family were staying. At times, the pain seemed unbearable, but God was with him. Fortunately, no serious damage had been done.

One of Cheryl's cousins, Jeff O'Neal, who owned a wholesale jewelry store in Atlanta, gave them $10,000. When he shared with one of his diamond suppliers, a Muslim man from Israel, the man wrote the Bakers a $5,000 check. A few weeks before he had resigned from the church, he had led a couple to the Lord. They owned Ticketmaster and lived in a high-end subdivision on Lake Lanier, just a few miles from the church. Because the church was in a temporary facility, they offered to host the going-away reception for them at their clubhouse. As they were leaving the reception, the man placed a $20,000 check in Baker's shirt pocket. Many people from the church donated to them. But with all the much-appreciated large donations, some of the most touching gifts came from the ones who were limited financially. Most memorable was a couple in their 80s living mainly on Social Security who gave them $100. Such sacrifice meant more to them than they could express.

Baker family (September1999).

Frankie and Joyce Tyson, along with their four children, returned to the States from Guatemala shortly before the Bakers' departure. The timing was such that the Tysons were able to buy much of the Bakers' furniture, along with a car. It was a win for both families.

Richard shipped down a Ford Bronco and Toyota van, along with a shipping container. On January 1, 2000, he and Christopher flew to Honduras to prepare for the arrival of Cheryl, Ryan, and Joshua. Ken Anderson had already secured a rental house, and their vehicles and container were at the port awaiting clearance.

The clearing process took a few days longer than expected, so the Bakers' belongings had not been released by the time Cheryl, Ryan, and Joshua arrived. Consequently, the family had to sleep on air mattresses and sit on folding chairs for about a week. But they soon felt an infusion of excitement and anticipation, as they began to unload the container at their new home in the suburbs of San Pedro Sula Honduras. A new life in Central America had now begun for the Baker family.

Richard and his three sons, Ryan, Chris, and
Ricky climbed to the top of Pacaya, an active volcano in Guatemala. They are standing only five feet from the rim of the crater.

27

A New Residence

After settling into life in a new country, Richard and Cheryl enrolled their two youngest sons, Ryan and Christopher, in a private Christian school that supposedly was bilingual. However, after a week, they realized that only one of the six teachers could speak any English. It became evident that the boys could not stay in the school and learn at an acceptable pace. So, the parents withdrew them and began homeschooling them through Abeka, after ordering the prescribed videos, books, and materials. They also enrolled them in Spanish classes, with one teacher teaching the four of them.

Because San Pedro Sula is not a safe place to live, the Bakers purchased a trained 100-pound Rottweiler. The dog was trained to only obey one person's command. One day, as the family was in the yard, three-year-old Joshua was doing something that prompted Richard to insist that he stop. After he continued to ignore his father, Richard lightly swatted him on the backside. Goliath–as the Bakers named him–walked over, got in-between him and Joshua, and looked up at Richard, bumped him, and growled. Richard admitted, "I knew then who the boss was, and it wasn't me. I immediately told Cheryl to never discipline Joshua in the yard."

While waiting for their first Men and Women of Action team in February to rebuild one of the destroyed churches from Hurricane Mitch, Anderson came up with a great idea. He purchased two heavy-duty flatbed trucks and a portable block-making machine. About one month before the team planned arrival from the states, a team of Hondurans would haul the sand, gravel, and cement to the job site, manufacture the blocks, and install the footers. Baker would bring a team in behind them, erect the walls, and install the roof system. Next, the local congregation would be responsible for finishing the inside.

The team drove about two hours from San Pedro Sula and spent five days building the church. They returned to the Baker home where the 10-member team had been invited to spend the night. The next day Baker drove them to the airport for their return trip to the states.

Around 5:00 the following morning, the sound of gunfire awakened Richard and Cheryl. Until this moment they felt reasonably safe, considering they lived in a two-story house protected by a 12-foot concrete wall with razor wire on top that surrounded the house. But now police officers were having a shootout with a gang.

A man had climbed the wall and was crawling over the razor wire when he looked down and saw Goliath waiting for him. Quickly deciding not to drop into the Bakers' yard, he chose rather to drop back down onto the street side. Although he escaped Goliath, he could not escape the wrath of the policemen. Richard and Cheryl watched as the officers shot him to death. Two of the men picked him up, unceremoniously threw him in the back of a truck, and sped off.

In the meantime, a sharpshooter was on a neighbor's roof to Baker's right shooting across the street, where more gang members lurked. In a couple of hours, the kerfuffle settled down. Baker walked outside, opened the gate, and asked a police officer if he could leave. After getting his permission, he drove to Burger King and bought breakfast for his family and guests.

When he returned, the police were gone, and the intruder's blood was visible in the edge of the front yard. Richard immediately thought, "Cheryl is going to pitch one more fit to go home!"

The Bakers had housed and fed the team and, even though the members were somewhat shaken over the early morning intrusion and tragedy, they all had a story to tell when they returned home. He got them to the airport and returned home. When he saw Goliath lying in the front yard, he walked over and patted him knowing that the $300 he had spent to purchase him was spent wisely.

Before the Bakers departed for Honduras, they received a donation toward building a church destroyed during Hurricane Mitch. The donor had previously asked Baker to find a church that really needed help. In response, he had gone over his list of churches that still needed assistance and quietly meditated over the list and asked the Lord to lead him to the right church. As he did, he felt impressed to call Tim Norman. Norman lived on the island of Roatan and served as the overseer for the bay islands and the jungle area of Honduras/Nicaragua, a region called La Mosquitia. The area, inhabited by an indigenous group called Miskito, was only accessible by plane or boat. The Rio Coco River served as the boundary line between Honduras and Nicaragua, and the Miskitos, who numbered close to 400,000, lived in both countries, with the majority living in Nicaragua.

When Baker called the overseer's office, Norman answered the phone. They had met only once when Anderson flew him and Cheryl over to Roatan during their initial visit. Baker asked him if he had a church in his territory that desperately needed funds to rebuild. He answered, "I do."

Baker replied, "I will release these funds into your World Missions account tomorrow."

Norman became very quiet. In a few seconds he asked, "Are you 100 percent for real, and can I be assured you will be sending the funds?"

"Tim, I am a man of my word, and we have the funds in hand," Baker answered.

The overseer then related to him the rest of the story. "The pastor of the San Isabella church located on the Nicaraguan side of the Rio Coco River came and met with me about three months ago. His village of about 500 people was destroyed. It took him three days to get to the territorial office, as he took boats, walked, and finally took a ferry to Roatan. I told him that the office was unable to financially assist him in rebuilding his church and to go back and do everything he could do on his own. I assured him that I would agree with him in prayer. He then departed for the long journey back home."

Norman continued, "The pastor came back and said to me, 'Brother Norman, we did all we could do. We cleared the area and dug the foundation for our new church with our hands and this is all we can do.' Brother Richard, he is sitting in front of me telling me this when you called. That's why I questioned if you were for sure going to send the funds. May I tell him the good news?"

Baker answered, "Please do!" As he relayed the message in the native language of the Miskitos—most don't speak Spanish, especially the ones living in the more remote areas—Baker could hear loud crying and rejoicing coming over the phone. Later reflecting, he said, "It never gets old witnessing God perform miracles, and it certainly never gets old when He kept using 'such a worm such as I.'"

The more Baker thought about it, the more he wanted to go and build the church. He mentioned it to a few of the men at Sawnee Mountain, where he had recently resigned. They agreed to be part of the project and planned a trip for March 2000. This time Baker was able to take two of his sons, Ryan and Chris, with him. His two dependable colleagues Foster and Till wanted to join the team, along with a retired pastor, E.L. Addis, who was a professional block mason. Another Georgia pastor, DeWayne Shaddix, signed up for the project, and a few other men, as well.

Homer Foster & Richard Baker.

The team flew into San Pedro Sula and from there took a flight to La Ceiba. Another flight followed–this one to Lempira, a small port that served the Mosquitia region. From there they had a seven-hour drive through part of the interior of the Mosquitia, on the Honduras side, to get to the Rio Coco River. The road was dirt all the way, and at times, it was just a path. The men set up camp on the Honduras side and took dugout canoes to go a couple of miles downriver to the village of San Isabella. All the building materials had to be brought on these large canoes, which had been built out of large trees.

After arriving the following day, the team immediately went to work. Baker had also secured funds to build the pastor and his family a small house. Most of the team went to work on the church, while he and Shaddix started building the house. Ryan and Chris bounced back and forth to whoever needed them. Baker was extremely proud of both his boys working as hard as they did with temperatures remaining in the 90s the entire week. The pastor and his congregation were so appreciative and were, themselves, helping in any way they could.

Baker asked about alligators and was told there were not too many in that region. As they were making the trip back upriver, one of his sons excitedly asked, "What's that in the water?" Of course, it was a gator. The sides of the canoes were only four-to-six inches above the water, so there would have been no problem for these reptiles to swim aboard.

That night they slept on air mattresses or sleeping bags in a small church on the Honduras side. The ladies of the church cooked their meals over an open fire in black kettle pots. There was no electricity or running water. However, there was a stream cascading down the mountainside, and the team put together a makeshift shower with some old tubing they found.

Ricky working with Richard, his dad, on Hogar Agape.

By the end of the week, the church, and pastor's home, had been built. The pastor, along with members of his church, had hand-dug a foundation bigger than the original church. That was most certainly remarkable faith on their part. They dedicated the church first and then his home. It was a very humble and small three-room wood structure, with a tin roof and dirt floors. When the pastor walked through the front opening, he fell on his face crying and thanking God for this wonderful blessing. The interpreter shared with Baker that he was praying, "In all my life, I never dreamed I would have a home this nice!"

Baker would later write, "I truly believe experiencing God's love and grace at this level was one of the most humbling things I have ever experienced, one that 20 years later is still very fresh in my thoughts and heart. Once again God used "such a worm as I."

Homeschooling was not going so well. The videos and material they received were outdated by 20 years. Cheryl shared with Richard how hard it was trying to deal with all the changes. She suggested they make plans to return to the States. She expressed, "I am so concerned for Ryan and Chris that they will not get the education they need, as we are just not qualified to homeschool them."

Building Hogar Agape orphanage in Nicaragua September (2000).

Richard reassured her that one thing he did know was that God had sent them to Central America. The five months they lived in Honduras would go down as the toughest time of their ministry. They loved Honduras and the people, but looking back on the experience, Richard explained, "I see so clearly how the enemy of our soul was working so intently against us trying to cause friction between Cheryl and me, and bringing some of the heaviest discouragement that either one of us had experienced. But deep down I knew the attack was coming from Satan, because he was afraid of the purpose for which the Lord sent us there."

Another team flew in from the US to host a medical clinic. Steve Brown, pastor in the Atlanta area, was the group leader. Richard met them at the airport, but the overseer of Honduras had arranged to host them, since he spoke English and was also a medical doctor.

On their last day in Honduras, they came by the Bakers' house. Richard had warned them not to pet or get to close to their dog, Goliath, since he would bite anyone who tried, except family members. Ryan was holding him by the collar as the team walked into the house. One lady in the group remarked, "All dogs like me; he won't bite me."

Before anyone could react, she walked over to Goliath and started patting him on the head. As she turned to walk into the house, he lunged at her, pulling Ryan with him, and bit her deeply in the buttocks taking a large chunk of flesh from her. The Bakers back bedroom became a trauma center. She was fortunate to be traveling with a medical team with a doctor and nurses. Richard said, "They had to stitch her up, and I'm sure that when she returned to the States, more treatment was necessary."

Soon, another man was shot and killed close to the Bakers' residence, this time about 100 feet from their entranceway. They had heard that Guatemala had a school mainly for missionary children, one started by a missionary. Baker had discussed their situation with Anderson and suggested to him that he felt their only option was to move to Guatemala. Anderson was very supportive of the idea and offered to help in any way he could.

Richard and Cheryl talked about the possibilities and knew it was either give Guatemala a try or return to the States. Richard contacted the national overseer for the Churches of God in Guatemala, David Munguia who, along with his wife, Maribel, spoke fluent English. He had received his doctorate degree from Asbury Seminary and upon graduation, he and his wife had come by the Baker home in Cumming, Georgia, a suburb of Atlanta, and stayed a couple of days. He also was the president of the Bible school Baker and his church had raised funds to build a few years earlier.

The Munguias now invited Richard and Cheryl to come for a visit. Upon their arrival at the airport, the couple was eagerly waiting for them. They hosted them for a couple of days and even helped them to find a house to rent, after which the Bakers returned to Honduras and began making plans to move to Guatemala. Moving from state to state is one-thing, moving from country to country is quite another.

Richard and Cheryl found a moving company that had the licenses to operate in both countries. On the appointed day, a 28-foot moving van pulled up and loaded all their furniture and personal items. Anderson, along with his wife, Karen, graciously offered to make the trip with them. They had to sell their Toyota minivan, since they needed the funds to move with.

While Baker drove his Ford Bronco, Anderson was in his vehicle following the moving van. They drove several hours to reach the border with Guatemala. After presenting their paperwork, passports, and letters from denominational leaders in Honduras and Guatemala, and after explaining who they were and what their purpose was, authorities on the Honduras side wanted to unload the truck. If Anderson had not been there, Baker said that they may still be hanging out at that border crossing.

After several hours, they received the green light to proceed into Guatemala. One of the pastors there had worked as a customs officer and had connections. Consequently, entering Guatemala was a breeze.

Upon entering the country, they traveled about 30 minutes and came upon a bridge under repair, forcing them to detour. The detour, which took them along dirt roads climbing high mountains, was so precipitous that when the moving truck that was in front of them went around a curve, sand would fall off the side of the mountain. It was a rough and bumpy ride, and Cheryl kept saying that they were going to have a lot of broken items.

The Bakers finally pulled into Guatemala City late in the afternoon and went straight to their selected hotel. The moving company wanted to unload the truck as early as possible, so they could return to Honduras. Richard agreed to meet them at the house early the next morning. The boys wanted to ride with Richard, but Cheryl wanted Ryan to remain with her and Joshua. It was still dark when Richard and Christopher left the hotel for their new home, which was about a 40-minute drive from the hotel.

As he and Chris were driving to the house, a taxi had an accident in front of them, which left the driver lying halfway out of the car. It was apparent that he was dead. Richard slowed down, not quite sure just what to do, considering that the person who caused the accident left the scene. He certainly didn't want to be accused of having any part in it.

Furthermore, the fact that his Spanish was limited only added to his anxiety. When a vehicle drove up and stopped, he, quite relieved, drove on to the house.

After the truck was unloaded, the Munguias brought Cheryl, Ryan, and Joshua to the house and the job of getting everything organized began. In a couple of hours, the family got to missing Ryan and Chris, and Cheryl went into panic mode. Richard finally found them a couple of blocks down the street playing basketball with Guatemalan kids in the neighborhood.

The Baker family soon noticed that the water was on for only two hours daily, and the holding tank was small. There simply was not enough water for a family of six, as Ricky was making plans to come and would be arriving shortly. As stressful as it was, they found another home which had more access to water. Consequently, they moved again. As Baker later reflected on this time in their lives, he said, "God love Cheryl's heart. As I am writing this, my appreciation for her has risen dramatically. The boys and I looked at all of this as an adventure, but I certainly don't think Cheryl did."

The Bakers' oldest son, 19-year-old Ricky, was missing them and they were missing him. Initially, he seemed to want to move to Central America and to be a part of what his family was doing, if only for a brief time. This was the first time that any of them had been separated for an extended period. Baker also realized that he had made a mistake in encouraging him to stay in Cumming and continue with the company for which he was working. He concluded that Ricky felt pressured to stay by his suggestion.

In August 2000, the family flew back to the States for a couple of weeks. While they were there, Ricky strongly indicated that he wanted to go back with them. Richard agreed. He resigned his job, sold his truck, and they all flew back to Guatemala.

They had received a request from the overseer of Nicaragua, Lopez, for an orphanage to be built. Anderson and Baker had visited Nicaragua earlier in the year and knew there were many children left orphaned in the country from the devastation left by Hurricane Mitch. The extreme poverty in the country was indescribable. Baker felt in his heart that they needed to build an orphanage, and Anderson fully supported the decision.

Baker began writing to pastors and prospective individual donors to share the need. Funds started coming in. The Church of God operated a clinic in the slums of Managua, and Lopez wanted the orphanage built next to it, if they could acquire the land. Anderson and Baker felt differently.

They believed that building it in a safer environment would be best. In the end, they made the decision to try and buy five small homes situated next to the clinic. After negotiating the purchase of all five properties, a retired architect from Texas agreed to draw the plans without cost, even making trips at his own expense.

In September, Richard and Ricky boarded a bus headed for Nicaragua to start the construction process. This nearly two-day trip included a stop in El Salvador to spend the night. A Men and Women of Action team consisting of 17 men from Arizona, Georgia, and Florida arrived the day after they did. Baker had made an earlier trip to Nicaragua to meet with the architect on the design and hired a local contractor to prepare the footers. With the footers installed, Richard and Ricky went to work laying block their first day. Baker also hired about a dozen locals to help them. The project consisted of a boys' dorm, a girls' dorm, and a third building which served as a dining hall, kitchen, offices, and a common area.

Richard Baker, Frankie Tyson, & Jack Till building church—Central America.

They raised the walls on all three buildings in eight days, which included building large steel reinforced columns every eight to ten feet along the walls, to give extra strength to the building in case of earthquakes.

Baker also hired ladies from the church to cook meals on site each day for the workers. One of the most touching observations to Baker was men coming up to the work site and offering to work four hours just for a plate of food. On the last day, the team took the day off and visited Masaya, a tourist area with shops and restaurants, and a place that gets its name from an active volcano close by.

The following day, the team departed for the States. Ricky asked his dad if he could stay, since Baker was planning another trip in about a month. In all honesty, he was surprised that his son wanted to stay that long, especially considering that he was not yet proficient in speaking the language, although he was doing better than his dad was. A couple of pastors assured him they would take good care of him, so Baker returned home leaving him in Nicaragua.

Baker desperately needed another vehicle, especially a truck. He called Meadows' daughter, Robin, who was now the general manager of the Ford Lincoln Mercury dealership and informed her that he needed a late model four-wheel drive truck for the mission field. He asked her to call him immediately if she found anything she thought would work. Within a few days, Robin sent him an e-mail saying that they had just traded for a pickup she thought would be perfect for him. She assured him that they would hold it as long as he needed them to.

Needing to act quickly for his own sake, Baker flew into Atlanta and was greeted by Foster, who picked him up and took him directly to the car dealership. Pulling into the car lot, they parked next to a beautiful emerald green, almost new, GMC Z71, with an extended cab loaded with all the bells and whistles. Baker turned to Foster and exclaimed, "Wow! That's a beautiful pick-up but too expensive and nice for the mission field."

The World Missions Department had given him $12,000 towards a vehicle, and that was essentially what he had to work with. As he walked inside, Robin greeted him and announced, "Preacher, your truck is out front and here are the keys. Take it for a spin."

Baker asked, "Where did you say it was?"

Robin replied, "It's the green one sitting out front."

Taken aback, Baker responded "Robin, I can't afford that!"

"Preacher," she rejoined, "Take it for a drive, come back, and let's talk."

Acquiescing, Baker drove it and fell in love with it. Still, he knew the price was out of his range. After returning, he walked back inside and again explained, "Robin, I love it, but I can't afford it."

Robin spoke up and said, “You told me the missions department was helping some. How much are they giving?”

Baker answered, “$12,000.”

“That just happens to be the price!” she exclaimed. She continued, “How are you going to get it to Guatemala?”

“I will drive it to Miami and ship it down,” he answered.

“How much does that cost?” Robin asked.

When Baker told her, she wrote him a personal check for the shipping. He left there that day amazed again at how God had provided so miraculously, even allowing the vehicle to be his favorite color.

He said his goodbyes to Foster, a brother in Christ who had become like a second dad, and departed for Miami. On the way, he stopped in Brunswick, Georgia, to visit his mother and sister. Upon arriving in Miami, he dropped the truck off at the port, took a taxi to the airport, and flew back to Guatemala. Within a couple of weeks, the truck arrived at the port in Guatemala, and the pastor that helped the Bakers with moving helped him get his truck out of customs.

One of the churches, El Papalonal, built in Nicaragua (September 2000) Medical clinic extending to the far right.

With projects underway in Guatemala, Honduras, and now Nicaragua, Baker found himself quite busy. He had managed to raise $125,000 toward the orphanage in Managua, which now had a name. Brother Lopez had asked Cheryl to name it, and she chose Hogar Agape. Although the goal was to have the children living there by Christmas, they were $100,000 short, and the stream of donations had dried up.

Eddie Roberts, a cardiologist from Brunswick, had contacted Baker about coming to Central America to set up a medical clinic for a few days, with just him, Baker, along with a nurse whom he wanted Baker to hire. The particular country did not matter to the doctor, who informed him that he was leaving the logistics up to him. After giving it some thought, he decided on Nicaragua, since he needed to go back anyway to get Ricky and check on the orphanage project. He also thought that the doctor might make a donation to help finish the building, or at least go back to the States and share the needs with others in his profession.

After processing the most pressing needs, Baker shared with Roberts that he felt Nicaragua would be the best place to set up the temporary clinic and noted that he would arrange a couple of locations. A date was set a couple of weeks out, and Baker returned to Nicaragua. Shortly after, the doctor arrived, bringing with him a good supply of medicines. He purchased more once he got to Managua.

The following morning, he and Baker departed for a remote village about two and a half hours from Managua. Roberts informed him that he was somewhat finicky about eating and would struggle eating certain foods. Consequently, they stopped and got some ham sandwiches, chips, and some other American favorites.

Upon arriving at the church where the clinic was to be operated, the pastor's wife told Baker that she would be preparing a lunch of beans and rice. She then asked him if he liked what sounded like "azucar," Spanish for sugar. He replied that he did and passed along to the doctor what the pastor's wife had planned, encouraging him to try to eat a little. He responded, "Richard, I will have no problem eating beans and rice."

They saw about 30 patients before lunch, with Baker serving as the pharmacist. Roberts would tell him what medicine and the dosage that the patients were to take daily, and he would dispense it accordingly.

When lunchtime came, the two men walked back to the pastor's home. Roberts left something at the church and went to get it. While he was gone, the pastor's wife sat a large container on the table and took off the lid.

Baker immediately recognized it as some sort of animal—what kind, he wasn't sure. He just knew that it wasn't beef, pork, or chicken. So, when he asked, she replied with a word that, again, sounded like "azucar." Sensing now that she was not saying, "sugar", he asked her if the dish had another name. She answered, "Armadillo."

El Papalonal, Nicaragua (First service of newly built church).

About the time of his discovery, Roberts returned and asked what the meat was. Baker told him, and believing him to be kidding, the doctor looked at him and replied, "Yea, sure Richard." He then put some on his plate and ate it. Several times that day, he would look at Baker and say, "Don't tell me I ate armadillo!"

Baker would simply reply, "Yes, we ate armadillo."

They spent another day there, then a couple of days in the slums of Managua. On Friday evening, they headed back to the hotel. Baker asked the doctor if he wanted to visit the orphanage project. He answered that he would very much like to see it. After arriving, Baker showed him around and shared with him the financial needs related to completing the project.

Roberts announced, "Richard, I brought you something." He took his backpack from his shoulder and began going through it. Baker was hoping that he was looking for his checkbook. Instead, he pulled out a little book entitled, *The Prayer of Jebez.* When he handed the book to him, Baker felt a ping in his heart. He felt impressed to stay at the construction site that night and read the book.

Baker said to the doctor, "I am going to take you to the hotel and then come back and spend the night here."

Roberts responded, "If you're staying, I am staying!"

"But there are no beds, only a thin mattress on the floor," Baker explained. But the doctor wanted to stay. So, he put him in a little room adjacent to his, while he lay down on the four-inch mattress and started reading the book. He didn't stop until he had read it through. He then got on his knees, broken and crying, and began praying and asking the Lord to let him be a conduit for His blessing to flow through to help the orphans, widows, and other impoverished people. He prayed directly for God to link him up with a wealthy person, or a foundation who had the same passion and vision that he had.

Baker then prayed, "Lord, they never have to bless me. I just want the blessing to flow through me."

The Holy Spirit spoke to his heart and asked, "You don't mean that you want them to bless you too?" What the Lord had just spoken to his heart broke him on the inside, and he began to cry and mourn in his spirit for nearly an hour. The next morning, he dropped Roberts off at the airport, and the following day, he and Ricky returned to Guatemala. But he knew something had happened that night in prayer, and peace surrounded and filled him.

In about three weeks, he received a call from John Nichols, who served as Director of Benevolence for the Churches of God. He asked Baker if he would assist him with a couple of projects in Central America. He responded that he would be happy to assist him anyway he could. After talking for a few minutes about the projects Nichols was giving assistance to, he asked Baker if he had any humanitarian projects he was working on. He immediately shared with him about Hogar Agape in Nicaragua.

When Nichols asked how much Baker needed, he answered, "Dr. Nichols, if I had $20,000, I could get it to the next stage."

"How much do you need to complete the project?" Nichols asked.

Baker answered, "$125,000."

Nichols inquired, "Where do you want me to send the funds?"

Amazed by the promised gift, Baker shared with him his project account number. Nichols assured him that within two days the funds would be deposited into his account.

After ending the telephone conversation, Richard shared the exchange with Cheryl. She asked, "Is he sending $20,000 or $125,000?

Richard answered, "I am not sure." He called him back and asked him.

Nichols replied, "Richard, you told me you needed $125,000, and that's what I will be depositing."

Little did he know at the time that these funds were coming from a foundation that he would later serve for years as the executive director.

28

Rebuilding

Now with enough funds in hands to finish the three building, Baker pushed the contractor, in addition to making a couple of trips back to Nicaragua himself to work on the buildings. He even managed to get another smaller Men and Women of Action team to come in early December. His goal was to finish the building and have children living there by Christmas. That goal became reality.

Somewhere around December 20, 2000, the first 16 children arrived to their new home, Hogar Agape. Baker and Anderson had planned to have Christmas with them and dedicate the home at the same time. A day or two after Christmas, Baker boarded a bus in Guatemala, and Anderson boarded one in Honduras. They met in El Salvador and boarded another bus for Nicaragua. Both had purchased items for the children: a large toy, a small toy, two new outfits, and tennis shoes, along with candy and other small items for each child.

When Baker had returned home from his last visit a couple weeks earlier, the tile had not been laid, nor had the sinks, showers, and kitchen been completed. His sister and her husband, Phyllis and Bruce Garrett, had shipped a 40-foot container down with bunk beds and mattresses, along with other items.

As the bus entered Managua, the intensity built deep within his spirit. He could hardly wait to see the finished project, which he had had the awesome privilege of designing. Much more than that, he was anxious to see the 16 children who were now living in this beautiful home that their heavenly Father had provided for them. Baker had visited the children a couple of times before and saw that their dwellings were humble, to say the least. They had been feeding them during the entire time they were building the children's home. He would share with them, during the few times he visited, that they would soon have a new home and live in peace and security.

When he and Anderson arrived at the home, Bishop Lopez had everything arranged for the dedication service. Even a couple of government officials were there, along with a couple of politicians. The children were nicely dressed and sitting close to the front during the service. Baker could not keep his eyes off them. He was so happy for them and felt such a sense of accomplishment in being allowed to be such a small part of what God was doing here.

After the dedication service, they had Christmas lunch with the children, who had requested pizza, colas, and ice cream. For some of them, it was their first pizza. After lunch Baker and Anderson began giving out the presents. Baker remembers, "I can still see them now as they opened their gifts and saw the new clothes. They immediately ran to their rooms and changed. Ken walked over to me crying and said, 'A child just walked over to me and thanked me for giving him his first home.' I responded that I too just had an eight-year-old boy thank me, not for his clothes and toys (although they were very much appreciated), but for giving him a home."

Over the next 16 years many homeless, hurting, deprived, and abused children would call Hogar Agape home. Unfortunately, in 2016 the Nicaraguan government mandated that all faith-based private orphanages be closed. It was truly a sad day for Baker, Anderson, and all who loved the orphanage and the ministry it provided to the homeless and hurting children of Nicaragua.

On Saturday morning, January 13, 2001, Richard and Cheryl, along with their sons, were home in Guatemala when a massive earthquake measuring 7.7 on the Richter scale struck El Salvador. The ferocity of the quake was such that in Guatemala City where they lived, the porcelain tile began moving like a wave rolling onto the beach. Baker got his entire family outside until the earth stopped quaking.

Within a couple of hours, Anderson called Baker and informed him that the epicenter of the quake was in El Salvador and that initial reports indicated there was widespread destruction, along with substantial loss of life. Baker immediately began making plans to travel to El Salvador.

Around 1:00 pm the following day, he pulled into Santa Tecla, a suburb of San Salvador where the national office for the Church of God was located. Because he was listed with the US Embassy as a disaster relief first responder worker, he was given a special permit that allowed him to travel anywhere within the affected areas. The four-wheel drive GMC that God had just provided for him was now put to the test, considering that many bridges and roads were impassable.

Surveying damage from earthquake in El Salvador (January 2001).

He spent that first afternoon encouraging the national overseer and his team. Some of the buildings, such as the dorms for the Bible school, were almost completed destroyed. He and Anderson had just stayed in one of the dorms a few weeks earlier, a dorm that now lay in shambles. Most everyone who was living on site had makeshift shelters to sleep in. However, Baker decided to sleep in the library, which turned out to be a bad choice. An aftershock measuring 5.7 struck during the night. The ceiling, lined with metal beams, seemed as if someone grabbed them and twisted them in different directions. He quickly jumped up but was knocked back down. After this happened three times, he decided to crawl out of the building. More than 2,500 aftershocks were recorded over the next four weeks, many of which he experienced.

Anderson arrived the next day, and the two began devising plans for relief efforts. World Missions initially sent $25,000 to help until some sort of assessment could be made. Because the Church of God has a centralized form of government—meaning that each country has a national overseer who has territorial overseers under him, who in turn have district overseers under them that give oversight to usually 8-12 churches—they were able within a couple of weeks to get a fairly accurate assessment of the damage and loss of life that the churches had suffered. They also gained a general overview of the magnitude of the damage the country as a whole had suffered. Out of the 430 churches that the Church of God had in El Salvador, 147 were destroyed or damaged. Not one city, town, or hamlet in the country escaped the effects of the quake.

Baker crossing a river to get to suffering people after a hurricane had destroyed all the bridges in a remote area of Guatemala.

The first priority, of course, was keeping people alive, especially in the remote areas where accessibility to commodities was limited. Richard negotiated with Pricesmart, a chain owned by Costco that operates throughout Central America, for seven staple goods: beans, rice, pasta, salt, cooking oil, cornmeal, and soap. They sold them these items at five percent under their cost. For weeks, Richard loaded his pickup to capacity several times daily, taking food to the pastors, who, in turn, delivered to all in their communities that needed help. Several others were also delivering food and water to those who were suffering.

Baker had met with one of the top architects and engineers in the country, who also taught at the main university in the capital. After meeting with him, he and Anderson met to devise a plan to reconstruct all the churches that were destroyed and repair the damaged ones. Only God could have given them the idea they came up with. And that was to hire the architectural firm and let them set up offices at the Church of God national offices.

Every Monday through Wednesday, Baker and the architect would visit several churches. The architect would make rough drawings for the new church building. Each day after returning, he would meet with his draftsmen who prepared the drawings. On Thursdays the pastors would come to the state office, pick up their drawings, and enough funds to have the footers and foundations installed. After this part of construction was completed, Baker, sometimes accompanied by the architect, would inspect the foundation. If all was good, funds would be released to erect the walls. Lastly, the final draft would be released for the roof system.

Every Sunday evening, Baker left Guatemala and would arrive late Sunday night in El Salvador. He would stay until late Thursday evening and return to Guatemala. He did this for one year. In the end, every church was rebuilt or repaired. They also built several dozen small homes for single moms and widows. At times they had as many as four construction crews from the States working simultaneously in different parts of the country. He personally worked on at least 25 of the churches.

On one of the trips, he took his son Chris, who was 15 at the time. They had been to a remote part of the country and were heading back to the capital. Chris piped up, "Dad, I am really hungry!"

Baker responded, "We will be back in San Salvador in an hour-and-a-half, and we will stop at KFC." About that time, a truck coming from the opposite direction cut in front of them crossing the highway and plowing over a guy sitting on a motorcycle waiting for the traffic to pass. The truck then sped away. They immediately stopped, but it took a couple of minutes to back up to where the accident happened. He and Chris, along with Carlos, the educational director, exited the truck to witness the man lying face down in a ditch full of water. Six or eight people were just looking on doing nothing. Carlos, Chris, and Richard grabbed the man by the shoulders pulling him out of the ditch. He was a large man, and it took some effort to pull him out. Once they did, they realized his right leg was detached below the knee, and his tennis shoe and sock were intact on the severed foot. Picking him up, they placed him in the back of Richard's pickup. He was praying the entire time, "God, please send a policeman!"

About that time, two police vehicles drove up and Carlos explained what had happened. They asked for a description of the vehicle that had fled the scene. While one police vehicle took off after the driver, another policeman got up in the back of Baker's truck to ride with the injured man while the other officer asked him to follow him to the hospital. Carlos, after picking up the severed leg and foot and placing it in the back of the truck, climbed in the back to assist the officer.

As Baker was preparing to drive off, a woman came to them crying out that she was the wife of the man that had been run over. After Chris opened the door to let her in, Richard sped away to the hospital. During the 20-to-30-minute drive to the hospital, she explained to them that she was a Christian and that her husband had just accepted the Lord a couple of weeks earlier. She said they had four children.

Upon arriving at the hospital, they found emergency personnel waiting with a gurney. As they took the man from the back of the truck and placed him on the gurney, a nurse reached and grabbed the severed leg and foot from the back of the truck, placing it on the gurney beside the man.

The police officers instructed Baker to back up into a certain area and park. Suddenly, fear struck him when he remembered that he had always been told not to stop if he saw an accident, since they may try and blame him, seeing that he was a foreigner. That is indeed a common practice in many countries. But to his surprise, five police officers took their shirts off and hand washed his truck. After putting their shirts back on, they stood in line to shake their hands and thank them for getting involved and helping this man.

A little later they arrived in San Salvador, and Baker asked, "Chris, do you still want KFC, or something else?"

Chris answered, "Dad, I'm not hungry anymore." Richard certainly understood that.

Baker later expressed, "Just the experiences of the 12 to 15 months I spent doing disaster relief in El Salvador would fill a book. There are so many stories flooding my heart. But it took its toll on me physically, emotionally, and even spiritually. I also coordinated trips for disaster relief teams from the United Methodist and Presbyterian USA churches, as they had no churches in the country but wanted to help with the relief efforts. We truly appreciated their assistance and support in the relief of the suffering."

In Santa Tecla just a very short distance from where he was staying, a mountain split in two parts and covered a subdivision killing hundreds of people. One family victimized by the catastrophe was a Church of God pastor and several of his children. His wife and two daughters had just left the house 15 minutes before the earthquake struck. Baker witnessed front-end loaders picking up debris laden with body parts. He visited a mass grave where, in an attempt to keep down the spread of diseases from dead bodies and body parts, the bodies were buried without any attempt at identification.

On one occasion, a Baptist missionary was traveling with him, and they were dropping off a pastor and his wife. As they were exiting the truck, four MS-13 gang members, who were standing close to where Baker had parked, began to taunt the couple, even going as far as to say what they were going to do to the pastor's wife. He could see shear fear in their faces, and before he knew what he was doing, he grabbed his machete and exited the driver's side door shouting at the gang members. Gary, the missionary, jumped across the seat, grabbed him, and shouted, "Richard, what are you doing?" They stayed until the couple was safely in their home, but if Gary had not been traveling with him that day, only God knows what may have happened.

Subdivision destroyed (500 died here along with a pastor and four of his children). Richard spent one year helping with the recovery and rebuilding.

Baker later related, "Apparently the gang members were not armed, or I probably would not be around to tell this story."

Realizing that he was totally exhausted and had allowed his old nature to rise up again (because his intention was to hack those gang members), he decided to return to Guatemala and spend much-needed time recuperating.

The 911 terrorist attacks struck a little over halfway through the reconstruction process in El Salvador. Richard said, "It was surreal to be living in a foreign country and watch on the news that your country was being attacked by terrorist and knowing that all flights had been grounded, and you couldn't return home if you wanted too."

By March 2002, most, if not all, of the 147 churches had been rebuilt or repaired. Today, Baker is still amazed at how the Lord gave such great favor. He marvels at the support of the Lazarus Foundation and the faithfulness of churches in the US who donated much and sent many teams to help rebuild or render humanitarian services.

In late March 2002, Baker received a call from Anderson, who arrived in Managua on March 27. Anderson shared with him that the national overseer of Nicaragua, Bienvenido Lopez, was deathly ill and not expected to live. Anderson added that he had come to preach his funeral and asked him to fly to Managua and join him.

Upon arriving at the Lopez home, they experienced an atmosphere of sorrow and sadness. The overseer's pregnant wife and their three children were already mourning. Anderson asked for his medical test from the doctor treating him and sent them to Dr. Otoniel Collins. He and his wife, Dr. Xiomara, were both medical physicians. Collins also served as the national overseer for the country of Belize. After perusing his medical records, Collins believed if they could get him to the US, he would have a good chance of surviving.

Baker mentioned to Anderson that Dr. Goodson, whom he had pastored in Cumming, Georgia, before coming to the mission field, might also be able to give them an assessment. They sent the information to him and within a few hours, Goodson reached out to Baker asking him to get Lopez to Atlanta. If they could, he said the Baptist North Hospital would be willing to treat him free of charge.

God had given His "worm" a new assignment: "Get My servant to Atlanta." Anderson and Baker met with the family and shared the good news. They also informed the family about the risk involved in trying to transport him to the US. Baker agreed to take him, and Victor Lozano, a minister and right-hand man to Lopez, offered to go with him. Their flight would take them from Managua, Nicaragua, to San Salvador, where they would change planes for their final flight to Atlanta.

On Easter Sunday, March 31, they departed for the US. The first flight was on a small commercial jet. As they rolled Lopez in a wheelchair to the plane, Baker began to wonder how they were going to get him up the steps. Shortly, he got his answer. Airport personnel informed them that the sick man would have to climb the stairs on his own, as far as airport staff was concerned. Knowing that the stairs were very narrow, and that Lopez was a large man, over six feet tall and weighing 300 pounds, Baker didn't know what to do. He again asked the man pushing the wheelchair if he could help. And again, he said he couldn't.

Baker helped Lopez to stand and asked Lozano to go to the top of the stairs. As he backed up to him, he asked Lopez to wrap his arms around and lean on his back. He replied, "I am too heavy for you, Pastor."

"I will not be carrying you; the Lord will," Baker answered. As his feet came off the ground and all his weight came to bear on Baker, he felt like a little child was hanging onto him. He easily walked up the eight to 10 steps and into the plane, where Lozano then helped seat him. The stewardess was crying, and the passengers started clapping.

They flew to San Salvador where they had a two-hour layover. From there they would be flying Delta into Atlanta. When the call came to board, the woman working the counter said he could not board without the airport nurse looking at him. She remarked, "I think he is too sick to board." Richard pleaded with her and shared part of Lopez's story.

Before his conversion, Lopez served as a driver and bodyguard for President Somoza. For 70 years the Somoza family ruled as dictators. During the overthrow of Somoza in 1979, Lopez was shot four times and placed in prison. For six years he slept on a concrete floor and was tortured. Church leaders and pastors were also arrested and witnessed to him in prison. He accepted the Lord.

One evening he and six others were led to a swimming pool, where they were blindfolded, handcuffed, and instructed to walk into the pool. When the water reached their waists, Lopez heard the order to turn around. He then heard instructions given to the firing squad and knew he was about to meet Jesus. The shots rang out, but he felt no pain and thought it impossible that they could have missed him, being so close. He heard the order again, and another volley came whizzing his way, but not one bullet struck him.

Reaching up, he pulled his blindfold off to witness the other six men floating in the water dead. The firing squad stood looking at him in total disbelief. He walked out of the pool, past the firing squad, and back to his cell. Within a few months, he gained his release from prison and started attending a Church of God, where he eventually became the pastor.

Baker explained, "This man gives oversight to more than 600 churches in Nicaragua. They need their leader, but most importantly, his pregnant wife and three children so desperately need him."

The attendant replied, "Even if I let him pass, the captain will not let him board, since a stewardess will see how sick he is and tell the captain."

Not about to be discouraged, he asked to speak with the captain and walked to where people were waiting to board. He explained the situation to him. With tears in his eyes, he said, "I am not supposed to do this, but if you agree that no matter what happens, I will not be able to make an emergency stop, then I will allow him to fly." Baker agreed and they boarded. Because of his size, they gave him two seats behind the bulkhead.

Lozano sat next to him, and Baker sat across the aisle. It seemed that all the flight attendants came up and engaged him about Lopez's story. He received special attention during the entire flight. About halfway to Atlanta, he experienced confusion and finally passed out. As Baker stood next to him and Lozano sat beside him, they began praying. As they prayed, they witnessed his eyes rolling back in his head. By now, a couple of the flight attendants and a woman passenger had joined in on the prayer meeting. An attendant summoned the captain. When he approached, he said to Baker that they were nearing Miami, but he couldn't stop. Baker nodded and whispered, "It's okay."

In a few moments, Lopez regained consciousness and many passengers in the cabin began to clap. They arrived in Atlanta where Goodson had received permission to board the plane. After all the passengers had disembarked, they loaded Lopez into a wheelchair and quickly headed off to the hospital.

Upon arrival at the hospital and a quick but thorough examination, the doctors determined he was in organ failure, had lost half of his blood, and was near death. Lopez received excellent care and spent approximately 10 days in the hospital. There is no doubt that the Lord was with him.

When the hospital dismissed Lopez, he and Victor Lozano were driven to the airport, where they boarded a plane to Nicaragua. Baker expressed his heart saying, "Special appreciation goes to Dr. Goodson and his wife, Kathy, for all they did in helping this great servant of God, and for allowing Lozano to stay in their home the 10 days Lopez was in the hospital."

When Lopez had arrived back in Nicaragua, their fourth child, a little girl, had been born. The family insisted that Baker dedicate her to the Lord, which he was thrilled to do. He reflected:

> What a joy and privilege it is to serve the Lord and to be His hands extended. I truly believe one of the main reasons so many Christians have no joy is that they have never learned to serve; they only want to be served. True joy comes when we allow ourselves to be the body of Jesus through our acts of kindness and sometimes sacrifices. Writing this story today has caused me to relive this experience. And what joy and true happiness it brings to me, when I taste once again the fruit of obedience. It was through obedience to the Lord, when he asked me if I would become a worm for his glory, to follow Him. Even today people ask what exactly do I mean by being a worm? It is a question that cannot be fully answered or explained with words. In fact, it really can only be understood by experiencing for oneself, as we yield ourselves to what God's love is leading us to do, and how through submission to His will, we are motivated to be servants one to another.

In June of 2002, a team from Missouri was scheduled to fly into Belize to do some remolding work on a church and parsonage. Ryan and Chris wanted to go with their dad and Gary, their missionary friend who served with another mission organization and had kept Baker from hacking on the gang members in El Salvador. They loaded the Bronco and set out early one morning for the 12 to 14-hour drive.

About four hours into the trip, they came to a place in the road that was under repair, which caused the closure of one lane. Baker pulled behind a semi-truck and waited for his turn to go. Looking into his rearview mirror, he saw a semi-truck barreling toward them at a high rate of speed. He shouted, "Brace yourself! We are about to get hit!" He knew the driver would not be able to stop in time.

He immediately threw the Bronco in reverse and lunged backward a few feet. Frantically turning his wheels sharply to the left, he thrust the shift into forward and was about to shoot across the highway to avoid being hit when the semi slammed into them, knocking them a couple of hundred feet down the opposite side of the highway. The collision threw them headlong into a four-by-four pickup, after which they rolled into a ditch. The semi then hit the semi they were parked behind pushing it into a 15-passenger van filled to capacity. The impact to the van was so great that the back six feet of the van was push into the front of the van. Even though people were seriously injured by the impact, the Bronco was still running. He put it in four-wheel drive and backed out of the ditch.

Chris and Ryan were sitting in the back with most of the impact being on Chris's side, forcing his seat forward and trapping him between the front and rear seats. It took them a few minutes to get him free.

Chris, Ryan, Gary, and Richard after the accident.

The police officers directing traffic witnessed the accident and told Baker that it wasn't his fault. But by the time the driver called his lawyer to the scene, the police changed their story and said Baker was passing. The police escorted them to Morales, the nearest town with a police department, where they were told they could not leave the station. Baker sensed that his boys thought it was exciting to be arrested with their dad. He kept thinking that if he had not backed away from the semi in front of him and turned the wheel to the left, they would all be dead.

He called his pastor, David Munguia, who in turn contacted a local Church of God pastor in Morales, who immediately came to check on them. Although they explained what had happened, the police informed them that they could not leave until they went before the judge. The pastor shared with Baker that he knew the judge and that just three weeks earlier, he had led her to the Lord. In fact, she was now attending his church. He said, "I will go see her and get back with you." Within a couple of hours, the judge sent word to have them released.

Munguia offered to come get them, so they waited for him at the church. He had a son about Ryan's age, and they soon struck up an acquaintance. They enjoyed their conversation enough for Ryan to ask if he could stay the weekend. Since Baker had to return the following Monday to appear before the judge, it seemed like a good idea. When Richard and Chris returned home, Cheryl asked, "Where is Ryan?"

Baker answered, "I left him in Morales with the local pastor."

She shot back, "You left my son where?" She was not too happy about her husband's decision. She decided to ride with them on Monday for them to appear before the judge and for her to get Ryan. As they entered the city, someone on a bicycle came alongside them. Seeing that it was Ryan, Cheryl felt greatly relieved.

The judge didn't order Baker to appear before her in court but offered to meet with him in her office. She asked for his side of the story. Once he shared it, she announced, "I am dismissing all charges against you." Once again, the mighty hand and favor of God was evident. He could have been found liable for all the damage, including those hurt in the van.

On the ride home, Ryan declared, "I got you beat (speaking of eating strange things). The pastor's son and I visited his grandmother who lives up in the mountains, and for dinner we were served fried cow utter. I was given the teats."

His dad asked, "How did it taste?"

"A little chewy, but it tasted fine." Ryan answered.

He graduated from high school in May, just before their planned trip to Belize, and was accepted into Lee University, located in Cleveland, Tennessee. Since the family was a missionary family, he received a 90 percent scholarship. Although he asked to remain another year in Guatemala, Baker encouraged him to go ahead and enroll, considering the scholarship he had been offered. So, Ryan departed Guatemala in the summer of 2002 to attend Lee. Now, two of their sons had departed

Guatemala—Ricky, who first moved to Phoenix, Arizona, but was now living in Brunswick, Georgia, and Ryan, who had just departed for Cleveland.

Baker's next trip took him to a place called Mango Tara (place of the mangoes) deep within the jungles of Honduras. Traveling with him were Mike Morgan and Mark—both missionaries at Casa Shalom Orphanage in Guatemala—and territorial overseer for the Miskito Coast, Tim Norman. They flew to Porta Lempira and took a bush plane to Kruta. From there they rode a canoe for another two to three hours. The village consisted of several hundred Miskito Indians living in wood structures six to eight feet above the ground due to predators and flooding. There was no running water and no electricity. The men took their baths in nearby Kruta River.

With a chainsaw, the men cut down trees for lumber to construct the wood church building. They had to build it four feet off the ground. A water purifier was purchased from the Red Cross and water ran through it twice. It took four days to build the 28 by 50-foot church building. The pastor and congregation were happy to finally have a place in which to worship, since they had been meeting in the open.

Baker wrote, "There is such a deep satisfaction in knowing you have been part of an answer to a prayer that was prayed by these precious people and that God would use such a worm as I to help fulfill their dream."

Following their completion of the project, the men boarded two canoes for the two-to-three-hour journey back Kruta to catch the bush plane to Porta Lempira. Upon arriving at Kruta, they had about an hour's wait for the plane, so Baker decided to get something to eat. The only thing he could find was scrambled eggs with some sort of meat chopped into it.

Since there is no runway in Kruta, the airplane makes a low flyover to alert the people about a landing. As Baker and his team waited for their flight, the pilot flew across the landing spot to announce his intention. On his second approach, he began his descent. Baker stood close to the landing area and just as the plane neared touchdown, a mare and her colt walked in front of the plane. Horrifyingly, the airplane severed the mare's head and cast the animal a hundred feet away. It also killed the colt. The plane almost crashed into some homes but managed to stop just in time. He ran to check on the pilot, who, although shaken up, was okay.

For the time being, the team had to stay put. There was no other quick way out of the jungle, and a plane would not be available for a couple of days. Tim Norman found a man with a boat large enough to take them to Porta Lempira and estimated the trip would take eight hours. After purchasing 30 gallons of fuel, they loaded up and took off for a very long boat ride.

After about two hours, the river had narrowed to the point where the men had to lift tree limbs to allow the boat passage. The boat's pilot finally admitted they were lost, and now darkness was setting in. Finally, the narrow canal opened into a large lake, but another 30 minutes were spent trying to find a way out. A creek came into view, and they followed it, riding all night not knowing for sure if they were even going in the right direction.

When daylight appeared, following a long night of consternation, they were able to ask some of the Miskitos that lived along the waterways, and they kept giving directions to the lost travelers. Around mid-morning, after spending 12 hours in a small skiff, they could see Porta Lempira. The Church of God had an office there, and the men were able to get something to eat and take a shower. Baker had given all his clothes, including his boots, to the pastor, since they were about the same size. Consequently, he had to put his dirty clothes back on for the three-leg commercial flight back to Guatemala.

Cheryl was waiting for them upon their arrival, and as he entered the vehicle, Cheryl exclaimed, "Richard, you stink really, really, bad, and I can't believe you got on the airplane looking like you do!" What could he say?

The next day, Mark reached out to Richard to inform him that the water purifier had been recalled. They were all suffering from constipation, which was not normal with most parasites they dealt with.

Two days after returning home, Baker was driving alone and began having excruciating pains in his chest. He felt like he might have pneumonia, so he pulled into a local hospital and asked to be checked by a pulmonary doctor. In Guatemala medical personnel checks everyone for parasites. So, while he waited for the doctor, they checked him. When the doctor stepped in to see him, he asked where he had been, because his intestines were full of four distinct kinds of parasites. Interestingly, one of them was not native to Guatemala and was quite deadly. The doctor reported, "The parasite goes from the intestines to the lung. That's why you're having chest pains. Then they travel to the liver and, if not treated, can cause death." By the grace of God, they had the medicine to treat him, and in a few days, he felt like a new man.

The remainder of 2002 found Baker and his team building churches in Guatemala and Honduras. He also was given plenty of opportunities to preach the gospel and had the wonderful privilege of also preaching the conventions in Nicaragua and El Salvador.

29

Disaster Relief and Children

In December 2002, Anderson and his family returned to the US to pastor in Anderson, South Carolina, after spending 11 years on the mission field. Baker had shared with Anderson that he did not feel qualified to assume his role as superintendent mainly because he had not mastered the Spanish language. Furthermore, he enjoyed the ministry role he presently filled and believed that he would be more useful staying in it. However, he did fill in from December 2002 until April 2003, when a new superintendent took over. He had the arduous task of moving the superintendent's office from San Pedro Sula, Honduras, to Guatemala City, Guatemala. There are 6,000 churches of God in Central America, and that translates into a tremendous number of files and hardcopy records, and other such things. He had to transport overland all the files, computers, and other essential items related to the superintendent's office.

He had no sooner got the office moved when massive storms struck Costa Rica causing horrific flooding, which destroyed 25 churches and several homes belonging to church members. Baker boarded a plane bound for Costa Rica and upon arrival was met by the national overseer, Martin Castillo. They spent three days inspecting all the damaged and destroyed churches.

When Baker arrived back to Guatemala, he sent Lovell Cary, director of Church of God World Missions, a report of the damage. Cary summoned him to Cleveland since the World Missions board was getting ready to convene. Baker addressed the board and answered any questions they had. When he departed, Cary had $250,000 deposited into his Central America disaster relief account to start the relief work.

Quickly, Men and Women of Action teams heard about the flooding and started contacting Baker about bringing teams down. In less than eight months, all churches had been rebuilt or repaired.

In June 2003, the director of Casa Shalom, Olga Gonzales, resigned, having served at the orphanage since it began in 1987, when Richard and Jan Waldrop founded the home. He and Cheryl were asked to attend a Casa Shalom Board of Directors meeting that was convened on a Friday. When the meeting was over, Cheryl was unexpectedly the new director.

When they arrived home to San Christabel, a suburb of Guatemala City, they received a call from the cook, Isalena, who shared with Richard that there was no food to prepare dinner for the children. He and Cheryl purchased enough food for the 28 children and the five or six staff members to last for a few days.

On Monday morning, he arrived at the orphanage around 7:30. Cheryl planned to come later. Around 8:00 that morning, a government official showed up demanding to see the director. Although Cheryl was now officially the director, Richard acted as if he was. The official began by telling him that the home had not been paying social security tax on the employees, and that they owed several thousand dollars in back taxes.

With his limited Spanish, Baker tried to explain to him that this was their first day and promised him that all back taxes would be paid. However, he noted that they would need some time to raise the funds. The official became belligerent and started threatening to close the home. Never one inclined to acquiesce to threats Baker asked, "Sir, where do you live?"

The man answered, "Antigua."

"What is your street address," Baker asked.

Feeling threatened himself, he shot back, "Why do you want to know my street address?"

Baker responded, "If you close this orphanage today, the children will need to eat somewhere tonight. I was planning on loading them onto the bus and bringing them to your house for dinner."

The government's representative hastily arose from his chair and brusquely departed. Baker never saw or heard from him again. Just as he promised, they eventually caught up all back taxes.

Casa Shalom was in dire condition. The wells had gone dry, and they had to purchase water that was brought in on tankers, which became quite expensive. All the plumbing needed to be replaced, and the children needed new beds and mattresses. There were electrical issues to address, and many of the children had parasites. Donations had drastically fallen off to the point where there wasn't enough money coming in to properly care for the children.

Baker sat down and wrote 25 pastors he knew on a first-name basis and shared with them the situation. Immediately, they collectively sent over $30,000. The home the Bakers would be living in needed a major renovation, so, with no funds available, they took funds from their 401k to make the necessary repairs.

In spite of all the work needed at Casa Shalom, Baker was still the coordinator of humanitarian and disaster relief for the seven countries comprising Central America. He was traveling nearly half the time responding to disasters, humanitarian crises, or hosting a team. They had hired Lesly, a 19-year-old woman who worked in the kitchen at the main Bible school in Guatemala. She became Cheryl's right-hand person and became like a daughter to the Bakers. Even though she couldn't speak English, she understood their elementary Spanish and at times interpreted for Cheryl. For example, when Cheryl had to appear in court to stand before the judge on behalf of the children, Lesly would interpret, if the judge didn't understand all Cheryl was saying. That was not too bad considering that she spoke no English. Surely, God was at work in all this.

By the first of August, conditions were starting to turn around. Donations were picking up, most of the repairs had been made, and the house the Bakers would be living in was nearing completion. The courts called and had a two-week-old baby boy they needed the orphanage to take. Of course, Cheryl quickly agreed. However, since Casa Shalom was not set up to take infants, little Antonio became part of the Baker household.

Within a couple of weeks, they received another call, this time requesting that they take a three-week-old baby girl. Once again, Cheryl accepted. They drove the three hours to San Juan Quiche and had the director of the hospital place the most beautiful little girl in their arms. Her name was Melanie, and she has been the Bakers' daughter ever since that day.

By the time a couple of months passed, they had eight infant babies living in their home, which was only 1,500 square feet. They had to hire another lady to live with them to help Cheryl and Lesly care for the babies.

At the same time, they were also taking older children in and by September, they had grown from 28 to over 50 children.

Mikey came to Casa Shalom shortly after the Bakers had gotten Melanie. A police officer heard a faint cry coming from a ditch he was passing and stopped to investigate. He found a newborn baby boy lying in several inches of cold water, still with the afterbirth attached. He was immediately cleaned up, fed, and taken to a pediatrician. Because he had lain in the cold water for a time, he had neurological issues and cried all the time. Both Cheryl's mom and Richard's mom visited them and would sit and hold Mikey for hours. They were deeply concerned for his future but knew that, if God's eye is on a sparrow, His eye is most certainly on an infant orphan.

Melanie at Casa Shalom—second Christmas.

They received a call that a Guatemalan couple, who were unable to have children, wanted to visit Casa Shalom and talk to the Bakers about the possibility of adopting one of their babies. When they arrived, it became apparent that they were people of some means. They owned all the Isuzu dealerships in the country and were also Christians. When they saw Mikey and heard his story, they were touched and chose to adopt him. God had answered prayers, seeing that he was now in a family which had the means to address his medical needs. About 18 months later, they came back and adopted a sister for him.

In September, Hurricane Isabel struck the Mosquito Coast of Nicaragua and Honduras packing powerful winds and causing extreme flooding. When Anderson returned to the States, he left his Cessna 185 bush plane, which had been donated to him by Jack Dyer, who had been a missionary in the Mosquito Coast. A missionary pilot from Norway, Jarle, along with his wife, had moved to this area of Honduras and had taken over Ken's duties as a missionary pilot. Baker arranged with Jarle to fly him around the affected areas. In most of the villages there was nowhere to land because of the flooding. He took pictures and together they would document on a chart the villages pictured.

However, they were able to land at a couple of villages. In one of those villages, as they walked around surveying the damage, a woman invited them for lunch. Knowing the people were struggling to sustain themselves, Baker wanted to decline but didn't want to offend her. As they sat on a small front porch, she brought them a small plate with a little rice, pasta, and a small piece of meat. Richard couldn't identify the meat, but it appeared to be a portion where the neck and shoulder come together. When he asked Jarle what it was, Jarle answered, "I was hoping you knew."

When the woman came back, they asked her what it was. She responded, "It's poca." That didn't help them to know what they were eating. All they knew was that it didn't taste all that good and it left a film in their mouths.

A few minutes later some veterinarians from the US walked up. They were there to try and save the cattle from dying from any disease they may have contracted by standing in floodwater for so long. Still curious to know what he was eating, Baker asked one of them if he knew what a "poca" was. The man answered, "I can do better than that. I have a picture!" That's when they knew they were eating a healthy rat.

They boarded the Cessna and continued surveying the damage. Once they were airborne, the thought of what he had just eaten began messing with his mind, and he started feeling nauseous. When Jarle approached the next village, he banked the plane hard left tilting it so Baker, who was sitting in the back seat, could take photos and videos. When he noticed that Baker wasn't taking pictures, he said something to him through the headsets. Baker replied, "There is a battle going on back here. The rat is trying to crawl up my throat and I keep pushing him back down. Right now, there is no time to take pictures!"

Sadly, many people died of starvation, because the storm washed all the crops out to sea, banana trees rotted, and the storm disturbed fishing for a long time. Baker arranged the purchase of a couple of railroad boxcars of rice from Louisiana and had it shipped down. Either a French or Italian relief organization brought in a small helicopter to transport the rice and other commodities to the villages in greatest need.

Baker returned to Guatemala to find Cheryl having received more babies and children into the orphanage. In a couple of weeks, he had to travel to Nicaragua. His instruction to her was, "Don't accept any more babies. We simply don't have the space or the finances to support any more babies or children."

When he returned from Nicaragua, he pulled around to the back of the house that featured a large picture window. Cheryl saw him drive up and ran upstairs. As he walked in the door, Lesly announced, "Brother Baker, your wife has you a new gift." It was baby number nine.

He went upstairs and asked, "Cheryl, why did you take another baby when we are out of space and funds are so tight?"

She answered, "The police drove up, rang the bell at the gate, and asked to see me. As I was walking from the house to the gate, I kept saying to myself, 'I must say we can't accept any more babies.' I opened the gate, and the officer was holding a two-month-old boy with him facing me. I tried not to look at the baby, told the officer we were filled, and couldn't take him. Then the baby asked me if I would be his mommy. And Richard, I just couldn't say no!"

Richard questioned, "How did a two-month-old ask you to be his mommy?"

She replied, "With his eyes. I looked into his eyes, and he spoke to me, 'I need a mommy; will you please be my mommy?'"

"How do you respond to that?" Richard thought.

He and Cheryl funded the babies the entire time they served at Casa Shalom, with the exception of donations that teams brought and left. It cost them $2,500 to $3,000 every month. At times they had to pull funds from their 401k, but if they had to do it again, there would be no hesitations. There is a special place in the heart of God for orphans and abused children.

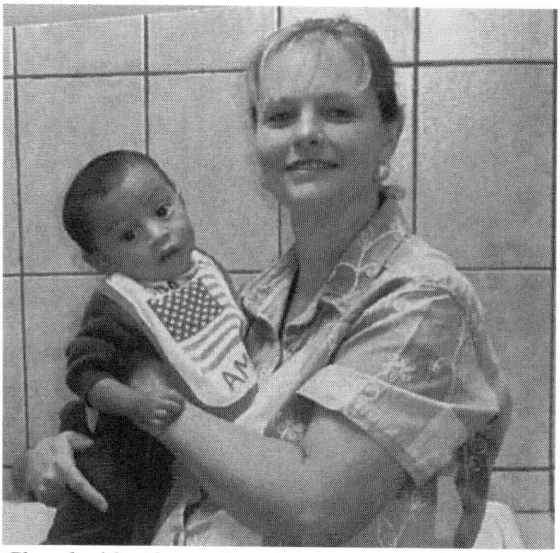

Cheryl with Alex at Casa Shalom, one of 14 infants she took in during her first six months as director. Alex remains there and is in his last year of school (2020).

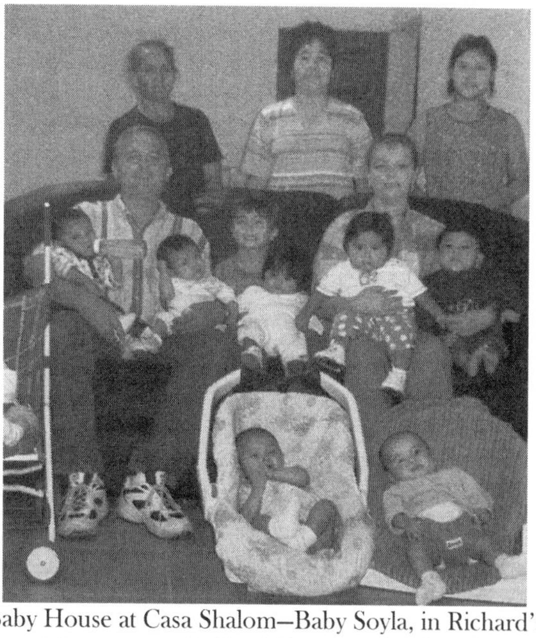

Baby House at Casa Shalom—Baby Soyla, in Richard's right arm, would die within a couple of weeks. Joshua is sitting next to Richard; Cheryl is holding Melanie.

Baker's sister and brother-in-law, Phyllis and Bruce, shipped a couple of 40-foot containers from the States loaded with hundreds of cases of Gerber baby food, pampers, wipes, new beds and mattresses, furniture, clothing, appliances, and other items. There were at least 10,000 to 12,000 jars of baby food, and they were able to share with other orphanages.

Ricky was now living and working in Brunswick, Georgia. As providence would have it, in December of 2001, he met a girl named Tiffany Owens at his home church there. Not long after they met, they fell in love. On November 22, 2003, Richard had the honor of being part of the wedding ceremony of his firstborn. Since their wedding, Ricky and Tiffany have blessed him and Cheryl with six beautiful and wonderful grandchildren: Jonathan, Brayden, Kylie, Isaiah, Karleigh, and Kingston. Richard and Cheryl are so proud of their love for God and for each other, and for the commitment they have made to put God first in their lives and to raise their grandchildren in a loving home.

Richard saw the need to build a home just for babies and toddlers. About 100 feet behind their house was the concrete foundation of what had been a barn for cattle. They cleaned it up and Richard, with Cheryl's input, drew a rough sketch of what she envisioned for the new baby house. They divided it into three areas: birth to toddler, toddler to three, and threes and fours.

When they had done all they could do, he received a call from Nichols asking him about helping with a project in Panama. After he inquired about Casa Shalom, Baker shared with him that they had nine babies all less than eight months old living in their home. He ended with, "We need a baby house built."

Nichols asked, "How much do you need?"

Baker replied, "$100,000 for everything."

"The funds will be in your account in a few days," Nichols answered. And so it was.

Baker reflected, "What an amazing God we serve. I have often thought if we had looked at it logically, we would have never taken the first baby, because logistically the home was not set up to take in infants nor was there any budget for infant care. But we knew we were not to turn any children away who needed a home. We knew God was with us and would supply our needs. And He did—every step of the way."

It took a few months to build the 4,200 square-foot facility. A few teams came from the States and locals helped, as well. Cheryl made a comment one day saying, "I wish we didn't have to get on our knees and bend over in the bathtubs to wash the babies. It would be nice if we could raise the bathtubs up, but you can't do that, can you?" They did, and there were some happy house moms.

The day they completed and dedicated the baby house was a bittersweet day for Cheryl, since she had taken great pleasure in now having 13 babies living with them in their home. She could hardly bring herself to put them in the newly constructed facility. She cried as she helped carry each one over.

Just after the home's completion, they received four babies at one time. They had been sold by their mothers or had been kidnapped to be sold on the black market. They ranged in age from two months to about one year.

Around 2:00 one morning, Baker heard a knock on the door and found one of the house moms holding the lifeless body of the two-month-old. He took the baby in his arms and he and Cheryl cried and prayed out to the Lord. He put his mouth over hers as Elijah had done with the widow's son and asked God to breathe life into her. He laid her down and lightly rested his body over hers asking for life to come back to her. As he held her close to his chest, the Lord spoke to his heart saying, "In her short life on this earth, she was abandoned and abused by those who should have loved and protected her. She is now in My loving arms, and I will not send her back."

Baby Soyla's funeral—Brent Potter, missionary to Guatemala, helping Baker hold casket

They had a white casket made and planned the funeral, asking a local pastor to minister at the service. Richard held the casket in his arms throughout the entire service, until the very end when he had to ask Brent Potter, a volunteer at Casa Shalom, to come over and help him. This precious baby's death shook them to the core of their hearts. No definitive cause of death could be determined other than crib death. The Bakers and staff just believed the Lord called her home.

When Joshua was about seven or eight, Baker was leaving Casa Shalom in his truck and noticed a number of boys in a huddle. He decided to pull up close to them to see what was happening. They had just accepted a boy about six years old the day before, and he was standing next to Joshua, who was doing the talking. He heard Joshua say in Spanish, "Friends, remember how you felt when you came here for the first time. This boy is like all of us. He doesn't have a mommy, but God has given us our new mommies and a new home, so let's pray for him." And with that, Joshua laid his hands, along with all the other little boys, on the new kid and prayed for him.

Baker was astonished at the words Joshua used and the tenderness of his heart at that moment, especially being so young. They never acknowledge his presence, and after they prayed, they started playing, while Dad drove off wiping tears.

One night around 9:00 pm, Juan the security guard, knocked on the Bakers' door informing them that the police were at the gate with three siblings wanting to know if they could take them. Richard walked down to speak with the officers and, as he drew nearer to them, witnessed three children, five, eight, and 11 shaking. Their faces portrayed fear. The officers told him that a gang had attacked their home killing their parents and two- year-old sibling. After shooting the 11-year-old Mateo in the face, they set fire to the house. Mateo was able to rescue his younger siblings, eight-year-old Isabella, and five-year-old Samuel, from the burning building.

Until now, Baker thought he had experienced all he could, relating to children suffering. But as he looked into the faces of these three devastated children, he knew they had experienced an unspeakable tragedy. The siblings were first taken to the Baker home where Cheryl and Leslie cleaned them up, fed them, and gave them new clothing. They accepted them into the Casa Shalom family that night where they found, not only food, clothing, and shelter, but found a loving group of caregivers who nurtured them and poured the love of Jesus into them.

Baker secured the top plastic surgeon in the country to remove the bullet from Mateo's left cheek, with several churches in the States sending funds for the surgery. The picture below was taken a couple of months after they arrived at Casa Shalom and is a testimony to what God's grace and love can do to heal the brokenness of hearts shattered from enduring such an ordeal. The amazing smiles on their faces tell it all.

They lived at Casa Shalom until they aged out. Isabella is married now with two children. They all three live within 30-45 minutes of Casa Shalom and stay in connect with Brent potter a missionary who served with us at Casa Shalom. It is utterly amazing what God can do with a willing worm.

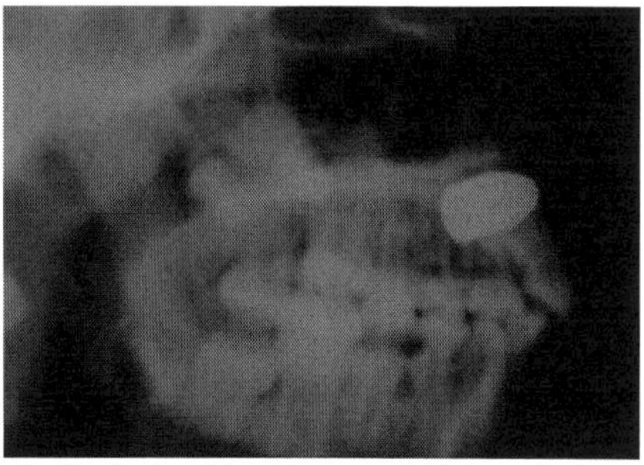

Bullet lodged in 11-year-old Mateo's face.

Mateo with siblings.

Upon entering 2004, the Bakers found themselves hosting more teams than ever. In total, Richard and Cheryl had the wonderful privilege of hosting upwards of 200 mission teams with 50 of them coming to Casa Shalom. Witnessing people experience the mission field was always an amazing experience for him. To see God first-hand transform people's lives and witness some being called into ministry was an awesome thing to be a part of.

In 2004, he ministered and hosted teams in all seven countries of Central America. He was invited to preach the national convention in Belize, and while he was preaching, seven or eight members of a gang walked into the service. The anointing was so strong in that place that as they walked down the aisle, the Holy Spirit prompted him to come down from the platform, even as he preached, and walk up to them. One of them broke down and accepted the Lord. The others left. The true anointing of God always makes the difference and will do one of two things—it will compel or repel. A person cannot encounter the true anointing of God without deciding one way or the other.

Baker also was invited to preach the opening service of the national convention in Nicaragua. They estimated the attendance to be upwards of 8,000, which up to that point was the largest venue he had preached in. T.L. Lowery, along with his wife, flew in on Tuesday morning to preach the evening service. The presence of the Lord electrified the meeting.

In July, Baker felt honored to be asked to preach the first service of the Arizona camp meeting, which was convened in Phoenix. He preached the 9:00 am service on Sunday, and Lowery followed him, preaching at the 10:30 am service. Paul L. Walker preached in the 6:00 pm service. Baker was so thankful to go first, since he did not want to follow these two distinguished ministers of the gospel.

He shared with the congregation that the Lord had given him a new ministry. He related, "A couple of weeks ago, Dr. Lowery flew down to Nicaragua to preach in the convention. I had preached the night before and now I have the privilege to preach ahead of him again. My new ministry is to remove all the binding spirits so it will be easy for him to preach." He said that Lowery looked at him bewildered, and Walker bent over laughing. A person would have to have known Lowery to understand that story.

Baker soon received an invitation to preach the annual convention in Puerto Cabezas, Nicaragua, for the indigenous Miskitos. They had rented a basketball arena for the meeting. As he preached, a demonic man armed with a knife walked inside and headed straight for the platform. Security personnel didn't seem quite sure how to handle the situation. The anointing was powerful on Baker as he preached. When the disturbed man came within 20 feet of the platform, Richard, without forethought, ran and leaped off the six- to seven-foot-high stage and landed within several feet of the detractor. As he continued to preach, the man tried to say something, but the anointing of God was too strong in that arena for Satan to speak. The spirit controlling the man became subdued, and he abruptly departed.

Baker loved these people and worked among them countless times. He and Cheryl even accepted the position of territorial overseer for Mosquito Coast and the Bay Islands, going so far as to pack up their belongings to move to Honduras. But the night before they were to move, the Lord spoke to both of them not to go. A few months later, Cheryl was appointed director of Casa Shalom. Then they understood why God had stopped the move to Honduras.

In January 2005, the field director of all of Latin America, Costello, informed Baker that he would be flying into Guatemala to attend some meetings in Quetzaltenango and wanted him to pick him up and accompany him on the trip. After retrieving him from the airport, the two began their five-hour drive. About two hours into the trip, they stopped at a rustic restaurant, one of Baker's favorites, and enjoyed a wonderful meal and fellowship. As they resumed their journey, darkness began to fall, and conversation waned. After about 30 minutes of quietness, Costello interrupted the silence suggestively stating, "Richard, I feel you need to move your family back to the States."

Costello's statement caught Baker totally off guard. He was not at all sure how to respond. They had no intention of moving and were making plans to retire at Casa Shalom. After a few minutes to collect his thoughts, he composed himself enough to ask, "Why?"

"I don't know why," Costello answered. "They love you down here, but in prayer I felt that you need to return to the States."

"When do you want me to depart?" he asked.

"Stay the rest of this year, if you like," Costello replied. "Return by January 2006."

All Richard could think of was that Cheryl was going to be devastated. The trip lasted three days, after which he returned to Casa Shalom to break the news to Cheryl. She indeed was saddened by the news. He continued fulfilling the tasks he had committed to, and Cheryl was busy as ever caring for the children.

In early July while in prayer, he felt impressed to call the Church of God State office in Lawrenceville, Georgia, and speak with Steve Brown, the evangelism director for the state. His secretary said he was in prayer and then realized that Baker was calling from out of country. She asked him to wait a minute to see if he could talk. Steve answered the phone and asked, "Richard Baker, what's up?"

Baker answered, "I don't know but I felt lead in prayer to call you."

Brown immediately responded, "I know why. I guess you know Pastor Green, who followed you at the church in Cumming, retired from full-time ministry, and the church has been without a pastor for six weeks. Things are starting to come unraveled. Bishop Donald Walker asked me to agree in prayer with him for 30 minutes that God would lead us to the right pastor for the church, and you called out of the blue."

Baker replied, "Steve, we didn't know Pastor Green had resigned. Nor am I sure God is leading us to return to pastoring right now."

About 30 minutes after talking with Brown, Walker called and shared just how desperate he felt the situation was. He said, "Just pray about it, Richard. If you can just commit two years, it would be great to get the church stabilized."

The Bakers sincerely prayed for a few days. However, their biggest obstacle was that they were in the middle of the adoption process for Melanie, and Cheryl wasn't going anywhere without her. He finally called Walker back and shared with him their dilemma.

Walker pleaded, "Richard, would you just come and preach and meet with the council before you say no?"

Not wanting to dismiss the possibility of this being God's will, he flew the next week to Atlanta and preached on Sunday morning. He struggled in delivering the message. The attendance was off by 100, and that was troubling. During the council meeting, the men were surprised that he was even considering coming back. Baker answered any questions they had and asked a few of his own.

On the return flight to Guatemala, he began to sense confirmation from the Lord that returning to Cumming was indeed His will. He called Walker and informed him that if he got the vote, they would come back. However, he said that he could only commit to one year. Although he was willing to stay longer, he could not feel released at the time to commit to any more than a year.

The next Sunday, the overseer preached in Cumming and took a vote. Although the vote wasn't what he wanted, it was a majority, and he felt God could possibly use him to bring healing in the body.

30

The Lazarus Foundation

During the first week in August, Richard and Joshua boarded a plane for Atlanta leaving Cheryl and Melanie at Casa Shalom, as the adoption had not been finalized. They temporarily moved in with Homer and Marie Foster, while one of the members, Diane Whitmire, loaned Baker a car until he could purchase one. He enrolled Joshua in school and went to the church to begin setting up his office. The atmosphere in the church was cold, not anything like the church they had left nearly six years earlier. He knew he had his work cut out for him.

Church attendance stood at a little over 200, and after a couple of weeks, the services began to warm up. Still, he knew something was not right. He began to pray and fast for God to show him where the hindrances lay. There were serious problems, and he needed to know what and where they were.

He later wrote, "The Lord showed me at least two extramarital affairs within the church, one being a leader. I braced myself for the inevitable storm I knew was coming and dealt with one of the situations. Within four weeks, five or six families left the church, which not only affected the attendance but also the finances. I had just hired a full-time minister of music. But God is always on your side when you take a stand for righteousness. By December, our attendance had dropped to the 150-range causing morale to sink. The only good news was that the adoption of Melanie was finalized, and I flew down and brought Cheryl and her home on December 21."

As the year 2006 began, the spirit of worship began to return to the church. With Cheryl now at his side and Melanie with them, his spirits were lifted, and he felt ready to dig in and try to rebuild the church.

Scott, the new minister of music, reenergized the music and attendance began picking up slightly. In early March, Nichols called and asked if he could fly down with him and a few other people to Quito, Ecuador. Baker explained that he didn't feel comfortable leaving the church on a Sunday but that he had no problem leaving on Monday and returning on Friday.

Nichols shared that he and John Gregory, who was unknown to Baker at the time, wanted his opinion on a couple of projects they were thinking about funding. He told Baker to meet them at the Chattanooga airport. When he arrived, he was escorted to a private jet. He immediately thought, "Lord, what in the world is going on?"

He boarded the plane and was introduced to Gregory. Also aboard were Bill Leonard, Gene Rice, and, of course, John Nichols. They took off for Quito, stopping in the Grand Cayman Islands to refuel.

L to R: Bill Leonard, Richard Baker, John Gregory, Gene Rice, John Nichols.

After arriving in Quito and checking into a hotel, Gregory asked to have a meeting with Baker. They met for a couple of hours and over the next few days visited several humanitarian projects and one seminary. By the end of week, Baker discovered that Gregory had been the CEO of a pharmaceutical company and was a philanthropist with a special focus on widows and orphans. On Friday, they boarded the jet and returned home.

A few weeks earlier, Angie Altamirano (McInvale), who operated an orphanage in San Pedro Sula, Honduras, had contacted Baker about struggling financially to keep things afloat at the children's home. As they were flying back to the States, he asked the pilot to let him know when they were over Honduras. When he later received a thumps-up from the pilot, he asked to speak to Gregory and informed him that they were passing over Honduras. He then told him about Angie and her children's home being in need.

Richard, Gregory, Nichols, & Rice at Casa Shalom (March 2006)
Construction on house for older girls.

Gregory asked, "Richard, what is her monthly budget?"

Baker answered, "Three thousand dollars."

The philanthropist looked at Nichols and instructed him saying, "When you get back, send her $18,000 to help her for six months." Gregory then resumed the conversation he was having before Baker asked to speak with him.

Upon returning home, he shared details of the trip with Cheryl and settled back into pastoring the church. He had invited Nichols to preach for him the first week in April. He and his wife, Doreen, arrived on Saturday, and Cheryl prepared a home cooked meal. As Cheryl brought the ham to the table, Nichols spoke up, "Richard, John wants to hire you to help us give better oversight to the projects we are funding." Cheryl almost dropped the ham. He continued, "If you are interested, he wants to interview you this coming Thursday."

Baker exclaimed, "I am caught completely off guard! I will need time to pray."

Nichols replied, "You got three days."

After spending the next three days praying, Baker felt he needed to speak directly to Gregory before he could make such a life-changing decision. He met with both Gregory and Nichols. Both appeared casual and explained in detail what his role would be. Nichols was serving as the executive director of the Lazarus Foundation, and he would serve under him as the director of field operations.

Baker asked, "When do you want me start?"

They answered, "Immediately."

He then shared with them that he had committed to Walker that he would give a full year at the church and didn't feel he could break his promise. Also, he was concerned about leaving the church so abruptly.

Gregory asked, "When is the year up?"

Baker answered, "July 30."

"Then you can start July 31 with us," Gregory declared.

Feeling the Lord was leading all of them in this direction, he agreed. After informing his overseer of his decision, Walker graciously accepted his resignation effective July 30.

In early June, Walker contacted Baker and informed him that there was a pastor in Maine wanting to come to the Atlanta area and start a church. Baker mentioned River of Life to him (the name had changed). After checking with the pastor, Walker related to Baker that they would be in town the following week and wanted to stop by, see the facilities, and speak with him. He had been praying that a pastor would become available before he officially resigned. Jason and Shannon Bailey met with him, and the rest is history. A week or two after Baker resigned, the church accepted the new pastor. Fourteen years later, they are still pastoring the church.

Resigning a church is one of the hardest things a pastor ever has to do. The congregation doesn't have all the pieces of the puzzle available to them to understand the dynamics of how God leads pastors and other church leaders to a different area of ministry. But a true servant of God knows when he has finished the task God has assigned, as he senses the plow moving in a different direction.

A decision was made involving the Lazarus Foundation, Church of God World Missions, and the Executive Committee to form a closer partnership, and that Baker's office would be in the World Missions Department. That, of course, meant moving to Cleveland. The Bakers had just purchased a home in Cumming seven or eight months earlier and were concerned about having to sell it so quickly knowing they would probably incur a significant loss. The home sold in less than two weeks, and they actually made a few thousand dollars. After purchasing a home in Bradley County a few miles out of Cleveland, they settled in to their new ministry.

Baker's first day in the office was chaotic since several staff members' offices had not been assigned. He still was not completely sure just how he would function in his new dual role. Already, he was thinking that if a conflict arose between World Missions and the Lazarus Foundation, he would be caught in the middle. He spent the month of August getting acclimated to his two new jobs. For World Missions, he would serve as project and disaster relief coordinator and as the liaison to the Lazarus Foundation. As for the foundation itself, he would serve as director of field operations.

In early September, he received an alarming call about the Phebe Gray Orphanage in Liberia. Dwain Pyeatt, who served as an educational coordinator, was visiting Bible schools in Africa and while in Liberia decided to visit the orphanage. Pyeatt shared with him that the children were suffering considerably, and rice seemed to be all they had to eat. He only had a limited amount of cash on him, but he gave what he could to help.

The Lazarus Foundation had built the orphanage in 1996 during the civil war that lasted from 1989 until 2003—a war in which 10 percent of the population was killed and many more wounded and suffering.

Baker reported the information to Gregory who instructed him to fly to Liberia as soon as possible. He also instructed him to take at least $5,000 cash with him to render immediate help, if it was needed. Since there were no direct flights to Liberia, he had to overnight in Ghana and catch a flight to Liberia the next day.

A church official, who had been the national overseer of Liberia and now was living and working in Ghana, offered to meet him at the airport, secure lodging at a hotel, and travel with him to Liberia. After dropping him off at the hotel and returning the following morning, the two sat in his room for a while just getting to know each other. The Lord began prompting Baker to ask him more direct questions about how the orphanage received funding under his administration and how it provided accountability to the donors.

Although Baker did not suspect him of financial indiscretions, the leader began crying and saying, "Your spirit is piercing my heart like an arrow. I must confess." As he shared certain information, Baker let him talk realizing God was giving him evidence he would need to expose even greater corruption moving forward, not just in Liberia, but in other nations as well.

They arrived in Liberia and went directly to the hotel. It had been two years since the war had ended and still generators provided their electricity throughout the country. The hotel was very rough, and, honestly, Baker was uncomfortable remaining there alone. Since the day had been long, he was tired and turned in for the night.

About 2:00 in the morning, he awoke and felt the Holy Spirit prompting him to stand up. As he did, he heard the door being breached, with one man stepping slightly through the door entrance. Without a second thought, he charged the door, hitting it with his shoulder, and pushing the man back out. The door closed behind him. He realized that three men had tried to enter his room. Unsettled, he was afraid to go back to sleep or to leave his room till morning. To this day, he believes a hit was placed on him, since he was about to expose a good deal of corruption.

The next morning around 7:00, a minister from Ghana and a pastor from Monrovia, along with a UN driver, picked him up for breakfast and then took him to visit Phebe Gray Orphanage. They were surprised to see him waiting in the lobby with his bags packed and ready to check out. After explaining to them the intrusion of the previous night, he informed them that he did not intend to remain there any longer. He asked them to find him more secure lodging before their visit to the orphanage.

Once they found a much nicer and more secure hotel for him and checked him in, they had breakfast together. During breakfast, the former overseer asked Baker his agenda and the purpose of his visiting the orphanage. Considering that they had had a lengthy conversation the morning before in Ghana, the question seemed strange to Baker.

Upon his arrival at the orphanage, Baker was unprepared for one of the coldest receptions he had ever received–not only by the staff but also by the children. He would later discover that the former overseer had informed them not to approach him. After spending about an hour at home, he asked a worker to assemble all the children together so he could speak to them.

Within a few minutes, all 112 children and most, if not all, of the 15-member staff were gathered in an open area. He began speaking to them about God's love for them and the provisions He wanted to bless them with. Further, he told them who he was, for whom he worked, and his purpose in being there. Baker shared with them that Gregory was so concerned for them that he asked him to leave for Liberia immediately. Detecting a change in their countenance, he asked the children a question he asked all children in orphanages he visited. "If you could have anything today your heart would desire, what would it be?"

Usually when he asked this question, the children would shout out, "A ball, clothes, ice-cream, candy!" He pointed at an 11 or 12-year-old girl and declared, "She will be the spokesperson. Talk among yourselves, and she will tell me what you desire most."

After discussing his question for a few minutes, the girl raised her hand indicating that she was ready to give their answer. She replied, "We have decided that if we could have anything today, our hearts' desire is that we would like to have a little piece of chicken with our rice."

Baker soon discovered that for the past four months, they had been mainly surviving on white rice occasionally supplemented with a few beans. Their only drinking source was a hand-operated well on campus that did not produce enough water for the children's home. As he stood there trying to comprehend the enormity of needs this children's home had, he sensed the Lord speaking to his heart saying, "I have seen the suffering of My children and have heard their cries to Me. That is why you have been sent."

After quickly pulling the leadership together, he inquired, "Where can we buy a truckload of food for the children, including chicken?" Seeing the orphanage had no electricity, he knew that any perishable items would have to be eaten immediately.

They drove to Monrovia, which was about 30 miles away, and rented a truck from a local man. After purchasing as many non-perishable food items as they could load onto the Toyota pick-up, Baker purchased 150 pounds of chicken, all with funds from the Lazarus Foundation. He also purchased the largest generator he could find, so the orphanage could at least have a little light at night. In addition, he also purchased medicines, since many of the children, having no mosquito nets for protection at night, had malaria.

When the truck returned loaded with food, the children and staff began to openly weep. The cooks immediately went to work preparing the evening meal of chicken, rice, beans, vegetables, bread, juice, and dessert. Baker expressed, "What an amazing privilege for me to be able to help serve these precious children a meal that most, if not all, had never sat down to before."

When Baker departed, he left $2,000 with the orphanage and gave strict instructions that the gift was to serve the wellbeing of the children and staff. Furthermore, they were to keep all receipts. He communicated with them that if they were trustworthy with donations, they would never find themselves in this predicament again. He knew in his heart that Gregory, through the Lazarus Foundation, would start sending support regularly.

Baker's schedule had him fly to Sierra Leone the next morning to visit an elementary school/feeding center that the Lazarus Foundation had recently built. He received notification that the airline had canceled the flight and that the next flight would not be for another three days. One of the local Church of God pastors informed him that he had access to a small four-by-four SUV in which they could drive to Freetown, the capital of Sierra Leone, in roughly 16 hours. Baker, always up for a little adventure, agreed. The pastor also had connections with the UN which provided them with a driver, since they were doing humanitarian work.

The team set off at 4:00 the next morning, arriving in about two hours at the Liberian/Sierra Leone border. After crossing into Sierra Leone, Baker found that roads were almost non-existent. They crossed game reserves and drove through small villages. Around lunchtime they entered a rustic village inhabited mostly by Muslims. At the center of the village, they found a man sitting under a shelter and asked if they could have lunch there—a lunch of broiled fish, potatoes, and bread prepared by the pastor's wife.

The man graciously obliged them. The temperature was around 100 degrees, and they were thankful for the shelter from the sun.

At one place on their journey, they had to cross a river on a wooden ferry, which was towed back and forth by several men pulling large ropes. The entire trip through Sierra Leone was on dirt paths often framed by brush on both sides scraping against the vehicle. Finally, around 6:00 pm, they pulled into Freetown, checked into a hotel, and refreshed themselves.

The following morning, they visited the school/feeding center and the small medical clinic. An African American couple from the state of Delaware served as directors. Baker was amazed with the ministry they were providing. Two hundred-fifty children, most coming from Muslim homes, lined up in front of him, quoted scriptures, and sang worship songs to the Lord. He was deeply touched by the presentation. The Muslims allowed their children to attend the Christian school because of the quality education offered. He visited the school three or four more times over the next eight years. On his last visit, the school had over 400 students, of whom more than 95 percent had accepted Christ. In fact, a church was built onsite because the children started witnessing to their parents, and many became Christians.

After a rewarding visit, Baker and his traveling companions departed on the 16-hour drive back to Liberia. He had become so weary being cramped in the back seat of the small Nissan SUV that it seemed that every few feet he felt another bump. About 10 hours into the journey, as they maneuvered down a path through thick brush, a large rope at least six inches in diameter stretched across the path in front of them, forcing the driver to stop. Four gunmen, two on each side, rushed out with AK-47s drawn. Baker turned to his right to see one of the gunmen with his gun barrel pressed against the glass pointed at his head. He remembers thinking, "We probably won't survive this, and Cheryl doesn't even know I am in Sierra Leone!"

In 2002, Sierra Leone had just ended a bloody civil war in which many were killed or maimed, some reports up to 300,000. No doubt these gunmen were part of the leftover rebel movement. The UN driver, who was not a believer, instructed his passengers to remain seated and allow him to try to talk with them. He exited the vehicle and began explaining their presence there. After about five minutes, an argument ensued, and the Ghanaian and Liberian pastors slowly exited the vehicle to reason with the men. Of course, Baker was intensely praying, considering that he still had a gun barrel pointed at his head.

After another five to ten had minutes had passed, the apparent leader of the gunmen began getting quite agitated. At this point, Baker really became alarmed. He thought, "If this doesn't end well, I prefer to be standing."

He slowly started opening the door of the truck, with the man continuing to hold the gun on him, although stepping back a little to let him exit. Slowly making his way to the other side of the vehicle, as he rounded it, the leader of group roughly asked in English, "What are you doing traveling through the back country?"

Baker answered, "We are with a humanitarian organization that is doing relief projects in several countries in West Africa."

He then ordered them to open the back of their SUV. The first thing he saw was a large canvas tarp with something wrapped up in it. He asked Baker, "What's wrapped up in the tarp?"

"One hundred fifty mosquito nets," he replied.

Accusingly he exclaimed, "You are trading on the black market!" With that, he ran his bayonet into the canvas tarp and demanded, "What are you doing with so many mosquito nets?"

Once again Baker explained the humanitarian nature of their presence. He remarked that since they were unable to find mosquito nets in Liberia, they had to purchase them in Sierra Leone and transport them to Phoebe Gray orphanage, where the children were suffering from malaria.

Still not satisfied with Baker's answers, the man asked suspiciously, "Why are you doing this? What's in it for you?"

At that moment, Baker felt led to share a little of his testimony with him. He declared, "I was a drug dealer and had been locked up five times. At an early age, I became bound to drugs and alcohol, but then I found Jesus and was completely set free. The Lord sent me here to help the suffering orphans."

The spokesman responded, "I am a Muslim, and we don't do this to help people in need." He then asked Baker what church he was a part of.

He answered, "The Church of God."

In quick response, he asked, "How do I become part of the Church of God?"

At that point, the Liberian pastor stepped in and explained to him that serving God was not about being part of a denomination but was about having a personal relationship with Jesus Christ. As this conversation was taking place, the other three gunmen returned to the bush and were seen no more. When the pastor asked the man if he wanted to ask Jesus into his heart, he broke down crying out, "Yes, yes, please!"

That day a Muslim rebel accepted the King of kings and Lord of lords as his Savior. The ministers asked him to stay in the area for a few hours to give them an opportunity to find someone to disciple him. After driving about an hour, they came to a river crossing and asked a local resident if there was a pastor close by. Confirmation that God had orchestrated this entire event came when another pastor rode up on his bicycle. The pastor explained what had just happened, and the newly arrived pastor agreed to go see if the newly converted Muslim was still waiting.

Baker handed the pastor a love offering and watched as he rode back down the path. The Liberian pastor had given his cell number to the local pastor and asked him to let him know if he contacted the man. After Baker returned to the States, the Liberian pastor emailed him informing him that the man was patiently waiting for him. Interestingly, the man lived not far the pastor's church. The born-again Muslim began attending and serving Christ.

"What if the flight had not been canceled?" Baker thought. "This Muslim man would probably still be lost today." He had been praying for God to let him lead a Muslim to the Lord. He remarked, "Be careful what you pray for, because God answers in ways you are not expecting."

After returning to Liberia, the troupe dropped off the mosquito nets at the orphanage. The next morning as Baker prepared to depart for the airport, the new national overseer for the Churches of God in Liberia, Moses Hart, came to his hotel to meet him. As they conversed, Baker discerned in his spirit that the overseer's heart was pure and that he could be trusted. He joyfully returned to the US amazed at the incredible journey and ministry the Lord had allowed him to be a part of.

When he arrived back home, he shared with Gregory the horrible plight that the children at Phebe Gray Orphanage were enduring. He then presented the budget he had put together while in Liberia to adequately care for the children. Gregory agreed to start sending monthly support immediately but wanted him to return the first of 2007.

Gregory also wanted Baker to launch an inquiry into how the Lazarus Foundation funds had been expended since the children's home had been built and had become operational. Baker's findings revealed that only about 70 percent of the total donated funds actually made it to Liberia. The mistake was rectified, and the funds were returned to the Lazarus Foundation.

Shortly after, Baker shared with Roland Vaughn, director of World Missions, the dire situation he had witnessed in Liberia and asked if he could do a promotional video to raise funds for the orphanage. He wanted to help rebuild churches that had been destroyed during the 14-year-long civil war. Vaughn agreed and a trip was planned for January 2007.

Baker's next trip would take him to Cambodia and Thailand. Fred Garmon, executive director of People for Care and Learning (PCL), a non-profit organization, asked him to travel with him to Southeast Asia. Bill George, who served as educational coordinator for Church of God World Missions and gave oversight to more than 100 Bible schools, accompanied them.

The team spent a week visiting different projects that PCL was spearheading. Baker was impressed. PCL also operated an orphanage in Siem Reap, Cambodia. The Lazarus Foundation a few years earlier had given the seed money to start this orphanage.

Once back in the States, Garmon asked Baker to serve on PCL's board of directors. He consented, feeling that it would be a worthwhile investment of his time. Also, knowing that the Lazarus Foundation had already invested heavily in the establishment of PCL added another layer of validity to the work.

Before the end of the year, Baker made a quick trip to El Salvador and Guatemala to visit the orphanages there. He was thrilled to visit Casa Shalom again but, sadly, some of the children were still perplexed as to why the Bakers left. Still to this day, Richard and Cheryl feel bittersweet about their departure.

By the end of 2006, Richard was getting adjusted to his new ministry role and was feeling more than ever that he and Cheryl were definitely in the center of God's will.

January 2007 found him back in Liberia, since Gregory wanted to make sure the children were receiving proper care now that the Lazarus Foundation was giving financial support. Church of God World Missions also had approved for him to produce two videos, one focusing on the Phebe Gray Orphanage and the other on the devastation the 14-year-long civil war had on the churches. Of the 65 Churches of God in Liberia, all of them were either destroyed or damaged.

World Missions dispatched a professional cameraman to accompany Richard. They were able to produce two powerful videos shot on location, which highlighted the plight of the orphans and the general population during the civil war. From these two videos, more funds were raised than through any video World Missions had produced up to that time—one-half million dollars. Immediately, churches began to be rebuilt, and improvements were made to the children's home.

On this trip Baker also got to spend some quality time with national overseer, Hart. Again, the Holy Spirit bore witness to him that Hart was a sincere and honest man. For the past 14 years, he had served in that position and had been a significant help to the children's home and was also a blessing to him.

While he walked around the Phebe Gray campus, a 16-year-old young man walked up to him and asked, "Can I speak privately with you?" After walking under a large tree away from everyone, he asked, "Are you are employed by the Lazarus Foundation?"

Richard answered, "Yes, I am."

The young man continued, "My name is John Gregory, and that makes me your boss. I am about to graduate high school (in Liberia, high school goes through the 10th grade. Their 11th grade is equivalent to the freshman year in college in the States). I need to go to college because in Liberia if you don't get a college education, you will live in poverty the rest of your life." Frankly, Baker thought that the young man was quite witty.

He told the student that he would speak with Hart and find to find the cost of tuition, room, and board. Hart informed him that the total cost per semester would be around $1,800. Baker checked his grades and found that they were good. He then went back to the 16-year-old "John Gregory" and announced, "I can authorize only one semester now, but if you keep your grades up, I will do everything in my power to see you complete your four-year degree in education." He wanted to be a schoolteacher.

When Baker returned to the States, he discovered the rest of the story of Liberian "John Gregory." As he met with Gregory to go over the details of his trip to Liberia, he mentioned, "Something funny happened at Phebe Gray. I met a 16-year-old John Gregory."

Gregory started laughing and said, "Let me fill in the puzzle for you. Back in 1997 or '98, John Nichols and I flew to visit the home for the first time. Two boys, both about seven years old, performed a skit. One played me and the other played Dr. Nichols. The one playing me asked, 'Dr.

Nichols, are we still supporting orphanages?' The boy playing Dr. Nichols answered, 'Yes, we are.' The boy playing me responded, 'Not those rich North American orphanages, but the orphanages that are in need like Phebe Gray.'"

He then related to Baker that the young man probably thought he knew about the skit they did. Gregory loved it and declared, "By all means, if he keeps his grades up, give him a full ride."

Four years later, August 2011, "John Gregory" finished college with high honors and received his bachelor's degree. Baker had planned his trip to Africa to coincide with his graduation but, because of changes beyond his control, had arrived the day after. The president of Liberia, Ellen Johnson Sirleaf, decided to have one graduation ceremony for all the high schools and colleges, which would convene at the national soccer stadium. She planned to give the commencement address but asked "John Gregory" of Phebe Gray Children's Home to offer the invocation. Baker reflected, "Such a worm as I could not have been any more thrilled." The new college graduate returned to the orphanage and started teaching at the school he had attended as a boy. He shared with Baker that he wanted to give back and help others who were less fortunate as he was.

On a humorous note, when Baker brought all the children together and asked them what they wanted, the answer caught him a bit off guard. They replied, "Spareribs and sweet potatoes."

He looked at Hart and asked, "Can we buy spareribs in Liberia?"

Hart responded, "Yes, we can." So, they drove to Monrovia and purchased 150 pounds of spareribs and sweet potatoes. What a feast they had that evening!

When Baker departed the children's home heading for the airport, he left a different scene than he had back in September. This time the children were laughing, playing, and eating three meals a day. And not one of them had malaria. Through the support of World Missions and a commitment from the Lazarus Foundation, that included the building of a new kitchen and cafeteria, Baker was able to oversee the shipment of a 40-foot container full of items the home needed: furnishings, computers, a desk, a large generator, and kitchen equipment. A highlight was the giving of Christmas gifts to the children. This was perhaps the first time these children had received a gift of any kind. As they unwrapped their presents, Baker started weeping. When Hart asked him if something was wrong, he answered, "Oh no, these are tears of joy."

31

Zambia and Kenya

Baker's next trip took him to Zambia. The Lazarus Foundation had contributed heavily to two orphanages there, and Gregory asked Baker to check on them. Before his departure, Gregory asked him to visit one of them without giving notification of his visit. That is, he was to show up unannounced. He contacted a missionary, David Mills, and asked him to help him by arranging a car and driver, and, if possible, accompany him for two or three days.

Upon his arrival, Mills was waiting for him with a car and driver. The driver was a Church of God minister and served on the board of directors for the first orphanage he was going to visit, an orphanage that Gregory had some concerns about. Baker was unaware of this until he mentioned where he needed to go. In response, the driver asked, "Does the director know you are coming?"

Baker answered, "No, he doesn't."

The driver expressed, "This puts me in an awkward position, and I will have to notify him first."

Since he was seven hours away on business and Baker's entourage was only two to three hours away, he gave him permission to call the director, who asked Baker over the phone why he didn't notify him. Baker informed him that Gregory had instructed him to show up unannounced. Not being in a position to resist, he gave permission for the board member to transport him to the orphanage.

Upon his arrival, it became evident that the report of 700 orphans living here was grossly overstated. The home was very rustic and not well maintained. Considering the $700,000 the Lazarus Foundation had poured into it, along with hundreds of thousands of dollars from other organizations, caused Richard to sense in his spirit that something was not right.

After spending about two hours at the home, a few other board members arrived. Baker asked Mills to speak to a couple of them alone while he spoke to the other two. He gave him several questions to ask–the same ones he would use. They would then compare notes.

One of the questions had to do with how many children lived at the home. Mills' group told him there were 600-plus, while Baker's group informed him that there were from 200 to 300. With all the questions Baker and Mills asked, the two groups never came close to giving the same answers.

The home only had 46 bunk beds, which meant that the maximum number of children they could accommodate was 92. They did appear to have 150 to 200 children on campus, but one of the workers shared with Baker that some neighborhood children came to play and get a meal.

Bidding farewell, they departed for the next orphanage, Emma's Kids, which was approximately a 12-hour drive. They overnighted in Lusaka, the capital, and arrived at the orphanage the following afternoon. Roger and Sandra Wyklund were the founders and directors of Emma's Kids. The Lazarus Foundation had invested $400,000 into this home with a large portion of it going to help build a school on the premises. An apartment complex adjacent to the home, which contained 20 two and three-bedroom apartments in decent shape, had come up for sale. The Wyklunds submitted a request for a grant to purchase the apartments with the intention of using four or five of the apartments for staff and visitors. The others would be rented to help support the orphanage's ongoing monthly expenses. Later, Baker presented the proposal for a grant to Gregory. The Lazarus Foundation invested about $250,000 in the acquisition of this apartment complex.

One of the first things on the agenda for Baker and Mills upon their arrival was touring the facilities. The home had 75 to 80 children and staff living 100 percent of the time at the home and another 200 to 300 who attended school and participated in the feeding program. The home also had a small clinic staffed by a nurse. As they entered the assembly area, the children began to sing and worship the Lord. Later Baker reflected, "I will never forget a little eight-year-old girl named Esther that came up to me, placed her hands over the top of my feet, and prayed one of the most powerful prayers that anyone has ever prayed over me."

The next stop on the tour was the medical clinic. As they entered, they saw a small girl about four or five years old lying in a bed. It was evident to them that she was in severe pain. When Baker inquired about her condition, Sandra said that a couple of days ago she fell into an open fire. As she removed the sheet, he looked in shear horror at her chest and arms, which were burned severely with second- and third-degree burns.

Deeply moved and disturbed, Baker emphatically asked, "Why is she not in a hospital?"

Sandra replied, "They won't take her without payment, and we don't have the funds available."

He cried out, "Take her to the hospital immediately. The Lazarus Foundation will cover all expenses!"

In response, she exclaimed, "They only take cash!"

Baker directed, "Take her and see how much they need today, and I will have the rest wired to them."

It wasn't until the next day that the child was transported to the hospital. They asked for $2,500 up front and on the day she would be dismissed, they agreed to accept a wire transfer. The precious little girl survived and recovered. She needed plastic surgeries and perhaps more when she gets older. A copper mining company owned the private hospital. After she spent a couple of weeks in the hospital, the Lazarus Foundation wired less than $10,000, which covered everything from the hospital bill to the doctors and medicines. When Sandra later sent Baker the pictures of the little girl holding a teddy bear with a big smile on her face, he knew that God had sent His "worm" on one more mission.

Upon returning to Lusaka, the director met them and offered to take him and the former overseer to dinner. He took them to an upscale Asian restaurant close to the US Embassy. As the party of three sat down, the first words out of his mouth were, "I know why Dr. John Gregory sent you here, and I don't blame him."

He appeared quite surprised that he had gotten away with so much fraud for such a long time. Baker's investigation ultimately revealed that he had received funding from the German Embassy, the Swedish Embassy, and a NGO based out of Tennessee, all for the same project at the orphanage.

After dinner, Baker asked him to take him to the office for the orphanage, which was conveniently situated just up the road within walking distance of the restaurant. The entire area was an affluent part of the capital city. Upon entering the office, Baker and missionary, David Mills, were shocked by the lavishness of the workplace. It was more luxurious than both Baker's and Gregory's. The desk was eight feet long and hand carved. He heard that it cost $8,000 in Zambia, which would have been $20,000 or more in the States. The Lazarus Foundation had given the funds to build the office but didn't know they were located hours away from the children's home.

Understandably, the director had just received his last dollar from the Lazarus Foundation. Baker notified the director of the NGO in Tennessee to share with him his findings. He was saddened to get the news but thanked Baker for informing him.

As he later reflected on the matter of corruption, especially as it related to giving to charitable organizations around the world, he wrote:

> I have been involved in humanitarian work/ministry since 1993 in some capacity. I have visited 70 countries, some of them as many as 50 times. I have made 400 site-visits to orphanages alone, not counting feeding centers and refugee camps. I have personally worked more than a dozen disasters, natural and manmade. I truly believe that most NGOs, even those based in third-world countries, are very honest and have compassionate hearts, and are very sincere in their efforts to relive suffering among those they are serving. Although I have no hardcore statistics to give, when considering all the projects and ministries I have visited around the world within many different cultures, I fully believe that no more than two percent are corrupted.

The next stop took him to Nairobi, Kenya. One of the office personnel from the Kibera Orphanage met him. The orphanage was located next to the Kibera slums, purportedly the second largest populated slum in the world with a reported 2.5 million dwellers.

In the early 2000s, Gregory, along with his family, and Nichols, traveled to Nairobi and visited an orphanage close to the Kibera slums. The orphanage was quite small and offered only humble dwellings packed with children. A pastor and his wife served as directors and shared with Gregory that there were many more homeless children needing a place to live, but they had no more space.

After arriving back in the States, Gregory and Nichols had a deeper conversation about the orphanage they had visited. Both felt the Lord leading them to build a much larger and better facility than the one that existed. In response, they made the decision to move forward. The Lazarus Foundation spent 2.5 million dollars to purchase the land and construct a large and immaculate campus capable of housing several hundred children, along with an on-campus school. Larry Jones with the Feed the Children organization said it was the most impressive orphanage in the entire world.

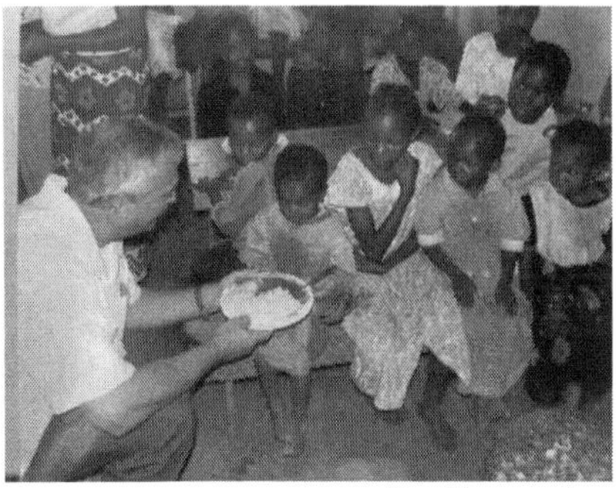
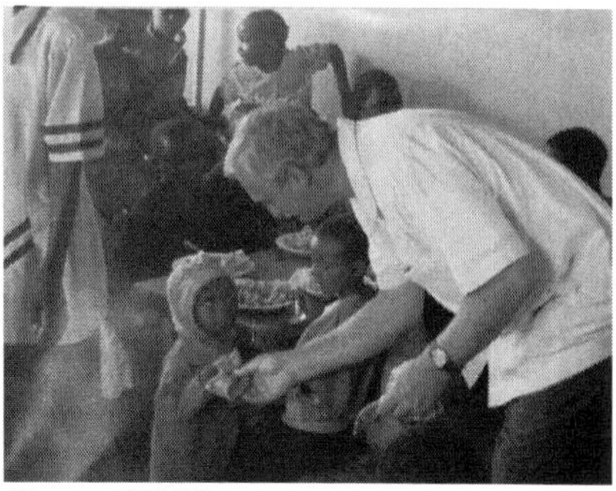

Feeding orphans in Kenya (2007).

At the time of Baker's visit, the director and his wife were in the States fundraising. The home had an in-house population of 160 children with another 200 attending school. There was also a large church on campus with a seating capacity between 400 and 500. He had not visited, before or since, such a facility. He remarked, "How blessed these children were to be able to live in such a nice and safe place, learn about Jesus, and get a quality education."

Over the next eight years, Baker would visit the Kibera orphanage seven or eight times, once with Nichols accompanying him and twice with Gregory. Unfortunately, there were some issues here as well, but presently those issues have been rectified, and the home is operating smoothly, caring for the most vulnerable of society, the orphans.

In 2002, the Lazarus Foundation funded another orphanage, school, and feeding center project which was located about a 45-minute drive from Kibera Children's Home. Tumaini (Swahili for hope) Children's Center was birthed in the heart of Pastor David Hinga and his wife, Alice. During Baker's first visit, he found that many of the children had been sent to stay with extended families or temporary families for a couple of weeks. He thought that the ministry had a wonderful approach to caring for orphans. They would locate families close nearby, most of whom were very poor themselves. The children would stay with them from about 6:00 pm until

7:30 the next morning, when the children would report back to Tumaini. All three meals and a snack were provided for them at the center, but also the family hosting them would receive food as well for their family. It was a brilliant concept.

While Baker served as executive director of the Lazarus Foundation in 2012, a position to which he was appointed in 2009 after the untimely passing of Nichols, they funded a building project that doubled the size of their capacity. At the height of their ministry, there were over 600 children were being caring for. He had the privilege of visiting this ministry more than a dozen times, once with Gregory and Nichols.

Before returning to the states, he had one more orphanage to visit, one located in Kampala, Uganda. Joseph Kagarma, who at the time pastored a church and served as national overseer for the Churches of God, and presently serves as the superintendent for East Africa, contacted him and shared the dire need of providing care for the children at Grace Home for Children.

When Baker arrived at the home, Kagarma shared with him that a few years earlier a pastor and his wife had died of malaria and left several children orphans. He explained, “My wife told me to go get the children, and we will raise them.” He looked at his American contact and said, “Brother Baker, she hasn’t stopped taking in orphan children since then. We managed to acquire a small piece of property adjacent to the church I pastor, with a few small buildings, but it is grossly inadequate.”

After touring the home, two things became evident to Baker. First, the Kagarmas loved and cared for the children to the best of their ability. Second, the home was much in need of major repairs. There was little in the way of furnishings, kitchen equipment, and bedding. The children needed clothing, school supplies, and the home had no electricity. He could truly sense Kagarma’s dilemma. On the one hand, he and his wife had a burden to care for orphaned children, but on the other hand, there simply were not enough resources coming in to adequately care for the children. Perhaps the most difficult task for someone called to humanitarian ministry is to discern what the will of the Lord is in each situation.

Baker knew that Gregory was counting on him to give wise counsel and direction just as well as the Church of God World Missions was. Many times, he felt immense pressure to make a recommendation one way or the other, which was especially difficult since there were only so many resources available. Under such circumstances, the person responsible has to ascertain if the leadership is willing, or even has the ability, to manage a ministry properly. He often came across people with compassionate hearts but simply lacked the ability to provide needed management. These were some of the loneliest times for him as he sought to know and discern the appropriate direction to take in each situation

After seeking God for His will, he felt impressed in his heart to immediately release some funds to help Kagarma, until he got back to the States and could meet with Gregory.

While he was there, he purchased fresh vegetables, meat, and as a special treat for the children, ice cream. He bought pots, pans, utensils, and other small items the home desperately needed. After returning to the States and meeting with Gregory, he agreed to have the municipality run electrical lines to the property and to begin making improvements to the buildings. Baker has visited this home many times since that first visit, and he is especially thankful that he could discern the voice of God for this orphanage.

In April he returned to Liberia to preach the national convention and check on the progress of churches being rebuilt. While there he knew that he could not pass up the opportunity to visit Phebe Gray Children's Home.

Many of the pastors live in rural areas and are unable to afford the trip to the capital. Funds became available for Baker to assist every pastor in the country who wanted to attend. Cooks were hired and food purchased to prepare all the meals on site. He asked Hart for a list of all the pastors and how many children they each had. On the last day of the convention, he met with each pastor privately in a small office and gave them a love-offering equivalent to three to four month's salary.

During the meeting a young pastor around 30 years old, who lived approximately eight hours away by bus, received a disturbing call from his wife informing him that their four-year-old daughter had contracted malaria. When the pastor informed Hart of his daughter's condition, Hart brought him to the front of the line. The pastors were not aware they would be receiving a love offering. They thought Baker wanted to speak with them one-on-one and pray with them individually.

As the young pastor came in to speak with Baker, he was clearly distraught and shared his disturbing news with him. Baker asked him if his wife was able to get medicine for their daughter. He replied, "No, pastor. It's too expensive for us."

"How much is it?" Baker asked.

He answered, "As much as $25, a lot of money for a pastor." Baker learned from Hart that in the remote areas a pastor's salary may only be $25 to $50 a month. Consequently, they have to do a lot of bartering and have to grow as much of their own food as possible.

The Holy Spirit spoke to him to give him extra, and when he placed several hundred dollars in his hand, he looked down at the gift and started quivering and exclaimed, "Never in my life had I dreamed I would have this much money at one time!"

Baker laid his hands on him and prayed for him and his family. At the close of his prayer, he declared, "Go and take care of your daughter." After returning to the States, he heard that she had fully recovered from malaria.

The average family in the Western World spends more money going out to eat than over half of the pastors in the world make weekly—some monthly. What a sobering thought!

Once again God had dispatched His "worm" to be His hands extended in rendering provision and care to his pastors and their families who were suffering.

At the beginning of the service that night, the Liberian church honored Baker and presented him with an outfit that a tribal king would wear on special occasions. They exclaimed, "You would bless us and make us very happy if you preached in it tonight!" He did.

Baker being honored with wearing
tribal king's attire in Liberia (2007)

32

Personnel Emergency

The Lazarus Foundation conducted a number of care conferences throughout the US and in several other countries. They were designed to bring awareness to the plight of the less fortunate, to offer training, and to provide useful resources to NGOs, churches, and individual believers to help them learn how to better minister and serve the disenfranchised.

The foundation was not a 501(c)3 non-profit and never solicited or accepted donations but rather was a private non-profit family foundation which at times provided funding to NGOs and other groups. Gregory would teach a class at these care conferences on how to write grants to such foundations.

A conference had been planned for India during the summer of 2007, and Nichols, his daughter, Judy, along with Baker, flew to Coimbatore, India. Over 2,000 pastors and church leaders assembled for the three-day event. Baker was excited to get to spend some personal time with Nichols.

One morning after both had spoken in the conference, Nichols said, "Richard, I am tired. Take me back to the hotel. I need to rest." As they entered the hotel lobby, Nichols turned to Baker and expressed, "Come to my room in 30 minutes and let's talk."

When Baker sat down with him in his room, Nichols began to explain to him that many people wanted the position that he (Baker) was presently holding. Some had even voiced dismay when he was chosen. He asked, "Do you know why we chose you?"

Baker answered, "Not really."

Nichols continued, "Because you have been reporting to us as an honest straight shooter. The fact that you have traveled, lived, and worked in underprivileged countries is also a big plus."

Baker's mentoring sessions began that day and continued until Nichols' death in March 2009. Gregory looked up to this man as a father figure and would not let him fly out of the country without Baker tagging along to assist him in any way he could.

The entourage left Coimbatore and traveled to Chennai, where a group of 200 Christian businesspeople had gathered. They spent an evening sharing about the blessings of being God's hands extended. Gregory spoke via livestream and shared the joy of being a philanthropist. Many of the attendees were challenged by his passion.

Their journey took them to the extreme southern part of India to dedicate an orphanage, Destiny Village. The Lazarus Foundation had donated the funds to purchase the land and to provide for the construction. Judy also received an invitation to speak to around 200 widows that had assembled at the orphanage. It was a wonderful evening of celebration and, again, Baker's heart was so full that the Lord had chosen him to be part of such an amazing and caring organization that truly brought comfort and peace to a hurting world.

In August 2007, Church of God World Missions convened a ministers' conference in Nairobi, Kenya, for the entire continent. Most of the World Missions leadership and personnel attended. Bill George, who had served as missionary, pastor, editor-in-chief of Church of God Publications, and professor at Lee University, was now working with the World Missions department serving in the capacity of educational coordinator with over 100 Bible schools and seminaries in his portfolio. He also had the task of writing and editing all World Missions' publications.

George arrived late in the evening, a day after Baker had. The next morning, Douglas Leroy, assistant director of World Missions, approached Baker privately and said, "Dr. George is very sick, and we need to try to get him back to the States, if possible."

Baker immediately went to George's room to find him in excruciating pain and sweating profusely. He asked the educational directed for Africa, Jurgen Rudolph, a dear German brother who lived in Nairobi at the time, to assist him. George expressed that he was apparently experiencing kidney failure. He did not want to go to a hospital in Nairobi because of recent reports of people being infected with aids from the practice of using previously used syringes.

They left for the airport as quickly as they could to try to book a flight for both him and Baker, since he would be accompanying him back to the States. But George was in so much pain that they had to stop at a doctor's office and have the doctor come to the car and drain fluid from him—with a new syringe. Because of his condition, they decided to check him into a hotel close to the airport. Jurgen would stay with him while Baker went to the airport to secure the flight.

After arriving at the airport at 10:00 am and trying to book a flight to the States, he quickly discovered that no flights were available. August was the main travel month to Kenya because of safaris. By lunchtime, he had explored every airline that flew to the US, but there were no seats available. He then called Leroy who directed him to try to find a flight to Europe, preferable Great Britain, France, or Germany.

Baker spent another three or four hours searching, but nothing was available on any airline. He went back to the hotel to check on George and share with him their dilemma, noting that he might need to take him to a local hospital in Nairobi. He asked Baker to try once more to find a flight. After returning to the airport around 6:00 pm, he found a small travel agency and confided in them his dilemma. He exclaimed, "We will take any flight leaving Nairobi going to any country in Europe or North America!"

After checking, the operative announced, "Sir, there is nothing available. Give us your cell number, and we will keep monitoring for any cancellations."

At 11:00 pm Baker received a call saying there were two seats available for a 1:00 am flight to London on Virgin Atlantic, but they were in sleeper class. "One-way tickets," the caller informed him, "are $7,000 for each person."

Baker felt he had no choice. He ran to the counter, handed them his credit card, booked the tickets, and immediately called Leroy, who used to live in London. Leroy assured him that he would arrange for George to be transported to the hospital upon their arrival.

Jurgen brought George to the airport. By this time, he could barely walk and was beginning to get a little confused. Baker said, "Bill, you've got to get the strength to walk up to the counter with me and check in. And keep a good poker face."

They made it to the gate and had about one hour's wait for their departure. By the time the call went out for first-class passengers to board, George had become seriously ill and continued to perspire profusely. Baker kept wiping his forehead as they walked to board the plane. One of the airport security personnel stopped them and declared, "He is sick. We can't let him board until he is checked out by a nurse."

Baker looked at the woman and exclaimed, "Ma'am, this is a man of God, and I am taking him home. Please do not stop us or call any nurse. In Jesus Name, I declare it!" They boarded without further incident.

He and George each had his own sleeper birth. This was the first time Baker had ever been on a plane with a sleeper class. After getting George situated, he went to his birth to prepare for takeoff. Once airborne, he felt greatly relieved knowing that, at least, he could get him to London. Within a few minutes, a smartly dressed woman came to his birth and said, "Mr. Baker, my name is Samantha, and I am the beauty consultant on this flight. Would you like a manicure, pedicure, or a head, neck, and upper back massage?"

Baker related that he looked at her like "a deer in headlights." Considering the tension that had built up in him over the past few hours, he quickly agreed to the massage. Behind the cockpit was a small area designed for massage therapy. After his massage, he stopped to check on George. Since each birth had a seat for a guest, he sat down and told him about the massages given on the flight and asked, "Do you want one?"

"Oh, heavens no, Richard," he exclaimed.

Baker replied, "Then can I have yours?" Later, after his recovery, George shared that scenario with everyone he could, and they had some good laughs over it.

Upon arrival in London, Baker located a wheelchair for George, and they got in line to pass through customs. George looked up at Baker and pleaded, "Richard, please take me home!"

He called George's wife, Nelda, to ask what he should do. She replied, "Richard, if he's that insistent, please try to get him home."

Baker approached British Airlines and asked if they had two seats on any flight to the US. They informed him that the only thing they had was to Washington, DC, and they were in first class. Without hesitation, he responded, "We'll take them."

As they waited for their flight, which was in about two hours, Baker bent down to tie his shoe and retrieve something from his backpack. When he stood back up, George was gone. He had simply wondered off. Baker panicked and started running up and down the corridor at Heathrow Airport. His problem was that he didn't know which direction he went. He frantically searched the bathrooms, even bending down to see if he could recognize his shoes. After looking for 30 minutes, there was no George, and their flight was being called.

Baker just stood in the middle of the corridor and prayed. Almost immediately, he saw him leaning against a pillar. He grabbed him and together they moved as fast as they could to make it to the gate. When they arrived, they found the gate had been closed; the boarding process had ended. Baker begged the not-too-friendly Brit to let them board. After he finally relented, the men settled in for their seven-hour flight to DC. George slept most of the way.

They arrived in Dulles around 6:00 pm. Baker was about to tell the stewardess that they needed an ambulance. George looked at him and again pleaded, "Richard, we've made this far. Please take me the rest of the way home."

And once again, he called Nelda. She agreed, saying, "If you can find a flight, bring him home."

Baker began looking for flights to Atlanta and found two on American Airlines. They arrived in Atlanta around 10:00 pm, where Nelda was waiting. She immediately drove him to a hospital where he was admitted. The following week he was transferred to the University of Birmingham in Alabama, where the determination was made that he needed a kidney transplant.

Years earlier, George had been a professor at Lee University and now several of his students came forth to donate a kidney, Fred Garmon being one of them. Finally, a match was found in a former student, Phil Hoover, who lived in Chicago. Richard and Cheryl bought a round-trip ticket for him to Birmingham. The surgery was successful, and George lived another ten years. He was a true friend and mentor to Baker and so many others. George greatly influenced and encouraged him to write his life's story and offered to help with the editing. Baker regrets not doing it while George was living.

33

Blindsided

The Bakers' second son, Ryan, became restless and wanted to return to Guatemala to work at Casa Shalom as a dorm dad to the older boys and as a physical education instructor for the school. In fact, he never wanted to leave. He applied and was granted missionary status. Gregory purchased a used Ford-150 for him with the stipulation that when he left Casa Shalom, the truck stayed. Ryan drove the truck to the Mexican border where the acting director of Casa Shalom, Carlos, who happened to be in the States, met him. Together, they drove the truck to Guatemala.

A few months after Ryan's arrival on September 5, 2007, Hurricane Felix struck Nicaragua as a Category 5 with sustained winds of 160 mile per hour causing unbelievable damage. It struck the indigenous area of Nicaragua and Honduras, which is home to the Miskitos people group. The storm affected 15 countries in the Caribbean and Central America, with the Nicaraguan coast taking a direct hit. Since Baker served as coordinator for worldwide project and disaster relief for Church of God World Missions, he immediately contacted Ryan and instructed him to get to the Miskito Coast of Nicaragua as soon as possible to give him a clearer understanding of the situation. As much as he wanted to go, he knew he could better serve by staying stateside coordinating and handling logistics.

Once Ryan arrived, he communicated with his dad that the area looked like a war zone, with so much destruction, injuries, and death. World Missions immediately began getting food supplies to the most vulnerable. Ryan said that the overseer for that region of Nicaragua, Gustavo Zavala, shared with him that one of the greatest needs was for a boat that could transport at least one ton of supplies at a time into the most remote areas.

These areas were only accessible by boat and the word was that people were starving.

Baker spoke with Gregory, and he immediately released the funds. Ryan, along with Zavala, negotiated with a local boat builder to construct a boat as quickly as possible. In short order, the builder constructed a 26-foot fiberglass boat and outfitted it with a large Yamaha motor. When Baker was finally able to visit Nicaragua about one month later, he was amazed at the quality and durability of the boat. It had been used in transporting food supplies and performing evacuations almost nonstop since being built. They also shipped three 40-foot containers of food and other essentials to this stricken area of Nicaragua, as well as many more containers to the other affected countries.

Baker was asked to travel with them to a remote village to take additional food and other items the village needed. A larger but much slower boat had left a few hours earlier and as the team arrived, they were just starting to unload the larger boat, which contained a few tons of relief supplies. Richard Becton and his wife, Carolyn, who were both pilots serving as missionaries at the time and living in Porta Cabezas, Nicaragua, traveled with him. The villagers were more than grateful to receive the humanitarian relief.

They traveled to another area and docked the boat. Walking inland to another village, they reached a pastor's wife who had been severely injured when their home partially collapsed on her, breaking her back. It was unbelievable that she had survived so long in such pain. They made a makeshift stretcher and carried her to the boat. Baker was extremely concerned for her, seeing they had to navigate the open sea to get her to Porta Cabezas, where the only hospital in the region was. As they transported her, she frequently screamed out in pain as they negotiated two to three-foot waves, which caused the boat to continually bounce. They got her to the hospital, and Baker spent a few more days visiting affected areas and helping as much as he could. He also tried to make an accurate assessment of the greatest needs.

The rest of the year he spent raising funds and trying to help the affected countries get the aid they so desperately needed. Men and Women of Action—whose main focus is sending response teams for disaster relief and doing building projects, such as churches and orphanages—began mobilizing to move into these affected areas and help in rebuilding.

In the fall of 2008, Baker visited the country of Guyana, which is located in the northeast corner of South America. Hugh Carver, who at the time was director of MWOA, was raising funds to help build a children's home in the capital city of Georgetown. He had requested assistance from the Lazarus Foundation, which he received. Bless the Children Orphanage was completed and dedicated on September 27, 2008, in memory of Carver's son, Tyler, who had been killed in a vehicle accident in June. Any projects to which the foundation gave grants required a visit from Baker.

Bless the Children orphanage—Guyana.

Baker found here one of the best run orphanages he had visited until this time. Guyana has a large Muslim and Hindu population, and most all the children coming into the home were from these two groups. Usually, within days of a child arriving at the home, he or she would accept Christ. Over the next seven years, he made several visits to the home. On one visit a group of Muslims brought food that had been donated. The children graciously accepted the food and replied that their custom was to pray a blessing over all the people that blessed them. They agreed. Baker stood there watching pure evangelism taking place. When they finished praying, the place was electrified with the presence of God, and all of the Muslims were weeping uncontrollable.

In early 2008, the Lazarus Foundation sponsored another care conference, this time in Quito, Ecuador. Gregory, Nichols, and Baker traveled down to attend and participate. The seminary hosted the conference, which many attended. Another area of ministry that Gregory had a heart for was chaplaincy. David Ramirez, the president of the seminary, had submitted a proposal to the Lazarus Foundation for assistance in building a wing onto the seminary for chaplaincy studies. During this trip, Gregory presented Ramirez a check for $150,000 with a commitment to do more once the project got under way.

They also visited Bread of Life Ministries, which was a feeding and educational center for poor children. Baker had visited the center with Gregory and Nichols back in 2006, seeing they wanted his input. The director wanted a new vocational addition with digital silk-screening machines, along with machines to make bolts and screws, welding machines, and several other types of machinery. The objective was to teach the older children a trade and to make a profit from manufactured items to offset the monthly operational budget. After listening to the proposal, Gregory committed $400,000. He informed the director that Baker would be making regular trips to check on the progress.

The project was completed just a little over one year later with obtaining the machinery being the biggest obstacle. Finally, the project came together, and the men flew down for the dedication.

On May 2, 2008, Cyclone Nargis struck the country of Myanmar (formally Burma). According to official estimates, 84,500 people died, along with 53,800 missing. The cyclone significantly affected 37 townships. Baker was still serving a dual role as the director of field operations for the Lazarus Foundation and as Project and Disaster Relief Coordinator for Church of God World Missions. Harold McLeod, who was serving as field director for Asia, accompanied him in mid-May to meet with pastors and assess the damage.

Since 1946, Myanmar has been headed by a military junta and has been called the second most repressive regime in the world, after North Korea. Baker took $25,000 cash with him, considering the difficulty in wiring or sending funds into the country at that time. The government rejected humanitarian help from the US and other countries, such as Great Britain.

Baker and McLeod flew into Rangoon and faced some difficulties getting through customs, since they could not announce that they had come to do religious or humanitarian work. They had to say that they were there to visit friends. Further, they had to affirm that they had visited the country before, and they had formed friendships while there.

After checking into their hotel, they secured a conference room and hosted pastors and church leaders to get a better picture of the situation. One of the pastors had a small orphanage that PCL had helped some. Garmon asked Baker to check on it while he was there. They did and were able to help them secure enough food to last until the Lazarus Foundation began giving monthly assistance, which continued for a couple of years.

They were informed that the government was downplaying the effects of the cyclone, and relief was not getting to those who needed it most. Because of government regulations, it was virtually impossible for Baker and McLeod to purchase food with US currency. If, on the other hand, they went to a bank to exchange $25,000 into the local currency, they would have been questioned as to their motives.

Appealing prayer to God to supply their needs was now called for. Both men were men of prayer and began seeking God to help them help the suffering. McLeod had been visiting Burma for eight or more years and had made friends with some of the hotel staff. Consequently, they felt comfortable enough approaching them for guidance and received the recommendation to speak with the owner of the hotel. The man, a devout Buddhist, seemed to have a heart for those who were suffering.

Baker was apprehensive to tell him how much money he had on his person but knew they had to trust someone. After informing him that their intention was to purchase as much bulk food as possible and deliver it to those in greatest need, he became excited and told them to convert the US currency into kyat, the Myanmar currency. He said the owner of the travel/car agency, which had an office in the lobby of the hotel, had connections with businessmen who will buy the dollars on the black market.

Now they had to trust another stranger, and as they were speaking discovered that he was Muslim. He promised the duo that he would do his best to get the most for the $25,000 on the black market, but he could not take them with him. Baker and McLeod retreated to their room to pray and discuss their options. However, the only one option seemed to be to trust a Buddhist and a Muslim businessman that they did not know.

Returning to the lobby, they reported to the Muslim that they would put their trust in him to make the exchange. After stepping into a private room, Baker gave the Muslim businessman the $25,000. He said it would take him two to three hours to sell the US currency. Six hours later they were still waiting. Just as Baker felt a spirit of heaviness come over him, the Muslim walked through the door with several bags filled with kyat. Then in a private meeting consisting of a Buddhist, a Muslim, and two Pentecostal preachers, the men devised a plan to feed hungry people.

The Muslim offered to provide two large trucks in which to haul the food, while the Buddhist volunteered 10 of his workers to go with them to assist in the distribution. The Muslim further agreed to provide a 15-passenger van for the workers. A Buddhist monk, who lived in one of the most affected areas, was contacted, given the task of notifying the people, and coordinating the distribution. The two businessmen helped Baker and McLeod in the purchase of the food by getting several of their employees to go to the local markets and purchase a few hundred-pound bags/boxes of beans, rice, and salt. The trucks parked close by and the food would be loaded onto them. Some of the food was purchased through the hotel. Altogether, they procured over 20 tons of food and thousands of plastic bags to use in dividing it.

Before they departed the hotel the following morning, McLeod asked if they could all pray together, and the men agreed. McLeod prayed a powerful prayer of protection and asked that God would blind the eyes of the authorities until all the food had been distributed. They arrived at 6:00 am and were met by the Buddhist monk and his team. For extra security, Baker and McLeod were chauffeured separately in a small SUV provided by the Muslim. They were told that if the military saw them, they probably would stop them, and possibly even arrest all of them.

As Baker exited the vehicle in which he was riding, he was introduced to the monk. Looking behind him, he saw a line of people stretching farther than his eyes could see. Looking at McLeod in consternation, he remarked, "I hope we have enough food."

McLeod responded in typical McLeod fashion, "Richard, let's pray that God will multiply it." They did, and God did! Thousands of people received food that day. Not one time did they encounter the military or even a police officer. Considering that no humanitarian organization was permitted access into the country to render assistance, they knew that God had been with them. He had spoken to two South Georgia preachers who feared God more than men.

The BBC news truck approached and stopped. Reporters came to the two men and queried, "Who are you with, and how did you pull this off? We have been here a week, and this is first time we have seen food distribution on this large of a scale."

Without going into detail, they simply answered, "Jesus organized everything. We just followed his instructions." Baker later exclaimed, "You should have seen the look on the faces of the BBC news crew when we shared that with them!"

Both Baker and McLeod helped with the distribution, either by placing the food into the hands of individual people or by bagging the food for distribution.

After all their efforts, over 5,000 people received food that day, because they put it in God's hands. Baker has had many people tell him after hearing the story that they would have never trusted those two businessmen with $25,000. He believes that that is why so few people witness miracles. He knows that not only those two businessmen, but their employees, the monk and his associates, and many others had had Jesus revealed to them in a real way. And after all, is that not what the Great Commission is about anyway?

Baker expressed, "It's such a blessing to be a worm, and it is only as we surrender our lives and wills to Him that we will witness His greatness and power."

Within a couple of years, 2010, SOW would be up and running and Baker would return to Myanmar several more times to help orphanages. What joy he found in visiting a few children's home and seeing them adopted into the SOW family.

Two Thousand Eight found Baker back in India, this time to attend the dedication of an orphanage that had been built in the city of Chennai. Thomas, a man that Gregory had been working with in humanitarian projects for a few years, met him at the airport. Baker had met him once before on his first visit to India.

The next morning, Thomas picked him up for the dedication. When they arrived, Baker began looking around and felt prompted by the Holy Spirit that something was not right. First, the facility was newly constructed and was not designed for an orphanage, but for a school. Second, the children's school uniforms were nicer than any orphanage he had ever visited, and the children did not conduct themselves as orphan children do—that is, humble-spirited. These children seemed to be from middle-class homes. Also, Baker thought about what Thomas had shared with him the night before on the drive to the hotel. And that was, that he was surprised that Gregory had sent him for the dedication. They went through a short dedication service in which even the children seemed to be a little confused.

The following day, he flew to Andhra Pradesh, which is located in the southeastern part of India. The Lazarus Foundation had built a large orphanage there with close to 500 children calling it home. They had never held a formal dedication service, so he went to pay a visit and to be part of formally dedicating the children's home.

During his visit, Jyothi Reddi—a pastor, church leader, and also founder of Jyothi's Home—felt comfortable enough to ask him about $100,000 that Gregory had promised him six months earlier—a donation he had never received. Baker promised him that he would immediately check on it when he arrived back in the States.

Baker wanted to buy all the children ice cream. Jyothi called the company and had them deliver over 500 individually wrapped ice-cream treats, something these children had never had before. It was a joy for the adults to see how a small act of kindness could go so far in a child's life, especially underprivileged children like these were. This home was designed and built for 300 children, but the first day it opened, it was over capacity. When Baker questioned him, Jyothi replied, "How can I turn a needy child away. It's better to be a little crowded than to be on the street alone and destitute."

All Baker could say was, "God bless you!"

After returning to the States, he drove from Cleveland, Tennessee, to Bristol, Tennessee, to meet with both Gregory and Nichols. He knew they had a lot of love for and confidence in Thomas, and Baker had a bit of trepidation in bringing up his concerns. They were already hurt and upset with the corruption the Lord had helped him uncover in Liberia and Zambia. There, he had proof. Here, he just had a feeling that something was not right.

He first brought up the $100,000 that Reddi had never received to pay off the last of the construction costs. Nichols immediately shared with Gregory he had wired the funds to Thomas months earlier. Baker felt another ping in his spirit, this time harder. He shared with the men his concerns about the orphanage in Chennai. They looked at each other and for the first time disclosed to him exactly why he had been hired. Gregory had been feeling for some time that accountability for the large sums of funds he was giving was lacking.

Gregory looked at Baker and instructed, "Get on plane ASAP and go back to India unannounced. I want you to investigate every ministry we have funded in India."

Over the next seven years, Baker would make 32 trips to India. He discovered that Thomas was fraudulent in his dealings with, not only Gregory, but with other organizations, as well.

Baker contacted an acquaintance of his in India who put him in touch with a Christian attorney. He picked him up at the airport and together they drove to the orphanage where Baker had attended the dedication ceremony just a couple of weeks earlier. When they arrived, his friend asked him to remain seated in the car while he spoke with someone there. He was told that it was a private school. They then went to an office that retained deeds and sales of properties to ascertain who owned the property. The lawyer was able to find that the property belonged to a man who operated several private schools. Thomas had sold him the land and the man had built the school.

While in India, Baker received a message from the pastor of a large church in one of the northern states in the US. He informed Baker that he had heard that the Lazarus Foundation was claiming to have given the funds to build Destiny Village Orphanage in South India.

Baker responded, "That is correct."

Deeply concerned, the pastor replied, "That can't be. We gave $250,000 to Thomas, and we came and dedicated it!"

Baker asked, "When did you dedicate it?"

"This past June," he answered.

Baker replied, "Dr. Nichols and I dedicated it this past May."

This was the hardest type of fraud to uncover, because the land was purchased with an authentic deed and bill-of-sale. The buildings were constructed with receipts to show the cost, and, finally, a genuine orphanage began operation. Thomas had simply double-sold it and pocketed a large sum of money. Baker would later discover that Thomas claimed there were 10 acres purchased when actually he had purchased 100 acres, with 90 acres being recorded in his name and in other family members' names.

He also discovered, with help from the attorney they had hired, that the 25-acre rice field the Lazarus Foundation had purchased years earlier was now in the name of some of Thomas's brothers, and the rice was not going to the orphanages, as was planned, but being sold for profit. Additionally, the foundation supported 500 widows with a monthly donation. Sadly, the widows were only receiving their donations every other month.

When Baker returned to the States and reported its findings to Gregory and Nichols, Gregory looked at him and declared, "Richard, he must be stopped! There are one million dollars on the table, if you need it, but solve the problem."

By this time, a particular pastor and Baker had spoken over the phone, and the pastor was having a hard time believing it to be true and wanted to know when he was returning to India. When Baker told him that it would be shortly, the deeply concerned pastor responded that he and his missions' pastor wanted to travel with him, if he didn't mind.

Baker's next trip was to the Ukraine, since the foundation had received a request to help an orphanage in Alexandria. He contacted a German pastor, Thomas, who offered to travel with him. Thomas had been several times and knew Eva, a missionary from Switzerland. She also worked at an orphanage, spoke Russian, and would be the perfect translator.

They contacted Eva, who was more than happy to help. She arranged for a Ukrainian couple, who attended the same church, to drive them around. They spent a week traveling the vast country of Ukraine and visiting three orphanages and several rehab centers. Baker also had the privilege of preaching in two of the local churches, with Eva serving as his translator.

When they visited Pilgrim Republic Children's Home located in Mariupol, Gennadiy, a local pastor, and the director of the home, shared an amazing story with Baker. Eight years earlier he had run completely out of funds and the picture looked bleak. He approached a Ukrainian businessman and asked for help. The man replied, "I can only help you with maybe one month's support. Let me buy you a ticket to the US, and maybe you can find support there." He related that he took him up on his offer, flew to New York, and caught a bus to San Antonio, Texas, since he knew the General Assembly for the Churches of God was convening there.

Gennadiy said, "I walked into a lobby where registration was taking place, but my English was not too good. I had run out of money and had not eaten in three days. A man walked up to me and asked, 'Can I help you?' I told him who I was, where I was from, and that I had come to get help for destitute children living in a children's home." Interestingly, this man happened to be a close friend of Baker's, Coleman Peacock, who worked at the time at the Smoky Mountain Children's Home in Sevierville, Tennessee.

The Ukrainian pastor continued, "He told me that he knew exactly who I needed to speak and said, 'He is here. Let me call his room and see if he can see you.' Coleman called Nichols and shared with him about me and the situation concerning the children's home. First, Dr. Nichols said he didn't have time, but then the Holy Spirit checked him, and he agreed to meet with me, but could only give me five minutes. As I entered the room, I was very nervous, but he greeted me with a big smile and offered me something to drink. I shared my situation with him, and he said, 'Yes, we will help you. How much do you need?' I said, 'I need a very large sum.' 'Well,' he said, 'How much?' I responded, '$10,000.' He said, 'No, that's not enough. I will wire you $35,000 into your account.' He then said, 'Have a good day,' and showed me the door. As I was leaving the building, Coleman asked me if I wanted a room. I said, 'No, I go back to my children. God has supplied our need.'"

Gennadiy then said to Baker, "Now, you are here standing in front of me representing the same foundation that helped me eight years ago. I tell you without that donation, we would have had no choice but to close the ministry."

Until now, more than 2,500 children have entered the doors of Pilgrim and found acceptance and love. Most of them were homeless and many were already drug addicts, but in the end, most found hope and redemption through saving faith in Jesus Christ. Pilgrim also operated a small home with eight to ten children who had AIDS. Baker's heart broke after spending a couple of hours with them. Tasha, an 11-year-old, captured his heart. As he was leaving, she grabbed his hand and held it tightly, begging him not to leave her. The Lazarus Foundation started supporting the ministry.

The next stop was Pearl Orphanage located in Alexandra. They had reached out to the foundation, since they were using a government building and needed to vacate it sometime in the future. The founder, Sergey, showed Baker an old, dilapidated building on a large piece of property that could be purchased for a good price and possibly renovated to accommodate an orphanage. Baker did a thorough walk-through inspection, determined that the sub-floors on the first and second floors were structurally unsound, and would need to be torn out. That alone would greatly affect the cost of renovation. In a couple of months, they were able to offer a rough estimate as to the cost. Baker presented it to Gregory, and he agreed to move forward with funding the Pearl Orphanage project.

Pearl Orphanage—Alexandria, Ukraine
(Built by the Lazarus Foundation and dedicated July 2011).

Sails of Hope Orphanage, where Eva worked, was their last stop. The children's home had a large two-story facility, and it was quite apparent that the children received excellent care and attention. In fact, Baker was impressed with the level of care that was given at all three of the children's homes. They also visited several rehab centers, and he gave his testimony at each one of them.

He and Thomas, a German pastor, flew back to Germany where Baker met with Gregory, who was flying in to speak at the European Theological Seminary. The seminary was located in the beautiful black forest, and Gregory had donated heavily toward their expansion. They spent a couple of days there and headed back to the States. Baker was glad to get home to Cleveland.

Nichols, Bakers' immediate boss, friend, and mentor, announced that he had been diagnosed with cancer. Both Gregory and Baker were devastated. He elected to receive treatment from MD Anderson Cancer Center in Houston, Texas. Baker visited him a couple of times before Nichols returned to his home in Knoxville, Tennessee.

In early February 2009, Baker drove to his home, picked him up, and took him to lunch. He ordered a bowl of soup and barely touched it. For two hours he poured into Baker, who later related,

> Dr. Nichols said to me, "Richard, when I was at the pinnacle of my ministry, I was at my lowest spiritually. For a few years I had lost my purpose for being in the ministry. Although no one knew it, I didn't get it back until I was given the opportunity to start the Division of Care and began seeing, touching, and ministering to hurting people. I really don't have a lot of talents. My success has come from surrounding myself with people who do and by empowering them. Richard, the greatest secret of leadership is being able to surround yourself with people smarter and more capable than you are and delegating them to the task they are gifted in."
>
> One of the last things he shared with me was this, as he slowly shook his finger at me with a half-smile on his face, "Richard, I have recommended to John Gregory that you succeed me. And so help me God, Richard, if you let him down, I will come back from the grave and haunt you!" He then let out a big laugh.
>
> Nichols died in March about six weeks after our lunch. His words have never left me. Some were personal and that is where they will stay. But God put a giant in my life for a few years to mentor me, give guidance, and perhaps most importantly, give encouragement to me.

Baker's mother was slowly succumbing to dementia. He asked Gregory if he would allow him to move to Brunswick, Georgia, where he could be closer to her and to two of his sons and grandchildren. Gregory told him that long as he was close to an airport, he was fine with it. He then asked the new director of World Missions, Douglas Leroy, who also gave his approval.

He and Cheryl put their house on the market, and it quickly sold. They found a house in Brunswick and made an offer. The sellers accepted their proposal, and the Baker's had a new home. In November they moved back to their hometown. They were now close to their mothers and their families. And they only lived one mile from the airport. They both thought they had probably returned home for the last time. Gregory was considering moving to Hilton Head, just an hour and a half up 1-95 from Brunswick. He had even built an office complex there. However, little did they know at the time that the Lord had other plans.

It felt good to be back home and around family. His mother still knew who he was, and Cheryl was able to spend time with her mother. Of course, living close to their sons, Chris and Ricky, along with Ricky's wife, Tiffany, and their only two grandchildren at the time, Jonathan and Braydon, was especially meaningful.

His first trip of 2009 took him back to India in early January. The above-mentioned pastor and his missions' coordinator, who thought their church had solely funded Destiny Village, met him in Chennai. They traveled together to Destiny Village. Baker had also asked the attorney and a well-known Indian minister that he had connected with at a care conference–a man who was well versed in Indian laws on non-profits–to travel with them. Also, Harold McLeod, who served as field director for Asia, accompanied them.

When the entourage arrived on site, the pastor showed Baker a plaque that he had permanently installed into the corner of one of the buildings listing the northern church as the donor. Baker pulled out his phone and showed him a photo of a similar plaque in the same location recognizing the Lazarus Foundation. After he spoke with the director, it became clear to Baker that the Indian pastor was in on the fraud. He later discovered that a few acres of the land had been placed in his name.

There were about seven people traveling with Baker. They were meeting in the courtyard of the orphanage when about 100 angry men showed up. No doubt, the director, who got his marching orders from Thomas, had invited them. Destiny Village is in a very remote area several miles from any town, so the team was most definitely in a precarious situation, seeing that some of the men had different objects in their hands.

Through their translators, the American pastor spoke, his missions' coordinator spoke, McLeod spoke, and Baker spoke last. They all were praying as each one was speaking. They shared with them that they had not come to close the children's home, as they had heard, but to investigate reported fraud. After spending about one hour speaking with them, they began to leave a few at a time until all had departed the premises.

The visiting men decided to bring the director and his wife to a neighboring city where they had secured hotel accommodations. They spoke with him for a few hours and convinced him that his only option to avoid prosecution was to tell the truth. Their attorney had prepared an affidavit that he finally signed. He admitted that there were never 150 children living at the home as reported to Gregory, but only around 40. Also, he admitted to having two dedication services, one for each donor. Further, he confessed that Thomas gave him a couple of acres of land to go along with the scheme to double sell the project. The American pastor was devastated, especially because he had even had Thomas visit his church and felt they had a close friendship. Of course, both Gregory and Nichols had developed that same relationship with Thomas and were themselves devastated.

Again, Thomas had approached different donors for many projects. In total, Baker made 32 trips to India trying to uncover all the fraud and to save as much of the investments made by the Lazarus Foundation and by others as possible.

Before the investigation had been completed, even the attorney hired by the Lazarus Foundation was paid off by Thomas and began working against them, only weeks before they were to go to trial. But God's faithfulness prevailed, and the Lord put two more Indian brothers in Baker's path—a pastor from Bangalore and another brother in the faith who held a PHD in social ministries and knew the laws of India relating to non-profits better than most lawyers did. He also found an honest attorney who represented them pro bono, except for court fees.

The foundation went to court and won their first court case with nearly all the 100 acres and buildings being transferred into a non-profit organization under the control of the Churches of God in the state of Tamil, Nadu. This was a miracle itself, considering that a Christian organization petitioned a predominately Hindu court, largely governed by Hindu teachings, and have that court rule in the organization's favor.

Over the next year, the Lazarus Foundation would continue the fight to retrieve Thomas's ill-gotten property and funds. The next court case was in Chennai where Thomas lived and had more influence. As mentioned earlier, the Lazarus Foundation had purchased a 25-acre rice farm for the purpose of growing rice and donating the profit to surrounding orphanages. Their attorney hired a private investigator to help sort out all of Thomas's fraud. The investigator discovered that the rice field had been placed in the name of Thomas's brother (he had a different last name), and it was being operated as a commercial enterprise with no orphans receiving benefits.

The case against Thomas went to trial and the foundation lost. Baker believed that the judge had been paid off.

Baker shared with Gregory that they could appeal to a higher court, but that it would be expensive. Gregory replied, "Go all the way to their Supreme Court, if that's what it takes to bring justice."

They appealed the lower court's decision and, in a few months, the three judges sitting on the appeals court reversed the ruling of the lower court. They ordered the land deeded to their India non-profit organization.

After much discussion, the foundation decided to sell the property and invest the funds into other ministries in India. This meant another trip, and Baker stayed at the same hotel he always stayed in while in Chennai. He was always treated well, and they had a great little restaurant.

When he checked in, the atmosphere was different than before, but he was tired and didn't think too much of it. Around 1:00 am, someone knocking loudly on his door awakened him. He jumped out of bed to find the pastor from an independent church group telling him he had received word that a hit had been placed on him. The pastor exclaimed, "You need to leave immediately! Don't even pack your suitcase. Just come now!"

Baker dressed as quickly as possible, and since he had not unpacked his suitcase, he grabbed it and ran out of the hotel into a waiting van containing several men from the pastor's church. As they departed, two vanloads of men drove up to the hotel and ran into the lobby. Baker initially didn't think the pastor knew what he was talking about. He soon found out differently, and he thanked God that night for putting that pastor in his life.

The pastor said to him, "You must only stay in four or five-star hotels, which have good security." He checked into a five-star hotel early that morning, where the room rates started at $320 nightly. The manager, knowing he was working with a humanitarian organization, only charged $99 nightly, a rate that stayed the same the next 20 visits he made to Chennai.

That next afternoon, Baker negotiated with three businessmen who were interested in purchasing the rice field. They eventually sold it for three times what the Lazarus Foundation had paid for it a few years earlier. The funds were reinvested in a couple of children's homes.

34

Democratic Republic of the Congo

In May 2009, Baker was promoted to executive director of the Lazarus Foundation taking Nichols place, which Baker said no one could ever actually do. His mind went back to that day in the slums of Managua, Nicaragua, at the sight where they were building Hogar Agape Children's Home, when the medical doctor, Roberts, handed him the book on the *Prayer of Jabez*. He had read it that night and had cried out to God for Him to let him be a conduit for His blessings—a channel to reach the needy orphans, widows, and others He would place in his path.

Just three weeks later, Nichols called him and asked for his assistance with a project in Central America. When Nichols had asked him if he had anything going on, Baker had told him that he was in the middle of building an orphanage in Nicaragua but had run out of funds. Nichols had sent every penny he needed to complete the project. The prayer he had prayed these nine years earlier continues to be answered, but in a much different way than he had ever envisioned.

Reflecting on those years, Baker said, "It would be impossible to share all that the Lazarus Foundation, through the philanthropy of Dr. John Gregory and his lovely wife, Joan, has accomplished over the last 30 years. On average, I visited 20 to 25 countries a year over the nine and a half years that I had the privilege to serve with the foundation."

As Baker entered the summer of 2009, his mother's dementia worsened. She had to leave her home, where she had lived since 1960, and move in with her daughter, Phyllis. In early August, the family called in hospice care knowing that she would likely not live more than a couple of weeks. Richard went over regularly to visit with her. She would point her finger at him and say, "My son, my son."

On August18, her breathing became shallow, and the family knew her homegoing was near. Richard sat next to her bed holding her hand. Ryan was lying next to her, and Ricky, Joshua, Melanie, and Cheryl, along with Phyllis and her husband, Bruce, stood nearby. They had a radio softly playing Christian music, and suddenly this beautiful saint of God opened her eyes, looked past Richard, and began speaking in a heavenly language. He could feel her hand grip his. The song playing on the radio was "Soon and very soon, we are going to see the King." When the song concluded, this godly mother passed from this world to the heavenly one. Richard expressed, "I would no doubt be in hell today if it had not been for the prayers of this righteous woman." A few days later, he had the wonderful privilege of preaching her homegoing service.

In the fall of 2009, the Lazarus Foundation sponsored another care conference, this time in Jakarta, Indonesia. With a population of 270 million, Indonesia is the largest Muslim country in the world. The conference was held at the newly constructed 18,000-seat Gereja Bethel Convention Center (church). Over 6,000 Indonesian pastors attended, as well as a delegation from the US and other countries. Gregory and Baker had the wonderful privilege of speaking. Baker said, "It will go down as one of the greatest honors of my life. To be able to speak to that many of God's chosen servants was humbling, to say the least."

On a given day, they distributed food in one of the slums, and the second highest-ranking Muslim leader in the country joined them in the distribution. They also visited an orphanage that was also located in the slums, which had been built on top of a former dumpsite. They left a love offering. Baker would return the following year.

Gregory informed Baker that Lamar Vest, president of American Bible Society, had asked for a meeting with them, but he didn't indicate what it was about.

On the day of the meeting, Vest arrived with his vice-president, Dr. Briggs, and the coordinator of special projects, Charles Lambert. The first words out of Vest's mouth were, "John, I didn't come to ask you for a donation." Continuing, he shared his heart. "In the nearly 200 years that ABS has been operating, we have printed and distributed the Word of God. Recently, the Lord spoke to me and said it was not enough to just print and distribute the Word, but we needed to live it out also. I feel the Lord is giving direction to launch ABS into humanitarian work as well. We have already selected Africa as our first continent, but are not sure just which country or countries. I am here to ask you to let Richard take a delegation from ABS to several countries in Africa where they are experiencing crises."

Gregory responded, "I have no problem with Richard doing it, if he wants to." Of course, Baker had no problem at all with it. Plans were made and the decision was made to visit Kenya, Uganda, Rwanda, Democratic Republic of the Congo (DRC), with the last visit being to Ethiopia. The trip was planned for January 2010.

The first stop was in Rwanda, where in 1994 nearly one million people were killed in a genocide brought on by ethnic tensions between the Hutus and the Tutsis, with most of the deaths being among the Tutsis. They attended healing sessions where members of each ethnic group would get up and apologize for what they had done. One man stood and declared, "I killed a family of eight." He then gave some description of when and where it had taken place.

A woman sitting behind the delegation began to weep. She stood up, asked him a couple of more questions, and then burst out crying, "That was my mom and dad and siblings you killed!"

The man humbled himself, getting on the floor and begging for forgiveness. She walked over to him as he was starting to stand, and the two embraced each other. Richard recounted, "I have never in my life witnessed such a level of forgiveness. I sat there wondering if I could have done what she just did. Then the Lord spoke to my heart saying, 'I did that and much more for you!' Forgiveness is the greatest and most powerful weapon in our arsenal against the enemy of our soul."

Leaving Rwanda, the team traveled to the DRC, where in the eastern part of the country over the last 20 years an estimated five million people have been killed, with millions more displaced. The first stop was Goma, a city of over one million on the Rwanda border. They spent a good part of the day at an orphanage that also housed 80 widows whose husbands had been killed. Many others had been tortured by various rebel groups, such as M23, a Rwanda-backed rebel movement, and LRA (Lord's Resistant Army), as well as others. The orphanage was located about 20 miles from Goma.

Richard saw a woman around 60 years old sitting on the floor and leaning against the wall, holding a two or three-week old baby, with perhaps a three-year-old girl standing next to her. There were hundreds of people there, but he was drawn to her. He got an interpreter and knelt down to engage this woman. She never acknowledged his presence but just sat there staring forward. After asking the interpreter to share with her that they were there to help, not tomorrow, but today, he walked away as the interpreter communicated that to her.

In a couple of moments, the translator waved him back over, and the grandmother began to tell him a story of unimaginable horror and sadness. She explained, "A few days earlier, my daughter, these two children, and I left our village to go scour for some wood to cook with. Twelve rebels came upon us, raped, and killed my daughter. Then all of them raped me and said, 'Grandmother, we are not going to kill you, as you have to care for the babies.' They left. I got my two grandchildren and walked 30 minutes back to our village where the chief said, 'Because you have been defiled, you can no longer live here (it was an ancient tribal tradition). I heard about this home for children, so I decided to bring my grandchildren here for help and walked two days with nothing but water, to give these babies a home. I was told they had nothing but a little rice to feed us, and the infants can't eat rice, so I am sitting here hoping they will die first, then me, as I don't want to die knowing they are still suffering."

The team did a quick assessment of the situation and sent a truck back to Goma with funds from the Lazarus Foundation to purchase baby formula and other staple goods to help feed the children and widows living there. With God's help, he was able to keep his promise to this grandmother that they were there to help today. Richard expressed, "This will go down as one of the most heart-wrenching experiences of my life. When the rebels would rape a woman, they would either kill her or, worse, take a machete and insert into her vagina, twisting it to cause them to become incontinent, and to inflict excruciating pain. Of course, many women did not survive this harsh and cruel treatment."

The larger Gregory family, John and his siblings, have a family foundation, Kingsway Charities, which provide medicines and medical supplies to third-world countries and also resources short-term medical teams with meds. When Baker visited a small hospital that was performing reconstructive surgery for these women, he asked for a list of medical supplies and medicines the hospital needed. Because of Kingsway Charities, every time Baker or someone from ABS headed to the DRC, they carried as many medical supplies as they could, to help resource this rural hospital.

On one evening, the team attended a meeting with the leadership of all the different denominations–Pentecostal, Baptist, Catholic, and everywhere in between. The purpose was to inform them of the situation that was transpiring in the eastern part of the DRC. Baker said, "It is amazing how trials and tribulations bring the body of Christ together when nothing else can. They showed us videos, shared photos, and told stories of atrocities that would be impossible to believe if the truth wasn't staring us right in the face."

Arrangements had been made for the following day for them to visit with and speak to some of the affected widows and orphans. An Anglican church, the largest church in the area, hosted the event. As the delegation of 10 to 12, counting a few local leaders, entered the church and was escorted to the platform, they were taken aback, as they looked around to see 2,500 widows sitting on the floor waiting to receive some hope.

One man, scheduled to speak for a few minutes, broke down in tears and said that he was not able to speak. They asked another, and then another, but all of them declined to speak. Dr. Bagu, a man raised in the DRC, who had attended university in the US, and who had been hired by ABS, came to Baker and expressed, "Richard, it's all up to you. No one else feels they can speak." Bagu's brief biographical sketch follows:

> Bagudekia Alobeyo (Bagu) was born and raised in Eastern Democratic Republic of the Congo (DRC), a country that has been devastated by wars in the past two decades, during which many young people did not have access to higher education but had only the opportunity to join the militia armed groups. Alobeyo believed in Jesus Christ as his Savior, developed the habit of being engaged daily with the Scripture, and received a call to serve the Lord as a minister, when he was yet a student in Christian schools established by mission work in Democratic Republic of Congo.
>
> He has a diploma in education and a master's degree in theology from the "Faculté de Théologie Evangélique de Bangui in Central African Republic (CAR). He also holds a master's degree in arts of religion and a doctorates degree in ministry from Westminster Theological Seminary in Philadelphia, Pennsylvania. He is fluent in five languages, namely, French, Lingala, Swahili, Zande, and English. In addition, he reads and translates ancient Hebrew and Greek.

> Before moving to the US in 1995, he pastored local churches in DRC for 11 years and served as the national vice president of a large denomination, the Church of Christ in Central Africa, CECA20. Alobeyo has also served as a church planter, youth pastor, Bible school director, and community development leader. Prior to working for Geneva Global, an international non-profit organization in the US, as the director of the West African region, he worked as family and children counselor in Philadelphia. He has extensive experience in international program development within the United Bible Society's global network, including matching innovative "holistic" humanitarian components with Scripture Engagement. He worked for American Bible Society in Philadelphia promoting national and global Bible-based trauma healing, Bible translation, and Bible engagement throughout US churches and global communities for about 13 years.
>
> Alobeyo and his wife, Suzanne, have five sons, five grandchildren in the US, and five grandchildren in Uganda, who have lost both parents. Alobeyo has witnessed firsthand in his own family the devastation and terror caused by the Lord's Resistance Army. In 2009, he had to arrange for his family's evacuation from his hometown of Dungu. He acknowledges what others in DRC have said of him—that he was spared from the ravages of the war in Congo and provided for in the US so that he could be their advocate and an avenue of hope and restoration. In 2010, Alobeyo led an unforgotten ministry assessment trip to DRC with a few people from American Bible Society and the Lazarus Foundation's representative, Richard Baker. The outcome of that trip laid down a path of partnership between the Lazarus Foundation and the American Bible Society to deliver a comprehensive ministry that impacted more than 10,000 orphans and widows in Goma and Dungu.

As Baker entered the pulpit not really knowing in which direction to go, the Holy Spirit spoke to his heart saying, "Remind them that they are not alone. I am the Bridegroom and they are part of my bride."

With that, he went through a short wedding ceremony explaining to them that as believers, we become part of the bride of Christ. At the end of his short message, he asked that if they were willing to accept the Lord's proposal to be His bride, to let it be known by standing and declaring, "I will!" As they all stood, the Holy Spirit began to flow among them, and many experienced spiritual and emotional healing that day.

When the widows exited the sanctuary, the place filled with orphans. Again, no one would speak. And again, Bagu came to him and said,

"Richard, you have the mantle again." He was told not to leave the platform, since most of the orphans were homeless and would possibly rush him in hopes of getting something. As he started speaking, he fixed his eyes on a little girl around seven or eight years old. He asked himself what Jesus would do, and he proceeded to do it.

Baker walked off the platform, eased up to this little girl, and while still speaking, extended his hands to her. As she fell into his arms, he picked her up and held her for the rest of his message. It was apparent that she had not had a bath in a while. She smelled, her clothes were tattered, and she was severely malnourished. But for those few minutes, God allowed His "worm" to be His hands, arms, and lips. As he put her down, he kissed her forehead and promised those children that day that they would do everything in their power to help them have a better life.

The team traveled by bush plane to a village of 50,000, Bagu's home, Dungu. Because of the rebel activity in the area, the pilot informed them that at the first sign of trouble, he would have to leave.

Baker preached three more times to several more thousand widows and orphans. The emotional strain of witnessing so much suffering was having a major effect on all of the team members. Bagu had selected a few widows to give their testimony, but one in particular caught Baker's attention. She spoke, "The rebels always attack at night, and a few months ago, they attacked and killed my husband and oldest son. But God has left me my two younger sons, and I praise His name."

A few months later, Baker would return to this village, and the same widow came up to him and related, "They have now killed another of my sons, and I am left with just one." On another visit a year or so later, the same woman came to Baker again and reported, "They've killed my last son. I am all alone, but I still have Jesus, and He is my strength and comfort."

Baker reflected, "The church in the Western world does not have the same faith, love, and walk with the Lord these precious saints do. We are so soft, not wanting to, or being willing to, suffer for the Lord. Too many of us are serving God for His benefits, seeking His hand but not His heart. Perhaps the greatest sermon I have ever heard preached was this one preached to me by this poor widow over a year-and-a-half span."

The team rescued a family by flying them in their 11-passenger plane to a safer area. Baker clearly remembers looking at this family, as they all became airborne, and thinking how they must have felt being out of immediate danger. But his next thoughts were, "How will they live?" He could not help but think of his own family knowing how safe and blessed they were.

Bagu &Lambert with Ryan & Richard on right.

They continued their trip to the other countries on their list, with each place having its impact on them. But Baker knew in his heart that ABS would pick the DRC in which to begin its humanitarian work.

In February of each year, the 55 nations of Africa meet in Addia Ababa, Ethiopia, at the Second United Nations Building. The meetings begin on a Sunday, and on the Saturday before, a delegation of 40 people from around the world are invited to attend a prayer breakfast. ABS was given four spaces and invited Gregory to be part of this momentous occasion. Gregory honored Baker by allowing him to take his place. He did this several times over the nearly 10 years he served with him.

The team arrived on Thursday with a planned tour of the African Union headquarters the next morning. All 40 of them were given an extended tour of the facility. As they entered the chamber where the actual meetings were held, they could see all the major news organizations setting up their cameras and equipment. Their guide was a believer, and someone asked him if they could pray. Muammar Gaddafi, the dictator of Libya, was serving as the president of the Union, but a vote was scheduled for Sunday morning. The guide answered, "Sure."

Baker walked to the platform with a couple of African women that he did not know, and they all started praying. The Holy Spirit moved in that chamber, and all the news organizations abandoned their equipment and left the meeting room. The Holy Spirit began interceding through most of the delegation, and they stayed 30 minutes or longer praying over all the seats where the 55 presidents of Africa would be sitting come Sunday.

On Saturday morning the prayer breakfast was being held at a five-star hotel, the security was tight. Baker was told the day before to bring nothing but the clothes on his back and his passport. He went through six or seven security screenings and finally was ushered into a large ballroom and was seated. Seven more people joined him, none of whom he knew. After everyone had assembled, prayer was offered for the meal and the meeting. Then they were invited to go to one of six buffet lines, each fifty feet long or longer.

The gentleman sitting on Baker's right struck up a conversation with him in the buffet line. Once they returned to their table, the man asked him what his function in life was. Baker shared that he was serving as the executive director of a humanitarian foundation called the Lazarus Foundation. He thanked Baker for helping the less fortunate. When Baker asked him what he did, the man started laughing and said, "I am the former president of Nigeria." Baker later said that if there had been a hole in the floor, he would gladly have jumped in. The former president grabbed his arm, still laughing, and said, "No problem. It's okay." They had a great time fellowshipping.

Also sitting at their table was a high court justice for the country of Malawi, who had just months earlier denied Madonna a petition to adopt a child. Baker would visit with her in Malawi later that next year. He knew that to say he had been honored to attend this prestigious event would be a great understatement.

After the prayer breakfast, he made contact on his own to visit an orphanage close by. The overseer for the Churches of God in Ethiopia picked him up and took him to a poor orphanage of about 50 to 60 children. Baker had arranged for the delivery of food to the orphanage, with plans to have lunch with them. It was surreal for him to be surrounded by such extravagance just a few hours earlier and now to be eating with orphan children in a dirt floor room. He looked into their faces and saw what innocence and humbleness really looked like. Although he knew that God had honored him by allowing him to attend the prayer breakfast, he sensed a special presence of His Spirit as he ministered to these precious children. If he could have only attended one of these events, he knew he would have chosen to be with these priceless treasures.

On Sunday, the news flashed that Gaddafi had been voted out as president of the African Union. The following morning, Baker departed and took advantage of the opportunity to make a couple of more site visits before flying back to the States.

Gregory was interested to hear how the trip went. By the time Baker had returned, they received word that indeed ABS had chosen the DRC in which to begin its humanitarian work. Gregory offered to partner with ABS, and, together, they developed a plan of action. In just a few months, Baker and Lambert, his counterpart with ABS, were heading back to the DRC to begin their work. They would eventually have nine large feeding centers located throughout the most affected area in eastern DRC. Food purchased in Uganda was transported by semis pulling two trailers through part of Sudan into the DRC. There were hundreds of tons of food shipped for three years helping to feed more than 10,000 orphans and widows. The Lazarus Foundation purchased all the food, with ABS handling most of the logistics on the ground—operating food distribution centers, providing trauma healing, Bibles, and other services. This incredible partnership helped many people.

DRC—widows and orphans (Bagu, far left in white shirt, Baker near center, Lambert in front far fight).

Kingsway Charities received a request from doctors working in the affected areas for medicines and supplies. A 40-foot shipping container was filled with the requested items and many other supplies. On one of his trips, Baker met a widow woman in Dungu who could not walk but had to pull herself around on the ground. He knelt and with an interpreter told her in a couple of months a container would be arriving. He assured her that he would see that she had a new wheelchair with tires made for the terrain. When he arrived back in Bristol, he went to Kingsway Charities and shared the story of this woman with Maryann, Gregory's sister, who directed the daily operation of the foundation. She immediately pulled a new wheelchair out, wrote the widow's name and the village she lived in, and promised him that she would personally make sure it was loaded in the container.

Baker and Dr. Bagu with woman for whom they provided a wheelchair.

Several months later, after the container had arrived, Baker went back to the Congo and witnessed that precious widow lady sitting in the wheelchair maneuvering around quite handily. He remarked, "Sometimes, it's the small things in life that mean the most, not only to us, but to God also. For if God sees all the sparrows and knows if one falls to the ground, how much more precious was this widow to Him? And once again he used 'such a worm as I.'"

35

Serving Orphans Worldwide

During the latter part of the fall of 2009 and leading into 2010, many of the children's homes that the Lazarus Foundation had built or had given help to reached out for help with their monthly budgets, something the foundation didn't normally do. But because Baker personally knew many of the directors, they began helping a few of them monthly.

In mid-2010, he visited Ecuador, Peru, Columbia, Paraguay, Uruguay, Bolivia, and Brazil and preached in the national convention in Argentina. He planned a meeting with Gregory in March and decided to drive the eight hours from Brunswick, instead of flying. During the meeting, Gregory asked him about the orphanages they were now assisting on a monthly basis. Baker shared that many were sighting the economy in the US slowing down as affecting donations.

Gregory remarked, "Richard, even with my resources, I can't be responsible for all the monthly expenses for the orphanages we have resourced over the years. Another thing, if they are solely looking to me for their support, and I lost most of my wealth or even died, where would that leave them? We need to find another way to help them with their monthly support."

Baker spoke up, "John, we could start another foundation focusing on precisely that."

Gregory responded, "That is exactly what I had in mind. We could do something on the order of Children of the World." That conversation laid the foundation for the establishment of Serving Orphans Worldwide (SOW). They immediately began the process of developing the structure relating to the purpose of the charity, board members, and officers needed to manage it. In a couple of weeks, Gregory called him and explained, "You know you will need to move to Bristol, as you will now have an office staff to manage."

Baker replied, "I know, but we will need to sell our home first."

Gregory asked him to bring Cheryl up as soon as possible for a visit. The following week, they drove to Bristol and Gregory showed them the first home he owned when he first moved to that city. It was vacant and he had just listed it for sale. He said, "You can live here until your home sells in Brunswick."

They committed to move in May, when the school year was over. Their move to Bristol was completed on May 28. He and Cheryl were so thankful to be able to live in Brunswick during his mother's final days. That brought great joy and peace to both of them.

In early July, their application for 501(c)(3) was approved, and they were officially in business. For the first few weeks, Baker used the personnel from Gregory's office, but then, Gregory hired Marsha Leonard who had just graduated from Lee University, to be his assistant. Her father, Bill Leonard, had led Gregory to the Lord back in the early 1980s.

A 15-member board was selected with Gregory serving as president and CEO, Baker serving as chief operating officer, and Bill George serving as secretary. Gregory and Baker went over a list of orphanages to begin partnering with and decided to call them "covenant orphanages." They initially started with 15. Baker visited each of the homes to go over budgets and to check out the facilities, ultimately to determine how much shortfall they were experiencing. They also developed a site report that would be completed by him as he made his annual visits. The orphanages also had to send them monthly reports and agree to annual visits by Baker or anyone from SOW. Furthermore, the visit could be unannounced. A representative had the right to show up at any time. The homes also had to reveal all other sources of revenue and donations they received monthly and had to give them permission to interact with their other donors.

The goal of SOW in relationship to donors was to provide complete accountability. SOW pledged that 100 percent of all donations would go to the orphanages, with the board of directors covering all the administrative expenses. Ten years later, that policy is still in place with not one donated dollar ever going toward the administrative cost of operating the ministry. Today, SOW's information booklet, in part, reports:

> There are approximately 150 million children around the world without a forever family. Although family is the ideal solution to the orphan crisis, we understand that it is not an immediate option for most children globally. In fact, the vast majority will never even be eligible for adoption. Orphaned children face extreme vulnerabilities including sex trafficking, forced child labor, HIV/AIDS and substance abuse. Many children have lost their parents due to illness, war, violence, and death. Some have been abandoned due to extreme poverty, stigma, and untreated mental illness.
>
> Global orphan care is complicated, costly, and sometimes riddled with corruption. When you make a gift through SOW, you can know that all of our partner homes agree to provide a high standard of care, and accountability. This includes announced and unannounced site visits, monthly reports, and other measures to ensure that your gift is making a difference and bringing the power of possibility to these children.
>
> When you give to Serving Orphans Worldwide, you are not only feeding their mind, body, and spirit. You are feeding the potential for greatness in that child. We believe that every resource donated to orphan care is a blessing and we take our responsibility to be good stewards of what is given seriously. That is why we have adopted a 100 percent approach. This guarantees that whether you sponsor a child or support a home, our promise is that every penny you give goes directly to the field and will never be spent on SOW's administrative costs. Through the generous support of our sponsors, everything from paper clips to staff salaries is totally covered. We even have a partnership with the bank so that all outgoing transfer fees are covered.

In the fall of 2010, Baker needed to visit a number of ministries in seven countries, on three continents. With SOW now up and operational, it became important to get quality photos and videos of the homes they were now sponsoring, to help in promotion. They also prepared to begin supporting a few more. They had begun receiving requests for assistant, and Baker needed to make site visits to do an accurate assessment.

On July 4, 2009, the Bakers' son, Ryan, married the love of his life, Mia. Gregory allowed them to use his beachfront home on Hilton Head Island. Baker had the wonderful privilege of marrying them on the beach. In time, they gave Richard and Cheryl two wonderful grandsons, Seneca and Everett. Ryan had enlisted about a year earlier in the US Army and was stationed at Fort Walton Beach. Mia was finishing her last year at University of Georgia. Being a gifted photographer, she seemed an ideal choice for Baker, considering he really needed someone to travel with him with her expertise. However, they had not spent much time around each other because of living hours apart. After deciding to call and ask her, he reached out to Ryan and asked, "Do you mind if I take your wife on a three-week trip to Africa and Asia?"

He answered, "Not at all, if you can get her to go."

Baker called Mia to discuss his thoughts with her. She was on board immediately. They departed in a few weeks with their first stop being Phebe Gray orphanage in Liberia. They spent a couple of days taking photos, shooting videos, doing interviews with both the children and staff in preparation for adding content to their web page, which would be used in promoting the children's homes to potential donors. He felt for the first time the pressure to get it right, to be factual in what they promoted on the webpage, knowing that if they failed to tell their story, their potential donors may not connect or give them the support they needed. Mia was an immense help to him in this area.

They took the same approach at each home they visited. Their second stop was Hope for the Children in Nairobi, Kenya, the largest ministry SOW sponsored, with over 600. It was structured differently than a traditional orphanage since most of the children stayed with adopted families in the evening and returned the next morning. The home provided meals and schooling, as well as for their spiritual formation.

From Kenya, Richard and Mia traveled to Zambia to spend a couple of days at Emma's Kids. There they met with Peter Thomas, a German brother who served as the field director for the continent of Africa. They rode with him to Malawi, which was about a 16-hour drive. There Baker met with the chief justice of the Supreme Court, who had denied Madonna her adoption petition. The justice had reached out to him and informed him as to when she would be in Malawi, since she wanted to meet with him. The next morning, she came to their hotel and met with him and Thomas.

Baker sensed that she had much compassion for the plight of orphans, seeing she was involved in a ministry that was building small homes and putting several orphans with a widow to form a family unit. The homes were built near each other to add security, as well as to form a greater support network. As they talked, Baker knew Gregory would love this concept and felt encouraged to learn that the highest-ranking judge in the country was a believer and had a heart for orphans.

The judge began to talk about the burden of her position and the corruption the countries had to deal with. She also discussed the burden she was carrying trying to help the underprivileged children in her own country. Baker asked, "May we pray for you?"

"Oh yes. Please do," she replied.

Thomas and Baker began to pray, and the power of the Holy Spirit came into that place. She wept and cried out to God. When the meeting ended, she shared with us how refreshed she felt and how her heavy burden had been lifted.

The Lazarus Foundation sowed some into the ministry she participated in, but Baker believed the main reason thy met in Ethiopia was spiritual. They had prayed at the African Union headquarters for Muammar Gaddafi not to be reelected as president, and now they were agreeing again in prayer for the well-being of orphans and for strength for a godly high court justice. Baker expressed, "We fail many times to understand the power of prayer, even at times when we see no answers or movement. When we pray in faith, something powerful begins to happen in the realm where warfare takes place."

Departing Malawi, the traveling companions headed to Uganda and spent a day at Grace Orphanage. As they flew from Uganda to Bangkok, Thailand, Mia, who loved animals and spent a lot of time rescuing them, turned to her father-in-law, and remarked, "I think I will start rescuing orphans now." Mia would play a significant role over the next seven years in helping SOW tell the story of the plight of the 150 million orphans around the world.

When they arrived in Bangkok, Lili and her husband, Samnuke, met them. They had two orphanages located close to the border with Myanmar (Burma), House of Hope and House of Faith, orphanages that SOW was considering supporting. They toured the sites, Mia did her amazing photography, and the troupe returned to Bangkok to fly to the northern city of Chiang Mai.

A North American couple was running an orphanage there and had reached out to SOW for assistance. The couple was nice enough and children precious, but Baker felt a check in his spirit by the Holy Spirit and decided not to consider supporting them. A brother from another ministry came to pick them up and take them to the hotel. He asked how the visit went, and Baker expressed that he did not feel peace about supporting this particular home. The brother announced, "I know another one a couple of miles from here. A Dutch family serves as directors. We can visit if you like."

Baan Zion orphanage for girls—Thailand.

Upon their arrival, they found the children (all girls) running and playing. The director was sitting on a picnic table watching them. Baker walked up to him, introduced himself, and shared with him his mission. For two hours, the director explained about the ministry he and his wife were passionately heading up. It was an amazing story. In Thailand, if a mother is sentenced to prison, she can take her children with her. Their ministry was to rescue these girls from prison.

When the team prepared to leave, Baker asked him, "Do you have any pressing needs?"

Immediately, the director broke down and began crying. He conveyed to them that they were in a serious financial strait because of a couple of situations beyond their control. In fact, he had just closed a smaller boys' home because of the lack of funds, and it appeared that the same fate may happen to the girls' home. At the end of the conversation, Baker did something he rarely did. He gave him $2,000 in cash and asked the office in Bristol to wire him an additional $3,000. The director declared, "SOW rescued the children's home from closing." Today, 10 years later, SOW is still supporting Baan Zion Children's Home. The ministry has flourished and helped many young girls over the years to have a better life.

House of Hope Children's Home–Thailand.

Leaving Chiang Rai, they flew to Chiang Mai, another city in northern Thailand. Connie and Richard, Baptist missionaries who had an orphanage that only took in infant babies, met them at the airport. One had been aborted but survived the procedure. She was so precious to Baker. He would push her and several other babies around in the stroller. This was, and continues to be, an amazing ministry. SOW is still providing support, and Connie's Home is used as a training center for workers in other children's homes.

From Thailand, they headed for Jakarta, Indonesia, with four new orphanages SOW would now be supporting once Baker returned and presented them to the board of directors. The board always asked questions but never denied the support of any orphanage he submitted to them for consideration. Baker never took for granted the confidence that Gregory and the board had entrusted in him to be their eyes and ears.

Connie's Home–Thailand (2013).

They arrived in Jakarta and took a taxi to their hotel. The next morning, Tommy Smith, a long-term missionary to Indonesia, along with his wife, Poppi, picked them up for a visit to the orphanage. Gregory and Baker had visited it on their last trip. A woman named Backer was the director. The home was built on top of a garbage dump, and the land was very unstable. With all the drawbacks, they had a great ministry work there. The work featured boys' and girls' dorms, a church, a small medical clinic, a small home for the elderly, and a feeding program for others in the neighborhood. They were running a deficit and Baker decided to recommend them to the board for monthly support, which they approved.

As Baker and his entourage completed their tour, and after Mia had done all the photography work, she collapsed. Her father-in-law managed to catch her before she hit the ground. She was completely exhausted from the hard work and the traveling by plane, bus, van, and car, not to mention a lot of walking and lugging her gear around in seven countries located on three continents visiting more than fifteen ministries. The good news was they were heading home the next day.

Within a couple of weeks after Richard and Mia returned to the states, he was again on an airplane, Thai Air, for a fifteen-hour nonstop flight from Los Angeles to Bangkok, where he changed planes for his final destination, Colombo, Sri Lanka. About one hour before landing, he checked his flight itinerary and discovered that he had a twelve-hour layover. He wondered what his travel agent was thinking and, frankly, became extremely frustrated.

After landing at 8:00 am, he went to the Tai lounge to take a shower and eat breakfast. That privilege came as one of the perks in flying as frequently as he did. He was a gold member with Thai Airlines, their top level, and a diamond elite member with Delta, their top level. For a few months, he stayed in the top five frequent flyers with Delta.

Orphanage in slums of Jakarta, Indonesia (2015).

As he checked his e-mails, he saw one from Fred Garmon, director of PCL (People for Care and Learning). Baker sat on PCL's board of directors. In his email, Garmon asked him to call him as soon as he could, which Baker did.

Garmon asked, "What part of the world are you in?"

Baker answered, "I just landed in Bangkok."

"Unbelievable!" Garmon exclaimed. He continued, "We have a situation in Phenom Penh, Cambodia. Matt Bohlman, director of the Pace Children's Home in Siem Reap, discovered that a children's home there, led by three Cambodian men, are in the process of selling the older girls to a brothel. Matt informed Bien Raneses, who is one of our leaders in Cambodia. He called me with the information. I can't travel to Cambodia anytime soon. Since you're so close, could you make time for a sight visit?"

Baker responded, "Fred, I will see if I can get a flight from Bangkok and go check the situation out for you, since I have a 12-hour layover." He immediately went to the ticket counter and found a flight that departed Phenom Phen at 10:30 am, with a return flight around 6:00 pm. He bought the ticket and boarded the one-hour flight. Bien and his wife, Faye, were waiting for him.

They drove Baker to the children's home, which was located about 45 minutes from the airport. Upon arrival, one of the three Cambodian men who directed the orphanage met them. There were probably 50 to 60 children in total. A couple of the older girls had told Faye that they were going to be sold to a brothel. These men claimed to be Christians and received some support from time to time from PCL, with a Mennonite group in the US also supporting them. In fact, some of the girls had already been sent to the brothel. Bohlman and a few men, at the risk of their own lives, had rescued them. After reaching out to Gregory, funds were immediately released to lease a two-story facility, and PCL started their second orphanage in Cambodia, House of Hope. In 2018, House of Hope merged with Pace Children's Home in Siem Reap.

About six months later, Gregory would make a visit with Baker to meet these precious girls who were now safe, being properly cared for, and learning about God's amazing love. The determination was made to find a different location. They saw a new building under construction, which they leased upon completion. It became the new home for House of Hope and now receives support from Serving Orphans Worldwide.

That afternoon, Baker flew back to Bangkok and connected with his flight to Sri Lanka. He could not help but ponder repeatedly in his mind that Ken Kennedy, his travel agent, who was one of the best in handling corporate clients, did not make a mistake. No doubt, he was unknowingly led by the Holy Spirit in booking Baker's flight with the 12-hour layover in Bangkok. It was all in God's plan, for He had seen and heard the distressful cry of these helpless orphan girls.

Baker remarked, "Once again, such a worm as I was used in a mighty way by his Lord and Savior. There is no better feeling than to know God trusted you with such an assignment, to be a small part of rescuing some of the most vulnerable people in the world, orphaned young teenage girls. The average age that girls, and boys to a lesser extent, are sex trafficked is 12 to 14, and internationally, there is an estimated 40 million that have been sold into modern slavery today, most to be exploited by the sex industry."

Destiny Village, Haiti—an unexpected kiss (circa 2014).

36

Thieves, Biting Mosquitos, Barking Dogs, and Praying Muslims

Two Thousand Nine found Baker back to Liberia, where he spent a couple of days visiting the children's home and several churches that had been recently built back. He then flew into the Sierra Leone airport, which was located on an island with three means of travel to Freetown, the capital–by helicopter, hover craft, or ferry. The national overseer, John Kun, was a Liberian who also served as overseer to Guinea, a neighboring country Baker was scheduled to visit next.

Because Kun and a delegation had purchased roundtrip tickets for the ferry, he felt he needed to take the ferry also. As they boarded, Baker noticed that he was one of only two or three who were not locals. The trip took about an hour, and he enjoyed the fellowship and scenery. There was even a little singing, and a comedian performed. He got a taste of a culture he had not experienced before.

When the ferry docked and people began disembarking, the process became a bit disorderly. Baker and his companions were on the third level and eventually made their way to the first level and to a 30-inch-wide ramp leading to the dock. Kun was carrying one of Baker's bags, and they had gotten separated. As Baker started down the ramp, he could see Kun exiting onto the dock. He only had his backpack. He observed four young men coming up the ramp that he assumed were porters. As they drew closer, he saw them staring at him and nodding at each other. Not knowing what to expect, he braced himself as they approached. Immediately, two of the men crossed to his side of the ramp and attacked him.

Baker had on cargo pants that had a zipper pocket inside the main pocket, which was designed to carry valuables. In it he had $16,000 for a project in Guinea. His cell phone was in his right pocket with the money in his left pocket. He did not think they expected him to fight back, but fight back he did, hitting both of them. As they managed to get their hands in both of his pockets, he focused on the one trying to get the money. He grabbed his hand and by pressing his thumb down hard on his wrist, made him relinquish his hold. Baker then pushed him back with his shoulder.

He believes that a number of factors saved him that day. Ultimately, he knew it was by God's help. From the natural perspective, the ramp was too narrow for the other two men to get to him. Descending the ramp gave him momentum. And being in 30 or more fights before becoming a Christian did not hurt either. His fear was that they were nearing the dock, and it could have been four against one. Thankfully, a taxi driver saw what was happening and began running for the dock, shouting as he approached. He was a large man, probably more than six feet tall and weighing around 250 pounds. When the four young men saw him coming, they fled. All they managed to get was his cell phone.

The taxi driver asked him what he was doing on the ferry all alone. About that time, Kun approached and asked him what had happened. The taxi driver ripped into Kun for allowing himself to become separated from his traveling companion and sharing what had just happened. Kun apologized profusely and was clearly shaken over the encounter. Baker was not physically hurt, other than a little stinging where he took a hit. However, he did expend a fair amount of adrenaline. The same taxi driver took them to a hotel, where Baker thanked him and gave him a healthy tip.

He had already begun to feel a bit under the weather, and by the time he had gotten to the hotel, he was feeling worse. The delegation had dinner together, and Baker turned in early. During the night, somewhere around midnight, the power went off and the room became unbearably hot. To find some relief, he raised the window and tried to go back to sleep. But with an open window, mosquitoes feasted on his blood the rest of the night. At some point, dogs began to bark and did not stop until the sun came up. As if all these disturbances were not enough, around 5:00 am the Muslims began to pray (Sierra Leone is over 50 percent Muslim). Baker reflected, "I am 63 years old at the writing of this book, and this night will go down as my worse night ever!"

At 7:00 am, the men met for breakfast and prepared for their scheduled 9:00 am visit to the school, where Baker was to speak at chapel. He was trying to keep a poker face but was sick and getting sicker by the minute. They made it to the elementary school that the Lazarus Foundation had built. There were now over 400 children attending. Many of the parents came, wanted to meet him, and thank the foundation for investing in their children.

After having a short meeting with the principle and faculty, Baker broke out with a high fever and could hardly stand. He spoke privately with Kun and informed him that there was no way he physically could preach. In fact, he insisted that they leave as soon as possible. After explaining his condition to the principal, Baker said goodbye to the children and gave them all a blow pop.

He asked Kun to take him to the nicest hotel in the capital hoping they would have a room available. As he checked in, he knew his condition was worsening. They had already purchased bus tickets and were scheduled to leave that afternoon for Guinea. Baker asked Kun into his room and explained that he needed to stay behind and rest a couple of days. He instructed him to take the $16,000 and make the trip himself.

Kun replied, “Pastor, I feel it is best that I stay with you until you get well.” Baker insisted, and Kun departed.

As Kun exited the room, Baker fell face first onto his bed and did not wake up until early the next morning. He perspired to the point where he was having cramps and was forced to drink water and juices. He knew he was in serious trouble and decided to call Douglas Leroy, director of World Missions, to see if he could get someone to him from a neighboring country. When he rang the hotel operator, he announced, “I would like to make a call to the US.”

The operator replied, “Sorry sir, we have not had an outside line since the civil war ended.”

With his cell phone stolen and with no international phone system functioning in the country, his fears began to mount. Feeling a sense of desperation, he walked to the lobby, sat down, and just watched people moving about. After about 30 minutes, he walked over to the desk and asked again, “Is there any way I can call the US?”

The clerk answered, “Only by cell phone that has international capacity.” He had been observing a certain bellhop, a young man in his early 20s, who seemed to have a good attitude and disposition. Baker asked for a moment of his time, told him that he was quite ill, and informed him that he needed to get to the airport. He explained that he was too sick to take an hour ride in a taxi with no air-conditioning, with windows down in 100-degree temperatures, and with stop and go traffic to get to the ferry or hovercraft.

The bellhop responded, “Sir, at the bottom of the hill below the hotel is a UN base, and twice daily they have helicopters coming and going. For $70 they will transport you if there is space. But you must purchase a ticket in advance.”

Baker asked, “Would you go for me if I give you the money?” He agreed, and Baker gave him a hundred-dollar bill. After the bellhop departed, Baker returned to his room and wrote down who he was and scribbled his contact information should anything happen to him. He waited and waited, but the bellhop had not returned. He decided to walk to the lobby hoping to see him, but the young man was not there.

Upon returning to his room, he laid down feeling hopeless and finding it difficult to pray. Finally, after three or four hours, the bellhop returned apologizing and saying he had to wait for one man to see if there was room that day.

“Here is your ticket and change,” he reported.

As he handed Baker his $30, Baker handed it back to him and asked, “How much do you earn a day?”

He answered, “Five dollars.”

Baker reached in his pocket to retrieve some additional cash, gave him another $20, and shared Jesus with him, to which he replied, “I am a believer.”

In an hour, Baker took a taxi for the 10-minute ride to the UN base. He walked inside a small building, but no one acknowledged his presence. Gazing at the window, he saw four large UN cargo helicopters and a couple of pilots. Thinking that that must be his flight, he exited the building with his ticket in hand and walked to the helicopter. The pilots were already in the cockpit, so he climbed into the cargo area. There were no seats but just a lot of cargo covered in a net. He sat down on the cargo and waited for takeoff. Within a few moments, the engine roared to life and the blades began turning, causing a considerable vibration. As the chopper lifted off, Baker, not knowing for sure just where this bird was flying to, felt anxiety grip him like he had never experienced.

In 15 minutes, they landed on the runway of the international airport at Sierra Leone. He hopped off and walked around to the front of the airport to gain entrance. Walking up to the Kenya Airlines desk, which was the main carrier at this airport, he asked if there were any flights departing for a major city in Africa or Europe. She informed him that their only flight was departing in two hours for Accra, Ghana, but there were no seats available. She continued, "Sir, there are no seats available on any flight until tomorrow afternoon."

Baker now felt that his only option was to try to purchase a ticket from a passenger and offer them a thousand dollars extra. But that did not work either. He walked back over to the desk to plead his case one more time. Now having stood in line for 20 minutes and feeling increasingly ill, he almost felt like giving up. A Kenya Airlines agent walked up to him and asked, "Where do you want to go?"

Baker shared with him that he was sick and needed to get somewhere with a decent medical clinic. The representative asked, "Will Accra do?" He then instructed, "Come with me." Taking Baker to the front of the line, he told the counter agent to give him a business class seat to Accra.

The woman responded, "Sir, we are completely booked."

Authoritatively, he commanded, "Then you will need to bump someone!" He then walked away.

Baker received his ticket, walked through the boarding gate, and was able to borrow someone's cell phone to call Leroy. When he heard of Baker's plight and received his flight information, he assured him that he would have someone waiting at the airport for him.

Upon arriving in Accra, Ghana, Baker exited to find a sweet couple, Ephraim and Margaret Shawa, standing and holding a sign with his name on it. He was serving as superintendent of West Africa, and she was a registered nurse. When Baker asked them to take him to the hospital, she replied, "Brother, let us take you to our home first. The hospitals here are not too good."

Margaret gave him five-star treatment and even hand-fed him soup. She also spoke with a doctor concerning his symptoms, and he prescribed an antibiotic. Baker stayed with them for three days, until he started feeling better. After deciding to travel back to the States, World Missions booked him a business class seat on KLM back to Atlanta. There he caught the 45-minute flight to Brunswick, Georgia, where he was living at the time.

When he arrived in Brunswick, Cheryl took him to urgent care where he discovered that he had double pneumonia. It took him a couple of weeks to fully recover. According to him, "This will go down as the most challenging trip I ever took, but God's faithfulness was with me every step of the way. I often reflect on this experience and feel in my heart that if we never face obstacles and challenges, our faith will never grow, neither would we be afforded the opportunity to see God work His miracles on our behalf."

37

An Interrupted Flight

In early 2011, Baker received a called from Roger Gillum, a member of Men and Women of Action, who back in 2004, was on a trip with another mission organization in Karako, Tanzania. While on this trip, he met Mama Warra and her husband, Nnko, who was a pastor. He developed a relationship that continues today. In 2004, Mama Warra had begun taking in orphan babies, and the outreach grew until the need arose for an orphanage. Roger, a commercial electrician in Atlanta, Georgia, helped them some and connected them with a church in the States, as well as with other individual donors. Through these combined efforts, Shalom Orphanage came into existence.

At the request of Gillum, Baker flew into Kilimanjaro in 2011. Pastor Nnko transported him on the two-hour trip to Karako. After arriving at the orphanage, he quickly saw that the home was struggling, since they had taken in more children. Yet, the children seemed happy and loved, despite their circumstances.

Shalom was a block building with meager furnishings and needing a lot of repairs. As they gave him a tour, he felt the Holy Spirit speaking to his heart to help. Other than what Gillum had shared with him, he knew nothing about them, nor did he know how they managed the home. He asked about their budget and was told that they were living day to day with no steady donations coming in.

The following day, just before Nnko was to take him back to the Kilimanjaro airport, he had a meeting with them and asked many questions. He also explained how SOW operated. Feeling released in his spirit to give them $2,000, he began counting out the money. Mama Warra burst into tears and shared with him just how desperate conditions had gotten. She related that they had been praying for a miracle of $2,000 to help with immediate needs. For Baker, the joy of being an answer to someone's prayer was beyond explanation.

Forty-five minutes after loading up and heading back, Nnko asked Baker if he wanted to see some wildlife. Of course, he did. Nnko pulled into a game reserve, and they saw several different animals. As they came up on several elephants, he espied one of largest bulls he had ever seen. As they drove in the bush, the bull elephant charged their vehicle, getting within 20 feet before he stopped. That gave Baker an adrenaline rush, quite unlike anything he had experienced before, but certainly not in the same way.

Shalom Orphanage--Tanzania
Mommy Warra with scarf.

After stopping in Arusha to spend the night, Nnko dropped Baker off at the airport early the next morning. Leaving Arusha, he flew to Zimbabwe and visited Rose of Sharon Orphanage directed by Fatima Maruta. From there, he flew to Kenya for more site visits and then returned to the States.

When he arrived home, Gillum called to tell him that when Nnko and son, Daniel, were returning home after delivering him to the airport, Nnko had an aneurysm and died the next day. This news caught Baker completely off guard. Nnko seemed healthy and was only in his late fifties. At that moment, all he could think of was that Mama Warra had all those children, and now she was a widow.

The Lord spoke to his heart quietly saying, "That is why I sent you at the time I did." In his heart he knew that God wanted SOW to support this home. After sharing the story with Gregory and getting board approval, SOW immediately began supporting the home, and continues to, nine years later. Baker visited the home several more times and even brought a professional video crew from Ohio to produce a video telling their amazing story.

Village close to Shalom Orphanage.

Ryan and Mia, without Baker's knowledge, scheduled a meeting with Gregory, whose office was only about 20 feet from his. When they walked by, they just looked at Dad and smiled. After thirty minutes, Gregory called him in and questioned, "Well Daddy, what do you think about your kids going and living in Cambodia as missionaries with the Lazarus Foundation and SOW?"

Baker was not surprised at his son, seeing that he had lived twice on the mission field. However, Mia caught him a little off guard. It became apparent to him that the trip she had taken with him, visiting seven countries, and three continents, had had an immense effect on her.

Within a few months, they moved to Siem Reap and were assigned the task of providing oversight to the orphanages in Asia. They would eventually move to Phnom Penh where PCL was spearheading the Build a City project. The Lazarus Foundation had invested nearly two million dollars into Build a City. In addition, Baker presented a one-million dollar check to Garmon and the PCL board of directors on behalf of John and Joan Gregory. John wanted Ryan to lend any assistance he could and give progress reports. Mike and Sandy Forbis, owners of F & F Construction Company in Memphis, Tennessee, also donated millions towards Build a City and toward operational support of PCL.

Build a City was a large multi-million dollar, multi-year project to literally build a small city for 8,000 displaced refugees. It included sewage drainage, paved streets, hundreds of small homes, police station, medical facilities, market, church, and much more. It was the largest project that he had ever been part of.

Cleveland, Tennessee, adopted Phnom Penh as a sister city. A political delegation from Cambodia that served in a similar role as the US president's cabinet flew into Chattanooga, Tennessee. Gregory afforded Baker the wonderful opportunity to fly them on two private jets to meet Governor Bill Haslam, Garmon and the leadership from PCL, and other representatives such as Kevin D. Brooks, who at the time served as a Tennessee state congressman. Today, he serves as the mayor of Cleveland. Brooks was very instrumental in forging this partnership between Phnom Penh and Cleveland and arranging the meeting with Governor Haslam.

After the meeting, they flew to Bristol, Tennessee, where they spent a couple days, with Gregory providing accommodations at the prestigious Olde Farm Country Club in Bristol, Virginia. They played golf and even attended the auto races at Bristol Speedway. This was the first for all of them. Baker said that he watched their expressions more than he did the race.

Both Baker and Garmon know that God brought them together in 2006, for since that time, they became close friends, traveled together, did ministry together, and served together on boards. Amazingly, their paths were similar, both having been involved in drugs and alcohol, as well as being arrested. But God wonderfully transformed both of their lives and put them together for nine years to help the less fortunate. God has since taken them down different paths, with Garmon holding a PhD in leadership and conducting leadership labs. Baker himself took Garmon's 72-hour leader labs course. Ultimately, God has used them both to accomplish His purpose. They also shared the same great mentor, Bill George, although Garmon enjoyed that mentorship longer than Baker did. Baker, with tongue-in-cheek, said that was because the Lord knew Garmon needed a little more.

In the early part of 2011, a strong storm struck Mexico on the gulf side severely damaging a couple of the roofs at Alpha and Omega Children's Home located in Poza Rica, Mexico. The Lazarus Foundation helped to expand this home back in the nineties and now SOW was giving monthly support. Gregory asked Baker to fly down with some cash to repair the roofs and see if the orphanage needed anything else.

Alpha and Omega Home–Poza Rica, Mexico.

He flew into Mexico City and took a 50-passenger commuter jet into Poza Rica. About 30 minutes before landing, the rain began to beat down intensely with no letup. On final approach, the wind tossed the plane from side to side creating a most uncomfortable landing. Baker sat in the first row facing the flight attendant. Although she was unable to see out the window, he could and sensed something was not right. The descent seemed much too steep. The plane hit the runway hard and sideways, lifted back off, and hit the runway hard the second time. However, this time the plane was completely out of control, spinning around and around, and eventually crashing into a wooded area. In the process it knocked down several small to medium size trees before coming to a jolting stop.

The smell of smoke permeated the air, and immediately the emergency doors opened. Unceremoniously, the flight attendant was the first person trying to escape. The captain had just opened the cockpit door and grabbed the back of her collar shouting for her to help people evacuate. They asked uninjured people to exit plane ASAP without taking anything with them. An elderly man and woman sitting behind Baker were both injured. After everyone had gotten off that could, he offered the captain his help, since no rescue personnel had yet arrived, it being a small airport. He thanked him and asked him to exit the plane.

When he turned to retrieve his backpack from the overhead bin, the captain exclaimed, "Sir, you are not allowed to exit with anything!" However, he had $25,000 in his carry-on luggage, and he was not about to leave it. As he walked to the runway, he found the water several inches above his ankles, and the torrential rain continued.

He pulled out his phone and called Garmon knowing that calling Cheryl would be too upsetting to her. At that point, he just needed to talk to someone. Understandably, his nerves were shot. Finally, a single 15-passenger van came to begin transporting the passengers to the terminal. He decided to walk, as did a few others. As they entered the terminal, the scene was chaotic. No one offered to see if he had sustained any injuries. Anyway, he just wanted to get out of the airport and get to the orphanage as soon as he could.

Finally reaching his destination, he was able to clean up, change clothes, and unwind the rest of the evening. Slowly, he began to feel soreness to the point he could hardly walk. The next morning, he toured the orphanage and surveyed the damage. He gave them the funds necessary to replace the roofs, bought the children pizza, ice cream, and drinks, and spent some time interacting with them.

The airport had been closed after the crash landing and did not reopen until after lunch. Baker arrived at the airport, received his boarding pass, cleared security, and waited for the boarding announcement. When the call came, there were probably 200 people heading for the plane, a Boeing 737. The boarding process took them outside and up a set of stairs to the plane. When the passengers looked over and witnessed the plane sitting in the woods, all but 15 or 20 turned around and walked back in the terminal. Although nervous himself, he continued up the steps and boarded.

After reaching 10,000 feet, the "Fasten Seatbelt" sign went off and the flight attendants began serving drinks and a meal. Baker wanted nothing more than to land in Mexico City. Without warning, the plane hit a severe downdraft which quickly thrust the plane downward a few thousand feet. One of the flight attendants fell in the aisle with food and drinks flying in every direction. Thankfully, they made it to Mexico City without further incidence.

When he tried to exit the plane, he discovered that he could barely walk. Since he had a three-hour layover before his departure to Guatemala, he slipped into the restroom, walked into a stall, shut the door, and sat there for two hours trying to pray and find some peace. At that point, he was not sure that he could get on another plane. Composing himself, he finally went to the gate and waited for the boarding call. Once again, when he started walking, he found it difficult to get on the plane.

The takeoff was delayed for 30 minutes, which only added to Baker's anguish. Fortunately, the flight was smooth and uneventful. He never had any trouble getting onto another flight since then, and he has been on hundreds. He has always given God the glory saying, "When His peace invades our fear and torment, His peace abides, and fear and torment are dispelled."

38

North Korea

In June of 2011, Baker received an invitation from Global Resources Services (GRS)—a humanitarian organization that works to build sufficiency by partnering with countries to develop health, education, and income—to travel to China and North Korea. At the time of his trip, GRS, whose director was Dr. Robert Springs, was one of only five NGO organizations allowed to work in the Democratic People's Republic of North Korea.

Gregory had supported GRS and had a heart to help the people of North Korea. In the mid-nineties, he invited a number of scientists and chemists from North Korea to King Pharmaceuticals, located in Bristol, Tennessee, for training in manufacturing antibiotics. Gregory disclosed to Baker that the North Korean officials repeatedly wanted to know what he expected in return. He kept responding, "Nothing! I just want to help the people of North Korea." Eventually the Lazarus Foundation would give the funds to build a factory that processed soybeans for making soymilk and another product they called "cornbread," which was fed to the school children. He learned that for many children, it was their only meal of the day. The waste product was used to feed hogs on a farm located on the same property.

Dan Jones, former president of the American Heart Foundation, and at the time of Baker's trip, was chancellor of Ole Miss (University of Mississippi), also accompanied the team of six of traveling to North Korea. He also brought a faculty member, who was from South Korea, to serve as translator. They flew into Beijing where Baker had to officially request permission at the North Korean embassy to make the visit. It took two days to receive permission and visas. GRS put him through several briefings on protocol–the dos and don'ts. One bit of information stuck clearly in his mind. Since the US had no official diplomatic ties with North Korea, breaking one of the country's laws could spell serious trouble. He was told to assume the hotels, restaurants, and cars would be bugged.

The team flew a North Korean airline to Pyongyang and was chauffeured to their hotel by government officials. After checking in, they met for dinner and retired for the night. Baker felt extremely isolated and quite unsettled being all alone in a North Korean hotel. Following breakfast the next morning, the entourage visited the main hospital in the capital. Ole Miss had been assisting the hospital by providing training with laparoscopic instruments. They even attended the live surgery of a 14-year-old girl who was having an appendectomy via laparoscopic surgery, all suiting up and standing around her. She was not yet under anesthesia and probably wondered what all these Americans were doing around her bed.

The hospital staff expressed deep appreciation to Jones and Ole Miss for their donations and assistance.

That evening, the guests attended a symphony in their honor, with several hundred people attending. It was an amazing experience. The following day they were driven in two older model SUVs five hours from the capital to the soy factory the Lazarus Foundation had built. The government officials informed them that this was the farthest into the interior of the country that any NGO had ever been allowed to travel. They witnessed firsthand the abject poverty of the vast majority of North Koreans. All along the road, people were on their knees pulling grass to eat.

The team arrived at the factory and was met by some of the friendliest and most hospitable people they had ever met. The plant manager took them on a tour showing how every part of the soybean was used. Baker reflected that the hog farm that was adjacent to the factory was as clean as any he had ever seen. While visiting a local school, they saw the children eating their lunch of "cornbread" that was made from soybeans.

Because of the poor nutrition, especially with pregnant women, GRS had shipped in thousands of cases of nutritional supplements. The shipment had arrived shortly before the guests did, and they were able to distribute the supplements to many pregnant women. Each one was given enough to last through her pregnancy. A look of amazement and a glimmer of hope that radiated on their faces lifted the spirits of these benefactors.

After being transported to a small seaside resort, the team checked into their hotel and met for dinner. Present were mostly high-ranking military personnel and businesspeople, although all could have been government personnel. Seeing people eat grass made it extremely difficult to sit down to eat a plate of seafood.

The following day, they arrived back in Pyongyang and did a little sightseeing. As they came to a large bridge that spanned a wide river, Baker saw to his right a US ship, the USS Pueblo, which was captured by the North Koreans in 1968 in what is known as the "Pueblo Incident." It became apparent that their driver was taking them there for a tour. Baker, along with the others, exclaimed, "No! We will not step foot on this ship!" The rest of the team traveling in a separate vehicle told the host the same thing. The driver changed course and drove them back to their hotel, no doubt frustrated that his guests did not allow him to gloat over North Korea's trophy.

That evening was their last one, and they gathered for a farewell meal function. The hosts instructed them on the time to eat and assigned their seats, although they all ate at the same table. At least two or three North Koreans always joined them. Everyone's table setting had wine and liquor. In their briefings in Beijing, the team members were encouraged to do everything they could to accommodate and please their hosts. But Baker's strong Christian values were not for sale. He shared with Jones, who was sitting next to him, that he could not violate his convictions and would not participate in the toasting and drinking. Jones looked at him and remarked, "Richard, me neither. Let's just take the glass, hold it up, and put the rim to our mouths without drinking the alcohol." He took the wise council.

As they enjoyed a seven-course meal that night, Baker struggled knowing that most people in the country were barely surviving. He noticed directly across from him was a place setting, but no one was sitting there. About halfway through the meal, a middle-aged woman came and sat down in front of him. She spoke perfect English and small-talked for a few minutes. She then asked, "How are Dr. Gregory and his wife, Joan, doing?" Continuing, she asked, "How are his children, Susan and James, getting along? We are sorry to hear he sold the pharmaceutical company (he purchased it back from Pfizer in 2014). And how are Cheryl and your five children? Are you enjoying living in Bristol?" Those and other questions quickly revealed to him just how good their intelligence was. Frankly, the level of their intelligence shook him considerably.

The woman then expressed her government's appreciation for all that Gregory had done in helping their people and asking for nothing in return. She also expressed appreciation for the Gregory family's non-profit Kingsway Charities sending the containers of medicines and medical equipment.

Baker was told that he and his team were some of only a 3,000 North Americans who have been able to visit North Korea since the Korean War. He knew that if it had not been for the philanthropy efforts of Gregory and his family, he would never have received a visa to enter the country. The woman also thanked GRS for their several trips each year to North Korea and to Jones and Ole Miss for all their help in donating much-needed equipment to their hospitals. She is one of the women who appears with the present leader Kim Jong Un and serves as his interpreter.

The entire party felt relieved to be on a plane the next morning bound for Beijing, even though China was itself a communist country. Some aspects of the trip to North Korea would have to remain confidential to keep from jeopardizing any humanitarian foundations that are still able to gain access to country. The people are beautiful and friendly, moms and dads who love their children just as Americans love theirs.

Baker challenges and cautions, "As the Lord impresses you, pray for the people of North Korea and for the people of every other oppressive country in the world. And pray for the United States, for if we are not careful, and if we don't turn back as a nation to God, this will be our fate as well."

39

Central and Eastern Europe

As Baker moved into July, his travel pace continued. SOW received a request to help a couple of orphanages in the country of Hungary and Romania. Baker flew into Budapest and transferred to a train for a two-hour ride to his designation. A newly appointed missionary, who had only been in the country with his family for a couple of months, met him. Since the missionary had not been in the country long enough to become conversant in Hungarian, communicating with the people was a challenge. Baker spent three days there and found the people quite hospitable, but no one spoke English, not even in the airport, the train station, or the hotels. They hired a young Christian woman, who was studying English in the university, to assist them in the evenings.

A serious language barrier creates some interesting situations. As Baker and the missionary walked around the town, they decided to get something to eat. Walking into a restaurant, they simply pointed at an item on the menu, since they were unable to communicate. The waitress began to laugh. Without any attempt to explain through gestures, she brought the order, a hamburger the size of a medium pizza in circumference and about four inches thick. It was meant to feed four people. She laughed, they laughed, and Baker believed the Lord smiled on them with this one order.

After visiting the two orphanages, one run by the government and the other by a private organization, his heart was touched. There was a seriously ill little boy, perhaps seven years old, at the home operated by the private group. It was evident that the staff there loved him and gave him the best care they could, with a worker staying with him around the clock. Baker was especially drawn to him and, with an interpreter, knelt beside him and spoke to him about God's love for him and how He would relieve him of his suffering. With such brokenness in his spirit, he began praying for his healing. The next day the angels ushered him into the presence of his heavenly Father. Baker cried out to God, "Why couldn't You heal him?"

The Lord responded, "I did."

Baker boarded a plane for Bucharest, Romania, where Gregory and his son, James, would be joining him to look at several ministries, including orphanages. He arrived a day early to make sure everything was in order for the visit. Upon leaving the airport, he didn't see any taxis available. A nicely dressed man in a coat and tie walked up to him and offered him a ride to his hotel. The man explained that he was with a private company and all their cars were luxurious. Baker had that small ping in his spirit, but it was middle of the day and, since everything appeared on the up and up, he accepted his offer.

The man led Baker to a nice car, although few people would consider it luxurious. After the driver placed his luggage in the trunk, Baker moved toward the front passenger seat. His experience had taught him, if possible, to sit in front with the driver. The driver suggested that he sit in the back because of more legroom, but he insisted on sitting in the front. The driver acquiesced and they departed for the Holiday Inn, which was about 20 minutes away. After driving for a longer time, Baker began to feel uneasy and asked, "How much further is it to the hotel?"

The man replied, "Maybe 20 minutes." When Baker asked him how much for the ride, he answered, "It will be $500."

Baker assumed that he was referring to the local currency, so he asked, "How much is that in us dollars?"

"Five hundred dollars," the driver answered.

"No way!" Baker exclaimed. "Take me back to the airport!"

Defiantly, the man responded, "If you don't give me $500, I am going to take you where you don't want to go!"

Baker then knew he was dealing with the Romanian Mafia. He felt stupid, especially since he knew about these scams. He snapped, "Listen to me. The moment this car starts to exit off this expressway, I will grab the wheel and cause us to crash. The same will be true if your hands leave the wheel."

Coolly, the villainous man retorted, "I don't think." He then acted like he was exiting. When he did, Baker grabbed the wheel with his left hand prompting the man to cry out, "Okay, give me $300 and I will drop you off at the hotel!"

Baker determinedly shouted back, "I will give $60 or we crash!" Seeing that his passenger was not a man to trifle with, he agreed and took him to within a block of the hotel.

The man declared, "Give me the money and get your bags out."

Baker had pushed him this far and was not about to let go now. He demanded, "You get my bags out, get back in the vehicle, and I will pay you!" He did.

When he got back inside, he asked, "Who are you?"

For the next 20 minutes, Baker shared some of his testimony with him and he began to cry. He prayed with him and the man even showed him pictures of his wife and two girls. They said their goodbyes, and Baker picked up his luggage and walked to the hotel. After checking in, he retreated to his room and crashed from the adrenaline rush he had just experienced. When asked if taking such a chance was worth $500, he answered that the possibility of someone robbing him and maybe even killing him left him with no option.

The next morning, he returned to the airport to receive the Gregorys. He had the hotel secure transportation, and they made the 20-minute trip there without interference. Later, their host met them in a van and transported them to their first ministry center. After spending a couple of days in the country, they departed for Ukraine where they were to participate in the dedication of the newly constructed Pearl Orphanage, which the Lazarus Foundation had funded. It was located in the city of Alexandria.

Because the Gregorys could be, especially in less developed countries, potential targets for kidnapping, one of Baker's assignments was to arrange security when deemed necessary. The Ukraine government, because of the Gregorys' philanthropy, provided two SUVs with chauffeurs, who were also bodyguards. They separated father from son putting them in separate vehicles, which is normal protocol in transporting high profile people. They put John in front with the driver, and Richard sat in the back. Off they went, sometimes driving 100 miles per hour. Every time John would try and put his seat belt on, the driver would wag his finger at him indicating, "No!"

Before going to Pearl Orphanage, they stopped at Pilgrim Republic Children's Home. This ministry is the one to which Nichols released funds to when Pastor Gennadiy traveled to the States looking for help. It was a touching time for them as they visited with the children, many of whom had been bound my drugs and alcohol, but through the ministry of Pilgrim had been set free by God's love and grace.

The center also operated a small home for children with HIV. Richard loved them all but every time he would visit them, one girl, gravitated to him and him to her. She would grab his hand as he started to leave, begging him not to go. Before they entered the house, they were told the house mom, who was pregnant with twins, had just given birth the week before. Sadly, one died shortly after being born, and the second one died that morning. As they walked inside, they witnessed one of the small girls that was sick sitting in the arms of the mother who had just lost her babies, and one that morning.

They had brought small gifts to give the children, loved on them, and prayed with them. Baker then asked the same question he asked every orphanage he went to: "If you could have anything today your heart would desire, what would it be?"

Tasha immediately shouted, "We need a van!"

The house mom quickly told her to be quiet. They had passed by a van sitting in the drive and were not sure what her request meant. Baker asked the interpreter if there was something wrong with the van in the yard. He said that it had quit running and was too old to put in more money. The children had no way to get to school or to the doctor. Of course, John and James were standing ten feet behind him laughing. He told Tasha that they would see what they could do, but it might take some time.

He continued asking what he could do for them right then. In a few moments, John asked him to step outside. He said, "Richard, go back in there and tell them you are going to buy them a new van, but don't tell them it's from me."

He replied, "John, it will be you buying it."

"Not if I buy it and give it to you first. Now go!" John directed.

Baker walked back into the house and assembled the kids. With a tremendous sense of gratitude and fulfillment, he announced, "God has already provided the funds for me to purchase a van for you!" An almost new Mercedes Benz 15-passenger van was imported from Germany. Later, the children's home sent pictures to them showing these precious children hanging out of it, waving, and smiling.

Baker remarked, "This was a special thing John did. He knew that I had a special connection to this HIV/AIDS home and them with me. I would return the next year and go for a ride with them."

Continuing their trip, they arrived in Alexandria for the dedication after about an eight or nine-hour drive. About two hours out, they had received information from the police and security personnel in Alexandria that they had intercepted some chatter about wealthy North Americans traveling to Alexandria. The drivers had pulled over, apparently to allow them to stretch their legs, but in reality, they wanted to share with Baker that information. A government official, whose first name was Gregory, recommended that they not spend the night in Alexandria and secured accommodations for them about one hour away. Extra security was put in place.

For Baker, the question now that he needed to answer was, "Do I tell John or not? Do I recommend that we don't attend the dedication?" With assurances that several government officials would attend and with plenty of security, he decided not to mention it at the time. This was a big decision that weighed heavily on him, seeing that John had counted on him to provide adequate security for him and his son.

The dedication service was amazing, and the home was beautiful and very functional. It exceeded expectations, and John could not have been happier with his investment. Richard then told him the situation and that they would be traveling another hour before they stopped to spend the night. Gregory, the government official, secured for them a nice bed and breakfast, and they were the only ones there. The next day they drove to Kiev, the capital, to catch their flight back to the US. It had been another amazing journey, as they witnessed God's hand of provision and protection.

40

Southeast Asia

Two Thousand Twelve found Baker traveling extensively, taking in more than 20 countries, doing site visits at the orphanages and following up on requests coming into the Lazarus Foundation for assistance. In fact, from 2008 until he returned to the pastorate in 2015, he visited 20 to 25 countries a year. Some of those countries such as India, Cambodia, Thailand, Sri Lanka, he visited several times a year because of the amount of ministry they were doing in those places. The stories, the visits to all the orphanages, and all ministries God had graciously allowed him to be part of, he would like to tell, but he knows that the book may never be finished.

Kingsway Charities had shipped another container of medicines and medical equipment to North Korea via South Korea. Gregory was invited to Seoul to attend a special celebration where he and his family were honored for their philanthropy. Along with Richard, they decided to tour a few of the Asian countries before arriving for the celebration. Susan, John's daughter, traveled with them.

Their first stop was Cambodia, where they spent time in Phnom Penh and visited the Build a City project. While there, they took in the House of Hope orphanage, where the girls had been rescued from sex trafficking. They also visited several other ministry projects there that PCL was involved in, such as a training facility. From there they traveled to Siem Reap and Pace Children's Home. Tonle Sap Lake, which is the largest freshwater lake in the country some 75 miles long where a reported one million refuges actually live, was also on their itinerary. PCL was heavily involved in rendering humanitarian aid and ministry to those living here.

Interesting, Cheryl was visiting with her husband once, and as they toured the lake in a boat, a young boy came paddling toward them in a large plastic container. As he came up behind Cheryl, he reached down, picked up a large five-to six-foot snake, and dangled it in front of her. Richard said that he was not sure if she was going to jump out of the boat or start walking on the water. The boy wanted Cheryl to put the snake around her neck for a photo—for a couple of bucks, of course. But Richard knew that a snake around his wife's neck was not going to happen, at least, not on purpose.

From there, their travels took them to Sri Lanka where they visited the City of Hope Children's Home. John had invited Ryan and Mia to join them. Harold McLeod, field director for Asia, had purchased the land and had some excavating done immediately after the tsunami that had caused major destruction and death there and in other Asian countries.

City of Hope (Richard with approximately a third of the children)—Sri Lanka.

Already having visited Sri Lanka with Garmon, who was the executive director of PCL, Richard knew there was a need for a Christian children's home. Premadasa, a former Buddhist monk and now a pastor and national overseer for the Church of God, along with his wife, Nelum, had a heavy burden to care for abandoned and destitute children. During a World Missions Board of Directors meeting, Baker was asked to give a report and updates on responses to various disasters relief efforts. After he reported the relief response to the tsunami in Sri Lanka, he shared the need for a children's home. Members asked a few more questions, and the board voted unanimously to give $350,000 toward building the orphanage.

Baker flew back to Sri Lanka to begin the process. He had with him a rough draft of the three buildings to be built and presented it to Premadasa for his perusal. They hired a contractor, and construction began in January 2008. In six months, the complex had been completed. Because of governmental policy changes, the opening had to be delayed until 2009. The Lazarus Foundation stepped in and covered the remaining $150,000 to complete the project.

After the first 25 children had arrived, Baker returned for the dedication and was astounded at how the project turned out. These precious children were so happy and content in their new home. Susan committed to support the home in the coming year. He felt so much contentment as he walked around the complex and saw the children playing. Each child had their own bed, and they were eating three meals daily. They also attended school, and most importantly, they learned about Jesus. Considering that Sri Lanka was predominantly Buddhist, witnessing these children finding faith and worshipping the Lord was especially touching. And once again, Baker marveled that God had used him, a worm, to be part of something so valuable and eternal.

Following a short stopover in Singapore, they continued to Seoul, Korea. Billy Kim, affectionately called the Billy Graham of Asia, hosted them and invited them to his radio station and operational center, where he gave them a tour and entertained them with a Korean children's choir. Richard, along with John and Ryan, all spoke a few minutes. That evening he and John attended a banquet where John received appreciation for the container of medicines and medical supplies he had sent to North Korea. Richard was assigned to a table where two ambassadors, one from Cambodia and the other from Indonesia, along with other dignitaries, were sitting. During such encounters, he reflected on how God had stretched a South Georgia boy to his limits.

The next evening, the entourage received an invitation to a special dinner with South Korean president, Chun Doo-Hwan, along with his wife and daughter. They arrived at the Korean steak house first, with security swarming all around. Suddenly, wailing sirens split the air and within a few minutes, the president and his family entered the restaurant and were seated. The entire dining party numbered only about 12.

Front & center: Former South Korean President, Chun Doo-hwan with wife & daughter to his right. To his left are Mia and the president's brother-in-law. Back row L to R: Gregory, Baker, Susan (Gregory's daughter), and Ryan.

After the exchanging of pleasantries, the party prepared for the meal itself. Richard and Ryan were sitting on the end across from each other, with Mia next to her husband. The president sat three seats down from Richard and, without any warning, turned, and asked him to give thanks for the meal. He said this was the only time he could not remember, or did not know, what or how to pray. Somehow, he got through it, and they enjoyed an incredible dinner. Afterward, they all posed together for a photo. This was especially meaningful, since Mia's mother emigrated from Korea when she was a teenager. In Mia's first and only trip to the country of her maternal ancestry, she dined and had her photo taken with the former president and his family.

41

Radical Muslims Believe

In 2012 and 2014, Baker was invited to speak in chapel services at Lee University in Cleveland, Tennessee. Because of the 5,000-plus student body, the chapel services were held concurrently in two separate facilities. His good friend and fellow missionary, Ken Anderson, was invited to speak in the second facility. In the 2012 service, eight students came to Baker and affirmed that God had called them to the mission field. Three students announced the same calling in 2014. As he reflected on his past, Baker felt humbled and honored to receive this invitation to speak at the university.

Two-Thousand-Two featured John Gregory joining with Denzel Washington to provide 1.5 million dollars to start Save Africa's Children, a nonprofit charity birthed in the heart of Bishop Charles E. Blake, pastor of the West Angeles Church of God in Christ and superintendent of the denomination. The main thrust of the organization was to support children affected with HIV/AIDS, by poverty, and by war throughout sub-Saharan Africa.

In December of 2012, Gregory received an invitation to attend a gala as one of the main speakers. Since he had a previous engagement, he sent Baker to represent him and the Lazarus Foundation. The prestigious City Club/Wells Fargo Center in Los Angeles hosted the event, and Baker was able to meet many people of influence in the Black community. At his table was Cookie Johnson, Magic Johnson's wife. She was the first of three speakers with him being the second. Also seated with them was Congresswoman Karen Bass and Joshua DuBois, executive director for the White House Office of Faith-based Partnerships.

There were several actors attending, as well as other politicians and professional athletes. Out of a gathering of nearly 500, Baker was one of only three white persons in attendance. A number of people came to him and asked, in one way or another, if he was comfortable.

He responded, "Absolutely! I have been in gatherings larger than this in Africa and was the only white person!"

The evening went well, and he could not have been treated any better. One of the top neurosurgeons in California and a devoted Christian spent over 30 minutes speaking to him about humanitarian ministry. Barbara Berry Cochran, a dedicated Christian and the widow of Johnny Cochran, spent another 20 minutes speaking to him about the same thing. They were two of several that wanted to make sure he was comfortable. Baker also found Blake to be a very gracious man and thoroughly enjoyed the time he was able to spend with him. For sure, Baker felt honored that Gregory trusted him enough to send him to an event of this caliber.

Save Africa's Children didn't do monthly support but asked if Serving Orphans Worldwide would consider monthly support for a few of the orphanages they were involved with. SOW adopted three, two in Tanzania and one in Zimbabwe. It is beyond amazing how the body of Christ coming together can accomplish so much for the kingdom of God.

In 2013 and 2014, Baker traveled extensively visiting each year all 40-plus orphanages SOW was supporting, as well as other humanitarian projects throughout Latin American, Eastern Europe, Asia, and Africa.

The Bakers' son, Christopher, joined the Navy in March of 2013 and, after basic training, was assigned to the aircraft carrier, Carl Vinson, based in San Diego, California. He met and fell in love with Ashley Frazier from the Dallas, Texas, area and became engaged. The wedding date was set for February 13, 2014. On Silver Strand State Beach in San Diego, with Cheryl, Ashley's mother, brother, and two close friends present, Baker had the wonderful privilege of pronouncing them husband and wife. They have given to them two beautiful granddaughters, Harper Reese and Willow Monroe, and a grandson, Brooks Alan.

SOW decided to do a promotional and informational video of the Pilgrim Republic Children Home located in Mariupol, Ukraine. A professional video team, Animal, led by Danny Yourd, agreed to come for expenses only. The team arrived on April of 2013. Bakers' son, Ryan, who was serving with the Lazarus Foundation, along with his wife, Mia, who was media coordinator for SOW, flew in with them. Baker was already in the country visiting the two other orphanages that SOW was supporting. He had flown from the capital of Kiev to Donetsk to meet the team.

Pastor Gennadiy picked them up and drove them the two hours to Mariupol. Upon their arrival at the hotel late on a Saturday night, Gennadiy asked Baker to preach for him the next morning. The team asked to be excused because of the long and tiring flight from the US. This would be his third time to minister to his congregation. At the time they were leasing a theater that held from 800 to 1,000 people, and it was full that morning. The service was powerful, and Baker thoroughly enjoyed ministering to people who had such a hunger for God.

Arriving back at the hotel, Mia mentioned to her father-in-law that she and the team had decided to walk around a little bit and take pictures. She explained, "The only problem was that we were in front of a KGB building taking pictures and were confronted. We immediately came back to the hotel to wait for you and Gennadiy."

The several days that the team spent videoing and documenting the story of Pilgrim Republic Children's Home were incredible. Baker departed for another assignment before they finished the filming, but the result significantly helped SOW in sharing about the plight of homeless and abandoned Ukrainian children.

Nearly a year later in March of 2014, Danny Yourd and his team visited Pilgrim again to do another documentary. This time they covered all their expenses because what their eyes had seen affected their hearts.

On March 18, Russia invaded the Crimea, which caused rioting in several places in Ukraine. The team was riding in a bus belonging to Pilgrim when a mob attacked them shooting the van, breaking out windows, and beaching the door. A tall nearly 300-pound young man, rescued by Gennadiy and Pilgrim Home, rushed to the door fending off those trying to gain entrance. The driver was then able to drive them back to the home. Immediately, the team returned to the States. Eventually, the Russians and their sympathizers destroyed the airport in Donetsk. The experience traumatized the production crew members but left them unharmed physically.

In 2014, Gregory and Baker were back in Seoul, Korea. They visited Billy Kim, chairman of the Far East Broadcasting Company who served on the board of directors for SOW.

Kingsway Charities had shipped another container to South Korea earmarked for North Korea. A presentation ceremony was held, and Gregory and Baker attended a concert of the Korean Children's Choir. The hosts planned a dinner in Gregory's honor with 16 invitees, in addition to Kim, Gregory, and Baker. The guests included the president's brother, the top two Air Force generals, a couple of ambassadors, and other dignitaries. To Baker's left was the top Air Force general and to is right, an ambassador. The gathering was surreal to him, as he thought where he once was and where the Lord had now brought him.

Before they flew back to the States, Kim arranged a meeting with Paul Yonggi Cho, pastor of Yoido Full Gospel Church, which is the largest church in the world with 800,000 members. There were just the four of them in the meeting, and as it ended, Baker was asked to pray over Cho. His mind went back to 1997 when he and Cheryl attended a conference in Montgomery, Alabama, where Cho taught on prayer. During that conference he wondered what it would be like to sit down in a private meeting with Cho and listen to him speak about prayer and serving the Lord. And now, 24 years later, God allowed him to experience it.

In January 2015, a particular ministry organization invited him to travel to an Arab country to help disciple former Taliban and al-Qaeda men who had accepted Jesus. He would be assisting three other ministers. Each one flew into the country on a different flight. A host picked Baker up at the airport and took him to a private residence, where the other three ministers were staying. They would go to another residence for breakfast and dinner.

On the first day, they were scheduled for training. Clandestinely, they were transported to a certain location where they exited the vehicle, walked a few blocks, and were picked up by another vehicle. On the following days, they may be dropped off at a store or mall and be told the place to go at a certain time. Sometimes they were asked to take a taxi and were given an address where another vehicle would pick them up. They followed this protocol morning and evening for three days.

After arriving on the first day at the residence where the training would take place, they were ushered into a large bedroom where they changed into Arab dress. Escorts then took them to a large room where 10 new converts to Christ from four different countries sat in a circle on a Persian rug. Although they all stood and greeted the men, it was apparent that they were somewhat skeptical or a bit uneasy.

Baker shared a little each day, but his main teaching would come on the last day where he would be speaking about spiritual warfare. The other three ministers mainly dealt with trauma, which was a major issue with these men.

When lunchtime came, the men sat in a circle, as food was set in front of them. They used their hands and ate from the dishes placed before them. Baker loved Persian cuisine, and this was as authentic as it got.

On the last day, his turn came to have a main part. The men had warmed up to them, and he felt they were brothers in Christ. They refused to call themselves Christians, instead saying they were followers of Jesus. These converts expressed that the Western church had polluted the name Christian. Baker later exclaimed, "Ouch! But so true to a great extent!"

As he taught on spiritual warfare, he explained about the Apostle Paul when he was Saul and consenting to the death of Stephen. In this part of his teaching, he was dealing with not allowing the devil to put condemnation on you thus robbing you of peace, joy, and contentment. Without any warning, they all jumped up, moved quickly toward the four of them, and sat down at their feet. The interpreter explained that this was a show of respect given to a teacher when the subject he was teaching resonated with them.

Within a few minutes, the class took a break and the youngest member, a 24-year-old former al-Qaeda member, came to Baker with the host and wanted to share something with him. He explained, "I have followed Jesus now for six months and have not slept a single night without waking up with nightmares of what I had done. I was trained as an assassin, and I have assassinated 40 men of different nationalities. Teacher, I thought I was doing God's will, but when Jesus appeared to me in a dream and revealed Himself to me, I knew He was the true God. But tonight, I will sleep with no torment from the enemy because I know now I have been truly set free."

In a different conversation, Baker asked him about his training. He replied, "I was trained to kill with my hands and by using a knife."

Baker, feeling impressed to demonstrate the meaning of forgiveness and trust, turned around placing his back to him and instructed, "Put me in a hold as if you wanted to break someone's neck. Just don't break mine!"

The young man hesitated, but the host encouraged him to cooperate. In response, he put more pressure on him than Baker was expecting. When he released him, he hugged him. Baker said that he believed that that act of trust he placed in the young convert helped to solidify his faith and to accept that the love of the Father and the blood of Jesus had gloriously changed him from the inside out.

One of the oldest men, perhaps in his mid to late 50s, had his village attacked by Isis fighters one night. As the people slept in their tents, AK-47 shells tore through this man's tent striking him and killing two of his children. He managed to get his surviving family members into the mountains. Baker recalls that possibly another child died in his arms.

The man testified that at some point Jesus appeared to him (all of these men, from four different countries, became followers of Jesus through dreams they had of Him). Jesus told him He was the real Messiah, the Savior of the world, and this man immediately accepted Him into his heart.

Former Taliban & al-Qaeda members who had accepted Christ.

After he had healed from his wounds and settled his family in a new village, Isis fighters also attacked it, but this time the villagers had weapons and fought back. He related that the battle raged all day but ceased when night fell. According to his account, the Lord told him that his enemy was hungry and that he needed to take them bread and water. After gathering provisions, he took a stick, attached a white cloth to it, and started marching toward their entrenchment. As he drew near, they asked him his intentions. He told them what Jesus had instructed him to do. Upon hearing his words, they permitted him to enter their small encampment, took the bread and water, and divided it among the eight men there.

The Isis fighters related that they took no provisions, since they thought they would overrun the small village in a short order and return to their camp. The spokesman said the men wanted to hear more about Jesus. When the meal was over, they all laid down their weapons and walked into the village so they too could become followers of Jesus.

Baker acknowledged, "This will go down as another one of the most amazing experiences God has bestowed on me. And I am also so appreciative of the ministry that had enough trust in me to invite me. In fact my good friend Ken Anderson, who is a pilot, flew me to a certain city here in the US to meet the director of this ministry that is helping disciple Muslims in general but, in particular, those who have been part of the Taliban, al-Qaeda, and Isis groups."

Continuing, Baker expressed, "I learned so much these three days. For instance, they shared with me that there is a great revival happened among Muslims. They told us when we see Muslims praying in a mosque, many of them are followers of Jesus and are praying to Jesus and not to Allah. They must participate in the times of prayer to keep their jobs and protect their families, but in their hearts, they are praying to the Lord God Almighty. Praise God and glory to the Lamb!"

In 2015, Isis was occupying most of Syria and the northern part of Iraq. All the men the ministry team was discipling were going either to Syria or Northern Iraq to be witnesses for Jesus. They knew there was a good chance that none of them would be returning to their homes. Even as Baker received criticism for ministering to these people, he stated, "Before too much criticism is leveled against them or against ministries that I connected with to share Jesus, ask yourself this question, 'If the Lord impresses me to witness to someone even here in the US, and I know there is a very high probability I will not be coming back home, will I go?'"

Baker cautions, "Even as this book is being written, it is looking more and more realistic, with all the anarchy that is happening in our country presently, that this is where we may find ourselves."

Once again, the Lord called His "worm" into service, and his servant, Richard Baker, rejoices that He did. He declared, "My heart wants to tell all the stories of all the places the Lord allowed me to visit and share all the ministry opportunities and miracles that took place, but that would make this book hundreds of pages longer."

The first seven months of 2015 proved to be some of his busiest times, as it relates to travel. He journeyed to Asia, the Middle East, Africa, and

Eastern Europe visiting multiple countries in each of these continents and multiple ministries within each country.

42

Support from Auto Racing

Back in March of 2011, SOW received an offering of several thousand dollars from Tom Pierson, owner of Pierson Construction Company in Kenner, Louisiana. Baker reached out to Pierson to thank him for his donation, and, during the conversation, Pierson shared about his ties to drag racing. Baker learned that he served as crew chief for Richie Stevens Elite Racing Team.

Pierson asked questions about Serving Orphans Worldwide operated and wanted to know some of the places where the organization supported orphanages. He then dropped a bombshell on Baker by asking that if he (Pierson) could work it out, would they like to have SOW as one of the sponsors for Stevens' upcoming races in Indianapolis in June. He continued, "SOW will be allowed to have advertisement on the car, and Richie will mention SOW on ESPN when he is interviewed. And, oh yes, the sponsorship won't cost SOW anything."

All the details were worked out and excitement began to stir in the SOW offices. Baker and his 14-year-old son, Joshua, headed to Indianapolis to be a part of an incredible opportunity to share the ministry of SOW with a completely different audience. When they arrived, they met Stevens, along with Erica Enders, also a drag racer racing in the Pro Stock Class. Although they were focused on their upcoming races, both were friendly and interested in the ministry of SOW. At the end of the races, Enders and Stevens presented SOW with a $40,000 offering.

Within a few weeks, both would be racing in Bristol at Thunder Valley. This was especially meaningful, considering this was home for SOW. Once again, Baker, and son, Joshua, received an invitation to hang out with the team and be a part of the race.

Stevens left the SOW logo on his car for the reminder of the season. Enders, who has won three championships in the Pro Stock Class, received a request to sit on the board of directors for Serving Orphans Worldwide, a position she still holds today.

L to R: Erica Enders & Richie Stevens (Pro Stock drag racers) presenting $40,000 check to SOW; Richard Baker, Tom Pierson (Stevens' crew chief)

Stevens' car with SOW advertisement.

In January 2015, SOW began planning their first gala and set the date for September, with plans to hold the event in Bristol, Tennessee. The staff met with other non-profits that had hosted galas seeking information. They set a goal of $600,000 and were told by everyone that the goal was unrealistic.

Sandy Forbis, one of the SOW board members, along with her husband, Mike, reached out to Baker and suggested seeing if Richard Petty would be willing to build a car for SOW to auction off. The Forbises committed to fund the car. In exploring the possibilities of such an undertaking, they planned a trip to Randleman, North Carolina, to visit Petty's shop and talk to his shop supervisor. Petty agreed to build a one-of-kind Mustang. A new Ford Mustang GT was purchased, and Petty's team turned it into a two-seater coupe with alligator seats and a 825 horsepower engine, protected by more than 20 coats of paint. It was projected to run the quarter mile in under 10 seconds, with a top speed approaching 200 miles per hour.

Richard Baker and Richard Petty standing in paint booth with the one-of-a-kind Mustang built for SOW (2015). Standing behind car is Mike Forbis; To the right are Petty's auto body specialists.

Baker and team made several visits to Petty's shop to witness the car's transformation. Petty also agreed to speak at the gala and sign a few of his hats, which would be auctioned. In addition, Chris Hill, owner of Lexus of Kingsport, donated a new Lexus automobile. More than $80,000 in raffle tickets were sold, and the winning ticket was to be drawn at the gala.

In addition, Charlie Warren, along with his wife, Donna, served food and refreshments at Gregory's skybox at the Bristol Motor Speedway and donated his Harley Davison motorcycle. They displayed it on their webpage, and a businessman offered the highest bid. When the man told his wife the bid and that it was the highest for a motorcycle, she refused to let him keep it. Consequently, he donated it back to SOW, who sold enough raffle tickets to receive donations about three times the bike's value. What makes this story so special is that doctors had diagnosed Charlie with terminal stage-four liver cancer. But he had such love for orphans; he was one of the hardest workers in helping decorate and set up for the gala.

Richard Baker, Charlie Warren on donated motorcycle, & John Gregory.

September 12 was quickly approaching, and excitement was building. SOW had over 400 people confirmed to attend. On the night the gala was held, everyone could sense that the Lord's hand was upon it. Remarkable synergy flowed through all involved. Every speaker spoke with passion. There were even a few former orphans present.

Kennedy McClendon, an eight-year-old girl from Douglas, Georgia, heard about SOW and the work the ministry was doing to help orphans, and raised over $2,000. Kennedy, along with her parents, came and presented the check in person at the event.

Eight-year-old Kennedy from Douglas, Georgia
Raised $2,000 for the first gala in 2015.

Petty had arranged with the Mecum Auction to auction the Mustang at their upcoming sale in Orlando, Florida. Mecum waived all the consignment and auction fees for both SOW and the buyer. Baker was given one minute to share about SOW and the Mustang. He later said, "It's a good thing I am a Pentecostal. We can say a lot in 60 seconds when we need to!"

The weather on the day of the auction was extremely cold and rainy for Orlando, which affected the attendance. The car did not bring the $200,000 they were all hoping for, but the exposure to a national TV audience and Petty's endorsement no doubt helped get SOW's name out to a greater range of people.

When all the proceeds had been tallied, the gala, along with auctioning the Richard Petty Mustang, brought in more than $750,000. It was a record for any gala for the Bristol, Tennessee/Virginia, area.

Chris Hill presenting new Lexus to John Gregory to be raffled for Serving Orphans Worldwide.

Hall of Famer Johnny Bench with Richard and Josh (2012) (Bristol Speedway).

43

Change in Direction

At the end of August 2015, just one month before the gala, Darrell Bewley, pastor of Grace Point Church of God in Bristol, Tennessee, where the Bakers were members, resigned and accepted an executive position in the state office located in Chattanooga. After Bewley's resignation, the deacon board met, and Baker's name came up. However, most felt he would not be interested because of his involvement with SOW and the Lazarus Foundation. When the state administrative bishop, Mitchell Corder, met with the board, someone mentioned Baker's name again. After the meeting, Corder gave him a call.

Frankly, Baker was surprised, especially considering he had only preached at Grace Point maybe three times over the five years he had been a member. Because of his hectic travel schedule, he was gone more than he was there. He expressed to Corder that he was honored that they would consider him, but there was no way he could contemplate resigning from the positions in which he presently served, especially since he had given Gregory a verbal commitment to stay at least another five years. Corder thanked him for his time.

Two Sundays before the gala, Corder came to preach and speak with the congregation about the process of selecting a new pastor. After preaching, he passed out to a blank piece of paper to every member and instructed each person to write any pastor's name that he or she felt would make a good pastor for the church. He then informed them that he would make the necessary contacts to see who might have an interest.

Following the dismissal of the service, Richard and Cheryl, along with Joshua and Melanie, returned home. Cheryl asked him what he thought.

Misunderstanding her question, he replied, "I wasn't surprised when Dr. Bewley resigned. I felt it was coming for a year or longer."

"No," she remarked. "I mean about you considering becoming the pastor."

Richard answered, "Cheryl, I couldn't if I wanted to. I committed to John 10 years when we started SOW, and I have five years left on my commitment."

Following lunch as the Bakers were relaxing in their sunroom, Corder called and said, "Brother Baker, I know what you shared with me a couple of weeks ago, but your name was about the only name submitted from the service this morning. And with such an overwhelming sentiment of the congregation asking that you be considered, I felt I needed to reach out to you once more. I have two pastors that have shown interest and are willing to be interviewed by the church council, and the interviews will take place this Thursday night."

Baker responded, "Bishop, I am truly honored and humbled by the church's confidence in Cheryl and me, but as I have already shared with you, I made a promise to John, and I must keep it. We have a gala coming up, and not only am I doing all the site visits, but I am also one of the main fundraisers speaking at Rotary Clubs, churches, other civic organizations, and am also meeting with individual donors. For me to resign now could prove to be counterproductive for the ministry." His last words to Corder were, "God would have to write it in granite!" He fully understood and supported Baker's decision.

Cheryl was feeling differently about the situation and said to her husband, "Don't act too quickly, and miss God. If God is calling us to pastor Grace Point, He is calling someone to give oversight to SOW."

The next morning, he went to his office around 8:00 am. As he entered, he found Gregory sitting there waiting for him. Gregory said, "Come in, Brother Richard. I need to talk with you."

As Baker sat down, Gregory declared, "I release you from SOW and the Lazarus Foundation. Go pastor the church."

Baker's first thought was, "Did someone communicate to Gregory that I was working to get the church without letting him know?" Cautiously he responded, "John, I have no control over who approaches me or asks me to consider being their pastor. I made a commitment to you, and I will honor it."

"You don't understand, Brother Richard," he countered. "I couldn't sleep last night, so I release you to pastor the church." With that, he got up and walked out of Baker's office. After sitting there dazed for about 10 minutes, his personal assistant, Jenny Wallace, came in for their usual Monday morning planning session. While sharing several items with him, she paused and exclaimed, "Richard, you're not listening to a word I am saying!"

He replied, "Sorry, Jenny, I need to leave for a little while."

Afet excusing himself, he slipped out and went home. As he walked through the door, Cheryl asked, "What are you doing home?"

Without hesitation, Richard answered, "I think I just got fired."

She shouted, "What!"

As he proceeded to tell her what had just transpired, she began to smile. Still sorting through the events at the office, he asked, "What do you find so funny?"

Cheryl answered, "Just think about your conversation with Bishop Corder yesterday." He still was not connecting, so she exclaimed, "Something hard; write on something hard!"

Befuddled, he demanded, "Cheryl, speak English! What are you saying?"

She shot back, "You told Bishop Corder that God would have to write it on..." Then it came to him. He had said, "Granite."

He drove back to the offices, went directly to Gregory's office, knocked on his door, and asked to speak with him. He said, "Sure, Brother Richard."

Baker sat down and asked, "John, did you just fire me?"

Gregory looked at him in disbelief and declared, "Heavens no! I just released you to follow the Lord in whichever way He is leading you. I hope you don't resign. But if you do decide to pastor the church, don't do or say anything until after the gala."

Baker walked out of Gregory's office truly feeling the direction of the ministry was about to change for them. He called Corder and shared what had just happened and let him know that he would be taking the next three days to pray and fast to get the mind of the Lord. Corder informed him that one of the pastors showing interest had withdrawn his name, so if he decided to submit his name, it would be a ballet with just two names, his and an unnamed pastor.

By Friday, he felt released to submit his name. For him, it was the hardest decision he had ever had to make in the ministry. But it was clearly God's will for him and Cheryl at this point in their lives.

44

Bristol Pastorate and SOW

After years of travel and ministry throughout the world, the Bakers had now been asked to return to the pastorate. The way God orchestrated the unfolding of the events made it undeniable to them that this was His perfect will. In all honesty, Richard had never felt comfortable or fully qualified to pastor a church. In fact, he had never asked to pastor, but the Lord had opened the doors for him and Cheryl to pastor four congregations.

Bewley's last Sunday was August 23, and his associate/youth pastor, Logan Justice, was given the task of filling the vacancy until a new pastor could be voted in. Although only in his mid-twenties, Justice had a great delivery coupled with good content. Richard and Cheryl enjoyed listening to him minister.

On September 27, 2015, Corder asked Baker to preach a short message at Grace Point, after which he gave the church an opportunity to express their pleasure through a vote. The Bakers left the sanctuary while the vote was taking place. Around 30 minutes later, the overseer informed him that he was overwhelmingly voted in with a vote in the high 90s percentage range. He immediately felt the weight and responsibility fall upon his shoulders.

Gregory had informed him that if he received the vote, the board needed to understand that he would have to serve a dual role until he could find a replacement. The attendance had fallen off by more than 10 percent, which often happens when the lead pastor resigns.

The next morning Baker went to the church office first just to get a little acclimated and to spend some time with the staff. Justice still filled the offices of associate pastor and youth pastor, while David Creger served as the church administrator. Matt Humphrey filled a volunteer role as music leader.

Steve Sneed, pastor of Connection Point Church of God in Bristol, Virginia, stopped by the office to meet the new pastor. When he left, Baker asked Creger a little about him, as he felt a witness in his spirit.

After spending a couple of hours at the church, he went to the SOW offices and began to understand just how daunting a task this would be trying to manage two major ministries at the same time. Fortunately, SOW's staff was amazing: Jenny Wallace, Baker's assistant, and office manager; Brooklynn Owens, bookkeeper and assistant office manager; Mia Baker, media coordinator; and Emily Glover, communications coordinator.

Kay Barker, who served as Gregory's personal assistant, helped Baker in many ways, especially with the Lazarus Foundation. In Baker's words, "Kay is the sweetest, kindest, and gentlest soul you will ever meet. If you look up the word, 'thoughtfulness,' in the dictionary, Kay's name would be the definition."

On a humorous note, when the Bakers first moved to Bristol in May 2010, Kay and her husband, Tom, a choice servant of the Lord, offered to come over and stay with 13-year-old Joshua and six-year-old Melanie one evening, while Richard and Cheryl went out for dinner. They had moved into one of Gregory's homes, which they eventually bought. Apparently, Kay had dropped something on the floor, and Melanie looked up at her and said, "Mrs. Kay, we must be careful not to mess up this home because it belongs to Dr. Gregory."

Baker soon discovered how amazing Grace Point staff was, perhaps the most dedicated staff he had ever been privileged to serve with in a local church setting. He began praying for God to give him and Gregory direction as to who should follow him as chief operating officer of SOW. There was only one name that repeatedly turned over in Baker's mind, Ken Anderson. Anderson was presently serving as regional superintendent of Southeast Asia and coordinator for Global UPG (Unreached People Groups).

Feeling that Anderson was the right one to lead SOW, Baker contacted him to see if he had any interest. Anderson asked for a little time to spend in prayer. Considering the years he and Karen had spent in Honduras as missionaries, his experience in traveling to various parts of the world, and perhaps the greatest reason of all, his undeniable love for children, made him the right fit in Baker's eyes. In addition, Anderson had considerable experience managing budgets.

Within a few days, Anderson called with a few questions and scheduled an interview with Gregory. Following the interview, Gregory met with the board and submitted his name for consideration. He was overwhelmingly voted in as vice president of operations for SOW. Although Anderson would not be available until December, Baker at least knew help was coming. He also had peace knowing that the day-to-day operations of SOW would be in great hands.

After a couple of weeks of pastoring, Baker began to get back in the groove. At 58, he did not think he would ever pastor again. Cheryl and the children were happy, and so was the church, expressing their approval by their complete support.

He began feeling the Lord leading him to deliver a mini-series on John 3:16. So, his first three Sunday morning messages were on God's love. Charlie and Donna Warren were at his first service, and when the altar call was given, both came forward for prayer. The pastor had the privilege of leading them in the prayer of repentance. That morning this husband and wife, both around 60 years of age, gave their hearts to the Lord. For seven years Baker had talked with them and shared God's love with them in the Gregory's skybox at the Bristol Speedway. A few people had told him that the couple had shared that if he were to ever pastor in the area, they would be there the first Sunday. He came to pastor, and they came his first Sunday. He has often marveled that God loved Charlie and Donna so much that he would send him to pastor Grace Point just so they would accept Christ as their Savior.

On March 10, 2018, Baker had the blessed privilege of preaching Charlie Warrens home-going service. Even though he was young in the faith, he had been voted on the deacon board, receiving almost every vote.

The next week, Baker gave Sneed a call and invited him to breakfast. They met at Cracker Barrel and hit it off so well that they almost stayed long enough to eat lunch. Baker shared a broad vision he had for the area and announced that he was bold enough to claim the Bristol Mall, which was closing down, or maybe the K-Mart building, which had closed. Amazingly, he had been thinking along the same lines. They began meeting weekly in each other's church to spend time praying, and from time to time would meet for breakfast or lunch.

In March 2016, SOW asked Baker if could do site visits at the three orphanages in Ukraine. He agreed and took Zack Wolfe, a young man in his church, with him. Olga Flex, a resident of Asheville, North Carolina, was in Ukraine when they arrived and offered to serve as their interpreter.

Upon arrival in Kiev, a couple that was part of a Christian ministry received them, took them for lunch, and then to the train station for their trip to Alexandria, where Pearl Orphanage was located. Traveling by train is the main mode of transportation in Ukraine, and the train station was bustling with activity. Baker, who rarely got overwhelmed, almost did as dozens of trains arrived and departed simultaneously, with everyone speaking Russian or Ukrainian. Thankfully, Olga was traveling with them.

They arrived in Alexandria in the early part of the night, where Sergey Drok, founder of Pearl Orphanage, met them and took them to dinner. Afterward, he transported them to an apartment he owned and used for family and guests coming to visit. The next morning, they arrived at the orphanage and thoroughly enjoyed their time with the children. For them to spend quality time there and experience the recently built home was special. It even turned out better than he had expected at the dedication. However, they were in need of mattresses, so Baker and Wolfe went to a mattress company that sold them 70 or 80 mattresses at wholesale. When the mattresses were delivered, the faces of the children radiated.

A little boy about nine years old took to Wolfe. He had an issue with one of his eyes and needed surgery, but the home did not have the funds to pay for it. Wolfe privately asked Baker what the surgery would cost. Baker inquired and found that it was less than $1,500. In response, Wolfe shared that he wanted to help and thought his family would also contribute. Consequently, they committed to paying for the surgery. Upon their return to the States, the funds were raised in just a few days. The surgery was successful, and the two men were so thankful and touched that God had placed them at the right place at the right time to be His hands extended.

A government official sent a Range Rover SUV to Alexandria, along with a driver/bodyguard, to transport them on the 11 to 12-hour drive to Mariupol, where Pilgrim Republic Children's Home was located. With the Russian incursion into Crimea in 2014, other areas of Ukraine, such as Mariupol, were affected.

When they arrived, they found that the city had recently been attacked by shelling. They rode by destroyed and burned buildings, only 15 miles from the front lines. After visiting the children's home, they stopped at several foster homes, which Gennadiy had started by taking a couple from his church, along with eight children from the home, and forming families. Baker says that this should be the goal of every orphanage, but, unfortunately, the laws of many countries prohibit it. Gennadiy also serves as a chaplain for Ukraine Armed Forces and was formally a Russian soldier, before his conversion to Christ. He asked Baker if they wanted to travel to the front lines with him to minister to the soldiers. Of course, Baker and Wolfe quickly agreed.

Sails of Hope Children's Home—Ukraine
(Unintentionally bombed by Russian troops).

Sails of Hope rebuilt.

They loaded drinks and snacks into the van and departed. After going through a number of checkpoints, they arrived in a town completely obliterated by Russian shelling. In the distant background, small arms fire penetrated the air. Baker soon realized that this was not at all a safe place for them to be. They were told not to walk in the open, as Russian snipers were in the vicinity, which brought even more apprehension.

While visiting several Ukrainian army outposts, each with six to eight soldiers, they were able to share their soft drinks and snacks and were freely allowed to pray with them. After returning to the orphanage, they spent a little more time with the children and then were dropped off at a hotel, where they were able to get a good night's sleep.

The next morning, they headed for Slavyansk, where Sails of Hope Children's Home was located. It was a grueling six-hour drive. Ukraine was experiencing some late snow, which made travel difficult even in the four-by-four SUV. This home was the one that Russian artillery largely destroyed, unintentionally, in the summer of 2014.

Eva Samoylenko and her husband, Andrej, were serving as directors. She came to Ukraine from Switzerland as a young missionary just out of school and committed her life to caring for these destitute children. Here she met and married Andrej, a Ukrainian with the same passion she had. Baker said, "They are an amazing couple doing an amazing job."

The two-story facility had been completely renovated. Their church with its video studio worked closely with TBN in Ukraine networking to help organize and solicit volunteers to rebuild Sails of Hope Home. She had a place for the guests to stay the night, and the next morning, they spent time playing and interacting with the children, who entertained them by singing and putting on skits. Eva shared several needs the home presently had, such as washing machines, a water-purifying system, bikes for the children, and other items.

They were scheduled to take the train back to Kiev, which departed at 6:00 pm. It was an all-night trip. After saying their goodbyes to Olga at the train station, he and Zack boarded the train. Had it not been for some well-meaning non-English speaking passengers motioning for them not to get off at a certain place, they most certainly would have. And that experience they did not want to have.

Arriving back in Kiev, a brother in Christ, who could speak a little English, warmly received them. Following breakfast together, their host delivered them to the airport, where they began the long journey back to the US. Baker reported, "It was an amazing trip, one I am sure Zack will never forget. There simply is no better feeling than helping those who, through no fault of their own, find themselves in desperate situations, especially the children."

Upon returning to the States, Baker asked for a meeting with Jeff Gregory, a businessman and philanthropist, and John's brother, to share with him the needs. He was already covering most of the monthly operational expenses of Sails of Hope and Pearl Orphanages, but without hesitation, he gave the funds to cover all their present needs.

Anderson, who served as vice-president of operations for SOW, and who, with his wife, Karen, lived in Bristol, asked Baker to travel with him to Africa. Although he had traveled extensively, he had never been to that continent. Grace Point was gracious in allowing him to make two missions' trips so close together.

Rose of Sharon Children's Home in Zimbabwe (2012).

In April of 2016, they departed for their first destination, the country of Zambia. While there, they visited Emma's Kids and attended a conference in the capital city of Lusaka. It was then on to Zimbabwe where they visited the Rose of Sharon Children's Home. Dr. Fatima Maruta, who could have held a good paying job, decided to dedicate her life to rescuing the most vulnerable children and seeing to their care in every way possible, while strongly emphasizing the importance of quality education.

For Baker, it was always a joy to visit her and the children. They loved to sing and worship the Lord when he and any traveling companions would visit. Ken fell in love with them. They gave them a special treat by taking them to a restaurant and feeding them fried chicken with all the trimmings, and with ice cream for dessert.

From Zimbabwe, they headed to Dar es Salaam, Tanzania, where they visited the Bethsaida Girls Children Home. This was another amazing ministry to orphan girls. They also put on quite a performance for their guests with their singing and dancing.

After flying into Kilimanjaro, Daniel, Mama Warra's son, greeted them and took them to Shalom Orphanage, about a two-hour drive away. On the way, they stopped beside the highway where vendors had barbecued a goat. Richard, Ken, and Daniel filled up on the delicious meat. Upon their arrival at Shalom Orphanage, a boatload of loving children met them, many of whom knew Baker, since he had visited many times through the years.

Buying bread for children at Agape Hope—Kenya.

Anderson immediately began playing with the children. Everywhere he went, regardless of the continent or country, children fell in love with him.

They spent a day and night there and headed back to the airport and on to Kenya. Arriving in Nairobi, Pastor Hinga met them and transported them to Hope for the Children Ministry Center, where they spent the rest of the day. The following day, they visited Agape Hope Children's Home located in one of the smaller slums in Nairobi. This home always touched Richard every time he visited it. Squeezed into less than one acre, the staff there ministered to over 300 children daily. Ken bought a few goats, and that evening all feasted on stewed goat.

Leaving Agape Hope, they visited the Oasis of Hope Children's Home located next to the Kibera slums on the outskirts of Nairobi, which also had a school on premises called Life Spring. After spending a few hours there, they caught a flight to Kampala, Uganda, and visited the Grace Children's Home. The trip was a marathon, but Richard and Ken enjoyed being with each other and doing ministry together. It brought back their times together in Central America.

Agape Hope in slums of Nairobi.

Baker received a call on June 8, 2016, from Dawn, Sneed's wife, that while he was making visits at the hospital, his right arm and leg became numb. He went to the ER where doctors examined him, diagnosed him as having had a stroke, and immediately admitted him to the hospital.

Baker checked on him and saw that he was having serious health issues. His tests came back showing that his heart was only functioning at 15 percent. Seeing that Dawn was struggling with her husband's sudden illness, he prayed for them both and excused himself. When he reached the parking lot, the Holy Spirit spoke to him to have a joint prayer service with their two churches for the following Sunday night, with the prayer meeting to be held at Connection Point Church.

Enjoying a meal at Agape Hope.

He returned to Sneed's room and shared his thoughts with Dawn. After she spoke with her husband, she called Baker to let him know her husband was thankful for the offer and was okay with the prayer meeting. Baker felt there should be just praise, worship, and prayer. As Michael and Tyler Sneed led worship, the presence of the Lord filled the church. More than 150 people gathered just to pray and worship the Lord. Almost immediately Sneed began improving and soon was released from the hospital.

Eventually the two pastors resumed their personal meetings and prayer times together. They had already spoken lightly about the possibilities of merging the two churches. But the obstacles seemed overwhelming. For one thing, one of the churches was in Virginia and the other one in Tennessee. The second obstacle was that 12 or 13 years earlier, a church conference went awry causing a number of members from Shelby Street Church of God (changed to Grace Point in 2004) to leave. Some of them had gotten together to form Higher Ground Fellowship Church of God, where Sneed became pastor on February 6, 2006.

Although almost all the original group that left had either come back to Grace Point, had died, or were attending other churches, Baker could see some opposition in trying to bring the two churches back together. But he truly felt in his heart that God was leading them in that direction. He and Sneed agreed to mention their plans to their leadership to get their feelings and input. Both were encouraged because they received truly little negative feedback. Most comments had to do with moving slowly, making sure they worked out all the details, giving the members of each church a chance to voice their thoughts, and allowing them an opportunity to express themselves through a vote.

The pastors decided to produce a list of items that both congregations would have to agree upon. The list consisted of 20 Articles of Merger. One item was deemed non-essential, and both churches separately agreed to the remaining 19 articles. They had already been in communication with their respective church leaders on the state and national levels. To their surprise, they received support to move forward, if both congregations were overwhelmingly in favor of merging.

A simultaneous vote was taken on Sunday January 29, 2017. Both congregations voted approximately 95 percent in favor of the merger. This was a major win-win for both congregations. Where Connection Point was weak, Grace Point was strong, and vice versa. Their first service together was held on Sunday evening February 6, exactly 11 years to the day that Steve and Dawn began their pastorate at Higher Ground Fellowship, now Connection Point. The state executive offices for the Churches of God in Virginia decided to sell their property and give a portion of the proceeds ($200,000) to Grace Point. At the writing of this book, three-and-a-half years have passed since the merger, and the union has proven to be the result of the Lord's hand. Both congregations came together as one, and there have never been any bickering and complications because of the merger.

Grace Point had now grown by 30 percent and was averaging 220 to 230 on Sunday mornings. Sixty-seven people transferred from Connection Point to Grace Point, which boosted the Sunday morning attendance to nearly 300. During this time of transitioning, they revamped the children's ministries and started the Awana program.

The church had already started serving a free meal on Wednesday evenings before service to help working moms. It also served as a ministry for the homeless. But everyone was invited, and, on some Wednesday nights, more than 150 people received a hot meal. With all the changes in the Wednesday night service, the church immediately saw their attendance triple to more than 200 in just a few months.

The church continued to grow through 2017 and 2018 to the point where the parking lot was not able to handle the number of vehicles. In response, the church purchased a six-passenger golf cart and received permission from a couple of nearby businesses to use their parking areas on Sundays. Shuttle service now began. Their highest monthly average has reached 372, with their largest number at one service being 500.

In the summer of 2017, Grace Point welcomed the Cardoso family—Samuel, Roxana, Matthew, and Nayeli—from San Paulo, Brazil. The plan was for them to come for a year to learn English, raise some funds, and then move to Mongolia as missionaries. The church was allowing a small Hispanic congregation to use their facilities and the Cardoso family became involved and started working with Pastor Isaac and his congregation.

After being in the States for six months, Samuel got word that Mongolia was not allowing missionaries into the country anymore. He shared the news with Baker who encouraged him to stay and continue working with Isaac. Isaac was living and pastoring another Hispanic congregation in Erwin, Tennessee, about a 45-minute drive from Bristol. This put considerable strain on his time, and the Hispanic congregation at Bristol began falling off. Baker met with Isaac and suggested he resign, allowing Samuel to assume the pastorate, which he did. Samuel and Roxana have done an outstanding job in ministering to the Hispanic community and have witnessed growth, salvations, and even some miraculous deliverances.

Interestingly, back in 2010, Baker visited San Paulo and needed a driver to take him to visit an orphanage about an hour-and-a-half away. The overseer asked Samuel to chauffeur him. Before he left Brazil, he invited

Samuel and his family for dinner to show his appreciation. When Church of God World Missions asked him if Grace Point could host a family from Brazil and told him their name, it had been seven years, and the name did not resonate with him. On their first day in Bristol, the Bakers had them over for dinner, and Richard kept looking at Samuel wondering where he had seen him before. Finally, the light went off in his head, and he asked him if he was the man that chauffeured him around in Brazil. Samuel smiled and confessed that he had also been looking at him wondering if he knew him. The amazing God they served had brought them together again.

In 2018 and 2019, Grace Point tried to purchase four different properties, but all attempts fell through. Baker now looks back and reflects,

> We are presently in this Covid19 pandemic with the rioting and everything else going on, and I realized the Lord was protecting us. As I saw the church grow, I couldn't understand why God wasn't allowing us to relocate. We are landlocked, with not enough parking and not enough space for our children's ministries.
>
> Grace Point is such an amazing church. We have a few millionaire members, but on any given Sunday, we will have a few homeless people or those living in shelters. A while back as I was getting up to preach, I happened to notice a homeless man sitting next to a millionaire. I knew they didn't know each other, but both seemed to be comfortable. It almost choked me up for a minute, and I thought to myself, "This is the kind of church Jesus died for." I can honestly say that everyone is welcome at Grace Point. We have witnessed at least a dozen set free from demonic bondages. God has delivered many from alcohol and drugs. We even have a special group—those struggling with any kind of bondage—that meets on Wednesdays in one of our on-campus homes we call "Victory House."
>
> Grace Point is not a perfect church. For one thing, I am there, and I am certainly not perfect. Remember, I am a worm, you know. Over the last two years, we have had two small groups of about 45 leave the church. Although it's painful and hurtful, it reminds us that we all are still human and live within the confines of this body of flesh, which is constantly at war with the Spirit of God. But Grace Point kept worshipping and magnifying the Lord. This is the key to living victoriously. Just keep praising and worshipping Him through the storms and His joy will sustain us.

> The church has enjoyed a revival spirit in almost every service since July 2015, which has resulted in over 200 conversions, nearly that many baptisms, and with over 200 new members joining the church. We have seen marriages restored and have seen many individuals finding true peace. It's all because of God's amazing grace and love for people. And this is all happening in a church that was started in 1921 and will celebrate its Centennial next July 11, 2021.
>
> If more churches would break away from their set traditions and allow the Holy Spirit to move freely in their services, revival would break out in our nation once again. In my opinion, the greatest hindrance to revival is not the devil or sin, but rather dead churches embracing iniquity and filled with complacency.
>
> In December of 2018 and 2019, two separate teams traveled to Hope House Children's Home in Honduras and had Christmas with the children. Grace Point is both a world and home mission-minded church supporting ministries which include: SOW; poor pastors in Liberia and Guatemala; missionaries; a ministry in Israel; Right to Life; Living Free, a ministry helping addicts; the Isaiah House, a ministry to help foster children; six widows needing monthly assistance, whose husbands were pastors; feeding the homeless and others, and much more.

In May 2019, Richard, Cheryl, Josh, Melanie, and a couple from the church, Britt and Courtney Stone, traveled to Guatemala. They rented a house in Antigua about 25 minutes from Casa Shalom, where Cheryl served as director from 2003 to 2005. Only a few of the children still there did they know since most of them had aged out. But they enjoyed their visit immensely. It brought back many fond memories. They also visited Frankie and Joyce Tyson, a missionary couple the church supports monthly.

They invited children that had left the home, because of age, to a lunch prepared especially for them. More than 20 showed up. This was an emotional time for them, as many of these children called Cheryl and Richard "Mama" and "Papa" when they were small. Some had married and now had children. It truly was a joy for them to see that most of these children that had grown were still in church living for the Lord. Their hopes that maybe in some small way they had made a difference in these lives now seemed realized.

Baker observes, "In March of 2020, the pandemic struck the world and changed life as we knew it. Because of the Covid-19, the unrest, the looting, and all the violence, we have had to change how we live and minister. We have stopped live services twice, resorting to livestreaming. Presently, September

2020, we are back to having live services. I have personally made a commitment not to stop in-person services again, but to also keep livestreaming and reaching out to people in other ways, since many still feel uncomfortable attending a live service. This past Sunday we had a woman delivered for demonic oppression, another one who was deaf in her right ear received a healing touch from Jesus. If we weren't having live services, these miracles would not have happened."

"God's 'worm' is committed to staying on the move until the Lord gives His command to come home, either by the rapture or the grave. Time is short and getting shorter. Only what we do for Christ will matter in the end. It is my desire, as well as Cheryl's, that this book will be a source of encouragement and inspiration. It is my strong prayer that many will witness the presence of a living God and see the possibilities of His greatness working in their lives."

"But now that we truly know Him and understand how deeply we're loved by Him, why would we, even for a moment, consider turning back to those weak and feeble principles of religion, as though we were still subject to them" (Gal. 4:9)?

Cheryl's Story

Cheryl was born on December 22, 1957, in Brunswick, Georgia, to Lloyd H. Davis, Jr. and Margaret E. Davis. She and her four brothers, Donnie, Charlie, Joey, and Kenny, experienced a chaotic home life most of the time, because of their father's alcoholism and their mother's issues stemming from her own dysfunctional upbringing. Lloyd and Margaret's instability led to frequently changing residences, which kept Cheryl and her siblings moving from state to state and constantly changing schools. And although her father had his problems, he was never abusive to her, and she has sweet memories of good times she experienced being with him.

Cheryl with mother & siblings: Front row left to right: Cheryl, Margaret, Kenny
Back row left to right: Joey, Charlie, Donnie.

Lloyd left Margaret and their five children when Cheryl was around seven years old. Margaret worked hard, often at two jobs, to support the family, while Donnie, Cheryl's oldest brother, had the responsibility of taking care of his four younger siblings while his mother worked.

In time Margaret began dating a man stationed at the naval base in Brunswick. Eventually, she moved in with him, and when he received a transfer to Norfolk, Virginia, she decided to move there with him. Margaret's choice meant that Cheryl and her three older siblings would need a place to live, since she took only the youngest child, Kenny, with her. Cheryl's three older brothers were placed in foster care with a good Christian family taking all three of them. Cheryl went to live with her paternal Uncle Merle and Aunt Vera, along with their three sons. He gave her the attention and affection so sadly lacking in her own dysfunctional home.

In time, she was transferred to another family member, her dad's sister, Janice. Cheryl began to feel that something must be wrong with her and that she must be a bad child. In her thoughts, her dad left because of her. Furthermore, her mom did not want her and neither did anyone else. Contributing to her emotional struggles were two family members who molested her during this time, a dark secret that she never shared with anyone until after she married.

For a short time, she was able to live with her father in Orlando, Florida. Although she remembers having some enjoyable times with him, she knew that the woman he lived with did not want her. When Cheryl's father heard Margaret had moved back to Brunswick, he took her there to live with her mother and her baby brother, Kenny. Because her childhood was so painful and unstable, she blocked much of it from her memory.

Once again, they were on the move. With no promise of a job or a place to live, Margaret, Cheryl, and Kenny departed for Virginia. They slept in their car until Margaret could find a job as a waitress. Only then was she able to move them into a small apartment. Because Margaret was an exceptionally diligent worker, she never had a problem securing employment. While she worked, Cheryl had the responsibility of caring for Kenny. Margaret gave her strict rules to follow and let her know that there was a price to pay if she didn't. Cheryl always felt that her mom, who never liked women much and had very few friends, did not like her because she was a girl.

Margaret soon began dating another navy man stationed in Virginia Beach, whom she married. He was good to her and Kenny, but with Margaret being so unsettled, the marriage only lasted a couple of years.

After they moved back to Norfolk, Cheryl one day saw, while walking home from school, a U-Haul truck loaded with their belongings. Her mother explained to her that she and John, the man she had divorced, were getting married again. Since he was being transferred to Jacksonville, Florida, they were moving again. Cheryl recounts:

> I didn't know at the time that God had a plan for my life. He was with me every step of the way and through everything I had to face. He was with me through all the agony of feeling loneliness, rejection, unloved, emptiness, and worthlessness. There are so many people that are searching for love and wanting to be accepted by someone. Too many times, we search in all the wrong places. God loves us so much that He gave His son Jesus to come to this world and die for our sins. I am so thankful that God loved me and had a plan for my life.

Around a year later, Margaret was feeling unsettled in her spirit again. This time she left Cheryl and Kenny with John, their stepfather. After a couple of weeks had passed and Margaret had not returned, Cheryl's second oldest brother, Charlie, drove to Jacksonville to pick up his siblings and bring them to his home in Brunswick, where they spent a couple of weeks. Richard Baker (Ricky) was friends with Charlie and had briefly seen Cheryl two years earlier at her cousin's house. Cheryl also saw him and from time to time would reach out to one of her cousins inquiring about him. When Charlie returned to Brunswick with his siblings, Ricky spotted them and fell in behind them on his motorcycle, following them to Charlie's house. They briefly spoke for the first time.

Cheryl reached out to her father, who was living in Dallas, Texas. He came and got Cheryl and Kenny. Unfortunately, he was living with a woman that had children, and the situation was not a good one. The two siblings were on the move again, but this time their father returned with them to Brunswick where their Aunt Dorothy, her dad's sister, took them in. Within a few weeks, her dad moved but stayed in Brunswick, where he moved in with another woman.

During this time, Ricky seized the opportunity to ask Cheryl for a date. She accepted, with her Aunt Dorothy's approval. Dorothy attended the same church as Ricky's parents. In approximately six months, Margaret moved back to Brunswick, and Cheryl and Kenny moved back in with her. Within months, Ricky proposed to her and on May 30, 1975, they were married.

Cheryl's parents continued to live turbulent and unfulfilled lives. In 1992, Margaret accepted Jesus as her Lord and Savior and became a Christian. She had a strong zeal to witness for the Lord. It mattered little to her if she was standing in line at a store or in a restaurant; she would witness of her Savior's love and grace. As she began to age and dementia began setting in, she would ask someone if they knew the Lord. If they answered in the negative, she would exclaim, "According to the Word of God, you are stupid!" She was quoting a particular translation of Proverbs 12:1, "Whoever loves instruction loves knowledge, but he who hates correction is stupid." Through the simple-mindedness in her later years, no doubt God used her to bring conviction to the hearts and lives of people who would have been highly offended by most people sharing that truth with them.

In 1994, just three years before his untimely death at age 65, Cheryl's father accepted the Christ as his personal Savior. Knowing that both of her parents had given their hearts to the Lord brought tremendous peace and healing to her heart, especially the last 30 minutes of her mother's life. Cheryl recalls:

> The first of October 2019, I received a call from the nursing home on Saint Simons Island, Georgia, where my mom was a resident, informing me that me she wasn't doing well. Richard drove Josh, Melanie, and me to Brunswick on Sunday after church. We arrived late that night. He stayed a couple of days and then returned to Bristol. The next morning, we went to the nursing home and quickly realized that Mom was not going to be with us very much longer. I experienced a rush of emotions that sprang up from my childhood, and even some from my early adulthood. Even though I knew my mom had accepted Christ, which brought me peace about her soul, I still needed more closure before she died. I needed her to tell me she loved me with all her heart, and that she was sorry for what she had put my siblings and me through. But standing next to her bed that morning and witnessing her declining health, both physically and mentally, to the point she could not communicate anymore, I knew that was never going to happen. I would have to live with pain in my heart, longing for my mom to show me love at a level she had never shown.
>
> For the next two weeks, I stayed all day with her. Joshua and Melanie never complained, as they loved her so much and she loved them. I was still hoping that maybe Mom would have enough cognition to at least

acknowledge me as her daughter or say my name, but it didn't happen. Richard returned to Brunswick on October 14 and shared with me that once while I was out of the room, he spoke into Mom's ear and shared with her how I felt. He told her that if she heard him to please try and communicate with me.

Two days later, on Wednesday, Richard and I made the decision to move her to hospice care in Brunswick. By 4:00 pm, they had transported her, and that night I spent alone with her. I talked and prayed with her all night. I still so desperately needed to feel my mom's love and hear her say my name. I will forever cherish that time I had with my mommy. A healing of our hearts began that night and a love began to flow between us that came through the Holy Spirit. Even though she could not speak, I could see in her eyes a deep love and concern.

On Thursday, her breathing continued to become shallower, and I was struggling to see her like this. I questioned God, "Why? Why couldn't she just go to sleep and wake up in Your presence?" But I realized that God has a plan for each of us, and we must learn to wait on Him and to trust him in all things.

As we moved into Friday, Mom was sleeping more and was not as responsive. I had determined not to leave her until she was ushered into the Lord's presence. Late Friday evening while sitting next to Mom holding her hand, the presence of the Lord invaded the room. It was a presence like none I had ever experienced before. It was so real. We try to imagine what God is really like. But there is no possible way in our earthly vessels to comprehend His greatness, His majesty, his power, His being, and His very existence. It is such a mystery to our minds. The pureness of God's endless love had invaded that room and entered the hearts of Mom and me simultaneously at a depth of which we had never experienced. Oh, how I love Him. He cares so much about every aspect of our lives from the simplest to the greatest things. When I think that the God of this universe—with so many people living on earth—would take time to orchestrate this time in my mother's passing and in my life to allow us to communicate with each other and allow healing to come to our hearts and soul, I am amazed beyond measure.

Many times, we question whether God really cares about us; does he really love us? Emphatically, I can answer that question in the affirmative. He cared so much about a dying mom who loved her children, although she regretted all the bad choices she had made in her life. So much did God care that He allowed her to share, while on her death bed, with her daughter just how much she loved her and her siblings. An internal healing came that night to both of us. Although my mom had accepted the Lord some 24 years earlier, she needed to share with me, her daughter, just how she felt. That night without any words being spoken except for the last 30 seconds of her life, a miracle took place, and we were able to communicate through the Spirit of God. A beautiful bright light filled the room like the sun, but it wasn't blinding. I could see beautiful silk fabric all around my mother, and she was so beautiful. I said aloud to her, "Mom, God is making you whole! You look young. Your eyes are bright, and your skin is smooth and lovely." I don't know exactly how long, but my mom and I spoke to each other through our eyes and spirits. There were no words spoken through these earthly bodies, but it was as if our spirits had transcended into a different world. My mother asked me to share with my brothers her love for them and asked them to forgive her for the wrongs she had done to them. She wanted them to please give their hearts to the Lord—that life was short and eternity so long.

Both of us felt such wonderful love and the power of the Lord, as we loved and forgave each other. Richard, sensing something was taking place, walked over to her bed where I was sitting. As I laid my head back on his chest while he held me, a more radiant light filled the room, much brighter than the first light that appeared earlier. I began to softly pray in the heavenly language for several minutes. Once again through our eyes, my mom and I continued to speak with each other for a few more minutes. You could see her facial expressions change when through her unspoken words she was conveying to me just how much she loved me. At one point, the nurse opened the door and took a step inside. Richard softly said, "Welcome to the presence of the Lord." She slowly backed out of the room.

The language God gave us that night was far more beautiful than any human language that has ever been spoken and on a level that simply wasn't possible in the flesh. I learned that night that it is through the Spirit that we must allow Him to work and fill our lives with His presence. We must also learn to put our complete trust in Him. At one moment, Mom turned her gaze on Richard, and he said to me, "Your mom just thanked me for taking care of you and asked me to continue."

I have so many emotions in my heart right now. I wish that I could describe what happened being with my mom as she was leaving this world, but there are simply no adjectives that could describe what I experienced that night. I just know that I will never be the same again. As her breathing became shallower, it became evident she only had possibly minutes to live, and after not hearing her speak my name audibly in a long time, she looked at me and said, "Cheryl." Then with each of her last three breaths she said goodbye. Richard also heard her say her last four words.

Cheryl with her mother, Margaret.

The entire time she was in hospice care, we had Christian music playing. The last song playing as she transitioned from this world into the presence of the Lord was *Blessed be the Name of the Lord.* Mom entered the presence of the Lord at 12:57 am Saturday, October 19, 2019. This story is about God's amazing love and forgiveness and how through experiencing His love, we can forgive one another. Mark 11:25: "Whenever you stand praying, if you find that you carry something in your heart against another person, release him and forgive him so that your father in heaven will also release you and forgive you of your faults."

With all that Cheryl experienced in life and the challenges she faced in ministry, she rejoices at how God has directed her footsteps, blessed her family, and used Richard and her for His glory. She is especially thankful for what she experienced with her mom in her mom's last moments on earth, and for the beautiful closure those brief moments in time brought her.

Afterword

I absolutely loved every minute of the ministry to which God called me, from being two worms in a puppet ministry, to youth leader, evangelist, associate pastor, lead pastor, missionary, and humanitarian worker. Additionally, I thoroughly enjoyed, and found great satisfaction and fulfillment, in serving as the executive director of the Lazarus Foundation and chief operating officer of SOW. My strong conviction is that God equipped me to do this.

To travel the world visiting and ministering in all the different cultures, being able to eat absolutely anything that was set before me, not needing a four or five-star hotel, but preferring to stay with the locals, when possible, was in my wheelhouse. I slept on coaches, cots, mats on the ground, in thatched huts with dirt floors, and spent once a week in the jungle listening to the wild animals crying out and loved every minute of it. My life has been so enriched because of my experiences in this world we live in. I have dined with presidents, dignitaries, and celebrities, and the same day dined with orphans. I have preached in more than 20 denominational settings from the Catholic Church to Charismatic churches and everywhere in between. I have had the wonderful pleasure of standing at the front of a line so long you could not see the end of it, giving out a little rice and beans to recipients who stood in line for over two hours to receive it. I have preached for pastors who didn't have enough to feed their families but insisted on me receiving the offerings they had taken in church that day. And when I would refuse, those pastors would rebuke me saying, "You are hindering me from obeying the commandment of the Lord to give." I would then take the offering and later gave it to a widow.

Once, I spent the better part of a day with a Liberian pastor who had 12 children living in a 200 square-foot hut, with an outdoor area where they cooked over an open fire. I finally got the nerve to ask him why he had so many children when he didn't have the means to care for them. His answer broke me up on the inside, and I cried profusely. He said, "Brother, nine of these children were orphaned from the war. What was I to do? Leave them in the bush?" Thankfully, I was able to come up with the funds to build him a small block home and was able to help him in other ways.

I have helped rescue girls from sex trafficking, boys from forced labor, and have helped disciple and teach ex-Taliban and al-Qaeda fighters—violent men who came to Jesus and realized more fully that grace is not something we just sing about, preach about, and talk about, but it is the most powerful aspect of the workings of the Holy Spirit in the life of a human being. I have witnessed Muslims, Buddhist, Hindus, and people in other false religions come to the amazing understanding of who the Messiah really is—that he is Jesus. I have been in harm's way many times and almost bitten several times by venomous snakes. I have been attacked by robbers, once having over 100 men surround me and several others that were with me and have been so sick that seeing home again seemed almost out of the question. I experienced what it is to be in a plane crash and walk away, and to being told my wife had six months to live, with five children still at home.

But God's grace was with us all the time. There has never been one time I considered giving up. When the thought would surface in my spirit, I would remember when God set me free from the bondages of the satanic strongholds that enslaved me. Sometimes the Lord allows the same presence to come over me that I felt the morning I was gloriously saved and delivered. When I gave my life to Jesus, I became His servant, and although I have failed him many times, I have endeavored to live for Him and answer His beckoning call with a resounding, "Yes Lord, I will go. I will do what You have asked of me." This is the secret to finding true peace, joy, and fulfillment.

As I reflect over my life, I am thankful for a praying and concerned mom and dad, and for a sister who, for a time, fasted every Tuesday for me. I am thankful for being part of a Word-based, Spirit-filled church, for the call of God upon my life, and for the degree that the Lord has used me in all the fivefold ministry gifts. Further, I am deeply appreciative that the Holy Spirit has flowed through me at different levels in all the nine gifts of the Spirit. To have been able to visit 68 countries and witness untold miracles is beyond description. At best, this book contains only 20 percent of all the Lord has allowed us to accomplish for His great Name. But the greatest appreciation I have is for the Lord Jesus Christ inviting me to do ministry with Him, picking up the mantle of a servant and knowing that one day I will hear Him say, "Well done; enter in!"

For even the son of man did not come expecting to be served by everyone, but to serve everyone, and to give his life as the ransom price in exchanged for the salvation of many (Mark 10:45).

Looking back and contemplating all the ways that God has blessed me and used me, I am once again reminded of the thought-provoking words of Isaac Watts' beloved song, "Alas and did my Savior bleed, and did my Sovereign die, would he devote that sacred head for such a worm as I."

Jim Elliot, a martyr for the faith, said, "He is no fool who gives what he cannot keep to gain that which he cannot lose."

Oh, my God, my prayer is for You to let your "worm" give his all that one day I may gain it all–eternity with You, my blessed Savior!

–Richard Baker

Ready to Know Christ?

If you are reading this book and do not know Jesus Christ, let me introduce you to Him. You have just read an amazing story of God's deliverance, mercy, and amazing love that he showed me. By most accounts, I should be dead. If that had happened, I would have been eternally lost and separated from God who loved me so much that He sent His only Son, Jesus, to die on the cruel cross of Calvary to pay the price for my sins. But not only did He die for my sins but also for yours. Through His grace, I have received life, eternal life, and it abides within my heart today. "But God demonstrates His own love toward us, in that while we were still sinners, Christ died for us" (Romans 5:8, NKJV). I accepted His passionate love, and you can too. Let me share with you how; it's so easy. I have taken the following scripture references from the New King James Version.

First, good works cannot save us. "For by grace you have been saved through faith, and that not of yourselves; *it is* the gift of God" (Ephesians 2:8-9).

Second, there is only one way to heaven. Jesus said, "I am the way, the truth, and the life. No one comes to the Father except through Me" (John 14:6). "Nor is there salvation in any other, for there is no other name under heaven given among men by which we must be saved" (Acts 4:12). "For God so loved the world that He gave His only begotten Son, that whoever believes in Him should not perish but have everlasting life" (John 3:16). "If you confess with your mouth the Lord Jesus and believe in your heart that God has raised Him from the dead, you will be saved" (Romans 10:9).

God made salvation simple. He loves us so much that He does not want us to die in our sins. So he gave us the gift of salvation. All you have to do is receive His gift while you still can. If you want Christ to save you today, all you have to do is trust God and receive Jesus as your personal Savior.

Pray aloud this simple prayer that I have written for you and mean it from your heart.

> Dear God, I know that I am a sinner, and I need a Savior. I want to repent and turn away from my sinful life to the life You have planned for me. Please forgive me of all my sins, cleanse me from my past, and make me a new person in You. I confess and believe that Your Son, Jesus, died and shed His blood for me, and He arose on the third day. At this very moment, I accept Jesus Christ as my personal Lord and Savior to rule and reign in my heart from this day forward. Thank You, Jesus, for Your grace that has saved me from my sins and given me eternal life. Please send your Holy Spirit to guide me, to empower me to live an overcoming life, and to help me do Your will for the rest of my life. In Jesus name I pray. Amen.

Let me be the first to welcome you to the family of God. I want to encourage you to do several things. First, start reading the Bible daily. I suggest beginning with the Gospel of John. Second, pray daily. This may seem awkward at first, but prayer is simply talking with God. Third, find a Bible-believing, Spirit-filled church, and jump in with all your heart!

If you are in bondage as I was, I want to share a verse of scripture that I prayed every day for weeks. It is 1 Corinthians 10:13: "No temptation has overtaken you except such as is common to man; but God *is* faithful, who will not allow you to be tempted beyond what you are able, but with the temptation will also make the way of escape, that you may be able to bear *it.*"

You will need the armor of God. "Finally, my brethren, be strong in the Lord and in the power of His might. Put on the whole armor of God, that you may be able to stand against the wiles of the devil" (Ephesians 6:10-11). Prayer for the God's armor:

> Jesus, I pray for the full armor of God, the helmet of salvation, the breastplate of righteousness, the shield of faith by which I will be able to extinguish all the flaming arrows of the evil one, the belt of truth, and that You would sturdy my feet with the preparation of the Gospel of peace, and for the sword of the Spirit which is Your word. In Your name, Jesus, I pray. Amen.

* If you have prayed and received Christ into your heart as a result of this book, please let me know through emailing me at:
suchawormasibook@gmail.com

Honoring and Remembering Cheryl

For 12 years Cherly and I were privileged to be part of Grace Point Church in Bristol, Tennessee. Having felt that the Lord distinctly spoke to both of us to return home to coastal South Georgia, we resigned the pastorate at Grace Point, with our last Sunday being May 1, 2022. In June we made the moved back home to costal Georgia. Initially, I took a five-month sabbatical only preaching a few times and sharing a few times at drug rehab ministry centers.

This autobiographical book, *Such a Worm as I*, quickly sold out of the original 2,050 copies. We had another 1,000 copies printed, which, as of February 2025, have also sold out. Consequently, we had to print another 1,000 copies. Because of the number of books sold, we have been able to donate $60,000 to Serving Orphans Worldwide!

In December 2022, we felt the Lord leading us to move to Douglas, Georgia, the birthplace of my parents. We quickly found a home, made an offer, and moved in within a couple of weeks. By the time of our move, I was preaching more regularly and began teaching every Wednesday morning at Still Waters, a women's substance abuse facility.

On a particular Saturday morning, Cheryl and I went to Still Waters for a causal meeting with the owner and director, Joann Lewis. Joann, who is Methodist, shared with us that she had a dream about a year earlier, a dream she believed was of a divine nature. In her dream a pastor, who was not from that area, came to her from the pastorate of a church called Grace Point Church. Until this moment I had never shared with her the name of the church I had pastored in Tennessee. Initially, what she was telling us did not register with me. When Cheryl stroked my arm and smiled, I spoke up and shared that our last pastorate was indeed Grace Point Church. She looked at me and excitedly exclaimed, "You're the man!"

One month later I was the proud owner of a 12-acre 15-bed women's substance abuse center with an annual budget of $200,000, which was running a deficit and needed major repairs. I met with a businessman in

Brunswick, Georgia, who shared that he believed in what we were doing, and that he believed in me. He said, "I have one question for you. How much more funding do you need weekly to fully operate the center?"

I responded that we needed $2,000 but $1,000 a month would be a huge blessing. Without blinging an eye, he asked for our banking information and began depositing $2,000 weekly into the Still waters account. He continued to do this for one year.

Often, I use the analogy of the plow when I am preaching and teaching. When you are in the field God has designed for you and you have your hands on His plow, you will not have to worry about the seed—the resources.

In late October 2023, an independent church in Brunswick, Georgia, had its pastor resign. One of the deacons called me and asked if I could fill in for a few weeks. I replied that I would not be able to at this time. A day or two later, he called again, and I gave him the same answer. When I shared this with Cheryl, she said, "Richard, you need to be careful. God is up to something."

A couple of days later, the deacon called me again, and I agreed to minister there for two weeks. God truly blessed in those two weeks, and I agreed to stay on until the first of January 2024. I felt that would give them enough time to find a pastor. On December 3, the deacon board met with me and asked if I would accept their offer to be their lead pastor. On December 17, the church voted for us to be lead pastors of New Life Sanctuary. It was a beautiful 25,000 square-foot facility situated on 20 acres in one of the fasted growing areas in Glynn County, Georgia.

The next Sunday, which was our first Sunday as official pastors, was Christmas Eve. We had leased a home and had already moved half of our clothes and household goods in and planned to complete the move from Douglas to Brunswick after Christmas. The Saturday night before, Cheryl shared with me how she felt God was going to use me in a distinct way at New Life Sanctuary. I quickly responded, "He will use *us*."

Sunday morning came and, in all honesty, I felt quite giddy. It is nearly a two-hour drive from Douglas to Brunswick, and I asked Cheryl to ride with me, while Joshua, Melanie, and Cheryl's brother, Joey, could ride together. At the last minute, Cheryl decided to ride with them saying that I would want to pray and mediate on my message. As I drove, I had a heavenly time praying and rejoicing in God's presence.

When I got three miles from the church, I received a call from a number I did not recognize. So, I didn't answer it. Immediately, the Holy Spirit prompted me to pull over and call the number back, which I did. A lady answered the phone and inquired if I was Richard Baker. I replied that I was. She continued, "Your family has been in a horrific head on collision with another vehicle." She shared with me that she had seen the accident and exclaimed, "It was not your son's fault!"

When I asked about my family, she responded, "Your brother-in-law is walking around, but bleeding. Your son is unable to exit the vehicle, but he is alert and talking. Your daughter seems to have suffered the greatest injuries but is conscious."

Since she did not mention Cheryl, I asked, "What about my wife?"

She replied, "I think she has lost consciousness."

I started to turn around, but the Holy Spirit led me to continue to the church. As I entered the parking lot, Joe Peoples, the deacon that kept calling me, was walking across the parking lot. I shared with him what had just happened. We jumped into his vehicle and headed the 25-mile distance back to the scene of the accident. The sight that greeted us looked like a war zone, with debris scattered over a large area.

As I approached the vehicle, I could see the paramedics working to get Melanie out of the back seat. I could also see the back of Cheryl's head, and she was sitting up still strapped in by her seat belt. At first, I felt some relief, so I started walking to the driver's side of the car. The paramedics had managed to get Melanie out of the vehicle and were transporting her to an ambulance. I walked beside her holding her arm. I said, "Melanie, Daddy is here. Everything is going to be ok."

She looked up at me and exclaimed, "I feel like a thousand needles are sticking me!"

They whisked her off to the hospital in Brunswick, and I walked back to the crash site. Joshua still had his hands on the steering wheel. I laid my hand on his arm and said, "Josh, I am here. It's ok."

Looking up at me, he said, "Dad, I am sorry I killed Mom."

I at once responded, "No son, the man driving that SUV over there killed you mom." That was when the reality of what happened hit me and hit me hard. The love of my life had transitioned from this world into the presence of her precious LORD and SAVIOR. I went to the back door and opened it. For the next several minutes, I sat next to her and thanked the Lord so much for giving me the opportunity to hold her and kiss her goodbye one more time. Now my attention turned to my two children who were severely injured, and to Joey, my brother-in-law.

As we were driving the 30 minutes to the hospital, I had the almost unbearable task of calling my three grown sons, Ricky, Ryan, and Chris, my sister, Phyllis, and Cheryl's two other living brothers, Charlie and Kenny, as well as other family members.

Upon arriving at the hospital, I quickly learned that Melanie's injuries were life threatening. She needed to be transferred at once to a trauma hospital in Jacksonville, Florida. The doctors gave her less than a 50 percent chance of making it to Jacksonville alive. Joshua's right foot was severely injured, and he also suffered some other bruising. Joey had a broken hand and lacerations.

Ricky and his family arrived a few minutes after I did, and they visited with Melanie before she was transported to Jacksonville. I stood in the emergency room trying to process everything that had just happened. By that time all the deacons arrived at the hospital and gathered around me praying for God's strength. Immediately, the Lord spoke to my heart so clearly it almost seemed verbal. These words flooded my mind: "I have not relieved you from the calling I have placed on your life for this time." That meant to me that I still had to pastor the church.

With tears streaming down my cheeks, I said to those men who were holding me and praying over me, "If you will accept a single pastor, I am still your man. As of this writing, I am 67 years old, and those were the hardest words I ever had to speak. The Lord seemed so unfair to ask me to pastor a church when I had just loss my wife and was not sure if my precious daughter, Melanie, was even going to live.

But as I spoke these words to the deacons, I could see Jesus hanging on the cross, and I knew then that I could continue because He was with me. "For the gifts and calling of God are irrevocable" (Rom. 11:29). First Corinthians 10:13 states, "No temptation (trials and tribulation) has overtaken you except such is common to man; but God is faithful, who will not allow you to be tempted beyond what you are able, but with the temptation will also make the way of escape, that you may be able to bear it."

Upon arriving at Shand's Trauma Center in Jacksonville, Florida, I rushed into the emergency room. I had only about five minutes with Melanie before one of the two trauma surgeons came to me and said, "Dad, we must go now."

Several more church leaders, along with their wives, had now arrived. My sister and her husband, Bruce, stayed with Joshua in Brunswick. After two surgeons worked on Melanie for seven hours, one of them called me and reported, "Dad, we have done all we can do today. She will be coming back to ICU still open. We will do surgery again on Tuesday."

I stayed with Melanie all night, holding her hand and praying over her unconscious body. I cried out to God, "I can't lose two in one day! Father, I just can't!"

The next morning was Christmas Day and at 7:50 am I received a call from one of the trauma surgeons letting me know he was going to do surgery again on Melanie. His words were, "We are going to try to put her back together." After speaking with him for a couple of minutes, I asked him what her chances were. He answered, "Forty percent or less."

In about 10 minutes, the other trauma surgeon called me saying, "I am at the hospital getting ready to do surgery on your daughter. If she survives the surgery today, we will need to do one more."

No doubt when these two surgeons left the hospital on Christmas Eve, they were not planning to come back on Christmas Day. BUT GOD...! After six to seven hours of surgery, one of the surgeons called and informed me, "We were successful in putting your daughter back together, but it will be touch and go for the next two weeks. We now give her a 50 percent chance to survive.

Both Melanie's large and small intestines were severely damaged, both to the extent that parts had to be removed. Her bowels were severed, and her spleen was also split in two. Almost every other organ in her body was bruised or suffered trauma. She had a gash on her left side 14 inches long, which cut into her six inches. Additionally, she had two crushed vertebrates. They shared with us at Brunswick Hospital that it was medically impossible for her to survive. BUT GOD...!

Now that Melanie was stable, I turned my attention to planning for Cheryl's funeral service, which we determined to be a celebration of her life. I planned it for New Year's Eve at 4:00 pm. The funeral director cautioned that the attendance would be off considering the holiday. I let her know that I understood. I asked two of my closest friends, Ken Anderson and Dr. John Gregory, to do the main part of the service. The service would be at my home church, Golden Isles Church of God, which seats more than 700 people.

The closer we came to the 4:00 pm starting time, the more people poured in, with a total of 450 in attendance. The top four members of the Church of God Executive Committee were present, with Dr. Tim Hill, Presiding General Overseer, and Dr. Raymond Culpepper, First Assistant, speaking at Cheryl's celebration of life service. We also live streamed the service, which was viewed by more than 1,000 from 42 nations of the world.

Those who knew Cheryl knew that she was not an upfront person and did not like the limelight, or any attention brought to herself. She would have been amazed beyond comprehension at the large number of people who came to pay their respects out of love for her and our family.

At the end of two weeks in ICU, Melanie was doing so well they released her. She went to my sister Phyllis's home, where Joshua had been staying since the accident and where they both received excellent care.

With Josh and Melanie out of the hospital, I now had to finish moving into our leased home in Brunswick. We loaded up the U-Haul and several vehicles and headed there. The house overlooked the marsh, and I remember that when we looked at it, Cheryl stood on the back deck and said to me, "Ricky, I will have my devotions right here." I lived in the home a couple of months before Josh and Melanie were able to move in with me. Every day I would go to the spot where Cheryl stood on the deck and talk to my heavenly Father. I had never felt such loneliness and lostness.

Except for the Sunday after the accident, I preached every Sunday, taught every Wednesday evening, and kept a few office hours each week. I also visited church members in the hospital. Within three weeks of Cheryl's passing, we lost two church members, one a spouse and another a mother. I was unable to take part in the services, but I did go to the viewings.

Before the church voted me in as their pastor, they were going through some stressful times. Attendance was down and morale was low, but after Cheryl's death, everyone sensed a different atmosphere in church. We began to grow and enjoyed some wonderful services. I believe that even in her death, God used her to help bring healing to this congregation.

I pastored the church for nine months and in early August 2024, I was standing on the back deck of our house. I cried out to God, "I am at the end of it emotionally, my Father!"

During that time, I felt the Lord leading me to drive to four churches, sit in their parking lots, and pray. When I got to the fourth one, I felt a ping.

Although I did not know any of the pastors or anything about the churches, I knew the fourth one was the one that God led me to. I contacted the pastor and in one month we had merged their congregation in with ours. Their pastor became the new pastor, and the name was changed to Turning Point Church. My last official Sunday was August 25, 2024. The merger has proven to be successful with new growth, salvations, and water baptisms. I am so glad God had once again used *a worm such as I.*

Having to deal with the loss of Cheryl and the needs of my children, as well as ministry work, I knew that I needed to get out from under the pressure of Still Waters. Thankfully, I was able to merge it with Shane's Crib, another women's rehab center, which, like Still Waters, sponsored a one-year program with a residency requirement.

We since have bought a townhouse in Brunswick, and Joshua is working for his Uncle Bruce while Melanie is in cosmetology college. I have recently been appointed by the Church of God World Mission Department as Missionary Evangelist. I will be ministering stateside, as well as in other countries. I still serve on the board of directors for Serving Orphans Worldwide, which now serves 8,000 orphans at 84 children's homes in 33 countries.

In late September Melanie was diagnosed with a small tumor in her pituitary gland. For sure it shook us up a bit. We prayed and asked many others to pray and believed God to bring His healing touch. In early December they did an MRI which showed absolutely no tumor. We give God all the praise for His wonderful love and mercy in preforming this miracle and for His constant strength and comfort.

–Richard Baker

American Bible Society

Sharing God's Word with the World

R. Lamar Vest
President and CEO

November 10, 2011

Mr. Richard Baker
340 Martin Luther King, Jr. Blvd.
Suite 200
Bristol, TN 37620

Dear Richard:

I wanted to offer my deep thanks to you for taking the time to engage in our 2nd annual Presidents Round Table. What a time we had together.

We placed a strong challenge in front of you—looking for you to draw directly from your significant experience as a leader, giving us your read of our mission for this important season of ministry. May I say, you rose well to our challenge and we are so grateful for the insights you shared. As you know, we captured your comments and we will be integrating those ideas and our plans going forward, and we'll use them to spur on our thinking and strategic planning.

This really is an exciting season for American Bible society. It is a time to listen carefully, seeking to understand well God's calling, and to act decisively to help resource both the church and culture with the larger influence of God's word. I am convinced we are up for the challenge and deeply appreciate this time for counsel and conversation as we set the path ahead.

I did want to share with you a good piece that Fox News ran, sharing more of my hopes and thinking about the needed expansion of God's word for our nation. I am encouraged by these ongoing opportunities to advocate for the best of the Bible in ever widening audiences. As I often tell our staff and partners, I continue to see the best days of American Bible society and God's Kingdom ahead of us.

I would also welcome hearing back from you if, as you reflect on our gathering, you have comments you'd like to share.

Yours Gratefully,

Lamar vest

American Bible Society
Sharing God's Word with the World

R. Lamar vest
President and CEO

January 10, 2012

Mr. Richard Baker
Lazarus foundation
P.O. Box 574
Bristol TN 37621

Dear Richard:

Thank you for your letter and for the good news about the continued joint venture with the Lazarus Foundation and American Bible Society. We are getting very encouraging news from our people on the ground in the DRC. This is one of the greatest partnerships I have witnessed since being at ABS. Thank you for your guidance and support.

It was a blessing to have you at the President's Round Table. I'm glad you were blessed by the meeting. I continue to be amazed that the Lord has opened for me such great doors of opportunity to impact the whole Body of Christ. We are committed to broader advocacy for the Bible and for people living out what it says. When people truly understand the Bible, there will cease to be any debate as to whether or not we are to care for the orphans, widows and poor of the earth. It is a basic and undisputable message that screams at us from almost every page of God's word.

Thank you again, Richard, for your support, prayers and involvement in our Lord's work. I am happy to partner with you in this endeavor.

I trust you and your family will have the greatest year ever in 2012.

Blessings,

R. Lamar vest

COUNTRIES VISITED
(Number of times visited)

1. Argentina (4)
2. Austria (1)
3. Bahamas (2)
4. Belize (4)
5. Bolivia (2)
6. Brazil (2)
7. Burundi (3)
8. Cambodia (25 plus)
9. Canada (2)
10. Cayman Islands (1)
11. Chili (2)
12. China (4)
13. Colombia (4)
14. DRC (Congo) (14)
15. Costa Rica (25)
16. Cuba (2)
17. Ecuador (7)
18. El Salvador (70 plus)
19. England (3)
20. Ethiopia (1)
21. France (3)
22. Ghana (8)
23. Germany (4)
24. Guatemala (lived over 5 years)
25. Guinea (1)
26. Guyana (5)
27. Haiti (5)
28. Honduras (lived 6 months)
29. Hungary (1)
30. India (32)
31. Indonesia (7)
32. Israel (1)
33. Jamaica (3)
34. Japan (3)
35. Kenya (50 plus)
36. Liberia (20)
37. Malawi (2)
38. Malaysia (2)
39. Maldives (1)
40. Mexico (10)
41. Myanmar (8)
42. Nepal (1)
43. Netherlands (70 plus including transiting)
44. Nicaragua (25 plus)
45. North Korea (1)
46. Palestine (1)
47. Panama (25 plus)
48. Paraguay (4)
49. Peru (4)
50. Philippines (6)
51. Romania (2)
52. Rwanda (10)
53. Scotland (1)
54. Sierra Leon (5)
55. Singapore (5)
56. South Africa (3)
57. South Korea (7)
58. Spain (1)
59. Sri Lanka (12)
60. Tanzania (10)
61. Thailand (50 plus)
62. Trinidad (Tobago (3)
63. Uganda (20)
64. Ukraine (12)
65. Undisclosed Arab country (3)
66. USA (live)
67. Uruguay (1)
68. Zambia (7)
69. Zimbabwe (8)
70. Senegal (1)

AIRLINES FLOWN

1. Aerolineas Sosa
2. Aerolitoral
3. Aeromexico
4. Aeroperlas
5. Air France
6. Air India
7. Air Tran
8. Alaska Airlines
9. American Airlines
10. American Eagle
11. Asiana Airlines
12. Atlantic Southwest
13. Avianca
14. Aviateca
15. Bangkok Airways
16. British Airways
17. Buddha Air
18. Cambodian Angkor Air
19. Caribbean Airlines
20. Cebu Pacific
21. China Eastern Airlines
22. Citilink
23. Comair
24. Continental
25. Continental Express
26. Copa Airlines
27. Delta
28. Eastern
29. Emirates
30. Ethiopian Airlines
31. GOL Airlines
32. Iberia
33. IndiGo
34. Islena
35. Jamaica Airlines
36. Jet Airways
37. Kingfisher Airlines
38. KLM
39. Korean Air -South Korea
40. Air Koryo - North Korea
41. La Costena
42. Latin American Wings LAW
43. Lufthansa
44. MAP Linhas Aereas
45. Northwest
46. Piedmont
47. Precision Air
48. Proflight Zambia
49. Singapore Airlines
50. South African
51. Southwest
52. SpiceJet
53. SriLankan Airlines
54. TACA El Salvador
55. TAME
56. Tarom
57. Thai Airways
58. Ukraine Airlines
59. United
60. US Airways
61. Virgin Atlantic